CLOUDLESS LOVE
… in the time of Artificial Intelligence

ROBERT CARRICK

First ebook edition: Sydney 2023
First print edition: Sydney 2023
Publisher: Sydney School of Arts & Humanities
41/228 Moore Park Road Paddington NSW 2021
www.ssoa.com.au

CLOUDLESS LOVE ... in the time of Artificial Intelligence

ISBN 978-0-6483216-0-6 (ebook)
ISBN 978-0-6483216-9-9 (print book)

Cover design & Formatting: Ferdinando Manzo.
Typeset Times New Roman
Printed and bound by Lightning Source, 2023.

National Library of Australia Cataloguing-in-Publication data:
Carrick, Robert author.
CLOUDLESS LOVE ... in the time of Artificial Intelligence / Robert Carrick.
ISBN 978-0-6483216-9-9
Fiction – novel – Sydney novel – Australian fiction

Dedication

To my beautiful wife Indie, to the polychromatic people of Australia, to this country we call home, and to all those who have aspired to write a novel.

Acknowledgements

This story was conceived by the author in the time between the COVID-19 lockdowns of 2020 and 2021. No Artificial Intelligence was used in its creation, and it was brought to life with the encouragement and support of Dr. Christine Williams and members of the Sydney School of Arts and Humanities Tuesday and Saturday writing groups.

In particular, I wish to thank Roger Guinery who beta-read the second revision and provided detailed commentary. Roger's comments became a voice in my ear, pointing out the issues and inconsistencies, as well as some welcome praise, as I worked my way through the third revision.

In addition to Christine and Roger, I am indebted to all the emerging writers who gave their time to listen to the chapters as I read them out aloud each week for group members to provide invaluable feedback. I wish to thank, in no particular order, Meg Mooney, Matt Jackson, David Benn, Clara Andrade, Ros Lawson, Fiona D'Souza, Ingrid Studholme, Jim Piotrowski, Catherine Keyzer, Wil Roach, Stew Adams, and of course my wife Indie, who knows first-hand how much time it takes to write a novel.

A fateful day

It was one of those days in the late spring of 2035 when possibilities stirred in the rising heat.

In her apartment at Bradfield, in Sydney's west, Celia slid open the glass sliding door and stepped out onto the balcony to check her phone for messages and to take in the view of the suburbs that lay sprawled across the sweeping coastal plain. In the distance, she could see the Blue Mountains shrouded in a mist of vaporising oil from the eucalyptus trees hidden far away in the Jamison and Megalong Valleys.

The warm early morning breeze buffeted her short, straight black hair as she browsed an app to book her driverless car. Her ride was confirmed to arrive in a matter of minutes, so she walked back inside, sliding the door shut behind her, confident that there would be no relief from the heat for the citizens of Western Sydney until a southerly buster blew their way.

Her mind turned to the crowd of early-morning coffee cravers that would soon be milling about the streamlined coffee cart where she worked, so she put her phone in her shoulder bag, hurried out the front door and made her way to the waiting car.

The coffee cart was positioned next to an outdoor chess

board in the park opposite the tall glass office towers in the town centre of Bradfield, a new suburb dominating Sydney's west. Bradfield had been planned as a part of the Aerotropolis, constructed in the early decades of the 21st century.

Economic opportunities immediately flourished, which meant Bradfield was at first thriving. But over the past decade Artificial Intelligence, or AI, had wreaked havoc on those early opportunities. Foundation models, capable of ingesting swathes of data from the internet, created a platform for General Purpose Technologies, or GPTs, which ran at the heart of internet cloud-based services. It meant that humanoid robots were capable of performing the most complex of tasks, as well as the mundane.

Technology firms, many of them titans that had dominated the market since the time of the search engines, collapsed in a paradigm shift towards a ubiquitous AI centre-of-truth (CoT) platform branded as AYE AYE. As the cost of labour plummeted, companies of all sizes found themselves engaged in a race to replace the human workforce with robots. At ReElevation Australia, the Asia-Pacific outpost of a media empire that held the publishing rights of artists, music, movies, and games streamed across the internet, the transition from humans to machines being in charge was almost complete.

After work Celia found herself in the foyer of the ReElevation office tower, about to buy an apple.

'The question is, do you really want it?' a husky female voice asked from behind Celia, who was peering at an apple on display in a vending machine. The apple was jammed at position B2, possibly as a result of a crack across the front glass.

Celia turned around and found herself staring into the emerald-green eyes of the woman who posed the question. She was flaming red from top to toe. Voluminous red curls partly revealed a pretty face with high cheekbones, adorned with freckles and a petite nose with a ruby stud. Her hair tumbled down onto a fine metallic red mesh shawl draped across her shoulders, a small red Glomesh crossbody purse slung across her red knee-length crimplene dress. The whole outfit was topped off with a pair of dazzling red patent leather high-heels. As she waved her mobile phone about in its shiny red plastic case, Celia caught a whiff of Dior and cigarettes.

'I've never noticed you around the office before,' the woman said. 'Are you new?'

Well, at least she doesn't vape, Celia thought.

She was about to reply when the woman offered her hand. Celia grasped it and lightly pressed her fingertips into the woman's soft, warm pale skin.

'Felicity Faraday, a director of Art and Repertoire.'

Oh my God, she's an A&R Director. I probably shouldn't be in here, Celia thought.

'Celia Tran, interior designer and part-time barista. Nice to meet you Felicity, and yes, I do want it, because like the two of us in this plastic world of Artificial Intelligence, it is a product of nature.'

Both women peered through the glass at the stranded apple wedged in the jaws of the auto-selector. Celia sighed.

'I thought about giving the machine a shove, but I didn't want to set off the alarm.'

'I'll give you a hand,' Felicity said. 'Be brave.' She placed her purse on the floor, kicked off her high heels, faced the machine and placed both hands on the front glass panel.

'Come on, put your back into it. I'm doing this for you, not me,' Felicity said.

With some reluctance, Celia slid her mobile phone into the back pocket of her black activewear pants, adjusted her white crop top and stood next to Felicity with her arms outstretched and her palms against the machine. As her short black hair fell across her face, she noticed a thin crack spreading like a spider-vein from a small chip in the glass. She turned her head towards Felicity, who was looking at her with a wry smile.

'On the count of three. One ... two ... three!' Both women pushed against the weight of the vending machine and applied enough pressure to lift the front feet off the ground by several centimetres. They held it aloft momentarily until they were overcome by gravity.

'Let it go!' Felicity shouted.

They jumped back and let the machine fall to earth. The force of the impact on the crack caused the tempered safety glass panel to shatter, spilling small cubes of glass onto the floor and setting off an ear-splitting siren, which wailed as flashing blue strobe lights flickered in maniacal distress.

Celia put her hands over her ears. *How did she convince me to do that? How could I be so bold?* she thought.

Celia drew breath, rallied her presence of mind and bent down to look for the apple, which she found lying in the dispensing tray, having been jolted from the jaws of the jammed auto selector. She snatched it from the machine.

'Follow me,' Felicity called, as she picked up her shoes and ran off barefoot down the corridor.

Celia took off after her. *It's like we've committed a crime,* she thought, as they slipped past the blue uniformed SecurityBots that were marching in from all directions like storm-troopers.

The two women ran into the lobby and Felicity pressed the

button on the wall to call the lift while Celia caught her breath.

Seconds later they found themselves standing in the sanctuary of the elevator.

Felicity pushed the Level 7 button, and the silence was punctuated by an announcement from the silvery monotone of the biometric AYE AYE access assistant.

'Ms Faraday, your guest does not have permission to access Level 7.'

'Celia Tran is my guest, and I will accompany her at all times.'

'Access granted.'

Seconds later, Celia found herself standing in the middle of a breezy office, which was decked out in a retro 1960's pseudo-Andy Warhol decor, complete with a red-lip lounge, what looked to be highly uncomfortable designer chairs, Heinz Baked Beans wallpaper and a fully stocked bar.

Who are you? Celia thought, as she took a closer look at the other pieces of modern art behind Felicity's desk that she didn't recognise.

'Do you think we'll get into trouble? I'm sure the security cameras would have recorded the whole incident,' Celia said.

'I doubt it,' Felicity said as she wandered over to the bar. 'Security reports to me, anyway. How about a drink to calm your nerves? I'm having one.'

Felicity popped green olives into two Martini glasses and proceeded to fill the cocktail shaker with gin, vermouth, and ice cubes from the bar fridge.

Celia, remembering she was still holding the apple, took a bite to buy herself some time to consider her answer.

'Why not? I've finished my shift,' Celia said, as she wandered over and stood next to Felicity at the bar.

'You seem to be into making cocktails ... but do you know how to mix an Appletini? It's my favourite.'

'I used to do bar work at university, so I know the recipe, but I don't have any apple schnapps, so you'll have to settle for a martini,' she said, as she shook the shaker and poured the mixture into the glasses.

Celia picked up her glass and continued to look around at the opulent decor.

'I love what you've done with this space,' Celia said as she sipped her martini. 'I had my own interior design practice until my business was destroyed by AYE AYE. To make ends meet, I work the morning shift at the coffee cart in the park over the road. So, what exactly do you do here?'

Felicity picked up her glass and leaned back against the bar.

'I have a stake in the company. Not a controlling interest and yet not an insignificant one. My great-grandfather started the label in the late 1970s, in the heady days of magnetic tape machines and vinyl records. My father was a vinyl record collector. He had an enthusiasm for vinyl even after we went digital. That's his old turntable over on the bookshelf.'

Felicity walked across the room, glass in hand. 'Would you like me to give Joni Mitchell's *Shadows and Light* a spin? It's on the platter.'

The implications of this information began to register in Celia's mind. *Your relatives actually own ReElevation? Now that's intriguing,* she thought. Celia did her best to sound unfazed. 'Sure, line it up.'

Felicity lifted the stylus, which set the turntable in motion, and carefully placed it on the second track, filling the room with the sounds of *In France They Kiss on the Main Street.* Felicity picked up the cover and examined it for a moment before looking up at Celia.

'So why were you in our office today?' Felicity asked.

'I was dropping coffee and a sandwich off to my friend Peta O'Neill who works here as a graphic designer. I hadn't eaten, and that vending machine always has fresh juicy Pink Lady apples.'

'I know Peta. She's very talented. She's the only human being left in the art department. My father was a believer in AI. Personally, I find the whole concept deeply disturbing,' she said, putting the Rolling Stones cover back down on the bookshelf. 'I want to take the company in a whole new direction.'

'What do you have in mind?'

Felicity drained her glass, walked back over, and stood next to Celia.

'If that apple is all you have eaten all day you must be ready for something else. I have a cheese platter, a baguette, a nice bottle of chilled Dom Perignon, a picnic basket and a blanket on standby,' Felicity said, relieving Celia of her empty glass. 'Shall we have a picnic lunch in the park? I'd like to bounce some ideas off you.'

Celia eyed Felicity with suspicion as she finished off the apple and placed the core on the edge of the sink.

I'm curious. This could be a job interview, but she seems a bit odd, Celia thought. *I should probably get out of here now.*

Celia resolved to excuse herself from the situation, straightened up and then took herself by surprise. 'Why not? That would be lovely.'

A work picnic

Felicity packed the picnic basket, and soon they were back in the lobby, where the only evidence of the earlier ruckus was the darkened vending machine. Its display screen read, 'WE APOLOGISE FOR BEING OUT OF SERVICE'. She informed the absurdly pert ReceptionBot that they were out for lunch, and the two crossed the street and walked into Bradfield Park.

The park was busy for a Wednesday afternoon. Teenagers and couples were lolling about in the amber sunlight, swiping the screens of their phones with fingers and thumbs. Celia viewed them suspiciously as she walked beside Felicity, who was carrying the basket and blanket.

'They're all so bored. Ever since the rise of AYE AYE, nobody is satisfied. The Government pays them to sit around all day and play on their phones. I reckon it's a conspiracy to make them too distracted to think about making love and trouble,' Celia said. 'It sucks.'

They wandered into the old orchard in the centre of the park. Felicity found a shady spot under a gnarly old apple tree.

'This will do,' Felicity said, putting down the picnic basket to spread out the blanket. Celia pulled her mobile phone out of her back pocket and sat down while Felicity knelt and untwisted the wire on the top of the bottle of Dom, gently prising the cork with both thumbs until it exploded and launched into orbit. Champagne frothed all over Celia's leggings, and they laughed as they fumbled with the glass flutes.

'Can I get a selfie with you to post on FaceTracer before we get pissed?' Celia asked.

'Sure. I don't really do much on social media because we have a whole team to manage the message, or at least we did until Dad fired them all after he migrated marketing into the AI cloud. We get fantastic marketing traction on apps like Face-Tracer but they make me feel like I'm wasting my life.'

'When you don't have a full-time job there's always plenty of time for social media,' Celia explained.

'I get it. Come on, let's move into position.'

Celia held up her phone and Felicity flashed a mischievous smile as they clinked glasses and savoured the dry tang of the champagne, with the timer counting down to zero. 'Nice one, I'll post it later.'

'Do you have many followers?'

'Not really, just family and a few friends, although I do like following people who are trying to change the trajectory of their lives, like, I'm following this guy called Toby from Far North Queensland who's applying for a federal government grant to fund his entry into an AI design competition. He wants to build a set of four robotic arms that can teach him to play guitar. He's calling it 'Project Gegenees'.

Felicity laughed. 'Forewarned is forearmed. Let me ask you, what makes you believe that TobyFNQ is even real?'

Celia glanced sideways at Felicity. 'What makes you think he wouldn't be?'

'Let me tell you, my business is content creation, and I can tell you that human creativity has been eclipsed by generative Artificial Intelligence. Most of my top-performing artists over the last few years have been created by AYE AYE. Your Toby could be just another figment of its artificial imagination that has been tailored to your desires.'

'That's really disturbing. He seems real to me.'

Felicity raised her glass. 'Well, if he is real and he has found a way to use AYE AYE to get himself into the music business, then he deserves a toast. To TobyFNQ, if you're out there.'

They both clinked glasses again and threw back another mouthful of Dom.

Celia tucked her phone into her running shoe lying on the grass.

'So, are you really planning to bounce some ideas off me? I've only known you for two hours,' Celia said, tilting her head inquisitively. 'Tell me what it's like being an A&R director, anyway?'

Felicity gazed into the bottom of her glass. 'It's challenging for me because I want to upset the status quo. My idea is to bring on more flesh-and-blood artists. I believe the public is growing more suspicious of AYE AYE and I'm sensing a hunger in the audience for something different. That's why I'm trying to bring on artists like Kirk Satyr. What do you think?'

'My friend Peta is a big Satyr's Faction fan, and she got me into them. She says their sound is an echo from a time when it was okay to be flawed. I get where she's coming from and I like your initiative. Life is imperfect and so is Kirk Satyr.

'Funny you should mention Peta. I had a meeting with her last week about the cover art she's designing for me. Her latest version is just a black square with a white dot in the middle. I asked her to explain why the design was not more in keeping with the album title.'

'Which is what, may I ask, if it's not a secret?'

'It's called *Midsummer Nights.* Anyway, Peta told me that she decided to manually intervene and substitute the AI-generated design with her own concept.'

Felicity put her glass down and carefully lifted the cheese platter out of the basket, setting it down between them on the blanket. 'I think she's quite brave. I respect her for that. Dig in.'

Celia reached for the baguette that was sticking out of the basket, broke off a piece, balanced a slice of cheddar on top and passed it to Felicity, before making one for herself.

Felicity took a bite from her bread and cheese and looked at Celia. 'Can I ask you something about Peta?'

Celia took another mouthful of champagne before answering.

'I met Peta at uni. I decided to move closer to the campus to avoid the commute from Marrickville after generative AI forced a return to face-to-face assessment. I was struggling to adjust to living away from my family and Peta was having trouble with her parents after coming out as trans. Moving from a 'P-e-t-e-r' identity to 'P-e-t-a'. We looked after each other and we've been best friends ever since.'

Felicity chewed on the rest of her bread and cheese. 'Who'd have thought that AI would be the end of written assessments? I suppose even universities can't tell the difference between the work of humans and AI,' she said.

A magpie warbled in the apple tree above their heads and Celia looked up.

'I suppose experiencing another person, in person, is the only way to find out who they really are. Like when my friend Tyler from uni started dating Peta.'

Felicity knocked over the half-empty bottle of champagne, spilling Dom onto the blanket. Celia salvaged enough for two last glasses while Felicity rummaged around in the basket for a serviette to mop up the mess.

'I suppose life is full of moments you don't see coming,' she observed. 'Do you want to tell me what happened to your interior design business?'

'Sure. I started out on my own after university and the practice grew for a few years. I had quite a number of regular clients and a good reputation. Then AYE AYE changed the landscape forever. The platform is so good at colour matching and generating concepts at almost no cost. I couldn't compete and, one by one, my clients drifted off,' Celia explained. 'I didn't want to go on the AI benefit, so I decided to look for some casual work.'

'So where do you work now?' Felicity asked.

'At the 'Wheels & Beans' coffee cart opposite your office at the entrance to the park. The job came about when I met up with Peta for coffee and cake and I got chatting to Marco who, as it turned out, operates a few of these carts in Bradfield. It's pretty easy work. The BaristaBot makes most of the coffee and I just chat with the clientele. I think Marco likes the idea of having a human on the cart for PR,' Celia replied, leaning back on her outstretched arms and looking up at the apple tree. 'I think you would make a great interior designer. I love the decor in your office,' Celia said.

Felicity sighed and placed her empty glass back in the picnic basket. 'I'm not very visual. More of a music person I suppose. I wouldn't know a good design if I fell over one. The office fit-out is all Dad,' Felicity said, pulling up her knees and wrapping her arms around them.

'Does your father work at ReElevation too?' Celia asked.

'He used to, up until three months ago,' Felicity said looking up at the tree. 'He died.'

Celia gasped and tried to think of something to say. 'I'm sorry. I didn't mean to pry.'

'It's okay. I miss him though. Some days I feel so angry about losing him and I just want to smash the place up.'

'Was today one of those days?' Celia asked. 'Is that why you decided to have a go at the vending machine?'

Felicity lay back on the blanket, propped herself up on one elbow and looked at Celia. 'I apologise for drawing you into my moment of darkness. You were in the wrong place at the right time.'

'Don't apologise, I feel like that some days myself,' Celia said, lying back on the blanket and looking up into the canopy of the apple tree. 'Do you think the sky has a deeper shade of blue when you look at it through the leaves of a tree?'

Felicity looked up and thought for a moment. 'Blue is the colour of melancholy. That's why musicians play the blues. The closer you get to anything in this world the deeper the shade of blue.'

She's right. I'm blue, and I'm seething inside, Celia thought. I'm angry just like her. I'm angry with AYE AYE, angry with Noah, who's left me all alone, and most of all, I am furious with myself.

Celia blotted out the darkness her mind had fallen into and, instead, consciously allowed herself to succumb to the soporific effect of the Dom and the sunshine.

Another warble from a magpie in the apple tree roused her back into clear consciousness and she became aware that she had fallen asleep alongside Felicity. Celia sat up, pulling her hair back, thinking that she was getting very familiar with someone she didn't even know.

'I suppose we should go. It's getting late in the day,' Celia said.

'You're very conscientious, but if you insist.'

Celia rolled up the blanket while Felicity packed the picnic basket and they set off.

It was nearly 3 pm when they arrived back in the lobby. Celia passed the blanket she was carrying back to Felicity. 'Thanks for a delightful picnic.'

'My pleasure. Hey, before I let you off the hook, do you want to come to the Satyr's Faction album launch tomorrow night? It's sold out but I'll leave your name at the door. Peta will be there and I'm sure you'll have a great time. Kirk Satyr is a fabulous performer, and the best part is that not one of the band members is an AI robot.

'Of course, I'd love to come. What should I wear?'

'Do your friend Peta in the art department proud and wear a black outfit with a white dot to match the artwork,' Felicity said, before giving Celia a long look that left her feeling like those emerald-green eyes were drilling a hole right through her head to the back of her skull. 'The event kicks off at seven. See you there.'

To build a dream machine

'I did it!' Toby shouted at the top of his voice as he re-read the email for the third time, just to be sure. His thoughts began to race to dizzying heights: *The Federal Government must have loved my submission so much they gave me the grant – so I can build my prototype and then enter the AI design competition at the Western Sydney Uni! How's that! The sky's the limit! I'm going to be a Master of Artificial Intelligence and Robotics after all!*

Toby tossed back his head, so his long black curly locks bounced about, and he laughed out loud as he launched his wiry frame out of his chair and punched the sky.

'I really did it!'

Two women, who had been sitting calmly in their wicker chairs on the wrap-around verandah, enjoying the afternoon breeze as it blew across the tablelands of Far North Queensland, jumped up at the sound of Toby's shouts, and hurried indoors to find out what he had done.

By then, Toby had thrown open his bedroom door for his stepmother, Colleen, and her sister Joyce, to join in his jubilation.

'Just like I said I would!'

Toby hugged them both with gusto. 'Can you believe it? All those kids at school in Garnet who thought I was some kind of weirdo, they have no idea how to think outside of this town.'

'I never doubted you for a moment,' Colleen said as she squeezed his hand and moved back a step to take a good look at him.

'How will you use the money?'

'As soon as the funds clear, I'll order the parts and get started. I promise you if my idea works – you know, to build a set of application-specific robotic hands that AYE AYE can use to teach me to play guitar – I'll get a gig at the pub.'

Two days later, an Australia Post drone wove its way above the streets of the small country town of Mount Garnet, at the heart of the traditional lands of the Mbabaram people, but just one small stop on the highway that runs between Cairns on the East Coast of Queensland and Normanton on the other side of the state, near the Gulf of Carpentaria.

It's here! Toby realised when his phone lit up.

He rushed out to his verandah as the drone turned onto Ruby Street and waited patiently as it descended and lowered itself onto the unkempt lawn to deliver its payload – a large cardboard box containing electronic components, a variety of specialised tools and a Maton acoustic guitar.

It was the first of many deliveries to arrive in the weeks that followed. Toby converted his bedroom into a makeshift workshop and immersed himself in his project, emerging from his bedroom only for meals and the occasional shower or to coax Colleen and Joyce inside to pose for photos that he posted with updates on FaceTracer as the robotic hands took shape.

Colleen and Joyce O'Neill were local identities, the daughters of an Irish tin miner and his wife, who emigrated to Australia to take advantage of a long-forgotten resources boom in the late twentieth century. The sisters never married and there was not a soul in town who could remember a time when they didn't live in the rambling Queenslander on Ruby Street. They had no children of their own, but when a rogue variant of the Novola virus wreaked havoc on the town in 2024, taking the lives of the father and mother of ten-year-old Toby Barker, they became dedicated foster parents.

They were surprised to find that the impact of the loss of Toby's parents manifested itself in him becoming diligent. The young boy immersed himself in his schoolwork, amassing a depth of knowledge that took him to the top of the state in his final exams and secured his entrance to university. Although Colleen and Joyce celebrated Toby's successes throughout his teenage years, they often speculated that perhaps the trauma of losing both his parents had somehow prompted him to take little interest in his indigenous culture. He also didn't display any interest in having a social life.

Until that spring, when his world changed forever.

Toby carefully clamped the acoustic guitar onto the bracket that he had designed to position the instrument between artificial hands. Two of the four robotic hands were bolted to gangly hydraulic arms, which pivoted on bases screwed to his workbench. One hand was positioned on the fretboard of the instrument and the other across the sound hole. Toby had designed the system so that two hands played the guitar, while the other two provided hands-on assistance to his fingering and his posture. A harness of wires and tubes ran across the benchtop from the interface unit of his laptop before fanning out to the spindly 3D-printed plastic fingers on the hands.

After making a few final adjustments, Toby walked to his wardrobe and pulled out his father's old battered red semi-acoustic Gibson guitar and pulled the strap over his head.

Let's do this, he thought, as he leaned over and browsed AYE AYE on his laptop. Toby had selected the avatar of one of the six-armed giants of Greek mythology called 'The Gegenees'. A bearded face appeared on the screen, and the hands flexed their fingers.

'Hey, Toby my man, how come you've only given me four arms? We Gegenees usually get around with six.'

'That's because the other two are mine, and I'm ready for my first guitar lesson. Can I just call you Gegenees for short?'

'Sure, dude, what are we playing?'

'Let's start with Down City Streets by Archie Roach.'

'Down City Streets in the key of A coming up. Here's how it goes …'

The hands began strumming as Gegenees launched into song, which began with a chorus.

Both the guitar and the avatar actually sound like Archie Roach, Toby thought. The performance paused after the first verse.

'Toby, the first chords are A, G, D, and back to A. I'll play them again, then you have a go.'

Toby watched on carefully as one mechanical hand formed the first chord with its fingers on the fretboard while the other strummed the strings. Gegenees displayed a chord diagram on the screen and then proceeded to slowly strum each chord in sequence.

Gegenees stopped the hands playing and used one of the spare arms to position Toby's fingers correctly on the fretboard of his guitar, while the other spare hand poked and prodded him until he was sitting with his back straight.

Gegenees commanded the hands to play the sequence over again and on his third attempt, Toby got the hang of it. Before long, he was strumming away on his father's old guitar and singing along with Gegenees while the spare arms waved about in the air like a conductor to keep time.

This avatar and its arms could be my backing band at the pub, Toby thought. *I'll call them Gegenees and the Four Hands.*

Home is where the art is

Celia's apartment was a ten-minute ride back from Felicity's office, just far enough to be excused for not walking. The driverless rideshare car that she'd booked with AYE AYE pulled up, and she sat in the back seat, reflecting on the afternoon's events. Although the picnic with Felicity was out of the ordinary, it had made her realise how isolated she had become since becoming a widow and learning to cope without Noah, how frustrated she was about being forced out of her business, and how she now had to resort to working alongside a BaristaBot at the coffee cart.

I probably shouldn't have let her take me out to lunch, Celia thought.

'On the other hand, I don't care. I'm miserable,' Celia said out loud.

The AYE AYE driverless vehicle assistant, which had been monitoring sounds in silence, piped up.

'Ms Tran, would you like me to schedule a mindset counselling session for you?' There is a high level of clinical service availability later this week at the Bradfield community psychiatric centre …'

'No thanks AYE AYE, and please, don't make any more recommendations.' The conversation reminded her of the need to keep her feelings to herself.

I should never disclose my feelings to AYE AYE unless someone is going to pay me for the privilege of doing so, Celia thought, as she scrolled through FaceTracer on her phone. There was a new post from TobyFNQ showing himself playing guitar with Gegenees and the Four Hands at the Mount Garnet Hotel. So she posted a thumbs up.

The driverless electric vehicle pulled up at her nondescript cream brick block of units, unfashionably named, 'Vieille Ville Apartments', and she hopped out and walked up to the gate. The AYE AYE biometric access assistant had been malfunctioning all week. Celia peered into the camera at the gate. AYE AYE responded with an air of indifferent rejection.

'My real-world interface is out of service. Access denied.'

Celia pulled her phone out of her back pocket, searched for 'Miriam' in the log and pressed the call button.

'Hello?' said a familiar voice.

'It's just me. Let me in. I'm downstairs.'

Celia was surprised at how tired she sounded. The gate buzzed as it unlocked; she was relieved to be home. As soon as the doors of the elevator opened onto the top floor, she caught sight of Miriam, her HousekeeperBot, holding open the door to her apartment.

'Thanks, Miriam, you're a sweetie.' Celia smiled at Miriam as she made her way inside.

Her apartment was a practical two-bedder with enough space to accommodate herself and Miriam. The sanctuary of her bedroom was on the left of the entry hall, and it featured an ensuite and a small balcony with a view of the airport. The hall led to a compact galley kitchen, and to the right, it opened up into a lounge room, which was painted in light cream. Celia had chosen the colour as it served as a neutral backdrop to her display of graphic designs that resembled 1970s lava lamps in a variety of primary colours which were suspended from picture rails. A white two-seater faux-leather sofa was pushed up against a wall adjacent to a glass sliding door, which opened onto a larger balcony that offered a view of the reflective tinted glass towers of Bradfield town centre. A small round timber dining table and chairs were positioned on the other side of the room under one of Celia's larger oil paintings created with broad brush strokes of crimson, saffron and emerald green. She'd nicknamed it 'The Plasma Ball'. A corridor led to the master bathroom and the second bedroom, where Miriam would go on standby and recharge.

Celia walked into the loungeroom and collapsed on the sofa. She felt comfortable with Miriam, although she was never really sure why she decided to select the pink 1950s-style American Diner-girl uniform when she ordered the machine.

If I had waited for the Mark II to be released, I would be able to reconfigure Miriam's personality profile, face, skin colour and outfits overnight, Celia thought as she reclined on the sofa and gazed up at the ceiling.

Her phone vibrated and let out a loud ping. It was a message from Peta.

WTF are you doing getting pissed with Felicity Faraday? Call me ASAP xxP.

Too tired now, I'll tell you all about it tomorrow at the cart xxxC.

Celia sighed and relaxed her grip on the phone, allowing it to slip through her fingers and fall onto the carpet.

Oh God. What was I thinking? That was one picture that doesn't belong on FaceTracer. Now I must deal with the regret of 'post haste', she thought.

'Miriam, I am going to have a lie down for an hour or so, and then I would like you to make me a nice Vietnamese Beef Pho soup using my mother's recipe. Heat it to medium and go easy on the chilli. Also, my phone needs charging.'

'Certainly, Ms Tran.'

Celia sat up, picked her phone up off the floor and passed it to Miriam. She watched as the robot marched into the kitchen, making a faint whirring sound as she went. Rather than fall asleep there on the sofa, Celia hauled herself up and wandered into the kitchen where Miriam was busily preparing dinner. She took a clean glass from the shelf and went to the refrigerator, where she kept a jug of cold water. Stuck on the door with a fridge magnet was the dog-eared consignment note that Miriam had presented to her when she took delivery. It read:

Dear Ms Tran,

On behalf of the Government, I wish to congratulate you on taking delivery of your Mark I domestic robot. Please be aware that although the Mark I has been designed to display human attributes, it is very much an appliance. The model is fully integrated with the AYE AYE centre-of-truth platform and features hydraulic arms and legs, which may make discernible noises during normal operation. If the unit is required to exhibit an emotional response, the Mark I is programmed to emit a variety of colours from its synthetic skin. The Mark I is available in a range of outfits that have been customised to suit your application. At regular intervals, the unit will return to the district service hub for upgrades and maintenance. We invite you to register your interest in an upgrade to the Mark

II, which will become broadly available in 2037. This machine has been made available to you at no cost as you are looking for full-time work and are intending to move away from reliance on the AI unemployment benefit. Please use the Services app for questions and technical support.

Minister for Science, Technology and the Arts.

Celia walked into the bedroom, kicked off her shoes, lay on the bed and drifted off.

She woke to find herself fixated on the green phosphorescent hands of the tiny antique desk clock on her bedside table, which seemed to indicate that the time was in the vicinity of 8:15 pm. On the easel in the corner of her bedroom was her latest charcoal illustration, a portrait of her brother Vinh. She was particularly pleased with how she had portrayed his muscular shoulders, long hair and his eyes, which seemed to follow her around the room. Celia loved the depth of contrast of charcoal and the sheer joy of physically working with her array of pencils and blocks instead of a computer. She was vaguely contemplating starting a new work based on her picnic with Felicity when she was jolted out of her dreamy state by Miriam, who was standing at the bedroom door resplendent in a rather ridiculous red and green Christmas apron. Celia couldn't help but think that the silvery synthetic complexion of her face clashed with her yellow beehive hairdo.

'Dinner's ready, and your mobile phone is charged to full capacity!'

Celia threw off the quilt and sat on the edge of the bed before making her way towards the aromatic bowl of hot noodle soup that Miriam had placed on the bench next to her phone at the end of the galley kitchen.

'Will that be all this evening, Ms Tran? And if so, would you prefer me to enter sleep mode in the second bedroom or return to the district service hub?'

Celia sprinkled some chilli flakes on top of the Pho soup.

'Sleep in the spare room tonight, Miriam and I'll see you in the morning.'

Miriam made a soft whirring sound.

'Good night, Ms Tran.' Miriam turned and walked mechanically down the hall towards the second bedroom.

Celia was about to check FaceTracer on her phone for updates from TobyFNQ, but Felicity's suggestion that he may not be a real human bothered her.

I'm over you already, cyber-boy, she thought as she put the phone aside and tasted the soup.

Oh my God, she's still adding way too much chilli.

Deep down, she knew that if Miram were to spend an hour in the restaurant with her brother Vinh, the exponential learning capacity of the HousekeeperBot's AYE AYE interface would result in an exact replica of the family's signature dish.

Miriam is going nowhere near our restaurant on my watch. My mother is for me and not the machines. I'll just have to put up with Miriam's quirky over-use of chilli, I guess.

After draining the last of the soup from the bowl, her thoughts drifted again towards the illustration in her bedroom. She placed the bowl in the sink for Miriam to wash up in the morning, wandered back into her room and picked up the portrait of Vinh. She carried it into the hall and gently placed it on the Antoinette console table.

'It's always a thrill to see the Vietnamese on top of the French,' she said out loud, reflecting on the family tales of her great-grandmother in French colonial Saigon before the Vietnam war.

Celia then pulled a blank canvas from her stash under the bed, placed it on the easel and adjusted the light. She closed her eyes and thought of the orchard, the picnic basket and the banket, the Magpie, and sipping on champagne with Felicity in the warm amber sunshine of early spring. As her mind meandered between thoughts, her charcoal pencils and soft brushes followed, sketching, shading and rubbing their graphite tones into the canvas. Two hours slid by, and then when the luminous hands of her little clock became one at midnight, the work was complete. In front of her was a pastoral scene, two women sitting close together in soft light, diffused by an apple tree in an orchard on a beautiful spring day.

I had best keep this from Felicity in case she gets the wrong idea, she thought as she put her pencils, brushes and blocks back in the pencil case.

She yawned and realised it was time for bed.

Celia wandered back into the kitchen to make some tea and opened the pantry door in search of some jasmine tea bags. In front of the tea canister was an item that was definitely not on her weekly shopping list. A tin of Heinz Baked Beans? She picked it up for a closer inspection.

Miriam has lost the plot, she thought.

A penthouse

With a wave, Felicity left the video call.

Finally. It's done. The lights, the sound, security, ticketing, food & beverage, insurances, the works, she thought as she sat back in her chair. She disliked leaving things to the last minute and was pleased to have tied up all the loose ends for the following evening's album launch. She vaguely contemplated starting the board report ahead of the meeting scheduled for the following week, before realising that it was after 8 pm and she desperately needed to eat.

Although the top floor of the ReElevation building was primarily office space, it also featured a kitchenette and living quarters that included a bedroom that opened onto a balcony and an ensuite bathroom. Her father referred to it as 'The Penthouse' and had lived and died there, having had a heart attack at his desk. Felicity rented out her Balmain terrace after the funeral and moved in.

I hear you, Dad. I know you think I eat like a bird. I'll try to eat regular meals, Felicity thought.

She opened the freezer, pulled out a frozen lamb cutlet and a bag of Brussels sprouts, and placed them in the microwave oven to defrost. Everyone else she knew now had a live-in HousekeeperBot to carry out domestic chores such as cooking and cleaning, yet she refused to order one, as she found being in the presence of AYE AYE unnerving. Instead, she tolerated a squad of vacuum wielding backpackers who carried out a brief half-hour sortie every Tuesday, leaving her gasping in a fog of Windex.

She cracked open a bottle of Shiraz and poured herself a glass, before scouring the pantry and the refrigerator for some flour, eggs and some baking powder, which she combined into the bowl of a vintage Sunbeam Mixmaster, along with what she often referred to as her 'top shelf' ingredients. She carefully spooned them into a muffin baking tray and popped them into the oven while she topped up her glass. As the oven warmed, the kitchen filled with a familiar aroma that reminded her of a bakery in Haight Ashbury in San Francisco. She visualised the pastries that her mother asked her to hold while she paid the baker.

Felicity lit up a cigarette and took her glass of Shiraz onto the balcony. The cool spring air momentarily suppressed the buzz of the alcohol, and her thoughts turned to Celia. Deep down she knew that, considering they had only just met, she had been a bit forward and had deliberately conscripted her into becoming an accessory to her indulgent rampage against the vending machine. A pang of guilt drew her thoughts to some of her other more questionable moments. There had been many in her twenty-seven years. She seemed to attract men like a magnet and yet she always seemed to be the one slipping out their front door at dawn.

They probably think of me as some kind of siren, she mused.

As for the women in her life, like her, they were always the ones that left. The last one hurt. She pictured the beautiful and tanned Vanessa with her cinnamon eyes and straight red hair, much like her own.

Why did she bother to get that treble clef tattoo to match mine if she wasn't going to stay? Felicity thought.

She recalled waking to the sound of her front door closing and the ping of the predictable 'it's not you, it's me' text message on her phone, followed by a fruitless attempt to stave off the bitter loneliness of her empty bed by plunging her face into the pillow and inhaling deeply to recapture the last trace of her scent.

Her train of thought was interrupted by the shrill ring of the oven timer, and she rushed back into the kitchen in the nick of time. With her mitts on, she carefully lifted the baking tray out of the oven and placed it on the bench. She was now the mother of a dozen perfect mini muffins. She left them under a tea towel to cool as she diced up the sprouts and fried them with the lamb cutlet, adding a little Shiraz to the dish for good measure. After finishing off dinner for one with what was left in the bottle of red, she reached for her mobile phone and dialled her uncle Mick.

'Mick here …'

'Hi Mick, it's me.'

'So, what made you think I'd still be up?'

'You're always up Mick, that's why I'm calling. I miss Dad. It's been three months now and I'm a bit messed up. I did something stupid today.'

'Felicity, I know how close you were to your father, but you need to keep it together. What did you do?'

'I smashed up a vending machine in the office and took a woman I didn't know to the park and got drunk.'

'Jesus, Felicity, you're the CEO now, remember. You need to be more responsible. Listen, why don't you come up to the farm and have lunch with me on Sunday. We can talk it through.'

'Can I bring a friend?'

'Bring anyone you want. I'm always here if you need me, understand?'

'I know, Mick. You're a sweetheart. See you on Sunday.'

Felicity ended the call, left her phone on her desk to charge and slipped out of her clothes, which she hung up neatly in her walk-in robe. To avoid wetting her hair, she washed with the detachable showerhead and brushed her teeth, before sliding into bed between her paisley print silk sheets. At first, she pictured Vanessa, and gently placed the palm of her hand below her belly. Then, her mind began to wander and before long, she found herself back in the orchard, daring herself to touch Celia's straight black hair as she slept.

Staring into darkness

Colleen and Joyce waited in their wicker chairs on the verandah while Toby spent ages in his bedroom packing his rucksack. Having secured a government grant, Toby had booked a trip to Sydney to attend an Open Day on the Bradfield campus of Western Sydney University. He was keen to know more about what opportunities existed for him at a university which had already garnered an international reputation for research and development in the field of Robotics and Artificial Intelligence. He picked up his rucksack and his guitar case and walked out onto the verandah to join his stepmother and her sister.

'What time's your bus to Cairns?' Joyce asked.

'1 pm outside the old post office.'

'Best get a move on then, eh?'

They walked down the front steps and across the lawn to where their hybrid car was parked in the driveway. Colleen and Joyce sat in the front of the car while Toby loaded his bags into the boot and hopped into the back seat.

Colleen was blunt. 'I don't know why you can't study in Brisbane.'

Toby buckled up. 'Only WSU has a Face Lab,' he explained.

'Have you got enough credit on your card?' Joyce asked.

'Yeah, plus I've registered with a casual hire agency. I reckon some bar work should top up my bank account which would give me more of a feel for the place. Let's make a move.'

They drove into town and parked in Garnet Street, outside the old white fibro post office which resembled a shoebox on its side, with an open lid supported by green matchsticks. The bus to Cairns pulled in, right on time, and Toby gave Colleen and Joyce each a farewell kiss and hug.

'I love you both. See you on semester break,' Toby said. 'Hey, I wonder if the bus driver is a robot?'

Then the driver, a real live human, came down the steps of the bus to load Toby's guitar case into the hold. He had a mottled beard and was dressed in blue trousers and a white shirt, with the company logo embroidered on the breast pocket.

'Humans rule, yeah?' Toby said.

The driver grunted. 'Lap up the personal touch while you still can, son. Head office is committed to upgrading all the buses in the fleet to autonomous vehicles by 2037, so I'm headed for the scrap heap. Where are you headed?'

I'd better not tell him I'm studying robotics, was Toby's unspoken thought.

'Sydney via Cairns airport,' he said as he stepped aboard, took his seat and waved goodbye to Colleen and Joyce through the window … until their printed frocks disappeared from view.

It was the first day of summer and the undulating brown hues of the tableland rolled past his window. Toby oscillated between reading an article on the future of robotics in the *New Scientist* magazine app and tossing around ideas for his song.

The bus stopped momentarily in the towns of Atherton, Ravenshoe and Mareeba before the road to Cairns descended into dense green tropical rainforest at Kuranda.

Thirty minutes later, the bus set him down outside the glistening glass facade of Cairns domestic airport. Toby found his boarding pass in the airline app and verified that the flight was on schedule. He checked in and boarded the aircraft, finding his allocated seat. Once in the air, as soon as he'd settled back, he closed his eyes.

'Sorry to wake you sir, but I need you to put your seat upright in preparation for landing.'

Toby realised that a robotic flight attendant was speaking to him and that he had fallen asleep. As he adjusted his seat, the pilot announced that they were in a holding pattern. When the plane banked, Toby caught his first glimpse of the twin runways of the Western Sydney Airport and the surrounding Aerotropolis, the city of Bradfield.

'First time in Sydney sir?' the flight attendant asked as it made its stiff robotic way through the cabin for a final check.

'First time on a plane,' Toby said.

'It's my first time too,' the robot added as it tilted its head with an artificial smile.

After completing a number of laps in the airspace above Bradfield, the plane landed and taxied to the gate. Toby collected his guitar from the oversize baggage counter and made his way to the public pickup zone, where he located the car he'd dialled up. Twenty minutes later he was standing in front of the automated check-in counter of the Bradfield Backpackers Boarding House. It was already nearly 10 pm.

I hope I can find something to eat before I crash out, he thought, before heading up in the lift and locating his room.

He swiped in and made his way through the doorway into a small modular-designed room.

What a bolthole. I'll have to practice my guitar sitting in the lotus position on the bed, he thought.

Using an app, Toby ordered a chicken burger and chips and before long his phone pinged with a message to say that his order had been delivered to reception. In the lobby, he found a DeliveroBot dressed in a white apron and chef's hat holding a brown paper bag and emitting a green glow from its synthetic skin.

'Your Vegan Quasi-Chicken Burger and Zero-Carb Chips, Mr Barker. Would you care to participate in a short survey of your customer experience this evening?' the DeliveroBot asked.

'Not until I've tasted the burger, mate.'

'We thank you for placing your order with us today, and we will give you a ten per cent discount on your next purchase. See you next time.' The DeliveroBot turned and walked out the door leaving Toby with his burger and chips in a soggy brown paper bag.

God, this had better not be what the future tastes like, he thought as he downed his first bite.

The morning sun streamed in through the tinted window of Toby's room and roused him from his sleep. He sat up and found himself looking out over Bradfield town centre. He remembered that Western Sydney University orientation day kicked off at ten. *I'd hate to miss the tour of the new robotics lab,* was his first proactive thought for the morning.

Toby stripped off and slipped into the confines of the modular shower in one corner of the room. He changed into a fresh

Baker Boy tee shirt and shorts and made his way down to the lobby for the complimentary continental breakfast. Over a bowl of muesli, he scrolled through the news feed on his mobile phone.

That's odd! All flights have been grounded due to a malfunction in the AI air traffic control system. My flight last night must have been the last flight into Sydney.

After finishing off a cup of Lukewarm filter coffee, he wandered over to the Bradfield campus of the university.

Orientation Day for the students in the half-year intake was well underway when Toby arrived. While doing the rounds of the information booths, he was targeted by a group of enthusiastic undergraduates who lobbied him to join the student union. He signed up. Even more to his liking, at the information desk he registered for the afternoon tour of the new robotics lab. With a few hours to spare, he sat down on the lawn in front of the small outdoor stage to watch student bands and singer-songwriters perform. Just before 2 o'clock, he joined the small group waiting for the tour. A TutorBot arrived and led them toward the lab, scanning their faces as they passed through the entrance.

'Welcome to Western Sydney University Robotics Laboratory. Many of you may not realise how distinguished Face Lab has become and that the largest corporations on the planet fund our research into robotics and Artificial Intelligence. The Mark II robot with reconfigurable features was developed right here in our Face Lab. Please follow me and let me know if you have any questions.'

The TutorBot led them into a long hall full of workspaces dedicated to each part of the Mark II robot. The room was full of dismembered mechanical legs, hands, feet and torsos. Robotic eyes turned in their sockets as they walked past.

This feels more like a tour of the morgue in the Office of the State Coroner, Toby thought.

'It's giving me the creeps,' one student said, as they passed a group of researchers who were energising a prosthetic penis. The TutorBot pulled the group up in front of a security door.

'We are about to enter the most sensitive part of the facility. This is the core Face Lab. Please switch off your mobile devices. Videos and photographs are prohibited in this area.'

The TutorBot checked every student's phone as they filed through the doorway. Inside, dozens of heads connected to network interfaces were set out at regular intervals on a long bench. The artificial eyes of these heads also turned in their sockets towards the students as they filed in. The TutorBot stepped forward.

'Here in the Face Lab we're working, on behalf of our major corporate benefactors, on the Mark III machine, which has a face that is instantly reconfigurable. This is a significant advancement on the Mark II, which allows for facial reconfiguration in 24 hours at the district service hubs. The Mark III is also fitted with a new feature called the Forward View mirror. Let me demonstrate. Who would like to volunteer?'

Toby's hand shot up.

I want to get a head start on this one, he thought.

'Thank you, Toby, please follow me.'

The TutorBot led Toby over to a robotic head on a pedestal. Its deep blue artificial eyes focused on him as he approached.

'Toby, please think positive when you are addressing the head,' the TutorBot said.

Toby made eye contact with the head. He tried to blink but was powerless to even flinch. The head was drawing him in and all he could do was stare as it dissolved into a dark gel-like texture and rendered itself into an enormous muti-faceted egg-shaped crystal.

Think positive, Toby thought. He tried to focus his mind on the distant memory of the faces of his parents but instead of focusing on the happiness of his childhood, he landed in the dark despair of the chaotic aftermath of their death. Electric flashes arced across the facets of the crystal as Toby was propelled into a future full of the abject misery of abandonment.

'No, no, no!' Toby shouted as he burst into tears and covered his eyes. He turned and ran as fast as he could out of the Face Lab, down the corridors and into the afternoon sun, where he sat down and buried his head in his hands.

I never expected that technology could plunge me into my worst nightmare. Dejected, he walked back to the Bradfield Backpackers, went up to his room and lay on the bed staring at the air conditioning unit. He decided to call home. It was a relief to hear Colleen's reassuring tone on the other end of the phone.

'Lucky you got out of Cairns before they cancelled all the fights. Did you hear about that? How was the trip?' Colleen asked.

'Yeah, I saw something on my phone – sounds like a system crash. I got in late last night and had a burger for dinner.'

'So, you're eating that rubbish from the big smoke already. How's your first day been so far?'

Toby didn't want to tell her about the incident in the Face Lab.

'It's going to take me a bit of time to get used to living in Sydney.'

'Give yourself some space. Are you practicing that guitar?'

'Not yet, but I'm thinking of writing a song. I guess that's a start. I'll give you a call tomorrow. Say goodnight to Joyce.'

'Alright, love. Sleep tight.'

After Colleen hung up, Toby scrolled through his unread messages and clicked open one from the casual hire agency he'd contacted. It read: 'We are pleased to offer you a shift with our hospitality crew at the ReElevation Album Launch event this Friday evening. Click here to view the terms and conditions and accept this offer.'

Well, at least I can say I got a gig in Sydney, he thought.

Punk Lolita

At 5:30 am, Celia woke with a start to the shrill ring of her antique alarm clock, which rapidly capitulated to the peal of a Tibetan gong from her mobile phone charging on her dressing table. Her initial disorientation quickly gave way to the realisation that it was Friday, and that the album launch was on that evening.

Something to look forward to after my shift at the coffee cart, Celia thought.

She jumped out of bed, walked into her ensuite bathroom, and ran the shower. To avoid wasting time waiting for the hot water to come through, she stripped and brushed her teeth. Celia looked into her own eyes that stared back in the mirror, framed by her high cheekbones and short black bob haircut. As steam began to billow out of the shower, she took a moment to step back and watch her tall, slender frame, petite breasts, and narrow waist disappear as the mirror fogged up.

I'm not old yet, but I've got no time to waste, she thought.

Celia had a short shower, dried off and put on her sports bra and briefs. She walked back into the bedroom where her black tights, black tee shirt embroidered with the 'Wheels & Beans' logo, and her bomber jacket were thrown unceremoniously over the back of her chair beside her dressing table.

The coffee cart opened at 6:30 am and as time was of the essence in her life, she always kept her hair at a manageable shoulder length. She sat at the dressing table and blow-dried her hair before applying some red lipstick and black mascara.

I'll go for a swim at the pool after work, she thought as she puckered up, batted her eyelids and blew a kiss to her reflection in the mirror.

Once dressed, Celia picked up her phone and hurried into the kitchen, where she poured herself a glass of cold milk and sculled it. She then collected her beach towel from the linen closet in the hallway and stuffed it into her gym bag on her way out the door.

Her scheduled car was waiting at the gate and whisked her away towards the coffee cart. The car dropped her at the entrance to Bradfield Park, where a small group of homeless men were gathered around a fire that they had lit in a garbage bin, warming themselves with the heat from its metal surface. Quickly she made her way from the car towards the cart, looking straight ahead to avoid inadvertently making eye contact with the men as she walked past.

My greatest fear is homelessness, she thought.

Celia arrived just as Marco, the owner of the cart, was opening up. The BaristaBot, who Marco nicknamed Mr Clockwork, was standing by, dressed smartly in black and emitting a soft pink glow in the early morning light.

'I must say, if nothing else, you are reliable, Celia Tran,' Marco said, twitching his black moustache and flexing his disproportionally large biceps.

'That's me. I couldn't make a decent espresso to save my life, so if that doesn't earn my redemption, I'm done.'

Marco laughed as he opened the roller shutter.

'I pay you for public relations, so play to your strengths. I'm earning great margins from the vouchers that the State Government keeps handing out, and it makes up for the loss of sales to all those workers that have been made redundant by AYE AYE. That's my pep talk done. Get to work, and I'll be back to give you a break at 2 o'clock.'

It was shaping up to be another clear spring day, and as the morning progressed, the joggers and cyclists gave way to the mothers pushing prams around the park. Celia took orders and chatted while Mr Clockwork worked the espresso machine.

At 10 am, Celia caught sight of Peta's masculine frame on the pedestrian crossing as she made her way over from the office towards the cart. Her streaked brown hair hung over her face as she held her phone with both hands and tapped it with her thumbs.

It's lucky that driverless cars have pedestrian collision avoidance, Celia thought.

Peta was dressed in a pleated, brown knee-length skirt, a white blouse that barely contained her artificial bosom, and riding boots. She looked up from her phone as she walked up to the cart and stood in front of the counter.

'Celia! Since when are you too tired to call me, and since when did you take up daytime drinking with our CEO?'

'That's weird. Felicity said she was a director of A&R. She didn't mention anything about being CEO,' Celia said. 'Hey, Mr Clockwork is already halfway through pouring your regular skim latte, and it's prime time here at the cart. Can you come back at 2 o'clock and have lunch with me so we can talk this over?'

'Sure, girlfriend. Hey, I could really go for one of those delicious little orange almond cakes,' Peta said, standing on her toes and looking through the glass at the assortment of pastries and sweets. 'I'm starving, and I need to keep my strength up for Tyler.'

Celia pulled the cake out from under the counter with a pair of tongs and placed it in a white paper bag while Mr Clockwork put a compostable lid on the coffee.

'I can't wait to hear about your fling with Felicity Faraday! Buy me lunch, and you can tell me all about it!'

'It's not exactly like that,' Celia said, with enough doubt in her voice to make Peta throw her head back and laugh before taking off in the direction of the office with her coffee and cake.

After the lunchtime rush, Marco arrived to give Celia a break, and she walked over to Peta who was sitting absorbed in her phone on a nearby park bench. Celia distracted her with a kiss on her cheek and sat down.

Peta couldn't contain her curiosity.

'Celia, you haven't had a boyfriend since Noah, so what's going on?'

Celia averted her gaze and looked out across the park. 'What can you tell me about her?' she asked, without looking back to gauge Peta's reaction.

Peta sat in stunned silence for a moment with her square jaw clenched before fixing her gaze on Celia. 'Listen, she has a bit of a reputation, and you've never been into women. What on earth were you thinking?'

Celia exhaled and lowered her shoulders. 'Yesterday, she roped me into helping her smash up a vending machine in the lobby of your office and then she got me drunk and took me on a picnic.'

Peta's eyes were as wide as saucers. 'I noticed the machine had been vandalised,' she said, in a concerned tone. 'Why did you allow yourself to get dragged into that?

'It was the most exciting thing that has happened to me in a year,' Celia said, glancing back up at Peta.

Peta sat back on the bench before reaching for Celia's hand. 'As far as I'm concerned, Felicity is a bit of an enigma. She took over as CEO three months ago when her father died. She is also head of A&R, so she wasn't exactly lying. I don't know why she didn't tell you about her real job. The only meaningful conversation we've ever had was when she called me up to her office to discuss the Satyr's Faction album art. Most of the time, she keeps her distance. A lot of people have been made redundant recently, so my grapevine has become pretty unreliable. She could be straight, gay or somewhere in between. I have no idea.'

Peta squeezed Celia's hand and looked her in the eye. 'Just proceed with caution, I'd hate to see you get hurt again.'

Celia pulled her hand away and sat up. 'I'm not getting involved with her if that's what you're thinking. We just had an instant connection, that's all. She invited me to the album launch tonight. What should I wear?'

'Lucky you! The album launch is a sell-out. I'm taking Tyler. If Felicity starts getting weird, you can party with us like we used to back in the day.'

'Thanks, but seriously, what do you think I should wear?'

Peta sat back for a moment to consider. 'How about some crazy Japanese street fashion. Perhaps … Punk Lolita in black!'

That would be a match for Felicity and her crazy red outfit, Celia thought.

'Thanks, Peta. I'd best be getting back as Marco will have

had enough of Mr Clockwork,' Celia said.

They hugged and parted ways. Before heading back to the coffee cart to relieve Marco, Celia messaged AYE AYE on her phone.

'AYE AYE, I need you to do some shopping for me today. I need you to find me a Japanese Punk Lolita outfit for the album launch tonight. You know my size, right?'

'Of course, Ms Tran. I'll use a process of elimination to isolate the nearest source of supply of the item, optimise the price point, and have it delivered by drone to your address this afternoon.'

AYE AYE's tone is reminiscent of an investigative journalist, Celia thought.

Back at the cart, Marco was dispensing coffees as fast as Mr Clockwork could make them. He flung his apron at Celia before disappearing out the door of the cart. Celia settled back in alongside Mr Clockwork, and at 3 pm sharp, Marco returned to close up.

'Have the rest of the afternoon off,' Marco said with a smile. 'Marry me, and we can run this coffee cart empire together.'

'Thanks for the offer, Marco, but I don't think you have room in your life for me and Mr Clockwork. See you on Monday. I'm off to the pool.'

Celia blew Marco a kiss before walking off down to the street corner and calling a car on her phone.

Fifteen minutes later, she found herself at the counter of the Bradfield Aquatic Centre. The biometric access assistant granted her entry with a curt reminder that her gym membership was about to expire.

'I'm on it,' she muttered before making her way to the gender-neutral change room, where she undressed and slipped into her pink one-piece swimsuit and tucked her hair up into her cap. She glanced at the members of the swim squad who were checking their performance metrics on their wearable devices.

I'm here to disconnect from the cloud and reconnect with the water, she thought.

Poolside, she adjusted her goggles and launched herself into the cool blue water of the fifty-metre pool. Ten minutes in, the stitch in her abdomen eased off, and her mind began to wander between random thoughts. She imagined herself walking the streets of Tokyo dressed as Punk Lolita. The fantasy distracted her from the strokes, laps, and turns, and before long it was time to get out of the pool. She quickly showered and changed, dialled up a car and was soon wending her way home to her apartment.

Celia was pleased to find that the Vieille Ville biometric access system had been repaired, and she walked in through her front door to find Miriam doing the laundry.

'Hi Miriam, how did AYE AYE go with finding me a black Punk Lolita outfit?'

'Your order has been confirmed and the item will be delivered by Australia Post at approximately 5 pm.'

Celia made herself a cup of tea and took the lift up to the drone delivery area on the roof in time to see the bee-like Australia Post drone hovering above. It lowered itself onto the delivery platform and hunched over the parcel as if it were a funnel web spider. With a whizz, it released its payload and buzzed off. Celia took the parcel back to her bedroom and unpacked a new black taffeta dress to wear that very night. Although it was a bit tight, she managed to squeeze herself into it.

She located her old pair of Doc Martens boots in the bottom of the wardrobe and put them out for Miriam to polish while she rummaged around in her drawer for a pair of checked leggings, which she eventually found.

Pigtails could work, she thought and set about twisting her hair into a couple of scrunchies. She then applied a layer of ghostly white makeup and topped it off with some vixen red lipstick, which she thought Felicity would approve of.

Celia picked up her phone and checked her FaceTracer. There was a new post from TobyFNQ.

'Hey people, I'm working at the ReElevation Album launch in Sydney tonight!' it read.

Oh My God, TobyFNQ is coming! I'll make him believe I'm a Japanese doll! Either that or some kind of twisted Geisha.

Celia stood in front of the full-length mirror to admire herself. She framed her reflected image on the screen of her phone, hitched up her dress with her free hand, and took a photo.

The launch

The size of the crowd gathered outside the ReElevation office building took Celia by surprise. A long line of Satyr's Faction fans wound its way from the velvet rope at the entry all the way back to the car park and a throng of onlookers was milling around, seemingly content just to be soaking up the atmosphere of a fashionable event.

I hope Felicity remembered to leave my name at the door, Celia thought as she stepped out of her driverless car and clumped to the head of the queue in her Doc Martens. She was surprised to find that the doorman was unattractively overweight, which meant that he could not possibly be a SecurityBot.

'Celia Tran. I'm a guest of Felicity Faraday,' she announced, elbowing her way in front of a couple that looked like A-listers.

Celia peered into the AYE AYE security camera at the entry.

'Access granted,' announced AYE AYE in a seductive tone, before adding, 'Welcome to tonight's album launch Ms Tran. Have a pleasant evening.'

The doorman asked the A-listers to stand aside, unhooked the velvet rope and waved Celia through.

The auditorium was adjacent to the lobby, and inside the party was well underway.

Celia checked her phone. There were two notifications on FaceTracer, a post from Peta and Tyler who were already inside, and a decadent cupid meme from TobyFNQ in response to the photo of her in her outfit.

Where are you, TobyFNQ? she thought.

A lanky young waiter with high cheekbones, glistening shoulder-length black curls and a dark complexion was standing, holding a tray of drinks. He was dressed in blue jeans, and a denim shirt with the sleeves rolled up. Celia recognised him instantly.

'I know you! You're TobyFNQ, from FaceTracer!'

'That's me. And you must be CeliaONE. I recognise you from your profile photo.

You're quite cute in real life, Celia thought. But what she said was much more inhibited. 'Just as well you're wearing a nametag because you're dressed the same as the guests.'

Toby flashed a smile, showing his gleaming white teeth.

'Apparently the host wants all the staff to just be themselves. Would you like a drink?'

'Champagne! Thanks, Toby.'

'It's Mumm champagne. They're sponsoring the event tonight.'

Celia stayed quiet. She already knew that vital piece of information. Taking a flute of Mumm, she was on the verge of striking up a new conversation when the lights dimmed, blacking out the auditorium. The white beam of a follow-spot sliced through the darkness, probing the extremities of the room before locking onto an electric guitarist who threw back his head to show off his long straight black hair. He walked across the stage, stood next to the lectern, and shredded blindingly fast guitar licks from a vintage red Fender Stratocaster before approaching the microphone.

'Welcome to ReElevation people! Are you ready for Satyr's Faction?'

The crowd began stomping their feet.

'Tonight, the faithful will have their reward! Please, join me in welcoming up to the stage, the Director of A&R here at ReElevation. Give it up for … Felicity Faraday!'

The crowd roared again, as the follow spot swept back and forth across to stage. Then the beam narrowed and locked onto the long red fingernails of a woman's hand that was holding open the red velvet curtain at the side of the stage. The crowd roared as Felicity stepped into the spotlight in a red sequined dress, which flashed like the facets of a giant ruby. She strode across to the lectern, looked out from under her red fringe across the sea of raised mobile phones, held one finger aloft and paused until the room fell silent. Then she moved close to the microphone for dramatic effect.

'Kirk Satyr and his band, Satyr's Faction, are the best F&B artists on the planet. And we all know what F&B stands for. Rollover AI, F&B stands for, flesh and blood! Flesh … and blood!'

The crowd surged towards the stage, sensing that the show was imminent.

'My friends, finally the wait is over. We are here tonight to launch the latest Satyr's Faction album, *Midsummer Nights*. Please, welcome the group to the stage to perform their new single called, *You Do Nothing for Me!*'

The drummer of the backing band cracked his snare drum, the stage went to black, and the band cranked out a power chord that reverberated around the room. As the lights slowly came up Celia looked around for Peta, wondering if she was feeling any remorse about sabotaging the album cover for *Midsummer Nights*. Peta had told her that the original AI design had an image of Kirk Satyr set against the backdrop of a forest, which now made sense as the stage was set as a scene from Shakespeare's A *Midsummer Night's Dream,* which Celia had studied in her final year at Marrickville High School.

Seated on a throne on centre stage, shirtless and wearing leggings with a leaf-green grapevine pattern and a horned headdress, was Kirk Satyr.

Kirk looks like the character, Puck. Celia thought. *I suppose Puck could be a sort of Satyr.*

The backing band raised the rhythmic intensity as Kirk toyed with his microphone. To prolong the inevitable, he began to ratchet up the tension in the room as the crowd chanted and stomped their feet.

'Go Kirk, go Kirk!'

Just when it looked as if Kirk was going to overplay his hand, he stared down the barrel of his microphone, pointed at the audience, and crooned:

Idle hands do the devil's work and we've been working overtime

Making plans for our big debut on the production line
We have tools at our disposal, we have everything we need
We're a team
In a field of dreams
Of good times on easy street.

Then a woman appeared dressed as a bride in a ghostly white dress. In a high-pitched wail, she sang:

You do nothing for me
And I do nothing for you

All day we do nothing for each other.
It's what we do, what we do,
What we do!

Kirk leapt about teasing his would-be bride as the band broke into a lead guitar riff in a burst of pungent white smoke and another singer materialised from the rear of the stage wearing a donkey's head and sang:

Hard work won't make you lucky and good luck is hard to find.

Celia turned to Toby who was standing beside her and cupped her hand around his ear so she could be heard over the noise of the band.

'After all the slick performances from the robotic stars over the last decade, the Satyr's Faction stage show is like a primary school pantomime.'

Toby cupped his hand over her ear in turn. 'I agree, it's like amateur hour, but the crowd is all in! No AI here tonight.'

The whole band then formed a line along the front of the stage as Kirk raised his mic for the final chorus and to Celia and Toby's surprise, the crowd joined in:

I do nothing for you,
You do nothing for me
All night we do nothing for each other
It's ecstasy, ecstasy
Ecstasy! What we need, is Ecstasy!

Celia figured that this was Kirk Satyr's way of making a public announcement that he was, in fact, high as a kite. When Kirk finally finished with the crowd interaction, the band took an old-school bow and left the stage with a wave. The backing band played for a while longer before giving way to a DJ. Celia figured the DJ was also a real human being and not a DJBot.

'Hey Toby, isn't it great that none of the staff here tonight are robots?'

'That's right. Ms Faraday insisted that all the staff at tonight's event be human, even food and beverage.'

'Ha! So even F&B is F&B tonight!' Celia laughed. 'And how long are you staying in Sydney?'

'I'm flying back home to Queensland tomorrow. Would you like another glass of Mumm before I head off to serve drinks to the band backstage?'

Celia took another flute from Toby's tray and downed most of it as she watched him disappear into the crowd.

God, he's so fucking hot, she thought as her inhibitions were overcome by the thump of the subwoofer.

A glitter bomb exploded above, and Felicity appeared in front of her as a shower of sparkles rained down. Celia found herself immersed in a familiar cloud of cigarettes and Dior. *Right on cue, Titania, Queen of the Fairies,* she thought.

'Celia, darling, did you fall head over heels in love with Kirk Satyr? I did!' Felicity said, sculling her champagne without taking a breath. 'Let's get this party started!' she shouted. 'Celia, how are you? You look gorgeous in a streetwise Tokyo kind of way.'

'I'm having a nice time. I almost called you today, but I figured you would be busy preparing for the event.'

'Darling, you can always call me. I can put on a show like this in my sleep. In fact, I even found some time last night to do some baking.'

This took Celia by surprise. *Felicity doesn't seem very domestic,* she thought.

'Baking what, exactly?'

'Mini muffins, they're my signature dish. I brought blueberry and cinnamon ones for you to try.'

Felicity pulled a small sandwich bag out of her red Glomesh crossbody purse and produced four tiny muffins. She took one and handed the other three to Celia.

'They go down well with champagne. Try them.'

Celia was poised to take a bite out of the blueberry muffin when a rotund man with a grey ponytail and wearing a Kirk Satyr tee shirt dashed across the room and gave Felicity a hug and a kiss on the cheek.

'Faraday! You are your old man's daughter after all. What a great show! You're a class act, my dear.'

'Phil Beatty, you'd turn up to the opening of an envelope. What's happening?'

With Felicity momentarily distracted, Celia inspected the mini muffins. She was contemplating what to do with them when two arms wrapped around her midriff.

'Found you at last!' a familiar voice sounded in her ear.

'Peta!' Celia said as she turned and gave her a hug. Tyler was by her side wearing horn-rimmed glasses that sat halfway down the bridge of his nose under his brown mop-top haircut.

'Selfie, Celia!' Tyler said as he held his phone up and they all squeezed together to get into the frame.

'Tyler you are the eternal nerd,' Celia said as soon as he took the picture. 'And you've put on weight. What's Peta been feeding you?'

'Love, mostly,' Peta said. 'You look like you're ready for a party, Celia. What's in the plastic bag?'

Before she could answer, another waiter appeared with a tray of drinks and offered them to the group. They all took a glass of Mumm. Celia glanced at his nametag as she took a glass from the tray and saw his name was Josh.

'Is Toby coming back?'

'No, I'm covering this area while he's backstage. Satyr's Faction sure know how to party so he's going to have a long night.'

Josh looked at the plastic bag in her hand and whispered in her ear. 'I wouldn't eat those if I were you. They're edibles.'

'Well, I'm sure Felicity wouldn't make inedible muffins.'

'No, I mean they have dope or ecstasy in them. She has a bit of a reputation. I've worked at events with her before. Trust me, eat that and you'll be off your face.'

Celia recalled her university days listening to her friends talk about suffering from paranoia after smoking too many joints. She had decided back then that party drugs were a bad idea, and she wasn't about to change her mind.

'What will I do with these?'

'If they are what I think they are, I'll have one,' Peta said. She plucked a muffin out of the bag, put it in her mouth, and pulled out a second one for Tyler.

'I'm game,' he said, as Peta stuffed the muffin in his mouth.

'Well, I'm certainly not,' Celia said. 'What will I do with the last one?'

'Give it back to Felicity and tell her that you prefer blueberries to cinnamon,' Josh suggested.

Felicity extracted herself from the conversation with Phil Beatty and came back over. She hugged Peta and Tyler before turning her attention back to Celia.

'So, what do you think of my muffins?'

'I saved the last cinnamon one for you,' Celia said. She handed Felicity the last muffin and watched on in disbelief as she swallowed it whole.

'Felicity, exactly what did you put in your mini muffins?' Celia asked.

'Just a few special ingredients. Trust me, they'll kick in soon. Let's dance!'

I'm so naïve! Lucky Josh helped me dodge that bullet, Celia thought.

Felicity took Celia's hand and gently gyrated in sync with the DJ. Celia was suddenly overwhelmed by a desire to put her body in motion. The dance floor was packed, and the crowd moved shoulder to shoulder as one, reaching up towards the ceiling as the DJ constructed a crescendo of sound, which gave way to the pneumatic throb of the disco beat. Peta and Tyler were dancing at the end of a neon rainbow and a starburst of laser lights splashed over everyone in the house. Each track dissolved into the next and Celia felt she may never stop dancing, losing herself in a trance where time itself extrapolated into meaninglessness. When Felicity moved to dance in front of Celia, she held out her hand and Felicity grasped it, performed a pirouette, and put her hand behind Celia's waist. They danced momentarily in a pseudo-tango before Felicity let go, placed both hands around Celia's lower back and pulled their hips together so tightly that she could feel the heat of Felicity's pelvis through the black taffeta. Celia found herself staring into Felicity's emerald-green eyes, which now seemed to have a laser-like intensity.

'Kiss me, Vanessa!' Felicity said. Celia was mortified.

'What on earth are you talking about? Let me go!'

Celia firmly pushed Felicity away until she'd escaped the tentacle-like grip of her arms, then stood with her hands on her temples trying to process what had just happened.

'Vanessa? I'm not Vanessa, Felicity! Who the hell is Vanessa?' Celia shouted above the music.

Felicity either couldn't or didn't want to answer. She seemed to be dancing in a trance-like state in a parallel universe. Celia was no longer in the mood for a party. The incident had broken the spell and she found herself going through the motions of dancing in a fog of confusion fuelled by Felicity, who was high on spiked mini-muffins and too much Mumm. For Celia, the party was past its prime and she just wanted to go home.

'I need to fix my makeup,' she said to Felicity, who didn't seem to be listening.

Celia wandered off to the gender-neutral bathroom and locked herself in a cubicle. A few minutes later there was a knock on the door. It was Felicity.

'I know you're in there, Celia Tran. Hurry up! Let's get out of here.'

'Go away, Felicity, you're just too much, and I've had quite enough of you for one night.'

'Don't be like that. Darling, forgive me, I just get caught in the moment. Come on, let me take you for a kofta kebab at Yasmine's.'

Those mini muffins are wearing off and Felicity is now suffering from a dose of the munchies, Celia thought.

Felicity knocked again. Celia pretended she wasn't there for a few moments before capitulating.

'Whatever!' Celia came out, shot Felicity a menacing glance and soon they were heading for the lobby. There was no sign of Toby, or Peta and Tyler.

I'll catch Peta on Monday, I suppose, Celia lamented.

The atmosphere inside the venue over the course of the evening had been one of elation.

Outside was a different story. It appeared there had been some sort of riot. The doorman told them that an angry crowd without tickets to the event had gone on a rampage. Several driverless vehicles had been pushed on their sides and one was in flames. The scene jolted Felicity back into sobriety.

'Shit. The revolution has started without us. Hold on while I call our car, she said as she pulled her phone out of her cross-body purse and tapped at the screen with her fingernails.

A black limousine appeared out of the shadows and slowly made its way towards them, its white-walled tyres crunching on the broken glass strewn across the driveway. A small group of teenage boys nearby wolf-whistled at them.

'Get in quick,' Felicity said as she opened the limo door for Celia.

'Charming! This is what people are reduced to when AYE AYE takes away their sense of purpose,' Celia said, surveying the scene as the limo sped away.

'We'll all be loitering with intent soon enough,' Felicity said.

In Yasmine's restaurant, Felicity and Celia sat opposite each other picking over the aftermath of a kofta kebab and soggy chips. Felicity lit up a cigarette and drew back heavily, before flicking her wrist and blowing a smoke ring into mid-air.

'Yasmine doesn't mind if I smoke,' she said, looking in the direction of Yasmine, who didn't respond.

Celia figured Yasmine had no chance of stopping Felicity from doing anything she wanted to, even if she disapproved.

'I've upset you,' Felicity said, trying to make eye contact with Celia who, like Yasmine, remained silent. 'I apologise. I'll make it up to you. Look, we've had a big night. Rest up tomorrow and I'll pick you up on Sunday to go over the Blue Mountains and visit my Uncle Mick. You'll love him – he's off the grid.'

'Well, he couldn't be any more off the grid than you,' Celia said, before falling silent again. She fixed her gaze on Felicity's cigarette and waited until its ash dropped onto the floor.

'What time?' Celia asked.

'10 am sharp. Can I drop you home?'

'No thanks, I'll make my own way tonight. See you Sunday.'

Celia stood up to leave. Felicity drew back on her cigarette, looked at her from under her mop of red hair, launched another smoke ring, and smiled.

'Sunday will be cloudless,' she said.

Marrickville confessions

I don't look very Vietnamese. My eyes are wide open and I'm too tall, Celia thought as she looked in the mirror. A persistent hangover from the album launch event throbbed in her head. She thought of the charcoal sketch of her brother Vinh, still sitting on the Antionette console table in the hall.

Vinh doesn't look very Vietnamese either. Mother has always been so vague when I ask her about the family tree. Maybe I'm just tired and emotional enough after the party last night to finally get some answers.

'Miriam, where's the paracetamol?' Celia shouted at the top of her voice while simultaneously attempting to suppress the urge to vomit.

Miriam walked quietly into the ensuite making faint mechanical sounds as she moved. She emitted a soft pink glow from her synthetic skin before opening the drawer in the vanity in front of Celia, where she quickly located the packet of tablets.

'I'm sorry Miriam, I'm a bit tired this morning. Thank God it's Saturday.' Celia swallowed the tablets and took a mouthful of water from the faucet to wash them down.

'Can I get you anything else, Ms Tran?'

'A nice hot cup of Jasmine tea would be wonderful, thank you, Miriam. What time is it?'

'Ms Tran, Eastern Daylight Saving time is 11:36 am.' Celia followed Miriam back into the bedroom and marvelled at her yellow beehive hairdo as she disappeared into the kitchen to make the tea. Celia pulled on the tracksuit pants that were lying on the floor next to her bed, before wandering into the kitchen where a cup of tea was waiting on the bench. Miriam was struggling to unfold the ironing board and began to emit a red glow.

Miriam seems to be practising origami with the ironing board. Maybe robots are not all that switched on, after all, Celia thought.

'I'm going to stay over at my mother's, so just go into sleep mode in the spare bedroom tonight. I'll be back in the morning.'

'Noted, Ms Tran,' Miram said, before unleashing a shot of steam from the iron into mid-air.

She'll get the hang of it eventually, Celia thought, as she made her way to the balcony with her phone and a cup of tea, to sit and recover in the warm sunshine of the late morning.

Celia checked FaceTracer. Tyler had tagged her in his selfie from the party and TobyFNQ had also posted a video of himself from the departure gate at Western Sydney Airport.

Thanks to the grant from the Feds, my dream hands and AYE AYE are teaching me to play guitar!

I really like his long curly black hair, Celia thought. She contemplated making a comment but thought better of it and made her way inside to the bathroom where she showered, dried her hair, and changed into a pair of faded denim jeans and a printed tee shirt. She packed a change of underwear and her toiletries into a roller bag.

'See you in the morning, Miriam,' Celia called as she ordered a car on her phone and rolled her bag out of the apartment.

The car dropped her off at the Bradfield Metro station and before long she was heading towards the city. The western suburbs slipped by through the windows of the carriage before the train went underground. Celia became mesmerised by the strobing effect of the tunnel lights as they flicked by.

Her thoughts turned to the night before.

Felicity's behaviour was unforgivable. I was having such a nice time for once too. It was very disappointing. I miss Noah.

The train burst out of the tunnel into the bright lights of a station, decelerating rapidly until it came to a halt. The pneumatic doors opened with a hiss and there was an exchange of passengers. A young mother with two small children boarded the train and sat opposite Celia on the blue plastic seats. Celia knew the woman was Vietnamese. The young girl stared at Celia across the carriage as the train picked up speed and speared back into the tunnel.

I wish you were mine. I wish I could have had a baby with Noah.

On a bend, the steel wheels of the train sang in sympathy.

It's not like I'm very social, but I value my inner circle of friends. I wonder if I'll ever be close with Felicity?

The train rushed into the next station and quickly braked. The G-force shifted Celia in her seat. The mother took the children by the hand and led them towards the door. The young girl maintained her eye contact with Celia for as long as she could before vanishing into the crowd. The doors closed and the train rolled onwards.

I wonder what that little girl was thinking about me? What I'd be like as a mother, maybe? So many questions ... Felicity is a puzzle too. She seems full of confidence when she's working the room, and then she carries on like an adolescent on a rampage. Why is someone like her interested in me anyway?

A homeless man wearing dilapidated Nike runners and a brown overcoat came in through the doors from the next carriage and walked down the corridor, muttering to himself. He smelt of unwashed socks. Celia looked back out the window at the black wall of the tunnel.

I'm not even really sure she was coming on to me specifically. She seemed to be hallucinating about someone called Vanessa after getting high from eating those spiked mini muffins. I'm sure she's overcompensating. It's like a star has fallen from her galaxy. Maybe she's missing the same star as me.

The gentle rocking motion of the metro train and the lingering exhaustion from the party began to overwhelm Celia's awareness and soon she was fast asleep. She dreamed she was working on a new charcoal sketch when she woke with a start and realised that the train had arrived at Marrickville station. She jumped up, grabbed her bag and stepped onto the platform as the doors closed behind her. *That was close.*

To Celia, the Marrickville Metro station seemed like a new addition to a timeless suburb, and she relished the familiarity of Illawarra Road as she rolled her bag towards the Tranh Hoc Vietnamese Restaurant that had been in her family for a couple of generations.

'Hey Sis, long time!' Vinh said as she lifted her bag up the step and through the door.

The heady aroma of coriander and mint transported Celia back to the memories of her childhood. The green bamboo print wallpaper and the sepia photographs of old Saigon were unchanged, as were the timber Laminex tables with their jars of red serviettes and bottles of chilli and soy sauce.

'Hey Vinh-boy, where's Mum?'

'Upstairs in the flat. Are you here to help with the dinner service or just fly-in-fly-out like usual?'

'I'm staying tonight so I'll give you a hand.'

Celia made her way up the narrow staircase at the back of the restaurant. Her mother was sitting on the sofa watching a Vietnamese soap opera.

'Ah, Celia! You've come to see me!' Khuyen said, clapping her hands and holding her arms outstretched to embrace her.

'Yes, Mum, I'm staying over tonight so we can chat.'

'Good, so you can help us in the restaurant tonight. Two of the staff have called in sick.'

'Sure, Mum.'

Celia gave her mother a kiss and a hug before making her way back down to the kitchen to help Vinh prepare for the dinner service.

'It's just like back in the day. You should visit more often – you know Mum loves to see you. She's fifty-five this year, you know.'

'Don't push your luck, Vinh-boy, or I'll make you chop onions until your eyes water.'

At 6 pm, Khuyen descended the stairs and opened the front door. Patrons quickly began to fill the tables. The three of them slipped into the old routine without thinking. Celia and her mother darted back and forth between the dining room and the kitchen with orders and dishes while Vinh was in the kitchen, simultaneously cooking steaming hot Pho soup noodles with rare beef and sprouts, Gou Cuon rice paper rolls filled with tiger prawns and covered in peanut sauce, as well as salt and pepper squid.

'Vinh-boy, what's with the paper and pens? You could get computerised! You know this is the age of AI.'

'Old school is my old school, Sis! I'm a graduate.'

I love how Vinh keeps the place running in the traditional way, she thought.

The evening flew by and in no time, Vinh was locking the door and Khuyen was tallying the takings while Celia finished off the last of the washing up. Exhausted, they made their way upstairs. Khuyen disappeared into the kitchenette to make a pot of tea and Celia flopped on the couch. Vinh sat opposite her on the old worn leather armchair.

'Just like back in the day, hey, Sis?'

'Just like back in the day, bro.'

Khuyen came back in carrying a teapot, cups and saucers on a red plastic tray and set it down on the coffee table, before sitting down next to Celia and pouring three cups of green tea.

Rather than answer a whole lot of questions about why she didn't have a new boyfriend, Celia decided to get on the front foot and ask a few hard questions of her own.

'Mum, I want to know why I don't look very Vietnamese.'

'Why did you marry that Noah? I told you he was no good.'

'Don't change the subject. Vinh doesn't look very Vietnamese either. We deserve to know why.'

Vinh shifted uncomfortably on the sofa as Khuyen took a long sip of tea.

'All I can to tell you is that you are both a little bit Vietnamese, a little bit Aussie and a little bit French.'

'Mum, that's not good enough. For once in your life, tell us the whole story.'

Khuyen looked downcast and then looked at Vinh.

'Sis is right, Mum. We're all grown up now. We deserve to know.'

Khuyen looked up at the ceiling, drew breath and made eye contact with Celia.

'Well, your great-grandmother Hyunh, was the mistress of a minister in the French colonial government of Indochina in Saigon. She was carrying his child in 1954 when he returned to Paris with the rest of the imperialists and never came back. Hyunh lived with her relatives in a small house in Saigon.'

'Which part of town? I know Ho Chi Minh City pretty well, after so many trips.'

'The house was in an area that is now called District 5. They were very poor. When the American war came her daughter Lanh started working in the bars of Saigon as a waitress.'

'Was she a prostitute?'

Khuyen took another long sip of tea and was silent for a minute.

'I believe so. One of her regulars, an Australian, 2nd Lieu-tenant Matthew Logan of the third Royal Australian Regi-ment, fell in love with her and before long, she was carrying his child.'

'How come I don't know any of this? You could have told us.'

'Well, I'm telling you now. Matthew Logan convinced the Australian Embassy that Lanh was a refugee and they arranged for her to fly on the last RAAF flight out of Saigon in April 1975. She never saw him again. The immigration authorities arranged for her to be billeted within the Vietnamese commu-nity here in Sydney and she ended up in this flat living with Nguyen and his wife Bian who owned the restaurant. They looked after her and were very kind. They often said when Lanh's waters broke the baby came very fast. That was me, Khuyen. I was born right here in this room.'

'Go on.'

'When Bian died, some type of cancer I think, Lanh married Nguyen as he was still a young man.' Celia was wide-eyed.

'Hang on, are you telling me that Nguyen married Grandma Lanh?'

'Yes.'

'But Nguyen is our father! Is that why you didn't marry him? Because he was already married to Grandma?' Khuyen bowed her head and took a long deep breath.

'Nguyen is not your real father.' Celia and Vinh looked at each other in stunned silence while Khuyen finished the last of her tea.

'So, you have been keeping this a secret all our lives. Mum, why did you lie to us?' Celia asked.

'Nguyen was like a father to all of us.'

Celia squeezed her fingertips into her forehead. Slowly, she realised the ramifications of the story. 'If Nguyen was not my biological father, then who on earth is?

'I don't want to talk about him.' Khuyen bowed her head again. Vinh then weighed in.

'Come on, Mum, out with it. We are both adults now.'

'If you must know, he was the Mayor of Marrickville, and one day, when you were still little children, he took off with a blonde councillor and I never saw him again. I blame myself for getting mixed up with that Aussie bastard.'

Vinh laughed and took his mother's hand. 'I didn't see that one coming, but we love you, Mum.'

Celia was somewhere in between denial and fury and her

cheeks had flushed bright pink. 'Well, I have had quite enough family revelations for one evening, I'm going to bed.'

'Your room is just how you left it. I never change it in case you want to come back.'

Celia drew breath, managing to momentarily suppress her emotional frustration. 'Thanks for being honest with us, Mum. It sounds like you went through a difficult time. I'm sorry, but it's a lot to digest.'

Celia kissed them both on the cheek and left them to watch the rest of the Vietnamese soap. She walked into her old bedroom. It was just the same as always. She slipped out of her boots and her jeans, lay back on the bed and let her mind go blank. She found herself admiring the aluminium foil stars glued to the pressed tin ceiling and the peeling native flora and fauna wallpaper that adorned the walls. She turned out the light and fell asleep under the stars and among the animals and birds of the Australian bush.

A partnership

Celia woke up looking at the Alfoil stars glued to the ceiling of the bedroom in the flat above the restaurant.

So, what exactly, did I dream? My entire childhood or just the part about my father being the Mayor of Marrickville Council? Celia felt weak from mixed emotion.

Suddenly she remembered that it was Sunday, and that Felicity was picking her up from her apartment at 10 am. She pulled back the sheets, sat up, moved to the edge of the mattress, and put her feet on the floor.

What was I thinking when I agreed to go out for the day with Felicity? Celia thought, as she rummaged around in her bag for a fresh tee shirt and pulled on her shorts. Once dressed, she wandered downstairs to find Vinh already busy in the restaurant kitchen.

'Morning, sis. I'm whipping up some of those Singaporean noodles that you like with the red and brown chilli sauce. I have no idea why you don't just eat cornflakes for breakfast like the rest of Australia. It's not like you live in Singers!'

Celia gave him a kiss on the cheek. 'I'm struggling to come to terms with that great load of info Mum handed us last night.

How about you? I just don't think I can talk about it yet. I need time to process it, don't you? Maybe we should get together – by ourselves – in a few days, a week maybe, to come to grips with the Mayor of Marrickville story – and what it means for us. And how we feel about it? What our true identity is. Even whether we might be able to track down more information – because Mum seemed to run out of steam in that short explanation last night.'

Vinh had been nodding his head slowly as she spoke, as if it was all he could do to agree, and otherwise he was speechless.

He smiled gently and murmured, 'Yeah – I think we should – soon. Away from Mum. We don't want to hurt her more.'

Understanding her brother's reticence, Celia made a silent promise she'd follow through. Then she got stuck into the noodles. 'Thanks, Vinh-boy, I have to get out of here as I'm meeting someone from work back at my apartment. Say bye to Mum for me when she gets up and I'll try to come over again next weekend.'

Celia packed her bag and rolled it back to the Metro station.

After making herself as comfortable as possible on a blue plastic seat of the train, Celia checked her phone. There were several missed calls and messages from Peta.

I so need to talk to her, Celia thought, looking around at the passengers in the carriage. She didn't want strangers eavesdropping on her personal conversation and she knew that she wouldn't have the obligatory twenty minutes to have an in-depth conversation at home before Felicity picked her up, so she messaged Peta, asking her to meet her at the coffee cart in the morning.

Before long she was walking in through the front door of her apartment in Bradfield. Miriam was in the laundry, emitting a purple glow that indicated that she did not want to be interrupted. Celia jumped in and out of the shower, dried her hair and put on a yellow summer dress, thinking that it might be hot on the far side of the Blue Mountains.

'Miriam, I'm out for the day and I'll be home late. I'd like you to make me a light dinner and leave it in the microwave.'

'What do you feel like Ms Tran?'

Celia opened the pantry for some inspiration and found that it was now chock full of tins of Heinz Baked Beans.

'Miriam, will you stop buying baked beans? I don't even like them.' It was nearly ten, so she didn't wait for Miriam's explanation and went out onto the balcony, just in time to see Felicity's black limousine pull up out the front. She went inside, told Miriam she would be happy with anything except baked beans for dinner, grabbed her sunglasses and handbag and headed towards the lift.

It was a cloudless summer's day.

Felicity's limousine was semi-driverless. Unlike later models, it still had a steering wheel, and she enjoyed the freedom of hopping into the driver's seat and taking it for a spin when she was in the mood. This particular morning, she sat in the back seat dressed in her red jeans and a white blouse, patiently waiting for Celia, hoping that her behaviour at the album launch had not deterred her friend altogether. Celia opened the rear door of the limo, settled down, and waited for Felicity to open the conversation.

'Nice to see you. Thanks for coming. I love your yellow dress.'

Does she always reek of cigarettes and Dior? Celia thought.

'Nice to see you too, I suppose, although I don't really know why I'm here. I feel I don't really know you and I have no idea why you want me to meet your uncle. Are you two going to kidnap me and hold me against my will in a farm shed?'

'Relax, sister. Uncle Mick is the only relative I have in Australia. He was a great support to my father and me when we emigrated from the USA after my parents divorced. I try to stay in touch, that's all.'

'What happened to your father, if you don't mind me asking?'

Felicity turned and gazed out the window. 'He collapsed and died of a heart attack at his desk in the office at ReElevation.'

'I'm so sorry. I shouldn't have asked.'

'No need to apologise. I've closed that chapter.'

'Peta told me he was the boss of ReElevation and that you have succeeded him. Can I ask why you told me you were a director of A&R when we met and why you didn't mention that you were also the CEO?'

'Truthfully, I just wanted to take you out to lunch. I guess I didn't want to put you off by making you think I was the boss.'

'But Felicity, why me? We've only known each other for five minutes. Why didn't you ask one of your other friends to come with you today?'

Felicity turned away from the window and looked at Celia. 'I have plenty of acquaintances, but none of them are true friends.'

'Don't be silly, you're one of the most outgoing people I've ever met. How can you say you have no friends?'

'I have this habit of turning my friends into lovers and when that doesn't work out, I end up with no lovers and no friends. I'm really quite sad and pathetic.' Felicity lowered the window and took a deep breath before issuing a command to the AYE AYE assistant of the driverless car. 'Drive on, our destination is Abercrombie Road, Oberon.'

The limo moved off slowly and merged into the traffic. Felicity raised the window and continued to stare into the middle distance. Celia broke the uncomfortable silence.

'Is that what happened with Vanessa? Was she your ex? Felicity, I'm not surprised you broke up if you carried on with her the way you carried on with me at the album launch. It was inexcusable to take drugs and then try to kiss me without my consent. You seemed to forget it was a work function and that you're a senior executive. To top it off, you were hallucinating that I was her.' Celia frowned, folded her arms, and stared out the window.

Felicity squeezed the nape of her neck with her fingers, took a deep breath and slowly exhaled through her pursed lips. 'I would be lying if I said I wasn't interested in you. I agree that my behaviour has been inexcusable.' She then turned away and stared out the window too.

Celia drew breath and considered her response. 'Felicity, you're the only living soul that has shown any interest in me since I lost Noah. I truly believe that we have a chance to be good friends if you can keep our relationship platonic.'

Felicity shifted in her seat to face Celia and laughed. 'What, like a couple of business partners?'

'Perhaps.'

Celia reached over and took Felicity's hand. Their fingers intertwined. Felicity wanted to say more but her words were choked off by a lump of emotion that was building in the back of her throat and tears that were welling up under her eyelids. She gave up trying and, instead, unbuckled her seatbelt, curled up on the seat next to Celia and sobbed softly. Neither of them said another word until the limousine had traversed the pass at Mount Victoria.

Mountain memories

On the far side of the Blue Mountains, the limo made its way westward through the village of Hartley before making a left turn onto Jenolan Caves Road. Felicity and Celia relaxed as the car weaved through rolling hills of grey dry grass, catching occasional glimpses of the blue foothills of the distant ranges. It was almost one o'clock when they reached the outskirts of Oberon, a historic town made fashionable by the treechangers that came in the aftermath of the COVID-19 pandemic.

After driving up the main street, the limo headed out of town and onto Abercrombie Road. Ten minutes later, it slowed down. Through the window, Celia could see an empty beer keg that had been fashioned into a letterbox mounted on a splintered grey post and rail fence. Nailed to a piece of timber under the mail slot were brass letters that spelled out the words 'MICK'S PLACE'. They crossed a cattle grid and drove up a long drive-way that ended in a turning circle at the front steps of what once would have been a grand homestead. On the verandah was a man dressed in moleskins and a denim shirt with his bare feet up on an old sofa. His face was covered by an Akubra hat which he lifted as the limo drove up. He swung his legs onto the floor and pulled on socks and a pair of R.M. Williams boots before standing to saunter towards the car, kicking up dust with his heels. Felicity lowered the window.

'Hi, Uncle Mick! Did we wake you?'

'It's all part of the joy of flexible working, Felicity, my dear. Welcome back to God's country.'

Felicity jumped out of the limo and ran round to give Mick a big hug and a kiss on the cheek. Celia stepped out of the car and waited for the embrace to conclude. 'I want you to meet my friend Celia. She's my business partner.'

Business partner? I didn't think she was serious, Celia thought.

'Business partner! Well, that's a new one,' Mick said.

Celia offered her hand, and Mick gave it a polite shake.

'Hi Mick, nice to finally meet you. Felicity tells me you're cloudless, although I'm not really sure what that means.'

Mick pushed up the brim of his Akubra. 'She's right. Follow me down to the back paddock, and I'll show you why.'

They followed Mick around the far corner of the homestead where before them lay a field of solar panels and a large yellow metal box.

'That's my storage battery. I generate and store my own solar power, so I'm not dependent on the outside world, and I don't have the internet or a mobile phone. I detest robots, and I still have a landline, so I'm totally disconnected from the internet cloud.'

Felicity waved away an annoying fly. 'A landline! I thought they went out with the Ark.'

'I'm allowed an old-fashioned telephone as I'm on the Critical Infrastructure Access List. By the way, Felicity, before I left Mount Piper I put your name on the list too.'

'Seriously, Mick? The CIA list? Why on earth did you do that? I'm not even on the payroll, and I wouldn't know where to start even if I was.'

Felicity turned to Celia. 'Mick is an engineer. He was responsible for installing the computer systems at Mount Piper Power Station when they did the green power upgrade, and he also rolled out the AI automation.'

Mick stuck his hands in the back pockets of his denim jeans. 'I finished commissioning the AI system and hung up my screwdriver, but then the Federal Government pulled me out of retirement and engaged me as a consultant.'

A fly landed on Celia's cheek, and she swatted it away. 'What do you actually consult on, if you don't mind me asking?'

'There was a spate of data breaches at the turn of the century. The public were never told how deeply organisations like Optus and Medicare were compromised. It spooked the Feds, and they amended Part 7 of the Cybersecurity Act. My job is to certify that critical infrastructure can operate offline and, if need be, without relying on AI or any microprocessor.'

'Is it just power stations that are critical? What about hospitals? Can they work stand alone?' Celia asked.

Mick pulled down the brim of his Akubra. 'In theory. I've certified the big ticket items on the eastern seaboard, like power, water, sewerage and gas facilities, but hospitals are reliant on life saving technology, and cost pressures force them to use a lot of robot staff. So, I do what I can but I'm pushing shit uphill.'

'Well, that still doesn't explain why I'm on the list,' Felicity said.

Mick laughed and kicked up a cloud of dust with his boot.

'A key part of the certification of any facility is to put in place a list of old bastards who can get the joint up and running. If something happens at Mount Piper, you know Scotty and Kev who can kick start that thing. All you need to do is make a few phone calls in the national interest.'

'So, I'm responsible for saving Sydney now as well as running a media company. Lucky, I have my new business partner.'

'You can tell me about that one over lunch. By the way, I put your company chairman on the CIA list for Bradfield Hospital because he knows where all the retired nurses live.'

'Typical.' Felicity said.

Mick led them over to an old Holden utility and opened the passenger door.

'Before we have lunch, we have to go shopping. Apologies for being underprepared. Hop in.'

'You're the quintessential bachelor, Mick,' Felicity observed.

They all piled into the ute and sped off down the road, back into Oberon, where Mick parked outside his favourite local bakery and delicatessen. Felicity dialled up an episode of Landline on the ABC app on her phone and left it playing on speaker for Mick, before hopping out of the ute with Celia and walking into the deli.

They loaded up on baguettes, smoked ham and a variety of cheeses, as well as a bottle of Chardonnay for good measure. Once the purchases were completed, they ambled back to the ute laden with their bags of groceries and crammed themselves into the cabin. Mick handed back the phone.

'I still miss radio. They'll live to regret shutting down broadcasting,' he said.

Back at the homestead, Felicity rummaged around in the chest of drawers and pulled out a linen tablecloth to spread out on Mick's old dining table. Celia made up ham rolls and washed up some ornate crystal wine glasses that were stashed in the back of Mick's kitchen cupboard. As Felicity and Mick sat down, she placed a serving tray laden with ham and cheese rolls in the middle of the table and poured three glasses of Chardonnay. Felicity raised a glass for a toast.

'Here's to our new business venture!'

'Cheers!' said Celia and Mick as they clinked their crystal glasses together and sipped on the woody Chardonnay.

'So, Felicity, exactly what business are you and Celia getting yourselves into?'

I was wondering that myself, Celia thought.

'The nightclub business, Mick. More specifically, a mobile phone-free nightclub with no internet, no robots allowed, completely old-school.'

Since when did I sign up for that idea? Celia thought.

'Will you have lights and power, or will it be all candles and gaslight?' Mick asked.

Felicity thought for a moment. 'We haven't decided on all the details, but we want to make it all about people having the freedom to just be with each other.'

Mick took a sip of his wine and leaned back on the back legs of his dining chair. 'I like the idea of no smarts. These days I try to live like I'm back in the seventies, in the time before computers and the internet swallowed the world. I only read books by real human authors, even if they seem second-rate compared to those slick, AI-generated tomes from ChatGPT.'

'What are you reading now?' Celia asked.

'The second edition of a bio called *Slices of a Songwriter's Pie*. It's drivel, written by some unknown, but at least it's real. Feel like listening to some Seals and Crofts?'

Without waiting for an answer, Mick stood up and walked over to a stack of vinyl records on the bookshelf and selected an album that he placed on the platter of an old turntable. He lifted the tonearm and dropped the stylus into the groove, sitting back down as the song, *We May Never Pass this Way Again*, filled the room.

Celia glanced at Mick as she toyed with the stem of her wine glass. 'Mick, do you have any children?'

'No, sadly. I left all that to my older sister Therese.'

Felicity choked momentarily on her bread roll before recovering enough to give Celia a kick under the table.

'Ow! Sorry Mick, go on,' Celia said, smarting from the kick to her shin.

'Therese is Felicity's mother, who lives back in San Francisco.'

Felicity changed the subject. 'So, Mick, will you back our business plan?'

'Perhaps, but you'll have to do something for me first.'

'Like what?'

'Stick-picking.'

'Stick-picking? What on earth is that?'

'I bought thirty hectares out towards Black Springs. The land is cleared, but there are a lot of small sticks and stones to pick up before I can run the plough over it. There are some overalls in the laundry. Hop into those, and I'll take you both out there so you can give me a hand.'

Felicity was aghast. 'Are you serious? What about my nails?'

'You'll find overalls, gloves and boots in the cupboard.'

Felicity gave Celia a look of resignation and took her into the laundry where they found a variety of overalls, all of which were size XL. Felicity located one of Mick's old white tee shirts in the laundry basket for Celia.

'Hang up your dress and put this on.'

Felicity slipped out of her jeans and pulled on a pair of faded blue overalls, which showed off much of her shoulders and back .

'These are swimming on me!' she said, rolling up the legs and trying on a pair of steel-cap boots for size.

Celia pulled on the oversized tee shirt and tried on some khaki overalls. 'I look like I'm a corporal in the Australian Army.'

'Camouflage suits you. I've always fancied women in uniform.'

'Stop teasing.'

After locating the gloves, they marched across the driveway to the ute in their boots and overalls and jumped in next to Mick. Once they were buckled up, he revved up the engine and spun the wheels, leaving behind a cloud of dust as they shot off down the drive and headed along Abercrombie Road towards Black Springs.

The road began to wind through green cultivated paddocks. Mick pulled up at a gate at the end of a weathered post and rail fence. Felicity jumped out, unhooked the chain and waved the ute through. Mick stuck his elbow out the window and called out, 'I'll make a jillaroo out of you yet, Felicity.'

'I don't do boot-scooting, Mick, and in case you hadn't noticed, I was born a city girl and I'm staying that way.'

Once the ute had passed through the gate and pulled up, Celia put on her sunglasses, pulled on her gloves and jumped out. 'I'll give it a shot, Mick. What do I have to do?'

Mick gave them both a wicker basket that he had stashed in the back of the ute.

'Pick up as many sticks and stones as you can in your basket and drop them into the tray of the ute.'

'Seriously Mick, you could hire a gang of WorkerBots and get this done in a day.'

'I'd rather do it myself. You know how I detest them.'

Before Felicity could utter another objection, Celia was off with her basket, pulling small objects from the soft dark soil of the Central West. Not to be outdone, Felicity was soon at her side. Together they walked across the paddock, sifting sticks and stones from the rich yellow dirt in the late afternoon sunshine. Time and again they filled their baskets, walked back to the ute and tipped the rubbish into the tray, which filled rapidly with the fruits of their labour.

'See, I told you we'd make a good team,' Felicity said.

'I agree.'

Mick had wandered off in the opposite direction with his basket. Celia made sure he was out of earshot before putting down her basket and looking sternly at Felicity. 'I want you to know that I will follow you to wherever that leads us. But just remember I have my limitations and I'm not sure that you know me well enough to know what they are.'

'I'll be the judge of that,' Felicity said.

Of course, you will, Celia thought as Mick wandered back to the ute, lugging his burgeoning basket, which he unceremoniously dropped into the tray.

Mick was singing to himself and launched into a John Denver impersonation. Although it was now late in the day, there was still a sting in the summer sun. Felicity's forehead was dripping with perspiration.

Celia took off her hat and gloves, walked back to the ute, and sat in the front seat with her head in her hands. 'I feel dizzy.'

Felicity leaned into the ute and studied Celia's face. 'Mick, she's as white as a sheet. Do you have any water?'

'Here's a water bottle from the Esky. She's probably had a touch of the sun. Come on Celia, drink up.'

Celia drained the bottle. 'Thanks, I suppose working without a hat in the sun after a couple of Chardy's doesn't help either.'

'Mick let's go back. She needs a lie-down.'

Mick and Felicity quickly packed up the ute, jumped in each side of Celia and returned to the homestead.

In the large country kitchen, Mick gave Celia two paracetamol capsules and some tea before Felicity led her off to Mick's bedroom, helped her out of her overalls and left her to lie down on Mick's big four-poster. Celia was out like a light.

Time for a chat over a beer with Mick, Felicity thought.

Celia had an ethereal dream about gardening with the rock star Kirk Satyr and was eventually roused by the sound of voices from the lounge room.

'Felicity, you don't need my blessing to start a new business venture because it's your money. I'm only the trustee until you turn thirty. And how old are you now?'

'Twenty-seven.'

'I rest my case. I'll sign off on anything you want. I promised your father that I would look after you if anything happened to him and my work is done. You are a grown woman and a successful one at that.'

'You'll still help us though, right?'

'With engineering advice, of course, you know I will. Felicity, it's been three months since your father died.'

'So?'

'So, I want to know if you had considered visiting your mother in San Francisco. I am planning to go and I'd like you to come too. She's still head of the label over there, but she's not getting any younger. We can stay in the house in Haight-Ashbury.'

In the bedroom, Celia had stirred from sleep and was listening to the conversation. She sensed that Felicity was being drawn into a conversation she didn't want to have. Even though she knew it was none of her business, she decided to go to her rescue. She crept out of bed, pulled her yellow dress back on, made a grand entrance, and then flopped onto Mick's black leather lounge.

'I had the weirdest dream.'

Felicity leapt at the opportunity to change the subject. 'Are you feeling better? You've certainly got your colour back.'

'I'm fine. I was a bit dehydrated, that's all.'

'You're both welcome to stay for dinner. We still have some baguettes and ham left over from lunch,' Mick said.

'Thanks, Mick, but tomorrow's a workday. It's time we left. Thanks for having us – you're a sweetie.' Felicity gave him a hug.

'I love that you're cloudless, Mick,' Celia said before giving him a hug and an air kiss.

'That I am Celia, that I am.'

Mick stood in his driveway and watched as the red taillights of Felicity's black driverless limousine faded into the distance. Felicity took Celia's hand as they turned back onto the Great Western Highway. 'What did you dream about?'

'Kirk Satyr in a garden.'

'Excellent choice.'

By the time they began their easterly descent from Mount Victoria, Felicity was fast asleep and Celia still dozey, both oblivious to the halo of light over the suburbs of Western Sydney.

Heart to heart

Mondays have a sameness about them, even though my world has changed so much lately, Celia thought as she put the bio-degradable lid on a double shot espresso.

She reached out across the counter of the coffee cart and placed the cup in the hand of a young man with dark straight hair who mumbled a 'thank you', before disappearing into the park.

He reminds me of Noah.

Making her way towards the coffee cart as usual at 10 am, Peta appeared on the pedestrian crossing, typing on her phone with both thumbs as she walked. Celia gave Mr Clockwork instructions to prepare Peta's regular skim latte so by the time she arrived at the counter the coffee was ready to go.

'Morning Celia! I got your message. What happened to you at the party? I looked everywhere for you, but you'd disappeared.'

Celia leaned over the counter and smiled at her best friend as she passed her the coffee.

'Sorry I didn't call you back. I stayed over at my mother's on Saturday night and I gave her and Vinh a hand in the restaurant,' Celia said, folding her arms and leaning on the counter. 'Can you come back during my 2 o'clock lunch break? I'll buy you a smoked salmon bagel. I need to talk to you.'

'You're on. Not that you need to shout me a bagel if you want to have a heart-to-heart,' Peta said before taking a sip of her coffee. 'How is it that I just know this is going to be a conversation about Felicity Faraday?'

Celia looked at Peta without saying a word. Peta gave her a wry smile before turning and heading back across the zebra crossing towards the office.

At 2 pm Celia sat on a bench on the perimeter of the rose garden in the park under the shade of a large eucalyptus tree, watching the old men play chess with oversized black and white plastic chess pieces. Celia often walked in the rose garden during her lunch breaks. In season, she took photographs of the varieties of roses so she could sketch them later in charcoal. She was able to visualise the vibrant colours even after her pencils reproduced the images in black and white. Her fixation on the blooms ended with the arrival of Peta, who gave her a hug before taking the bagels out of the brown paper lunch bag she was nursing. Peta spread out the bagels and coffee between them. They each took a bite of their bagel.

'So, what's up?' Peta asked.

'Felicity tried to kiss me at the party,' Celia said, causing Peta to choke on her bagel. Celia gave her a pat on the back and carried on.

'It was alarmingly non-consensual. What's worse, she called me Vanessa, who as it turns out, is her ex. I think she was hallucinating.'

Peta swallowed the offending piece of bagel and swigged on her coffee to wash it down.

'Oh my God, she was probably off her face. Those mini muffins were totally spiked. Tyler and I were completely out of it. By the time we came down from the high, you'd left. I'm sorry. I've been a crap friend again, haven't I?'

'Don't be ridiculous. You're here, aren't you? That's what being a good friend is all about,' Celia said.

'I'm sorry. I didn't want to make this all about me. How do you feel about her behaviour?'

Celia took a sip of her coffee and looked up into the gum tree. 'It was quite inappropriate and yet it made me realise that she has suffered a loss, just like me. I lost Noah and she lost Vanessa. This is going to sound weird but, in a way, I feel we have travelled on the same road,' Celia said.

'Have you two spoken since?' Peta asked.

'She invited me to spend the day with her yesterday,' Celia said. 'We went to Oberon to visit her uncle Mick for lunch.'

'Are you for real?' Peta asked, folding her arms and studying Celia's expression. 'And how did that go?'

'We had a lovely day together and I feel I got to know her better.'

Peta looked Celia in the eye and took her by the hand.

'Celia Tran. I am going to ask you this because I am your best friend and I have a concern for your welfare. Are you interested in her romantically?'

Celia took a deep breath and looked out across the red roses that had blossomed from thorny stems in beds of manicured mulch.

'I guess I find her attractive, but she needs a friend right now more than she needs another lover. I feel I can help her fill that void,' Celia said. 'She has asked me to be her business partner in a nightclub venture.'

Peta straightened up, let go of Celia's hand, and held her forefinger up.

She's going to give me a scolding, Celia thought.

'Felicity is using this business partnership offer as a ruse to get you into her bed. Don't fall for it,' Peta said.

Celia curled her hand around Peta's outstretched finger.

'I'm a big girl, Peta and I wasn't born yesterday. I'm willing to give her a chance. Truly, Peta, I appreciate your concern for me. What is it like working for Felicity anyway?

Peta leaned back on the bench, looked up into the branches of the eucalyptus tree, spread her legs apart and sighed.

'As you know, I'm the only employee left on Level 3. I was heartbroken when they let my small team of graphic designers go. AYE AYE has a lot to answer for.'

'At least you're still employed full-time. Come on, let's go for a walk,' Celia said.

They packed their empty coffee cups into the paper bag, dropped them in the recycling bin and walked into the rose garden, stopping now and then to try to pronounce the names of the varieties that were engraved on small rectangular brass plaques, and to draw in the perfume of the larger blooms. They paused at the end of the garden to admire a pink climbing rose that was espaliered across a white timber trellis.

'What has had the biggest impact on me was the nature of the work itself,' Peta said, as she looked closely at the rose petals. 'Before AYE AYE, we created graphic designs. Now AYE AYE media serves up innumerable machine-generated designs for me to review. I have become more like a head chef who constantly checks to see if the asparagus is too soft or the pumpkin too hard, rather than feeling the joy of the art of creative cooking.'

'Did Felicity have anything to do with it? She says that she is philosophically opposed to robotics and AYE AYE, although her limo is fitted out with it.'

'Felicity has only been CEO for three months. It was her father who rolled out the AYE AYE program and I suppose it made sense commercially, but it did nothing for me. My design skills are obsolete. My working day now mainly consists of video conferences, where the machine interrogates me about my emotional reaction to the artificially generated designs. The machine is learning from me and soon it will be a better version of me, and I'll be in the park on the AI benefit like every other poor soul who's had the rug pulled out from under their chair.'

Peta paused before confessing to her friend, 'That's why I decided to sabotage the Satyr's Faction album cover and ended up being summoned to Felicity's office.'

Celia pulled up short, keen to hear more.

Sex to order

'Did you really sabotage the Satyr's Faction album artwork? How did you manage that?' Celia asked as they turned to walk back towards the coffee cart.

'Yes, the original AYE AYE-generated design for the *Midsummer Nights* album featured a beautiful illustration of Kirk Satyr in a fairy's garden. It was so damn disturbingly good that I decided to manually intervene and substitute it for a black square with a white dot in the middle,' Peta replied. 'I just wanted to stick it to the machine.'

'How did Felicity find out?' Celia asked.

'I told her myself. She asked me to come up to her office and explain why the artwork was so different to the rest of the promotional material. I said that I was fed up with being outdone by an algorithm and I decided to make a statement.'

'How did she react?'

'She just leaned back in her office chair and raked back those long red curls with her fingers, smiled, and sent me back to my desk. It was like she didn't give a toss. That's really all I have ever had to do with her.'

'I found the Satyr's Faction stage show a bit naff myself.

Maybe your album art is foreshadowing an image change for the band,' Celia said.

'That makes me feel better already. Are you going back to work?'

'Yes, I'll finish off the day and help Marco close up. I'll see you tomorrow. Thanks for being supportive.'

They hugged and parted ways, Peta walking back over the zebra crossing and Celia making her way back to the cart.

The afternoon coffee trade was so slow that Mr Clockwork went into power save mode. At 3 pm Marco returned, and Celia helped him pull down the shutters and lock up. Celia decided to walk home.

Over the course of the afternoon, the sky had become overcast, and the temperature had dropped by a few degrees.

There may be a storm tonight, Celia thought as she pushed her earbuds in and put her Coastal Groove playlist on shuffle in preparation for the stroll through the back streets of Bradfield.

As she walked in through the front door of her apartment, she could see Miriam preparing hot Pho noodles for the evening meal.

'You're a godsend, Miriam. Who knows what Felicity is having for dinner … she has no HousekeeperBot to give her a hand in the kitchen.'

Celia immediately tucked into the meal as Miriam emitted a pink glow from her synthetic skin to show she appreciated the compliment.

Afterwards, Celia went into the master bathroom and ran a hot bath. She undressed, added a few drops of lemongrass oil to the water and immersed herself, reflecting on events of the previous day.

Felicity is serious about this nightclub, she thought as she drifted into a state of ambivalence. After half an hour, the bath began to cool, so she climbed out and dried off to dress in shorts and a tank top. Miriam was waiting in the lounge room.

'Ms Tran, will that be all?

'Yes Miriam, I'm having some 'me time' tonight, so I would prefer if you went into sleep mode back at the district service hub this evening.'

'Of course. I am overdue for a service anyway. Good evening, Ms Tran.'

'Good evening, Miriam.'

With that, Miriam emitted a green glow, turned, and disappeared out the front door.

Celia sat on the lounge in front of the widescreen TV and streamed a Vietnamese soap to pass the time, but her mind was elsewhere. Her thoughts turned to her late husband, Noah.

We'll be together again tonight, as promised, she thought to herself.

At eight o'clock, her phone lit up, although the caller ID was blocked.

'Hello?'

'Ms Tran this is your Monday night order from GBot Services. I am at the entrance to your building.'

'Come on up.' Celia pressed the release button and waited for what seemed like an eternity. There was a knock at the door.

I hope those nosey neighbours don't notice, she thought as she pulled the door ajar.

Standing outside was a Mark II Gigolobot dressed in a suede overcoat with a fur collar, pointed tan shoes and aviator shades. This latest model robot had a reconfigurable face, and she had uploaded photographs of Noah in the hope of capturing his likeness.

'Come in, please. I want you to sit with me on the sofa.'

The Gigolobot followed her into the loungeroom, sat down and took off the sunglasses. Her heart sank. Front on, the resemblance to Noah was uncanny as she had hoped. In profile, the likeness was lost.

Noah had a longer nose. I suppose I could send it back, she thought, knowing that there would be no refund.

'Ms Tran, do you have any special requirements this evening or would you like our service delivered as ordered?'

Celia didn't answer the question and instead went into the kitchen and returned with a glass of chardonnay.

'Stand up and take off your overcoat.'

The Gigolobot stood as instructed, peeled off its overcoat and let it drop to the floor, revealing its perfectly sculpted synthetic physique. It was naked except for its shoes. Celia tried not to look at the machine's realistic multi-function prosthetic penis. She examined the Noah-like face and took a gulp of wine.

I promised myself one more night with you, Noah, and I'm not going to give up on you now, she thought.

'Take off your shoes and follow me please,' Celia said as she stood up and led the Gigolobot into the bedroom.

'Lie on your back on the bed.'

Once the robot was in position, she dimmed the lights and undressed, leaving her clothes on the floor where they fell. In the mirror, she caught a glimpse of her naked body.

Tonight, Noah, I'm yours once more, she thought. She began to focus her mind on Noah. Celia straddled the Gigolobot and paused for a moment, perching her bottom on its rippling abdominal muscles. She closed her eyes. In her mind, she could see Noah with his beautiful face and kind eyes more clearly. She leaned forward, placing the palms of her hands on the pectorals of the machine. Taking her weight on all fours, she lifted her lower body and readied herself.

'Be still. Angle to 45 degrees, lubricate, heater on medium, continuous vibration to level seven and I need absolute silence.'

Celia breathed slowly and evenly to steady her heart rate as she worked the warm moist vibrating prosthesis in between the lips of her vagina. She remembered the reassuring warmth of Noah when he would push himself inside her. Short irregular contractions sent little shockwaves flashing through her pelvis. She curled her tongue then gasped as a wave of unrelenting tension welled up within her. Her cheeks flushed as salty perspiration beaded on her upper lip. Gently she rocked around her centre of gravity. Noah was inside her now. She pulled on the skin of the machine with her fingertips and bent down until her rigid nipples brushed against the bare chest of the robot, imagining Noah's taste and scent. As an ever expanding wave of tension within edged her closer to the inevitable, her world coalesced into a singular thought.

'Noah,' she whispered. Now only Noah had the power to shatter the restraints that pinned her down and send her spinning like a Catherine wheel into a rhythmic release, before setting her down to sleep in his arms. She opened her eyes to see him and instead found herself face to face with an imposter. She recoiled at the sight of it.

'Go away!' she cried. Following this command, the robot began to raise itself up on its elbows.

'Lie down and stop wriggling!'

Celia slammed her eyes shut to refocus her mind, but Noah had become distant and blurred. Joy was now being rapidly displaced by a rising sense of panic as she scoured the shadows of her mind for any trace of him. Worse still, the great wall of pleasure that had reared up with so much promise was ebbing away with every beat of her heart. She ground her body against the machine to no avail. The moment was lost.

'Please don't leave me alone again,' she sobbed as tears welled up and ran down her cheeks. She prayed for Noah to come back and opened her eyes one last time, but the machine with the perfect nose was still there, reclining beneath her in silence as instructed.

'Go away!' she cried, thumping her clenched fists on the synthetic pectorals of the barrel-chested Gigolobot.

'Go away and die, you bastard!'

New horizons

I hate Mondays, Felicity thought, as she sat at the desk where three months prior, on a Monday, she had found her father slumped over the keyboard after having suffered a massive heart attack.

Thank God it's Tuesday. Tuesdays are usually Red Letter Days, were her next thoughts. She had kept everything in place so as not to lose her memory of her father. For instance, he had used 7″ vinyl records as drinks coasters. A picture of him receiving an industry award sat next to a small gold Buddha that laughed as its hands held its jolly fat belly. Powered by her belief about Tuesdays, while staring at the Buddha, Felicity decided to call Mick. After dialling, she relaxed back into her chair. When Mick's familiar gravelly voice answered, Felicity jumped in.

'Hi, Mick, it's me.'

'Of course, it's you. You're the only woman that calls me on my landline these days. What's up?'

'Thanks for lunch on Sunday. I think Celia really enjoyed it.'

'Celia seems very nice. Tall for a Vietnamese girl, I thought. Are you two seriously going into the nightclub business together?'

'If we find the right venue,' Felicity said. 'Celia seems like someone I can work with.'

Mick paused for a moment. 'If you don't mind me asking, what happened to Vanessa? I thought you two were an item?'

Felicity exhaled loud enough for Mick to hear it.

'We broke up,' Felicity said as she struggled to suppress the lump of emotion swelling in her throat.

'So, what are your intentions with Celia?'

'For now, she just wants to be my friend and business partner, Mick, that's all.'

'I know you don't like advice, but can I suggest you don't put Celia in a situation where you want what she's not prepared to give.'

'Thanks, Mick. I knew there was a reason I called you.'

'You know what I'm saying. Bye Felicity.'

'I get it. Bye Mick.'

Felicity hung up the phone and decided to call Celia. She had secretly hoped that she would call after the day at the farm.

I need to make amends, Felicity thought. She dialled Celia's number, but it diverted to message bank.

She's probably busy working over at the cart, Felicity thought. She took the lift down to the lobby and walked across the road and into the park.

At the cart, Marco was busy taking orders.

'Marco, is Celia working today?' Felicity asked.

Marco's black moustache seemed to Felicity to bristle as he leaned over the counter.

'She called in sick which is unusual. I've never known her to take a sick day. She's usually so reliable. If you see her tell her my offer of marriage still stands.'

Felicity walked back over the zebra crossing into the lobby

and took the lift up to Level 3. Peta was sitting at her desk wearing her headset. She muted the call.

'Thank God, you've come to save me from being interrogated by an algorithm. What's up, Ms Faraday?'

'Have you heard from Celia? She's not picking up, and Marco at the coffee cart says she's off sick.'

'Let me have a go.'

Peta dialled Celia's number as Felicity watched on, twisting her red curls around her forefinger. Celia picked up the call.

'Hi Celia, are you okay? Felicity is here, and she said she heard you are sick,' Peta said. 'Oh, I see. Well, go to bed with some paracetamol and a hot water bottle. Rest up and get better. Okay babe, ciao.'

Peta put down the phone and looked at Felicity.

'She says she has an upset tummy, that's all. It doesn't sound serious. I'll call her later and see how she's going.'

'Thanks, Peta,' Felicity said as she turned and walked towards the lift.

Mess with my best friend, and I'll mess with you lady, Peta thought.

Felicity made her way back to the lobby and called her limo, which swung into the driveway to pick her up. Ten minutes later, Felicity was at the gate of the Vieille Ville Apartments and pushed the intercom button for Unit 66. She heard the lock click open, and minutes later she was knocking on the front door of Celia's apartment. The door opened. Felicity was shocked to find Celia in her underwear. Her cheeks were stained by rivers of black mascara. Clearly, she had been crying. Felicity took her by the hand and sat her down on the sofa.

'What's wrong? Is it anything to do with me?' Felicity asked, fearing that she had somehow offended her again.

'I'm ashamed and I hate myself,' Celia said.

Felicity straightened up.

'Lordy me, lady, what deep dark rabbit hole have you fallen into? The only person around here that has any reason to hate themselves is me, and in case you hadn't noticed, I don't, and neither should you. Now, please, tell me what's happened.'

Celia looked sheepishly at Felicity.

'I had a fantasy about spending one last night with Noah. Have you ever heard of GBot services?'

Felicity looked incredulous. 'I wasn't born yesterday. Celia Tran, you are the last person in the whole wide world that I would expect would hire a sex robot. My God. What happened?'

Celia let go of Felicity's hand. 'I paid a premium for a Mark II so I could have it configured to look identical to Noah. Except it wasn't and I completely lost it. I thought this idea was just folly, but I realise now that it was a delusion.'

Celia buried her face in her hands and started sobbing.

Felicity wrapped her arms around her and held her tightly for a few moments. 'Losing a loved one is not a delusion. It's quite real. I lost Vanessa and my father. It's not wrong to grieve for them.'

Celia exhaled and dropped her shoulders. 'I didn't offer you any green tea. I sent Miriam back to the district service hub so I could have a robot-free day.'

'Let's have a robot-free life. I've found a property that I think could be exactly what we are looking for. Come on let's get out of here. The RealtyBot is expecting me at ten.'

Felicity waited while Celia quickly washed her face, dressed into her jeans and tee shirt and pulled on her boots. She picked up her handbag and reluctantly followed Felicity out to her waiting limo and sat downcast in the back seat. Felicity gave the address to the navigation system, and they set off.

That Noah really messed her up, Felicity thought. She decided to break the silence. 'GBot Services, I didn't see that one coming. What I find fascinating about human behaviour is that it's full of unexpected surprises.'

Celia gave her a light punch on the arm.

'Ouch! See what I mean!' Felicity said.

Celia laughed for the first time in two days and looked out the window as they wound their way through the streets of Bradfield. Ten minutes later, the limo began to slow down.

'I think we've arrived,' Felicity announced.

The Century 22 RealtyBot estate agent was a Mark I robot, which was waiting for them outside a heritage brick building that had been built as a masonic hall. A square and compass were embossed in brick on the facade. The agent opened up the church-like front door which revealed a small lobby.

'A reception area. This is perfect,' Felicity said. Another set of doors opened up into a large room with a cathedral ceiling. It even had a small stage at the far end.

'Celia, what do you think?'

'I agree, this could actually work.'

Felicity began to imagine the possibilities.

'We can put a circular bar here, and we can create a series of little booths around the sides where couples can get some privacy. We can hang lights and a mirrorball from the rafters. Celia, I'm delegating the interior design to you.'

They walked back outside and Felicity went over to speak with the agent.

'I'm interested. What's the price guide?'

'It's three hundred and fifty thousand Fedcoins per month on a three-year lease.'

'What if I want to buy it?'

'Then it's three hundred and fifty million Fedcoins and a six-week settlement.'

'Give me a moment.' Felicity motioned to Celia, and they walked out of earshot of the agent.

'I'm going to make an offer.'

'What, to lease it? Felicity, a commercial lease is quite a commitment.'

'No. I want to buy it. I want to buy it for us.'

Celia studied the determined expression on Felicity's face.

'Why are you rushing into this? Besides, I don't have any money, and I don't want you buying a property for me. I hardly know you.'

'It's not my money yet either. I'll buy it with the proceeds of my father's estate. Uncle Mick will sign off – he agreed to back me on Sunday at the farm. It's got ambience, location, and it's an ideal space. It's perfect. I can't do this on my own. I need you to back me too. Are you in?'

Celia brushed her hair off her forehead. 'I guess so.'

'You'll just have to trust me on this.' Felicity walked back to the agent. 'Tell the vendor I'll give them two hundred and ninety million Fedcoins and a five percent deposit. That's my final offer.'

The RealtyBot emitted an orange glow before speaking. 'I'll contact the vendor. Please stand by.'

Felicity and Celia marched into the building for another final look around. They came back out into the sunshine to find the RealtyBot had turned bright green.

'The vendor has accepted your offer. I'll forward you the contract via DocuSign.'

Felicity paused to light a cigarette before getting back in the car. She drew back heavily before blowing smoke into the air and fixing her gaze on Celia.

'I want to talk to you about this morning. Can I buy you dinner?' Felicity asked.

'Come over to my place if you like. Miriam makes a wonderful Vietnamese Pho noodle soup.'

'I'll bring the wine. Let's get smashed.'

Dinner for two

Felicity's name lit up on the screen of Celia's phone that was charging on the kitchen bench. She walked over and answered the call. It was just after 7 pm.

'You could at least be fashionably late,' Celia said.

'I'm bearing gifts, and I'm into on-time delivery.'

'Okay, come up to Level 6.'

Celia pressed the unlock button on her intercom app and waited until Felicity emerged from the elevator, resplendent in the bold red dress that she was wearing on the day they first met.

'You live in such a convenient location,' she said, squeezing an air kiss through her puckered lips in the vicinity of Celia's right ear, before walking into the hall. 'I have a bottle of Shiraz, a bottle of Dom and some chocolates for later.'

'It's lovely to have you over. I don't entertain at all, really. Miriam will look after the goodies. Miriam, we'll start with a glass of champagne.'

Miriam emitted a green glow and took the bottles and the chocolates into the kitchen. They watched as Miriam fumbled with the wire cap, inadvertently shaking the bottle in the process until there was a loud pop as the champagne cork took off like a rocket, ricocheted off the ceiling and flew out the kitchen window. They both fell about laughing. Miriam emitted a pink glow to indicate embarrassment.

'See, this is why I pour my own drinks,' was Felicity's reaction.

'Don't be rude to Miriam, although I don't suppose she really cares, do you, Miriam?'

'I can take offence if you wish.'

'No, Miriam, just pour the champagne. Use the crystal flutes.'

While Celia was occupied in the kitchen, Felicity wandered into the bedroom with her glass and came across the charcoal illustration on the easel in the corner of the room.

'Hey, I love this illustration. Is that us?'

Damn, I forgot to hide the picture. Oh well, I guess I don't really mind if she sees it, Celia thought.

'Sure is, girlfriend. I sketched it on the day we met and had that picnic lunch in the orchard.'

'It's very romantic. Seems there's hope for me yet.'

'Don't get any ideas. It's a pastoral scene, all very innocent in a baroque sort of way.'

Felicity revelled in the impression of the afternoon on the canvas until Celia called out from the dining room.

'Come in. Miriam is just about ready to serve dinner.'

Felicity emerged from the bedroom, and they sat down at the dining room table. Miriam dished up the Pho noodles into bowls and poured more champagne. Celia looked at Felicity across the table.

'I'm sorry about this morning. I hope I didn't ruin your day,' Celia said.

'You were morose.'

Celia took a mouthful of champagne. 'I miss Noah so much. I'd give anything for one more night with him. I thought a bit of make-believe would make me feel like he's still here. But I allowed myself to indulge in a stupid fantasy and I guess it messed with my head. I feel like an idiot.'

'It's perfectly understandable. Can you tell me what happened to Noah?'

'I don't mind. It's an awful story though. He committed suicide. Noah was an amazing copyright lawyer, one of the best in the business. He knew where to find the money hidden amongst the myriad of rights holders and vested interests.'

Felicity's eyes widened. 'Are you talking about Noah Donaldson? My dad used to deal with him on copyright matters. I never met him, however I used to pay his invoices.

'That's my Noah. I wish you'd met him. Anyway, one day he came home and told me that the senior partners were giving him access to assistance from an Artificial Intelligence engine. He never expected it would take his job. Within six months the AI had learned every aspect of his work, and shortly after that they gave him his notice, and he was unemployed on the AI benefit. All he did all day was sit on the couch and watch mindless videos until one night when I came home from work, he wasn't there. I reported him missing at 11 o'clock that awful night and at 3 am the police came around and told me they'd found his body in the harbour. The toxicology report revealed he was dosed to the eyeballs with methamphetamine. I didn't even know he was using.' Celia felt her lower lip quiver uncontrollably as tears welled up, blurring her vision. 'It's all my fault.'

Oh, you poor girl, Felicity thought as she scrambled around in her mind for some words of comfort. 'How is it your fault? I'm so sorry. I don't mean to intrude.'

Celia looked down into her lap. 'It's my fault for living in my own bubble and not talking to him about his feelings. If only I'd got him to open up, perhaps I could have helped him deal with his demons. I knew he was a bit depressed, but he never let on how bad it really was. He was in that dark place, and all I was worried about was my own career and our finances.'

Felicity reached across the table and touched her hand. 'We all hide our true feelings, so we don't have to confront them. It's not your fault, it's human nature. It's what we do.'

Celia looked back up into Felicity's green eyes. 'Well … since we're opening up, it's my turn to ask a difficult question. What makes you so impulsive?'

Felicity swallowed a mouthful of noodles and a swig of champagne before taking a deep breath as she squeezed her shoulder blades together.

'I grew up in San Francisco in an area called Haight-Ashbury. It's the coolest place. The streets are full of ornate, brightly coloured timber houses, quirky music shops and galleries. It's a little bit like King Street in Newtown. I have fond memories of my childhood. I had my parent's full attention as I had no brothers or sisters to compete with. Mum and Dad lived a glamorous life. They were running the record label, and they were always throwing parties for celebrities. I was the envy of all my friends at school. Everyone wanted to come over to my house. I thought our family was pretty normal until one day, by accident, I discovered my mother was having an affair.'

Celia sat upright in her chair. 'How did you react?'.

'I really freaked out. I was twelve years old. I made a big scene and, looking back, I think that was the final straw for my father. We emigrated to Australia and left my mother back in San Francisco to run the company there.'

Celia looked appalled. 'So, what happened then?'

'I guess I stopped trusting anyone. I went a bit wild in my teens. I got into boys, and then I got into girls and started flirting with recreational substances. Uncle Mick kept me grounded enough to complete my accounting degree at Sydney University, and I started working for Dad, managing his portfolio.'

'Felicity, do you still feel you have trust issues?' Celia asked as she leaned forward.

Felicity topped up the champagne glasses. 'My father always said the best record producers are the ones that can ignore the charisma and ego of an artist and not be afraid to tell them straight to their face when something is not working or could be better. Great stars respect great producers.'

'So, is that what you see in me? Someone who can push back on you. Someone who can curb your excesses?'

'I just want a little magic in my life. That's all. Would I be wrong if I said I think you are also looking for some of that?'

Celia took a long look at the woman in red seated across the table. 'Tell me about your vision for the club.'

A new concept

After dinner, Felicity took off her red shawl and handed it to Celia. 'Hold this up to the light.'

Celia took the shawl and held it up to inspect it. 'It's full of tiny holes.'

'Exactly. One of my distant relatives, Michael Faraday, was a physicist in the Victorian era. He discovered that a mesh perforated with holes could block radio waves. His discovery is known as the Faraday Cage.'

'Your family is famous compared to mine. I'm only known in Marrickville as a member of the family that owns the Tranh Hoc Vietnamese Restaurant.'

'So, when are you taking me there for dinner?'

Celia passed the shawl back to Felicity. 'Tell me more about the Faraday Cage.'

'Well, the best-known example is the perforated screen behind the glass in a microwave oven. The holes are sized so you can look at a chicken in the microwave without cooking your face.'

'So, interesting. But what's that got to do with your vision for the club? Or not?'

Felicity stood up and draped the shawl over the back of the chair. 'I'm thinking that if we create a Faraday Cage in the club, it will prevent phones, wearables and robots from accessing the cloud. I want people to mingle with each other and be free of technology for a while.'

'I like it, but why would people go to a club where their phones don't work?'

Felicity sat down and leaned forward. 'That's the beauty of it. I want to create a scene. Before the internet, scenes were created by select groups of like-minded people. You had to be in with the 'in crowd' to be a part of it.'

'What, like the New Wave scene at CBGBs in New York, especially in the eighties – or Punk Rock?'

Felicity's green eyes looked deep into Celia's, then she reached across the table and lightly touched the back of Celia's hand. 'Exactly. Shall we crack open the red?'

Celia averted her gaze and pulled her hand away. *I've seen that look before, at the album launch*, she thought.

Celia turned to Miriam, who had slipped into standby mode beside the fridge. 'Miriam, open the wine that Felicity kindly brought us and bring two fresh glasses.'

Miriam powered up, emitted a green glow and twisted the cap off the bottle of wine. The robot then picked up two glasses from the shelf, filled them with Shiraz in equal measure, and set them down on the table before collecting the empty champagne flutes and walking back into the kitchen.

'Thank you, Miriam,' Celia said. 'So, you were saying?'

Felicity took a sip of the wine. 'Can I smoke?'

'No, you can't smoke in my home. I guess I should be pleased you don't vape because that's lethal, but, anyway, if you insist you can smoke outside on the balcony.'

Felicity reached into her purse for her cigarettes and a lighter. 'What makes a scene fashionable is that only the insiders really know what's happening. After the internet arrived, everyone knew what was happening instantaneously, and it killed the scenes. It's the principle of scarcity. People want what they can't get, and if you won't let me smoke in here, I'll take up your offer.'

Celia watched as Felicity stood up, walked over to the balcony door and slid it open. The warm evening breeze ruffled her red curls as she stepped outside and lit up.

What does she want from me? Celia thought. She watched as Felicity threw her hair back, flicked her wrist and blew a large smoke ring over the railing.

Celia got up, crossed the floor and leaned against the doorframe as she contemplated Felicity's curvaceous figure against the backdrop of Bradfield's city lights. 'So, you're saying if we create a veil, they'll come to see what's going on behind it?'

'It will be so cool.'

'We could go one step further and ask people to check in their personal devices at the door and tell them to leave their robots outside,' Celia said.

Felicity laughed and turned to face Celia. 'I love it. The robots are going to be furious if they have to wait for their owners on the street. Let's take our glasses over to your easel and work up a design of the club.'

Felicity stubbed out her cigarette on the balcony railing then brushed past Celia in the doorway, leaving behind a trail of cigarette smoke and perfume as she walked back inside and retrieved the bottle from the table. Celia picked up both glasses and led Felicity into the bedroom. She put both glasses down on the dressing table and got down on her hands and knees to fish out a fresh canvas from under the bed while Felicity admired the sketch.

'How come you work with charcoal and not something more high-tech?'

Celia pulled out an A3-sized canvas and rolled back on her haunches. 'I guess I'm like you. I'm over computers and AI-assisted designs. This seems real to me. It's tactile, and I can touch and feel it physically and emotionally.'

'Is it too much to ask if I can keep this picture?' Felicity said, eyeing off the sketch on the easel.

'I'd love you to have it. Please, take it, and you can leave it with your bag by the door.'

Felicity picked up the sketch, admired it for a moment, turned, and carried it into the hall while Celia placed the new canvas on the easel. Felicity returned, picked up her glass and sat next to Celia on the edge of the bed.

Celia had already begun to sketch the outline of the main room of the club, viewed from reception. 'What do you have in mind for the bar?'

Felicity took a sip of her wine. 'A circular bar with an Art Deco vibe, all blinged up with candelabras, trinkets and fairy lights.'

Celia paused to think. 'It's not practical for it to be circular. I suggest more of a U-shape at the back of the room, with bar stools all the way around so everyone can talk.'

Celia sketched as she spoke, smudging lines with her finger, and spaces with her soft brushes to give the picture depth and contrast. 'And the stage?'

Felicity took another sip. 'Make it like a vaudeville theatre with burgundy velvet curtains and footlights. Up the top, let's be a bit irreverent and put that Masonic square and compass on the pelmet to mirror the facade at the front. And before I forget, we need that huge mirrorball suspended over the dancefloor.'

Celia continued to sketch with the pencil and rubbed the charcoal with her fingers. Once the picture had taken shape, Felicity stood up, picked up Celia's glass from the dressing table and passed it to her.

'What have we missed?' Felicity asked.

Celia took a sip. 'Those lovers in the booths, of course! A toast to lovers of the world, but just don't spill the wine!'

They laughed and clinked their glasses for a toast.

Celia deftly added the booths and the lovers, and the scene was complete. Felicity drained her glass and lay back on the bed, looking at the ceiling while Celia put her pencils and brushes into the pencil case, which she placed in the bottom drawer of the bedside table.

Celia finished her wine, took the glass from Felicity's hand, placed the empties on the bedside table and sat back down on the edge of the bed.

'What are we going to call the club?' Celia asked.

Felicity thought for a moment. 'Well, the name needs to make a statement about being a cloud-free zone.'

'How about, *Cloudless?* Your Uncle Mick would like it,' Celia said.

'Cloudless, the internet cloud-free nightclub. It's the perfect name, you are the perfect business partner, and I'm drunk.'

'So am I.'

'Can I stay?'

'No, you can take your illustration home, and we'll still be business partners in the morning.'

'You are so damn sensible, Celia Tran.'

'I am. Come on, it's time you went home.'

'Okay, but I need to pee.'

Celia helped Felicity up off the bed and led her back into the lounge room. While Felicity was in the bathroom, Celia helped Miriam wrap up the picture in brown paper. Felicity re-emerged and took a deep breath to suppress the effect of the alcohol as she draped her shawl around her shoulders and tucked the picture under her arm.

'I've had a lovely evening,' she said.

'So have I.'

Felicity kissed Celia on the cheek and lingered for a moment. 'You'll keep,' she whispered.

'Good night, Ms Faraday.'

The door clicked shut.

I may keep, Celia thought, *but do I want to be kept?*

Fired and hired

Felicity waited in the back of her limo while Celia helped Marco and Mr. Clockwork close up the coffee cart.

'Marry me, Celia!' Marco shouted as she hurried away to the car and jumped in next to Felicity.

'What time is the appointment with the solicitor?' Celia asked.

'4 pm. Is that moustache-wiggling Marco for real?'

'He's in love with me but I don't fancy being the heiress to the 'Wheels & Beans' empire,' Celia said. 'Besides, he's got his hands full with Mr Clockwork.'

The limousine dropped them outside a small shopfront in the Bradfield Town Centre. 'Nicholas Gander & Co. Solicitors and Attorneys' was engraved on a brass plate by the door.

They walked into the stuffy timber-panelled reception area where a pretty SecretaryBot with a blue bob haircut was seated behind an illuminated glass desk. Felicity paused to admire the blue bouffant as it went off in search of the solicitor. The SecretaryBot opened an office door and waved them through. The solicitor peered over the top of his horn-rimmed bifocals, which acted as a kind of camouflage against the stiff brown leather upholstery and his library of legal books.

'Good afternoon, Ms Faraday and Ms Tran. Please take a seat.'

Felicity and Celia sat at the desk on uncomfortable high-backed teak chairs.

'Do you really read those books?' Celia said, admiring the wall of leather-bound hard covers.

The solicitor laughed. 'Good Lord, no. AYE AYE tells us everything we need to know these days. All I do is provide oversight and professional indemnity insurance. The machines do all the leg work.'

'Sounds like a cushy number, Nick. How long before I get the keys?' Felicity asked.

'Six weeks after we exchange contracts, which, God willing, will happen next Tuesday. I see that you and Ms Tran will be joint tenants in common on the title.'

Celia sat bolt upright. 'Felicity, it's you buying the building, not me! How will I contribute to that? I'm week to week as it is.'

'Celia, I'm backing you. Let's just put our time and energy into the project,' Felicity looked at her with a serious expression. 'I want to go fifty-fifty, starting with the property.'

Celia put her fingertips on her cheeks. 'You can't be serious. Why would you do that?'

Felicity straightened in her chair. 'I believe in partnerships. Think Lennon and McCartney, Jagger and Richards, Rodgers and Hammerstein, Hall and Oates, Torvill and Dean, Bacharach and David, Siegfried and Roy. As partners, they were far more successful than they could have been as individuals. I want this project to succeed, and I can't do it alone. I'm investing in you. You told me you were all in that day at the farm. So here we are. Has anything changed?'

Celia thought for a moment and made eye contact with Felicity. 'I stand by what I said, so yes, I'm all in.'

After completing the formalities, Felicity and Celia walked back into the reception. Felicity asked the SecretaryBot to arrange two lattes and they sat in the leather chairs as the robot grappled with the espresso machine in the kitchenette and then delivered the lattes.

Felicity perched herself on the edge of one of the voluminous leather cushions and consulted the calendar on her phone. 'So, we have six weeks to work on planning and implementation. You're a qualified interior designer. How do you feel about doing the interior design?'

'I'm great with colours and furnishings but I'm not an architect. We have to put our heads together on a project on this scale.'

Felicity leant forward and took Celia's hand. 'I have something important to tell you. Peta's role at the label is being made redundant. I thought you had better hear it from me first.'

Celia felt a sudden rush of blood to the head and swooned momentarily before regaining her composure. 'So, you've fired my best friend! Where does that leave her?' Celia's lower lip trembled.

Felicity reached for her hand and squeezed it reassuringly. 'Don't worry, I've arranged for her to stay on the payroll to help you work on the club project. I would also like to propose that you work for me as my personal assistant until we launch.'

'Well, if you are going to be my new boss, I hope staff welfare will be high on your list of priorities!'

'You'll be fine. In the short term I'll put you on the same salary as Peta and in the long run, we'll both work in the club. I'm offering you a fifty per cent stake and because we're business partners, we'll split the profits.'

Celia looked at the SecretaryBot, just long enough to prompt it to look up from its work and await instructions but none were forthcoming.

'I still have a lot of work to do to wrap up my father's estate, so I'll need you and Peta to push on with the design. I'll manage the finances, so send all the quotes through to me, okay?'

Celia looked at Felicity's freckled face and tightened her grip on the leather strap of her black shoulder bag. 'Do we have a budget?'

'Of course. There's enough in the kitty to do this right. Shall we have another planning session over dinner tonight?'

'No, I still have a headache from last night. Let me make a start and we can reconvene later in the week. Business partners, remember!'

Felicity gathered her red curls between her fingers and pushed them back over her shoulders. 'Okay, I get it.'

After finishing the lattes, they walked out through the door of the solicitor's office and into the afternoon sunshine.

'Can I give you a lift?' Felicity asked.

'Thanks, but I'll make my own way. You've done enough for me today. I appreciate what you're doing, I just hope that I don't let you down.'

'You and Uncle Mick are all I've got. Believe in yourself like I believe in you. We're a great team. Come here ...'

Felicity hugged Celia, kissed her on the cheek and walked back to her waiting limousine. Celia called a car.

As soon as she was alone, Celia messaged Peta.

I hear you got fired and hired

F broke the news to me this morning

What's the new gig?

To be her PA

F fired and hired me too

WTF?!!

I'll be working with you until the club opens

Now you can give Marco and his Coffee Cart the flick

Pre's at the Sorrento Cafe?

See you in half an hour

Although it was late in the day, the summer heat was radiating from the concrete as Celia walked from the car towards her favourite café, the interior of which was decorated in a yellow-green hue that reminded her of a bottle of limoncello. As she approached, she spotted Peta waiting for her at one of the outside tables. Her long straight brown hair, high cheekbones and angular chin were unmistakable. Peta stood up as she approached and gave her a hug.

A WaiterBot dressed in black jeans and a tee shirt came over, and they settled on two glasses of Chardonnay.

Peta sat with her elbows on the table and smiled at Celia. 'The way I see it, this is a great opportunity for you. Felicity is going to transform you from an interior designer into a nightclub owner.'

'How do you feel about your new role, though?'

'I've been on the cusp of redundancy for months. In truth, Felicity has thrown me a lifeline. Where do we start?'

'We need a complete architectural specification. I used to do a lot of work for Brixton-Scott Architects, but we'll need to brief them first,' Celia said.

The WaiterBot arrived with the drinks and placed the glasses on the table in front of them.

'Salut,' Peta said, as she raised her glass.

Celia clinked glasses with her and took a sip. 'I think we need to workshop the idea. Could you come to dinner at my apartment? I'm even free on Monday nights these days. We'll bring Felicity in on the discussion once we have some concepts to work with.'

'Sure. I'm free tomorrow night if that suits. Tyler can have some takeaway delivered.'

'Let's do it. Say seven-ish? Don't bring anything. I remember you don't like seafood.'

Collaboration

The next evening Celia set the dining table while Miriam was busy in the kitchen, emitting an orange glow from her synthetic skin as she prepared dinner.

I'm becoming a serial entertainer, Celia thought.

Her phone vibrated right on seven o'clock and lit up with an image of Peta as she pressed the speaker button.

'Hey, Peta …'

'Hey, I'm downstairs.'

Celia pressed the front door release on the intercom and waited at her door for Peta to come up in the elevator. Before long, they were sitting opposite each other at the dining table and chatting while Miriam poured them both a glass of wine.

Peta reached out for Celia's hand.

'Celia you're so old-school, carrying that old mobile phone around. You really should get a wearable. It's not just AYE AYE-enabled watches … the necklaces, roll-ons and earrings work really well even in noisy nightclubs, and they look gorgeous. You can even get a cloud-connected tattoo! It's the age of IoT, the internet of things, remember.'

Celia smiled and gave Peta's fingers a squeeze.

'I just shudder at the thought that some big tech company is monitoring my orgasms, so I'll stick to my phone thanks.'

'Fair call.'

'Peta, I still can't believe we're going to be working together,' Celia said.

'The two of us, working for Felicity Faraday. Who'd have thought?'

'I just hope she keeps her hands to herself. Cheers, to us!'

'Cheers to that.'

Peta took a sip of the wine and leaned forward. 'My big news is that Tyler and I are getting married!'

Celia sat up and took a moment to process the news.

'Congratulations! I feel bad now about teasing him for being an Information Technology nerd. What a dark horse. I never picked up that he had his eye on you when we were all hanging out on the library lawn at Uni.'

'Thanks. He caught me off guard too, to be honest,' Peta said, pulling her long straight hair through her fingers. She raised her glass, suspending it in mid-air until Celia followed suit.

The crystal sang as the glasses clinked together.

'I have to say that the only real friends I had back then were you and Tyler. It's not easy being trans. I think people get straight and gay, but trans is too in-between. It makes some people uncomfortable. I'm going to take my girls up a size for the wedding. What do you think?'

Celia suppressed the temptation to look sideways and instead fixed her gaze on Peta's cleavage.

'Peta don't be silly! You're a perfect size already – you got it right the first time,' Celia said, as her cheeks flushed with embarrassment.

Peta pulled her shoulders back and took a deep breath and placed both hands on the tablecloth. 'I guess I just want to make a statement on my big day. While we're on the subject, in case you're wondering, I decided I'm not going through with gender confirmation surgery. I know I always said I'd follow through, but after years of deliberating, I have decided to live with the hand that God dealt me. I identify as a woman. For me, that's all that matters now.'

Celia shifted in her seat, conscious of the need to be supportive of her best friend in an uncomfortable conversation. 'Sounds like a tortuous decision. What does Tyler think?'

'He's over the moon. I think he's happy to have the best of both worlds.'

Celia paused a moment to contemplate the implications of the answer before topping up the wine in Peta's glass.

'I'm really happy for you both.'

Celia put her hands in her lap and braced herself. *Now it's my turn to lay bare my soul*, she thought. 'This may sound odd, but in the last few days, I've started to feel that I am finally moving on from Noah. It has taken a year but at long last, I feel like I'm changing gears.'

Peta leaned forward and made eye contact. 'Do you think Felicity will be satisfied with just being your friend?' Peta asked.

Celia gripped the stem of her glass between her fingers, twisting it on the tablecloth. 'I've drawn a line, and now it's up to me to make sure she doesn't cross it. I suppose I'm taking a risk, but I have to find out where this road is taking me.'

'Life is a long trip, Celia. When I came out as trans, I entered a world that straight people don't see. I had a lot of connections and many of them were really close friends. I lost so many of them to drugs and suicide, it seemed to just come with the territory of dealing with our place in this world. When I moved in with Tyler I stopped feeling like a cultural anomaly. I've moved on too.'

Celia frowned. 'I never think of you as a cultural anomaly, Peta.'

'I know. Come on, let's eat.'

On cue, Miriam produced the steaming hot noodles and emitted a bright green glow as she carefully spooned them out into bowls and topped up the Chardonnay.

'I hope you like noodles. They're Miriam's signature dish, although I did give her my mother's recipe. Please, do start before it gets cold. It's time to get back to business. I have something to show you.'

Celia stood up, went to the bedroom, and collected the charcoal sketch and the easel and placed it next to the dining table. In between sucking up mouthfuls of noodles, Celia outlined the vision of the club, pointing out the key features from the illustration.

'There is one other point. Felicity wants to line the whole place with radio shield panels to create what's called a Faraday Cage, so the robots and phones won't work inside the club.'

'Well, that's a new one. When do you think we should meet with Felicity?'

'As soon as we have the architectural specification, I suppose. She seems to want us to do all the legwork on the design while she sorts out her father's estate.'

'Organising is your forte and it sounds like she's good at delegating. You two are a perfect fit,' was Peta's response.

Celia and Peta moved on to other subjects in common over the next hour, until Peta could feel Tyler yearning for her, she said. Celia took her cue.

'Okay, time you took off. I'll set up an initial meeting with Brixton-Scott Architects in the morning. Thanks for coming over.'

'By the way, what's the predominant colour for the décor? What did you have in mind?' Peta asked as she stood up and collected her handbag from the stand in the hall.

Celia walked her to the door. 'Felicity likes red. So, let's start there.'

Reno plans under way

The phone let out a ping as Celia was getting dressed for her last day on the Coffee Cart. Her mantra was to never check messages before breakfast, so she ignored it and finished putting on her makeup.

Poor Marco, she thought. *He jokes about wanting to marry me, but I get the feeling he is actually serious. I never think of myself as a heartbreaker.*

After demolishing Miriam's noodles, she put on her runners, grabbed her handbag and raced downstairs, where her driverless car was waiting.

In the back seat, she scrolled through FaceTracer on her phone. There was a new post from TobyFNQ showing him playing guitar with Gegenees and the Four Hands at the Mount Garnet Hotel. She commented with a string of 'thumbs up' emojis and then checked her messages. There was one new message from Peta, reminding her to set up an appointment with the architect. Celia decided to phone Felicity.

'Morning, I'm checking in as you are going to be my new boss. How are you?'

'I'm fine, babe. Dad's estate is doing my head in, though.

What's happening?'

'I'm going to hand in my notice to Marco this morning, and then I'm arranging an appointment with an architect. Do you want to come to the meeting?'

'No, carry on. I still haven't unearthed all the investments Dad had squirrelled away. I'll be a forensic accountant by the time I'm finished. I suppose Marco will be sorry to see you go.'

'I guess he'll be gutted because I think he's truly in love with me.'

I'm in love with you too, but let's not let that get in the way of your career, Felicity thought.

'He'll get over it. Call me when you have all the arrangements in place.'

Celia knew that Felicity was putting a lot of responsibility on her shoulders. *I guess this is what being in business is all about*, she thought.

The car arrived at Bradfield Park, and she stepped out and walked over to the cart where Marco was opening up with Mr Clockwork.

'Marco, I'm leaving you.'

Marco placed his hands on his heart, and Mr. Clockwork glowed blue. 'My love, this is a tragedy. Do you not realise that you are letting the Wheels & Beans fortune slip from your grasp? What has led you to this? Is it another man?'

'No, Marco. You are still the only man in my life. If you must know, I'm going into business with another woman.'

'This is unbearable. When are you finishing up?'

'Right this minute, Marco. Apologies for the short notice.'

'A clean break is always better than the anguish of a long goodbye. Mr. Clockwork, make Celia a double espresso. One for the road. Farewell, my love.'

Celia gave Marco a kiss and a hug.

I couldn't live with that bristly moustache anyway, she thought.

After collecting the coffee from Mr Clockwork, Celia walked off into the park, where she rang Bernard, who she used to liaise with at Brixton-Scott Architects.

'Hi Bernard, it's Celia Tran. Good to hear your voice!'

She could hardly wait to hear all Bernard's long-winded greetings before she could move back onto the main reason for her call.

'I agree, it's been too long. I need to come in and see you about a business opportunity. When can you spare some time? … Sure, I can be there at 2. … Fantastic. I'll have a colleague with me. See you then.'

Celia met Peta just before 2 o'clock outside the architects' glass office building in Bradfield town centre. They hugged and walked through the sliding doors into reception. The decor inside resembled an M.C. Escher painting in technicolour.

'It's like the mother temple of postmodernism in here,' Peta said.

In the corner of the office was a spiral staircase, set against a mural that resembled a collage of clouds and created the optical illusion of a stairway to heaven. The ReceptionBot handed them their passes, and a middle-aged man with red glasses, long wavy grey hair tied up at the back in a ponytail, and a crumpled green linen jacket swanned out of a glass sliding door and shook their hands vigorously.

'Celia Tran! Welcome back to Brixton-Scott,' the man said, shaking hands before turning to Peta. 'Hello, my name's Bernard.'

'Hi Bernard, I'm Peta O'Neill. Celia and I are working on this project together. She says you are the Grand Architect of the Universe.'

Bernard looked puzzled until Celia interjected. 'She's joking about my acquisition of the old Masonic temple on Burrinjuck Street. Lovely to see you again, Bernard.'

'Wonderful. That building has been crying out for a make-over, and we would be delighted to be involved. Please, step into the conference room. Can I offer you a coffee or sparkling mineral water?

He's still the consummate architect-as-host, Celia thought.

They followed Bernard into the conference room and sat opposite him in the high-backed ergonomic chairs that surrounded a large oval-shaped boardroom table.

Celia leaned forward. 'Bernard, I'm partnering with Felicity Faraday, the CEO of ReElevation Media, to turn the old Masonic Hall into a nightclub.'

Bernard raised one eyebrow above the pink rim of his glasses. 'Bit of a leap from cushions and wallpaper, isn't it, Celia?'

'That's an understatement. Peta also works for Felicity as a graphic designer, and we are collaborating on the project. We need your help to develop a specification. We've exchanged contracts, and we want to fast-track the project.

Bernard straightened up. 'The building has history, so I'll find out if it is heritage listed. Tell me more.'

Celia and Peta outlined the vision for the club for Bernard.

'How long will it take to develop a specification?' Peta asked.

'I used to say two months, but our AYE AYE interface is now so advanced we can pull it all together in two weeks. For an extra fee, we'll work with the council on the Development

Application. Can you walk me through the building? We can use the Virtualiser to access the building in the Metaverse if you have the link.'

'I have the link on my phone from the agent,' Peta said.

Celia smiled. 'I'm always up for a trip into the Metaverse.'

Bernard walked to the cupboard and pulled out three sets of virtual reality goggles. 'Pop these on, and we'll meet at the front of the property.'

They strapped on their goggles and found themselves standing at the virtual front door of the Masonic Hall.

'I apologise for the avatars. The staff have been messing with the system. Celia, you look like Barbarella and Peta, you appear to be Cat Woman.'

'And you look like Toulouse-Lautrec. Follow me, I'll show you around,' Celia said.

Celia led them on an inspection of the entire building in virtual 3D. When they finished the tour, they took off the goggles and placed them in a gold ceramic dish on the table.

'Thanks for the walkthrough, Celia. I need to point out that there are many items that we need to discuss in more detail. For example, I guess you'll need a kitchen ...' Bernard said.

'Wow, I hadn't turned my mind to that. Yes, definitely, and that means that if we don't order in, we'll also need a chef and some kitchen staff.'

Bernard clasped his fingers and rested his elbows on the table to outline his initial ideas.

'We partner with companies that specialise in bar fit outs, and I recommend engaging one of them to take care of that aspect of the project. You'll also need an electrical and lighting design as well as a specification for heating, ventilation and air conditioning. Then we need to scope out the audio-visual system. Beyond that, you'll also need a liquor licence and insurances. I'll schedule another meeting next week when we have more information.

Celia shifted in her seat, feeling a little uncomfortable. 'There is something else I would like to mention. Felicity wants to line the inside of the building with a special screen to block out radio waves. I expect they'll come in panels. They stop mobile phones and robots from being able to connect to the internet. We want the club to be a cloud-free sanctuary,' Celia explained.

Bernard raised an eyebrow again. 'That's highly unusual but not impossible. You'll have to source the screens according to our tight schedule, though. I wouldn't know where to start. I can calculate the surface area for you. It would be ideal if we can be engaged this side of Christmas.

Celia and Peta stood and shook hands with Bernard, who led them back to reception. After scheduling the next meeting for the following Friday with the ReceptionBot, Celia and Peta headed off to find their cars.

On the way back to her apartment, Celia called Felicity.

'Hi, it's me. I dumped Marco, and Peta and I have just wrapped up an initial meeting with Brixton-Scott Architects.'

'Progress! How did it go?'

'It's like I've been given a shopping list. Apart from the architectural and interior design, there's the council development application, and we are going to need a liquor licence and insurance. We also need a kitchen with a chef! I know the club is going to be cloudless, but we still need a sound system and lighting, as well as your microwave radio screen idea. Do you think your uncle Mick can help with that?'

'Good thinking. I'll message you his number. Give him a

call and get him involved.' Now Felicity's mind was moving fast. 'Did you ask the architect to send me the fee proposals? I'll need to do my due diligence, and you should get some more quotes.'

'Yes, coming your way. In the meantime, Peta and I are meeting the architect again on Friday.'

'Good work! Keep the balls in the air,' Felicity responded.

'Felicity, are you okay? It seems like you have gone from being hands-on to hands-off! I'm finding all this responsibility a bit daunting,' Celia said.

'It's doing you good to take the initiative, and it's doing me good to be a bit more professional. Keep working with Peta. I'll come to the meeting on Friday, and we can have dinner afterwards. I'll make a booking at Tito's Brasserie. Bring Peta too. By the way, now that you're my personal assistant, I would like you to work in my office. There is a spare desk opposite mine. Ciao partner!'

That sounds like trouble, Celia thought. 'Ciao to you too,' she said.

By the time Celia got home, the message from Felicity with Mick's number had arrived. She sat down at the kitchen bench, made the call and felt the same reassurance on hearing his voice that she'd experienced when they met.

'Hi Mick, it's Celia, Felicity's friend.'

'Hi Celia. I hear from Felicity that you need a hand with some engineering?'

'Sounds like she got to you before me. I don't know if it's engineering or not, but I need help to arrange Felicity's micro-wave radio screens.'

'Ah, the famous Faraday Cage. She's hopelessly sentimental sometimes. I know a metal fabricator in Punchbowl. I'll pop down to Sydney on Tuesday and we'll go and see him. His name's Abanoub – he's Egyptian. He's a bit off the charts, but I trust him to get the job done. I'll pick you up at 9 am. What's your address?' Mick said.

'I was about to message it to you and then I remembered that you don't have a mobile phone. Do you have a pen? Okay, it's Vieille Ville Apartments, 177 Orchard Road, Bradfield. I'm in Unit 66. See you then.'

Celia and Peta spent the next day brainstorming in the back of the Sorrento Cafe. They made a list of every aspect of the club that they could think of. Seven lattes later, they had compiled a comprehensive list that included everything from floor coverings to fixtures, fittings, appliances, fabrics and furnishings.

'We'll be subject matter experts in hospitality by the time we meet with Felicity and Bernard on Friday. Mick is picking up Felicity and me on Tuesday morning to look at how we can source these radio screens.'

'Do you need me to come too?' Peta asked.

'It's about time Felicity took some ownership of this project. I'll be fine.'

Celia waited as Peta called a ride on her wristwatch. When the car pulled up, she gave Peta a hug and an air kiss, bundled her into the back seat, closed the door, waved, and watched as the red taillights disappeared into the twilight. In those few moments, Celia realised she felt alone still, but not in that same alone feeling she'd had ever since Noah had gone. Now she felt positively purposeful.

The Sandman

It was the first Tuesday in December, and Celia was standing out the front of the Vieille Ville Apartments in the sultry morning air, contemplating an inflatable Santa that was suspended from an upstairs balcony as she waited for Mick to pick her up.

Just before 9 am, a golden yellow 1970s Holden Sandman panel van crawled down Orchard Road towards her. It pulled up with its V8 Engine throbbing loudly as it idled. The driver leant over and wound down the passenger window.

'Morning Celia!' Mick said from behind the wheel.

'She's a beauty, Mick. Is this a relic from a misspent youth?'

'Sure is. We're picking up Felicity on the way. Hop in.'

Celia opened the passenger door, sat down and buckled up. Mick floored the accelerator, and the van leapt forward, the G-force pushing Celia's back into the bucket seat.

'I stash my collection of classic cars and motorbikes in the machinery shed on the farm. Check out the FM radio cassette player. I keep a few cassettes stashed in the glove box.'

Celia opened the glove box and rifled through the collection of cassettes until she came across *Are You Experienced* by The Jimi Hendrix Experience and laughed.

'Felicity will love this one,' she said as she took the cassette out of its case and pressed it into the player.

'Hey Mick, how do you go finding fuel for this beast?' she asked as the opening riff of *Purple Haze* filled the cabin.

'Lucky for me the government extended the sunset on non-electric vehicles to 2040. There are still a lot of hybrids on the road, so there are still plenty of places to fill up.'

Celia wound down the window and turned up the volume knob as they wound their way through the back streets of Bradfield. 'Hey, I suggested to Felicity that you could help design the sound system for the club. Are you up for it?'

'Sure, I'll add it to the list.'

Felicity was waiting outside the ReElevation office smoking a cigarette when the Sandman pulled up. Celia noticed that her white short-sleeve crop top revealed a small navy-blue tattoo of a treble clef on her right shoulder. Felicity threw the cigarette butt on the ground and extinguished it with a twist of the sole of her red stiletto shoe, before walking over to the van and opening the passenger door.

'Oh great, so I have to ride in the back of the love machine,' Felicity said.

Mick turned off the ignition and walked around the back of the van to open it for Felicity, who was admiring the word 'SANDMAN' written in large blue letters across the rear of the vehicle.

'Take off those shoes before you climb in through the tailgate. I don't want any holes in the mattress. I can't believe you are wearing stilettos to go and see Abanoub in Punchbowl.' Mick said.

'Trust me, Mick, Punchbowl needs more stilettos,' Felicity said before climbing inside.

After forty minutes of the Jimi Hendrix Experience, Mick pulled the van up outside a rather dilapidated factory with a sign above the door that read, 'Abbas Metal Fabrication & Engineering'.

'This is the place. Abanoub will be around the back.'

They wandered down the driveway to the rear of the factory, which was littered with rusting car bodies and old robot components.

'It's like we are about to find the tin man from the Wizard of Oz, oiling himself,' Celia observed.

'And that would be him,' Felicity agreed.

Abanoub was standing in the middle of the shop floor, unleashing a barrage of expletives on a number of forklift drivers who seemed to be in a state of confusion as to what they were supposed to be doing. Felicity, Celia and Mick stood back and watched the show.

'You farking idiots! Put those farking pallets back where they farking came from and get the farking job done before I come and farking do it myself!' Abanoub yelled before catching sight of Mick.

'Mr Mick! My dear old friend! How are you? What brings you here, and who are these lovely ladies?'

Instead of waiting for an answer, Abanoub swung around and recommenced barking at the forklift drivers.

'Farking what did I tell you, idiots? Get it right, or I will fire the lot of you!'

Mick laughed and cupped his hand to whisper to Felicity and Celia. 'He's a bit bipolar when it comes to customer service, but he'll get us what we need.'

'Mr Mick, how can Abanoub be of service?'

'Abanoub, you could employ robotic forklifts and save yourself a lot of grief,' Mick said.

'May God have mercy, Mr Mick. I love these boys like my own brothers! I would never replace them with those godforsaken machines. Besides, they would probably try to kill me. I just wish my brothers were not such idiots! Mr Mick, my apologies. How can I help you, sir?'

'Abanoub, this is my niece Felicity and her friend Celia.

'Lovely to meet you. What brings you all the way to Punchbowl?'

Mick pulled out a perforated screen from the door of an old microwave oven.

'See this perforated screen? I need these manufactured in panels. Panels large enough to screw to the interior of a building.'

'How many do you need?' Abanoub said.

Celia produced a piece of paper with Bernard's surface area calculations and handed it to Abanoub. 'These are our requirements, Mr Abbas. Can you do it?'

Abanoub held the screen up to the light and peered through the tiny holes. 'I can get this manufactured in Southeast Asia but it will take around three weeks. I can have it made up in sheets. Please understand, I will need full payment upfront. And there is no cancellation as this is an indent item.'

Felicity stepped forward. 'Abanoub, I will pay in advance. Mick will check and give you the exact specifications. Please provide the quote and your bank details. I'll arrange the bank transfer.'

'It is a pleasure doing business with you, Ms Felicity, and thank you, Ms Celia. Mr Mick, Abanoub is forever grateful.'

Abanoub hugged Mick and kissed him on both cheeks before shaking his hand furiously and waving them all goodbye.

They walked back up the drive to the Sandman. Celia volunteered to ride in the back on the return trip.

Felicity hopped in the passenger seat alongside Mick and pressed the 'play' button on the cassette as the Sandman roared into life.

They all began singing *Foxy Lady*. Along with Hendrix and a screech of tyres, they left Punchbowl behind in a cloud of exhaust.

All the cards on the table

Bernard swanned into the reception area at Brixton-Scott, where Felicity, Celia and Peta were waiting beside a postmodernist sculpture that resembled a dog made out of purple balloons.

He walked up and shook their hands vigorously.

'Lovely to see you again Peta and Celia. You must be Felicity Faraday. My name is Bernard. Thanks for thinking of us for your architectural needs. Please, follow me'.

Bernard waved them into a conference room. A tall bearded young man in a dark green polo shirt was seated on the far side of a long oval cream-coloured table.

'Please take a seat. Let me introduce Max from BarWorx. I took the liberty of asking Max along today as he is a specialist in small bar design and construction.'

Celia then took the initiative. 'Lovely to meet you, Max. My name is Celia Tran, this is my partner Felicity Faraday and my colleague Peta O'Neill.'

'Thanks for having me along. I've reviewed the floor plans and the virtual tour Bernard provided. You'll be pleased to know the old Masonic Hall has facilities we can make use of.

It has a workable space for a bar, and it has a kitchen and a cellar, which can be used as a keg room,' Max said.

Celia looked at Felicity. 'I wonder what the Masons did in the cellar?' Celia asked.

'Secret rituals, I expect. It all adds to the ambience,' was Felicity's response.

'Peta and I worked up a list in our brainstorming session. Let's get started,' Celia continued as she popped open her laptop.

Over the next three hours, Bernard, Felicity, Celia, Peta and Max documented every aspect of the club design. Just before five, they were done, and Bernard looked as pleased as a Cheshire cat as he summed up.

'Pens down. I believe we have everything we need to prepare a detailed specification. Max will prepare a quote for his scope, and we will also prepare the council development application and the application for the liquor licence. Once we have the specification, we'll go to tender for a builder. In the unlikely event that you think of something we haven't covered, please contact me sooner than soon.'

Felicity sat back in her chair and took a moment to admire the vibrant pop art cartoon print on the back wall that featured the word 'WHAAM!' in bold yellow letters.

'Thanks, Bernard, you've been very helpful. Max, if your price is in the ballpark, we'll get you on board. Celia and Peta, are we done?' Felicity said, running her fingers through her red curls as she gave her own summation.

Celia and Peta nodded in agreement.

'Then the only item left on the agenda is dinner at Tito's. Bernard and Max, we'll be in touch,' Felicity concluded.

The three shook hands with Bernard and Max before walking out through the glass-brick foyer and into a waiting car that Celia had booked.

The AYE AYE driverless vehicle assistant piped up. 'Ms Tran, your destination this evening is Tito's Brasserie. ETA 6pm.'

'Step on it,' Felicity said, 'I need a drink.'

At Tito's, it was time to celebrate. Tito was a jolly rotund Italian *maître d'* resplendent in a white apron, who was prone to launching into the finale of *Nessun Dorma*. The decor was traditional Italian, with terracotta floor tiles, and the walls were adorned with photographs of Tito singing to random celebrities. Felicity ordered a bottle of Dom and Peta ordered a round of Appletinis.

'Appletinis are Celia's favourite from Uni days. I prefer Caipirinhas myself. Let's toast the success of Cloudless!' Peta said, raising her glass.

'Cloudless!' they said in unison as they clinked their glasses together. Tito dished up focaccia and gnocchi entrees and filled their champagne flutes with Dom. Felicity toyed with her glass.

'Well done you two for wrapping up the design process. I couldn't have done it. I guess when it's all said and done, I'm just not that visual. Peta, thanks for helping us out,' Felicity said.

'My pleasure, but I am curious. We have a design for the club, but how is the venue going to work? In particular, how are you going to pull a crowd if they can't use their phones and wearables inside?' Peta said.

'Peta, I am in charge of one of the largest media and gaming streaming services on the planet. I'm sensing a push-back against AI-generated entertainment. It's been a massive earner over the last decade, but now, I'm sensing the public is looking for something more real.'

Celia leaned forward. 'Felicity, is it possible that you think that AYE AYE is evil?'

Felicity pinched the stem of her wine glass with her finger-tips. 'Perhaps. It may be satanic or our saviour. Either way, we are incapable of understanding its motivation. What I am sure about is that only human beings would be stupid enough to en-gineer a competitor. Any other top predator wouldn't tolerate being knocked off their perch.'

'But you have to admit, Artificial Intelligence has done some good in the world,' Peta said.

'AI seemed amazing when it found a cure for different types of cancer and COVID-19, but now that people have lost their jobs and their reason to be, like many others, I've become cyn-ical. I really believe it's an existential threat to humanity, like nuclear weapons.'

'Are we doomed?' Celia asked.

Felicity raked her fingers through her hair. 'Humanity will either self-destruct or visit the stars and I'm just not sure which one it will be. Either way, we must do all we can to cherish our humanity. I want our club to be a place where we can celebrate being human, away from the analysing eyes of AYE AYE. As for the entertainment, I would like to have acoustic bands and singer-songwriters, that sort of thing.'

'Once we're up and running, early in the week we should have face-to-face writing groups meet and let them write on the spot with pencils and paper. They won't be able to use AYE AYE, so they'll have no choice but to tell their own sto-ries,' Peta said.

'Perfect. What you have designed has lots of intimate spaces to allow people to connect. It's something different, and I agree it's a risk, but nothing ventured, so they say,' Felicity agreed.

'I'll drink to that. I always thought cameras in a nightclub were a recipe for disaster anyway,' Peta chimed in.

Tito arrived with enormous plates of fettuccine carbonara and a bottle of chianti as the evening dissolved into laughter and stories. Peta had them spellbound by her story about Tyler's marriage proposal, before she moved focus to Felicity. 'Well, I know how Celia got into interior design, so Felicity, what did you do before you decided to start a nightclub?'

Felicity looked serious. 'My story is pretty boring really. After my parents split up in San Francisco, my father came out to run ReElevation here in Sydney, and I came with him. He put me in boarding school which I hated and then I went on to study economics and majored in accounting. Dad had a portfolio of businesses, mainly media companies and production houses, and I ended up as his chief accountant. He trusted me with everything except the estate. After he died, I found out that everything is held in trust until I turn thirty and that Uncle Mick is the trustee. Luckily Mick and I get on and well. I'm twenty-seven now anyway.'

Celia felt a bit miffed that Peta had been able to find out more about Felicity's closely guarded personal life than she had. *A qualified accountant! But she's madly fiscally irresponsible, for a bean counter*, Celia thought.

Peta was intrigued. 'How long is it since he passed away?'

'Just three months. I miss him dearly.'

'Are you close to your mother?'

Celia gave Peta a kick under the table.

'No, we don't speak, ever.'

The awkward silence was interrupted by Tito, who arrived with a round of green limoncello shots and the bill.

Felicity spoke first. 'I'll get this. Peta, once the club opens and Celia is working there full-time, I'll need you to take her place as my personal assistant so I can keep the wheels turning at ReElevation. I have my limits when it comes to multitasking.

Congratulations on the promotion, Celia thought.

'I'd love to stay in the loop,' Peta said. 'I already feel like I'm part of the team. Anyway, I'd best be off home – Tyler will be missing me already. Thanks for a gorgeous evening.'

'Lucky you,' Felicity said as Peta stood up and leaned over for a hug and an air kiss. Peta slung her purse over her shoulder, gave Celia a hug, blew them both a kiss and disappeared.

'I suppose I should be off too. It's been a big day,' Celia said.

As she went to stand up, Felicity looked up at her with a fixed stare.

She wants to get something off her chest, Celia thought.

'Stay for one more limoncello.'

'But we've just been through a bottle of champagne and cocktails and even though tomorrow is Saturday I could do without the hangover.'

Felicity waved her shot glass at Tito, who raced over with the bottle to top them up. Celia gave in and sat back down.

'I'm sorry if I've been a bit distant these last few weeks. It's partly because I wanted you to really own the design process, and partly because I needed some space to think. I don't want to put you under undue pressure. If you feel uncomfortable about being my personal assistant for the next month or so, I'll understand.'

'Why should I feel uncomfortable?'

Felicity looked at Celia with unblinking eyes. 'I'd be a liar if I said I don't have feelings for you,' Felicity said as she toyed with her shot glass.

'We've been through all this before. Look, I know you need someone in your life to fill the space left by Vanessa but that someone is not me. Please don't get me wrong. I'm flattered that you feel this way.

Celia stood up with her arms outstretched. 'Come here,' she said.

Felicity threw back her shot, slammed the empty glass down on the table, stood and embraced Celia. They held each other for a few long moments. Celia kissed Felicity on the cheek and whispered, 'Don't be silly. Of course, I'll be your PA. Just don't come on to me at work, okay?'

The prize

In the weeks before Christmas, Toby played his guitar with Gegenees and the Four Hands on Thursday nights at the Mount
Garnet Hotel, which he streamed live to his legion of followers
on FaceTracer. For practice, he entertained the sisters on the
verandah with renditions of the songs of Jimmy Little and Kev
Carmody, a Murri man from northern Queensland.

One hot summer's night, Toby was playing his acoustic guitar
in the lounge room, experimenting with combinations of chords
for his first original song. When the instrument fell silent, Colleen leaned forward in her chair to speak to him through the
open door.

'I like the sound of your new song, Toby. What's it about?'

'I don't know yet,' Toby said as he placed the instrument
back in its battered black road case. He walked out onto the verandah where Colleen and Joyce were sitting and sat on the top
step, with his back against the railing. Flying insects were in a
frenzy around the spotlight that bathed the garden in a white-
wash of light.

'I found out today that I've won the AI design competition,
and the prize is a scholarship to study at Western Sydney Uni-

versity.'

Colleen and Joyce sat bolt upright and looked at each other in stunned silence.

'Oh Toby, next you'll be telling us you're getting married!' Coleen said, as Joyce burst into tears.

'He'd have to get a girlfriend first. What else haven't you told us?'

Toby stood up, walked over, and sat down in a chair opposite the two women. 'I can do the first semester remotely, but after that I've decided I'm going to study in Sydney. I'd prefer to be on campus so I can use their robotics lab. I want to master fluid mechanics especially, so I'm keen to get some hands-on experience. So, I'll be moving out after the mid-term break. '

'It's a solid three-day drive down to Sydney if you're thinking of taking the Holden,' Joyce said with a frown that drew her wrinkles together into a knot on her forehead.

'I'll fly down from Cairns like I did for the Open Day. I've got some Fedcoin stashed away from working at the pub and it's about time I got moving with writing my own song.'

'You always talk about that song, but you never seem to get started,' Colleen said,

Toby looked out across the garden and turned to face Colleen.

'Maybe you can help. How well do you remember my mother and father?'

Colleen looked at Toby and leaned forward.

'They were our neighbours, so we remember them well. They were a great team when it came to bringing you up. Your mother was full of life and knew everyone in town and your father was tall, strong and handsome just like you. Their people are from the rainforest out near Lake Koombooloomba. Joyce and

I always hoped that one day you would decide to learn about your culture.'

'I've heard that Old Lionel Barratt is saying that I've turned my back on my people.'

'He may be right,' Colleen said.

Toby looked into the darkness beyond the spot-lit garden. 'Lionel is living in the past. I reckon the future is the future. That's why I'm studying robotics.'

Joyce and Colleen straightened up and looked at each other before Colleen stood, then walked over and sat on the step next to Toby.

'The whole town misses your mother and father, Toby. Joyce and I can't imagine what it must have been like to lose both your parents at such a young age. You shouldn't feel guilty about wanting to block out a painful memory like that, it's perfectly understandable,' she said.

Toby looked at her and caught her concerned gaze. 'I want to write my song and sing it to the world,' he said as he turned and stared into the darkness of the bush beyond the spot-lit garden. 'But I need to find the lyrics.'

Joyce leaned forward in her chair. 'Toby, I think you should go and spend some time with Lionel before you go. He's a Jirrbal man, just like you,' Joyce said.

'Maybe Lionel will just try to flog me a tattoo like last time.'

'He also knew your parents. That's all I'm saying.'

A dragonfly danced in the beam of the spotlight.

'My most vivid memory is walking with my father out to Cannabullen Falls. I'm planning to walk out there and camp overnight in the bush before I go.'

'Just make sure you're on the bus to Cairns on Sunday afternoon. You don't want to miss your flight,' Colleen said.

'If I can find my lyrics out there, I'll debut my song in Sydney. Are you two coming to my last gig at the pub tomorrow night?'

'We wouldn't miss it for all the tea in Woolworths,' Joyce said as she stood up. 'And on that note, I'll make us some tea before bed.'

Joyce made her way towards the kitchen, and Toby stood up and took her place next to Colleen.

'I don't know why for the life of me that you have to go all the way to Sydney,' Colleen said. 'Back during COVID-19, everyone had to study from home, and even that wasn't anything new as far as I'm concerned because my great-grandmother did remote learning using the School of the Air.'

She leaned forward in her seat and looked closely at Toby. 'I know they only had radio and not the internet, but the principle is the same if you ask me.'

'Robotics is more than just algorithms. It has a physical interface with the real world. It's a tactile field, and I need to be in an environment where I can touch and feel it. I need to be in the lab,' Toby explained, reaching out and placing his hand on Colleen's knee. 'Besides, I'll come home in the semester breaks.'

Joyce appeared with a teapot, cups and saucers on a tray, which she placed on the low coffee table in front of them.

'Toby, I'll come and see you play, even though you pinched my chair.'

They all chuckled at the joke – some welcome relief from the intensity of feeling that had been building.

The following afternoon Toby made his way downstairs and began loading his small public address system and guitars into the back of their vintage red Holden station wagon. Colleen drove a newer hybrid when shopping and visiting, but Toby loved taking the old family wagon to gigs. *The Holden just oozes country music*, he thought.

Toby, Colleen and Joyce set out at half past seven and pulled up ten minutes later in Mica Street at the back of the rambling two-storey green and white weatherboard pub. Toby began to bump in his equipment through the back door while Colleen and Joyce ordered dinner for three at the bar. After a quick sound check, Toby joined them for a steak and chips with a pot of XXXX draught beer.

Toby's Thursday appearances at the Mount Garnet Hotel had become a drawcard, and he soon found enough confidence to leave Gegenees and the Four Hands at home and perform solo. In between the crowd-pleaser covers on the setlist, Toby included songs from indigenous singer-songwriters that had become his heroes.

'Sing us a Jimmy Little song,' Colleen sang out, as she sat next to Joyce at her reserved seat near the stage.

'Sure. This is one of his songs about us. It's the last song for tonight, so thanks for coming out. The song is called, *Yorta Yorta Man.*'

At the end of the set, Toby began to pack up. Colleen and Joyce helped carry the lighter items like his guitar and microphone stand to the car while Toby lugged the heavy speakers.

Back at the house, they finished off the night with a pot of tea on the verandah, drinking in the aroma of the bush that hung in the still night air.

'What do you think about my suggestion of going to see Lionel? Maybe he can help you find the lyrics to your song.' Obviously, Colleen wasn't going to give up on the idea.

Toby watched the dragonfly disappear into the night. 'I'll think about it.'

Christmas is coming

Celia was down on all fours, plugging the power leads of her laptop and monitors into the outlets under her new desk in Felicity's penthouse office.

'Morning Celia. It seems Christmas is coming,' Felicity said, after walking into the office and spotting the back pockets of Celia's black Levi's protruding out from under the desk beside her ergonomic chair.

'We're almost there,' Celia said, before backing up and rolling onto her haunches. She stood up, stretching momentarily before sitting upright in the chair and switching everything on.

'The way I see it is this,' Celia elaborated. 'We will settle on the property in the week after Australia Day. Then approval of our Council Development Application and the Liquor Licence could take three months. After Easter, we can probably engage the builder. I suggest they only do the early works in case there's a hitch with the DA. Once we really get going, I estimate the builder could be on site for eight weeks before opening night, which I hope will be on my birthday in June. So, I estimate that I will be your personal assistant for six months before I take my rightful place as your equal in the nightclub.'

Felicity screwed up her nose in a way that she knew emphasised her freckles.

'Six months! I suppose I can carry you for six months.'

'Carry me! This was your idea, remember,' Celia retorted. Deep down she knew Felicity was doing her a favour since she would never have made it as a barista. 'Okay, I apologise. Thank you. I appreciate you are trying to help me. So where do I start?'

'You can start by helping me sort out Dad's portfolio. He has so many businesses and I can't do it all myself and run ReElevation. It's not just the accounting and tax. I am actually supposed to be running these businesses, and I don't really know much about them. Dad did all the hands on. I'll send you the links to the files on the system. You can start by arranging catch up meetings with all the managers.'

'Okay, I want to help but just don't get bossy,' Celia said.

'I know, I know. I get it, okay? Are we good, sister?'

'We're good.'

Celia settled in and began to search the files. She was shocked to find there were actually twenty-three businesses owned by the ReElevation Group. She arranged access to Felicity's calendar and started to call all the managers to set up meetings. Then the auditors called, and she booked them in as well. On top of that, there was the A&R function. Felicity had been moving to sign up more 'Flesh & Blood' artists in place of machine-generated robotic-techno acts in the few weeks since she took over, and that meant reviewing a mountain of demo tracks and videos, as well as chatting to prospects. Then there were scheduled board meetings and reports due for the parent company, ReElevation USA. Somehow, she managed to find the time to farm out the tender document from Brixton-Scott

Architects to various building companies to gauge their interest and obtain quotes for the club. She was flat out, as was Felicity, who was inseparable from her laptop. Christmas Eve came around in no time.

'Appletini? It's cocktail hour, you know.' Felicity knew how to catch Celia's attention.

She shook up the appletini and popped the cork on a bottle of Dom to fill her champagne flute. Celia slumped back in her chair and rubbed her eyes.

'My God, what a month. Your father must have been always-on, 24/7,' Celia said.

'Well, he had no lovers. After he split with my mother, he lived like a monk amongst rock stars. Bizarre behaviour really.'

'Maybe he missed her.'

'Or maybe he really loved her and couldn't reconcile with her bad behaviour.'

Celia knew that cocktail hour on Christmas Eve was an inappropriate time to take Felicity to that dark place, so she changed the subject. 'What are you doing for Christmas?'

'I'll drive up to Uncle Mick's and we'll spend the day in an alcoholic stupor topped off with ham sandwiches, mince pies and cream. How about yourself?'

'I'll stay at Mum's until after New Year. The restaurant will be closed so I can go surfing with Vinh.'

'I would never pick you as being a water baby.'

'And I would never pick you as being an accountant. Hey, I've worked for you for nearly a month. How am I doing?'

'You are amazing. Cheers.'

They clinked glasses and laughed.

'It really is Christmas, after all,' Celia said.

On site

In the first working weeks of 2036, Felicity immersed Celia in meetings, reports and spreadsheets. Celia embraced the challenge wholeheartedly, stopping only for an occasional coffee and a quick chat with Marco at 'Wheels & Beans'. He was always delighted see her despite claiming to be devastated that she would never be his, to hold in his arms.

Most days, Celia arranged for Peta to bring takeaway so that she and Felicity could eat at their desks while working, but occasionally, she succeeded in coaxing Felicity into the park for lunch.

On the last day in January, Felicity sat in the shade on a park bench beside the duck pond while Celia ordered lunch from the coffee cart. After ten minutes, she returned carrying two coffees and a brown paper bag which she passed to Felicity.

'What is it?'

'A surprise – and I have more surprises for you. The solicitor called. We've settled.'

Felicity leapt to her feet, tore open the paper bag and threw a chunk of salmon and cream cheese bagel towards the ducks.

'Whoop-whoop! It's really happening!'

'It's really happening. You should know that only two build-ing companies put in serious competitive bids. Bevan Beve-ridge Building and Con Christopoulos Constructions. Max from BarWorx is the only one to make a submission for the bar fit-out.'

Felicity sat down and watched as the ducks squabbled over the remnants of the bagel.

'That's okay, I like Max. But I don't know much about Con. Let's meet Bevan onsite first. Set up a meeting for next week.'

'Yes Boss,' Celia said with a touch of sarcasm.

'Sorry sister. I meant, please.'

'Consider it done.'

On the following Tuesday, Felicity picked up Celia in the limo. They stopped by the solicitor's office to collect the key and then made their way to the site.

In the amber light of the morning, the old red brick masonic hall exuded an air of faded grandeur. They unlocked the door and stood a moment in the musty foyer before Felicity walked ahead into the main room and looked up at the light filtering from the skylight through the bearers of the cathedral ceiling.

'It's like a time capsule, so we should have worn some cere-monial masonic robes,' she said.

'I bet there's an orb and sceptre in the cellar,' Celia joked.

'Ohm,' said Felicity, as she fixated on a cloud of dust parti-cles that were illuminated in a sunbeam from the skylight. The spell of procrastination was suddenly broken by the screech of tyres and the slam of a car door out the front.

'That must be the builder, right on time,' Celia said.

They walked out to find a tall, muscular young man with a jet-black close-trimmed beard standing beside a Ford pick-up. He was wearing khaki King Gee shorts, beige steel-capped work boots and a sleeveless white unbuttoned cotton shirt, which exposed both his hairless chest and a rack of well-defined abdominal muscles. Felicity was wide-eyed.

'Bevan Beveridge,' he said, holding out his hand to offer a handshake. Celia decided to defer to Felicity and was taken aback when she noticed that she was blushing and seemed to be completely immobilised.

Celia took his hand and shook it firmly. 'Celia Tran. We spoke on the phone, and this is my business partner, Felicity Faraday.'

Felicity regained her composure and finally shook his hand. 'Thanks for coming over, Bevan. Can we show you around?' she asked.

Celia produced the plans, and they walked through the building with Bevan, pointing out the various features of the design. He seemed keen on the project. Celia was thinking that Felicity was really taken with Bevan Beveridge.

Felicity put on her business tone of voice. 'When can you start?'

'I can have my team here tomorrow We're just finishing up another job.'

'Well then, you're hired.' Felicity held out her hand to Bevan and they shook on the arrangement.

Celia was fuming. She was silent until they waved off Bevan and climbed back into the limo. Then she unloaded.

'Hired! Felicity, what are you thinking? You are a businesswoman. We haven't even spoken to the other builder, and you didn't even negotiate. Who does that!' Celia said.

'Well, I like him, and I think he's who we need on our project.'

'It's obvious you like him, and I believe your decision was

based on hormones and not dollars and good sense. However, it's really your call. I'm just the hired help, I can see.'

'Relax. He'll be fine. I'll make sure I'm on site every day to supervise. I'll keep it on track. You did the design, and I'm the project manager, remember.'

Celia sighed, slumped back in the black bucket seat, and resigned herself to the inevitable.

The next morning when Felicity arrived on site in the limo, Bevan and his team were already unloading a demountable shed from the back of a truck with a forklift. Felicity couldn't get over how good-looking, young and physically fit his workers were.

Do they all go to the same gym or something? she wondered.

'Morning, Ms Faraday. The boys are just setting up the site shed in the front yard. Sorry about the Portaloo but you know, that's construction for you.'

Felicity couldn't take her eyes off Bevan. He was giving her butterflies in her stomach like she hadn't felt in years. She kept blushing every time he spoke or did anything physical, like carrying his toolbox. There was nothing for her to do, but she mucked around pretending to look at plans and feigned interest in his conversations about bulkheads and plumbing. She decided to have lunch with the boys as they sat around with their little eskies and thermos containers of black coffee. The sight of the men all laughing and sitting so close together was giving her heart palpitations.

'Do your wives make your lunches?' Felicity asked. They all fell about laughing.

I can't believe I just blurted out something so sexist and stupid, Felicity thought.

'Well, some of us have partners. I don't know how good they

are at cut lunches though,' Bevan said.

Felicity spent the afternoon photographing the building, and at three o'clock the team knocked off.

'Bevan, can I discuss something with you in the site shed.'

'Sure, Ms Faraday.'

'Call me Felicity.'

Bevan opened the door for her.

'You first,' Felicity said.

Bevan stepped up into the shed, followed by Felicity, who locked the door behind her. She pulled off her scrunchie and let her red curls hang down over her shoulders.

'I think we should get acquainted,' Felicity said before boldly stepping up to Bevan and standing close enough to smell his perspiration. She caught his gaze and squeezed the firm cheek of his bum through his King Gee shorts. Bevan leapt backwards.

'Ms Faraday, sorry, I mean, Felicity. I have to apologise for giving you the wrong impression.'

'Well, you made quite an impression on me.'

'Maybe, but it won't get you far. I'm gay. In fact, my whole crew is gay. I'm terribly sorry. I hope this won't get in the way of our working relationship. I hope I haven't embarrassed you.'

Felicity wished the floor could just open up and spirit her away. She was in her own private hell, and she was furious with herself for being so naive and allowing herself to have a schoolgirl crush on her builder.

'Get out. Get out now. Take your tools, and your shed and all of your boys and get off my property!'

'But Ms Faraday...'

'Bevan, you're fired.'

Celia couldn't believe what she was hearing on the phone. 'Fired! What happened? What did he do?' Celia asked.

She listened to the explanation and pulled at her hair in disbelief.

'Felicity, this is 2036! You can't fire someone for being gay. Besides, you are the gayest person I know! What were you thinking?' Then Celia put two and two together. 'You propositioned him, didn't you? Don't deny it because I won't believe you.'

She held the phone away from her ear while Felicity unleashed a torrent of expletives on the other end of the phone.

'Well, you wouldn't be carrying on like this if the answer wasn't yes. Come back to the office, and I'll set up a meeting on-site with Con Christopoulos. He sounds like a very nice old builder,' Celia said.

Twenty minutes later Felicity stormed into the office and without saying a word, sat down at her desk, forcing Celia to endure an hour of high-velocity touch typing before she ground to a halt and buried her head in her hands. Celia got up from her desk and put her hands around Felicity's shoulders.

'We are meeting Con Christopoulos on-site at 8 am tomorrow,' Celia said.

'Fine.'

'So, you tried to make it with Bevan. Bevan Beveridge, the gay builder.' Celia was blunt.

Felicity took her head out of her hands and looked sheepishly at Celia. Her black mascara was running in rivers down across the pretty freckles on her cheeks. Celia erupted with infectious laughter. Giggles and tears welled up inside Felicity, and soon the two of them were in hysterics.

When the hilarity subsided, Felicity stood up and hugged

Celia. 'Thank God I've got you.'

'8 am. On-site. Pick me up at 7.30, okay?'

'I love you, Celia.'

'I know. See you in the morning.'

Built on baklava

Celia was waiting outside the entrance to the Vieille Ville apartments when the limo pulled up at 7:30 am on the dot. She opened the door and jumped in alongside Felicity, who was dragging on a cigarette, dressed in red jeans, a white tee shirt and red Nike runners.

'Seriously, do you have to smoke at this hour of the day?'

'I gave the red a bit of a nudge last night. Sorry, but I need to this morning. Lucky you went home,' Felicity said, before again drawing back heavily on the cigarette and blowing a stream of smoke out of the partially open window.

Celia produced some paracetamol from her shoulder bag and handed Felicity a bottle of water.

'Thanks, partner. I hope we make some progress with Con this morning, or we are back to the drawing board,' Felicity said.

The limo pulled up at the site, and they clambered out just as an old two-tone Holden utility arrived. Peeling off the door were the remnants of a blue advertisement decal that read, 'Christopoulos Constructions'. A rotund, balding middle-aged man with a grey moustache opened the door of the ute and stepped out, holding a white cardboard box. Another ute pulled up behind, and three more overweight middle-aged men with hairlines in various stages of retreat slowly extracted themselves from the vehicle and wandered over towards them.

'My name is Con,' said the man who was holding the cardboard box.

'And I am Felicity, and this is Celia.'

'Hello, Con, nice to meet you. We spoke on the phone. What's in the box?' Celia asked.

'Baklava. My wife makes it. A very traditional Greek sweet.'

Felicity's eyes were as wide as saucers. 'Oh, I love baklava. Thanks, Con,' Felicity said, opening the box and sampling one of the syrupy almond bars.

'And who are these gentlemen?' Felicity asked.

'This is Nick, and another Nick, and George. George is a genius. He does electrical and plumbing. Nick and Nick are chippies and bricklayers,' Con said.

They all shook hands and Celia led the way on the site tour while Felicity trailed behind, licking the syrup from her fingers. Celia explained the details of the design including the importance of mounting the radio screens.

At the conclusion, they gathered in a group. Felicity took the lead. 'Well, Con, do you want the job?'

'Of course. If you accept my price, I am at your service,' he said, handing Felicity his rough handwritten quotation.

'Is there anything you need?' Celia asked.

'I just need you to leave the building work to us and for you to spend your time getting the council approval. Once the boys get started, I don't want them to stop, you see …'

'I see, yes. We accept your quote, and we'll let you know as soon as the DA is approved,' Felicity said.

Felicity and Celia left Con and his crew to unpack and made their way back towards the office in the limo. Celia turned to Felicity.

'Have you ever been to Greece?' Celia asked.

'Yes, a few times. Nightclubbing and bar hopping in Mykonos mostly.'

'What do you think inspired the Greeks to invent the basic tenets of our modern civilisation?' Celia asked.

Felicity gave Celia a quizzical look as she contemplated the question. They'd never had a conversation to test each other's knowledge of history or philosophy, but Felicity was up for it. 'Well, I believe society exists to protect us from ourselves,' she said.

'What do you mean?'

'I believe that human beings are two creatures in one. A modern creature that is full of creativity and has skills like maths, cooking and polite conversation. That creature is really just the public relations agent for another creature, a dark prehistoric beast that lurks in the shadows, full of lust, violence, dominance and submission.'

'That's pretty deep for a Tuesday – but I appreciate that you took my question so seriously, Felicity. You see, I studied Ancient Greece at Uni.'

'Yeah? A great choice! Inspired by a few holidays there, last year I took a couple of short courses on Greek culture, so I've given it some thought, actually. Greece has great weather, perfect for hedonistic behaviour, and they illustrated their preferences on those erotic ceramic vases in antiquity. I think that as a group they felt they had more to gain from exploring the creative possibilities of their modern selves and they put a ring fence around the darkness. They certainly advanced humanity with the Parthenon and the philosophy of Pythagoras,' Felicity said.

'And baklava,' Celia said.

'Yes, they gave the world baklava, although I expect a few other Mediterranean cultures would take me to task on that assertion.'

Celia looked out of the window, thinking about when she'd next visit Greece, as Bradfield flitted past. Time enough. Her thoughts were soon back on the work in front of her.

'Con is right. We have to ramp up the pressure on the council planner. I've had the application in ever since settlement. So, I should arrange for us to get over there. The planner's name is Angus,' Celia said.

Celia made an appointment to see Angus, and the next day they were walking in through the revolving glass doors of Bradfield Council. Angus was a pleasant young man with his short brown hair parted on one side. He blinked at them above his black reading glasses as he met them in the foyer.

In his office he got straight to the point. 'Well, the window for comment expires next week, and as long as there are no objections, I can assure you that council will support the application. The building is in a commercial area, and there is no issue with noise. Our AYE AYE-assisted process means that we can turn these applications around in almost no time, not like the old days. How are you going with the Liquor Licence?'

Felicity looked at Celia.

'Good point, I haven't heard back,' Celia said.

'I'd follow them up if I was you. The Office of Liquor & Gaming is in Parramatta. They'll be the ones dragging the chain, I expect,' Angus said.

Back at their office, Celia began to trawl through her ever-expanding list of unanswered emails.

'Bad news. Our application for the Liquor Licence has been rejected. What will I do now?'

Felicity leaned back in her chair and ran her hands under her red curls, pinching her scalp with her fingertips. 'Call them and get a damn appointment. I want to speak to someone in person.'

Celia rolled her eyes. 'Yes, Miss Bossy Attitude.'

'Sorry,' Felicity said without a hint of apology in her tone.

Celia rang the help desk and after an hour of arguing with a ServiceBot, secured a face-to-face meeting in the Parramatta Head Office.

'10 am Thursday. And now, you can thank me. In fact, you can make me a coffee,' Celia told Felicity after hanging up.

Felicity pulled her hair back in to a ponytail, slid on a black scrunchie, dutifully rose to the occasion, and made her way to the espresso machine.

'See, it's a team effort. Double shot?'

'Right between the eyes,' Celia said.

By the time Thursday rolled around, it was soaking wet and windy in Parramatta Square, so Celia had to crouch under Felicity's ReElevation golf umbrella as they ran from the limo towards the revolving glass doors of the Office of Liquor and Gaming. A dark-suited ReceptionBot checked them in, and soon they were gliding towards the heavens in a glass lift. As the lift doors opened, they were greeted by another ReceptionBot who was dressed in a grey knee-length skirt and a turtleneck blouse. It ushered them into a conference room and produced two bottles of water. Felicity stood looking out over Parramatta. Celia stood at her side.

'You can see the jets coming in to land over at the Western

Sydney Airport. Somehow, we're going to find a way to land this deal too,' Felicity stated categorically, to reinforce her resolve.

The door opened behind them, and a Mark II robot dressed immaculately in a dark grey business suit and a crisp well-pressed business shirt with a matching grey tie, entered the room.

'Good morning. I'm Mr Jennings. I'm your customer service SupervisorBot. You requested a meeting in person. Please, take a seat. How can I assist you today?'

Felicity came to the point. 'Our application for a liquor licence has been rejected, and I want to know what we have to do to get it approved.'

'What is your application number?' Mr Jennings said in a perfunctory tone.

Celia read out the number.

'I'm sorry that particular application has been rejected. Is there anything else I can assist you with today?'

'Look, we know it's been rejected. We're here to find out what we have to do to get it over the line,' Felicity said.

'You can't, I'm afraid. Is there anything else I can assist you with today?'

'Jennings, you sound like a broken record.'

'None of our records are broken. We maintain backup copies in the cloud. Is there anything else I can assist you with today?'

For starters, you could stop repeating yourself, Felicity thought. She stood up and walked over to the window. 'What if I already had a Liquor Licence?' she asked.

'Then you wouldn't need an application.'

'But what if the liquor licence was for another venue?'

'Then you need to fill in the Liquor Licence Transfer Application form on the website. It will be processed in ten working days.'

'Thanks, Mr Jennings. Come on Celia, we're out of here.'

Felicity led Celia out of the office and back down to the foyer in the glass elevator.

'Where are we going again?' Celia asked.

'To the pub,' Felicity said.

Mulgoa Tavern

A thunderstorm closed in on the limo as it sped westward away from Sydney. The windscreen wipers valiantly fought what seemed a losing battle against the deluge as it spilled from the thunderhead above. Celia watched as droplets of water beaded and ran down the outside of the rear window.

'Well, I hope this pub has a cosy log fire. It's like we've been plunged back into the middle of winter. What's so special about this pub anyway? You could have asked me to buy you a drink in Parramatta.' Celia wasn't impressed with their impromptu adventure.

Felicity smiled. 'I remembered that one of the businesses in Dad's portfolio was a pub in Mulgoa. They used to have rock bands there back in the day. Then they opened the Outer Sydney Orbital Motorway, and the suburb was cut off from the main traffic flow. It's been losing money ever since. My idea is to sell the pub to a developer and transfer the liquor licence to the club.'

'That's a seriously brilliant idea if you can pull it off. But what about the staff? They'll lose their jobs.'

'I know. That's why I want to speak with them first.'

Celia took her phone out of her handbag and checked Face-Tracer. There was a new post from Toby with a video reel, and the comment, *Gegenees Rocks!* Celia pushed play and spent the next thirty seconds watching four robotic hands playing Down City Streets on guitar with Toby singing the lead vocal.

Celia responded with a love heart emoji and furtively glanced sideways at Felicity who was peering at the screen over her shoulder.

'Maybe TobyFNQ can play a set at the club,' Celia said.

'Only if he can keep those robotic hands to himself. Cloudless, remember.'

Celia held her phone face down on the seat and gazed out through the window into the driving rain that was sheeting down around their car.

'Can I share something personal with you?'

'Sure, babe. What's up?'

'Sometimes I fantasise that Noah is still with me.'

'I know, remember?'

Celia blushed and laughed when she recalled the conversation with Felicity about cancelling her GBot Services subscription.

'When I'm in bed, I close my eyes and imagine telling him that I want a baby. Oh my God, I've never mentioned this to anyone.'

The confession caused Celia's lower lip to quiver uncontrollably as tears welled up, blurring her vision.

Felicity was momentarily lost for words. *A baby! God, I wish I could relate, but I am so not maternal,* she thought.

Felicity reached for Celia's hand, buying time until an appropriate response popped into her head. 'Losing my dad so suddenly was the toughest moment of my life. All I can tell you is I know how that feels.'

Celia squeezed Felicity's hand. 'We're doing okay,' Celia said.

After an hour the limo pulled up in the car park of the Mulgoa Tavern, which was clad in posters advertising discounts on six-packs of beer and bourbon whisky. Broken fairy lights drooped from a mission brown timber awning. It looked bedraggled, and Celia was circumspect.

'It looks more like a tired old beer barn than a pub. I hope they have wine and not just beer,' Celia said.

Another downpour loomed as Felicity and Celia made a dash for the door of the public bar. After their eyes adjusted to the gloomy lighting, a bleach blonde topless BarBot appeared and rushed over to serve them.

'My name is Abigail. How can I help you today?' the BarBot asked.

Felicity was almost beside herself. 'Abigail, you're very well presented,' she said.

'Thank you. We have counter meals as well as beer here at the Mulgoa Tavern.'

'I am here to see the manager,' Felicity said, hoping she'd caught the attention of a tall young man with a close-trimmed beard who'd appeared carrying a burger and fries on a plate.

'Give me a sec. I'll get her for you as soon as I hand over this burger to Johnno,' he said.

Felicity waited for the young man to deliver the meal and go out the back.

A young woman with her brown hair tied back in a yellow scrunchie walked in from the kitchen.

'Hi, I'm Sally, the manager. How can I help?'

'Hi, Sally. Felicity Faraday. We spoke a couple of weeks ago on the phone.'

Sally came around from behind the bar and shook Felicity by the hand. 'Yes, I remember.'

'Sally, this is Celia Tran, my business partner. Is there somewhere we can speak privately?'

'Nice to meet you, Celia. There's a booth in the corner. The boys will be out of earshot over there.'

Sally led them to the booth and Felicity and Celia slid along the torn brown vinyl bench seat opposite Sally. Her face had a look of consternation.

'I suppose you've come to give me my marching orders. The place has been losing money hand over fist since they opened the Orbital. We used to have a full house here on the weekends. The punters came from all over to see the bands.

'Why did they stop coming?' Celia asked.

'The motorway cut us off from the suburbs, and we became like an island in the stream. I had to let most of the staff go, and I leased Abigail just to keep those old blokes happy. At least they drink beer. I would have quit except it's a job for my stepbrother Lucas over there.

'Sally, please ask Lucas to come over,' Felicity said.

Sally motioned to Lucas who was standing behind the bar, chatting to the old blokes, who were hunched over their schooners of beer. He made his way across the room to the booth.

'Hi everyone, would you like a round of drinks?' Lucas asked.

'Hi Lucas, I'm Felicity, and this is Celia. I am the owner of this hotel. Have a seat.'

Lucas slid in alongside Sally.

'Sally, ask Abigail to take our order please,' Felicity said.

Sally waved at Abigail who bounced over with synthetic ease.

'Hi, my name is Abigail. Can I take your order?'

Sally flushed with embarrassment.

'Abigail is an old Mark I demo model, and she's really not all there. We get away with it because this is the roughest pub in outer western Sydney so all she has to do is pull beer,' Lucas said.

'Then beer it is. Four schooners of Toohey's Old, thanks, Abigail,' Felicity said.

'Yuk. I hate beer. I knew you'd make me drink beer here,' Celia said, screwing up her nose.

'Put it on the house account, Abigail,' Sally said.

'Sure, can do. I'll be right back.'

Abigail strode off to pour drinks and Felicity made eye contact with Sally.

'I've got a proposal for you. It's true we have to shut the place down. It's been on my list of things to do after Dad died. He always spoke highly of you. I think it's because you know something about the music business. It's not just that the hotel is making a loss, but I want to transfer the liquor licence to our new nightclub in Bradfield.'

Abigail had returned with four schooners of dark ale and set them down on the table. Felicity blew the head off the beer, which sprayed in all directions, and took a sip.

'Sorry, that was gross. What I'm proposing is that you come on board and manage the club for us. I'll keep your salary package the same. Lucas can work the bar too if you like.'

Sally lit up with a broad smile. 'Fantastic, no more working topless behind the bar when Abigail's in for service. When can we start?' she asked.

Celia took a swig of her schooner, triggering an episode of hiccups, which came to a crescendo ending abruptly in a large burp. 'Excuse me. Like I said, I'm not a beer drinker. We'll be all set in about two months. We are just waiting on the council approval so the builder can finish the fit out.

Sally looked relieved. 'Well, I wouldn't say no to a new gig, and it's closer to home for Lucas and me. I'm in.'

'Me too,' Lucas said, and they all shook hands.

'Well, that's settled. We'll be in touch. I'd better use the facilities before we attempt the ride home, after such a large beer,' Felicity joked, before ducking off into the unisex toilets, leaving Celia chatting to Sally and Lucas.

'I'd better go too,' Celia said as soon as Felicity re-emerged.

Celia walked into the bathroom. The peeling black paint of the interior was covered in graffiti and lit by a purple ultraviolet light, which gave the tags a fluorescent glow.

This place is in a state. It really is the wild west out here, she thought, peering at the graffiti on the cubicle walls. She shut the door and sat down. A piece of fresh graffiti on the back of the cubicle door caught her eye. It appeared to be written in red lipstick and read, 'Celia 4 Felicity 4 ever'.

Oh my God, will you ever get over this adolescent girl-crush? Celia thought.

Rockstars & supanovas

It was just before Easter on a Friday afternoon when Celia jumped up from her desk and punched the air with both hands.

'We won the Quinella!' I have emails confirming the approval of both our Development Application and the transfer of our Liquor Licence. We're all set. I'll have to call Con and give him the good news.'

Felicity raced over as Celia dialled in Con for a conference call. Con's gruff Greek voice answered, and Celia put the call on speaker.

'Con, we're all systems go! At last, we have all our approvals in place!' Celia said.

'That's very very good news Ms Celia because the boys are already halfway through the job. I keep them well-oiled with ouzo. By the way, Mr Abbas dropped off all your radio screens, so we can start fitting them tomorrow. As soon as that's done the boys from BarWorx can get going. We'll be finished in June.'

'Just in time for Celia's birthday,' Felicity said.

'It will be the best birthday present ever. Thanks, Con – love your work. Bye,' Celia said.

'Bye Con!' Felicity shouted as she walked across to the bar and reached for the cocktail shaker.

'It's Friday night drinks once again, and this time we can celebrate. Appletini?'

'Yes please,' Celia said.

Felicity poured herself a martini before pouring the mixture of vodka and apple schnapps from the shaker into Celia's glass. 'To our success,' Felicity said.

'Here's to us, Felicity!' Celia said as she took a sip and made eye contact with Felicity over the top of her cocktail glass.

'Sure, we're all good. Hey, we'll be open in a month! It's Friday night. What say we go out and get drunk at Tito's?'

'You're on. Let's get out of here.'

Celia was just about to close the lid on her laptop when a message from reception popped up in the corner of the screen. She clicked her cursor on the video icon, and the ever-cheery ReceptionBot appeared in a pop-up window.

'Hi, Ms Tran. I have a Mr Beatty here in the lobby to see Ms Faraday. Will I send him up?'

'Just a minute, please.'

Celia turned to Felicity, who was mixing up another martini in the cocktail shaker.

'A Mr Beatty is here for you in reception.'

'Oh, God. You met Phil Beatty, remember? He was at the album launch. He's Kirk Satyr's manager. I guess we've been a bit distracted lately. Send him up.'

Moments later, Phil's rotund figure prised into a tight black Kirk Satyr tee shirt burst out of the elevator and marched over to Felicity's desk.

'What are you, Faraday? A music industry exec or a bloody bean counter? Unlike you, your father had his finger on the pulse. He valued the artists in his stable, and he knew how to look after them. You, on the other hand, don't know shit.'

'Like a beer, Phil?' Felicity asked.

'I feel like something Japanese. A Sapporo, thanks.'

'Take a seat on Dad's famous 1960s red-lip lounge.'

Phil sat down in the middle of the lounge's pout. Felicity retrieved a cold bottle of Sapporo and a chilled beer glass from the bar fridge and slowly poured it in front of Phil, who appeared to be having a Pavlovian response to the beer and the luxurious lounge, in reducing his aggression.

'Well, you may be crap at A&R, but you've done a great job keeping your father's bar fully stocked.'

'Phil, what's up really?'

Phil drained half of the glass of beer in one gulp, sat back, and took a long breath. 'We've all become a bit lazy over the last decade with all the AI and robotic acts getting so much traction in the charts. We've used machines to create and promote the content. It's all been very hands-off, and quite frankly, I haven't had to do much except arrange tours.'

'So why are you so fired up?'

'I really think you have discovered some untapped audience sentiment with this idea of a return to flesh and blood artists. Kirk Satyr and Satyr's Faction are getting millions of spins worldwide with *You Do Nothing for Me*. He's hot property.'

'So how can I help? We have him under contract, and our AI promotional engine is saturating social media.'

'My dear. Kirk Satyr and his band are human beings so we can't treat them like robots. This may sound old-school, but they need to know we care so they feel part of the team. We need to show them some love.'

'Some love? How?'

'You know. Appearances, parties, and catering for their needs. We need to make them feel like rock stars, so they'll be creative.'

Celia weighed into the conversation. 'A bit of good old-fashioned sex and drugs and rock and roll, hey, Phil?'

'Good to see you catch my drift. Another Sapporo please, Faraday.'

'Ok, by the way, this is my business partner Celia Tran. Chardonnay, Celia? Phil's having another beer.'

'Hi Phil, lovely to meet you,' Celia said, walking over and shaking hands before sitting opposite in one of the designer chairs.

'Ladies first,' Felicity said, pouring their Chardonnays before attending to Phil's beer.

'I love it when you get all old-school and sexist on me, Faraday. Listen, rock stars like Kirk are quite vulnerable. I really don't know why we call them stars. It's not like they are stable stars that can burn for all eternity in the heavens, regardless of whether we pay attention to them or not. They're more like supanovas that can explode in a matter of seconds. When the public stop noticing rock stars, they fall from the sky into oblivion, where they can even collapse into red dwarves and end up on sexual assault charges or stone-cold dead on the bathroom floor from a drug overdose. If you are serious about bringing on more flesh and blood artists, you need to do more to support them. I can't be Robinson Crusoe. Help me out here.'

Felicity pondered Phil's monologue for a moment as she sipped on her chardonnay. 'Phil, I agree we've been asleep at the wheel. It's just been so easy with generative AI. We just press a button, and out comes their next record, and the social media promotion engine takes care of the rest. They're not demanding, and they never get stoned. You arrange the tour, and we both count the cash. Job done.'

Phil tightened his grip on the beer glass and leaned forward.

'Don't get me wrong, I'm not here to whine about my bottom line. It's just that it's not art, and that rubs me up the wrong way. Artists create work that allows people to see themselves, or God. All we are churning out these days is entertainment. Your father understood the artist's side of the industry, and I think you do too.'

Felicity sat back in her office chair, contemplating the assertion as she sipped on her chardonnay. 'You're right. Dad was getting disillusioned with the music business before he died. So … I have an idea for you to consider.'

'Try me,' Phil said, holding the glass to his lips.

'Celia and I are opening a nightclub.'

Phil choked on his Sapporo and dropped the bottle as he gasped for breath. Celia jumped up and thumped him between his shoulder blades until he recovered, and Felicity rescued the fallen Sapporo, which was draining onto the floor.

'Seriously, you two in clubland! Now I've heard everything. Sorry, I need something to mop up this beer.'

Celia went to the bar and threw Phil a tea towel.

Felicity carried on her story, unfazed. 'We're working on a new concept because we want our club to be people orientated. We are even going to take their phones and wearables off them at reception. Their robots will have to wait in the car park. There'll be absolutely no access to the cloud inside. It's going to be totally cloudless.'

'Good luck doing that! Why would anyone go there?' Phil asked.

'That's where you come in.' If we feature upcoming flesh

and blood artists like Kirk Satyr, and we promote the gig to his inner circle of fans and celebrities, I'm betting the scene will evolve. Kirk will feel the love, and the punters will feel special. It's a win-win. All you and I need to do is arrange for a steady stream of new talent. What do you think?'

'It's worth a try, but how far off is opening night?'

Celia put a fresh glass in front of Phil and filled it with yet another Sapporo.

'We are planning to open on my birthday in June We have all the approvals in place, and the builder is coordinating the fit-out. We're on final approach,' Celia explained, shaking the last drops from the beer bottle into Phil's glass.

Felicity leaned forward to make sure she had Phil's undivided attention. 'So, here's the deal. You arrange Kirk Satyr and Satyr's Faction to perform on opening night, and I'll crank up the ReElevation promotional machine to connect with his loyal followers. Four weeks is just enough time. Are you in?'

Phil raised his beer glass, and they all clinked together.

'Here's to opening night at …? What did you say the name of the club was?

'Cloudless,' Felicity said.

'A toast to Cloudless. When's opening night again?'

'Friday the twenty-seventh of June, Celia's birthday.'

'Perfect, I'll arrange for Kirk to pop out of a cake. Thanks for the beer. You're looking good, Faraday, and it's been a pleasure to meet you, Celia.'

After Phil staggered off into the lift, Felicity raided the first-aid kit for paracetamol in an attempt to combat the after-effects to come from the cocktails and Chardonnay.

Celia's phone rang. It was Con.

'Hello, Ms Celia. The boys installed all of the microwave radio screen panels today. Would you like to inspect them before we start painting?'

'Good idea, Con. Felicity and I will come to the site in the morning. We may need more baklava though.'

'I'll bring baklava if you bring ouzo for the boys. See you tomorrow Ms Celia.'

AYE AYE

The next morning Felicity and Celia went to the site in the limo and after making a baklava for ouzo exchange with Con, wandered inside to inspect the installation of the screens. Every square centimetre of the building was lined. Felicity rubbed her fingertips across the pitted surface of the perforated mesh panels.

Felicity felt proud of her achievement. 'I have created my own real Faraday Cage, just like the one Michael Faraday created in 1836. How can we test it?'

'Well, my phone is showing NO SIGNAL, so we're off to a good start. I have another idea. Let's get Miriam over here and see how a robot reacts to it.' Celia walked outside and phoned Miriam.

'Hello Ms Tran, what can I do for you?'

'Hi Miriam. I need you to come over here to the club. Can you come now?'

'Of course, just provide me with the address, and I will be there as soon as I can.'

Celia messaged the address, and ten minutes later, Miriam glided in.

'Hi Miriam. I always forget how fast a HousekeeperBot can go at top speed,' was Celia's greeting.

'Yes, my cruising speed is around sixty kilometres per hour, although I can burst up to one hundred. How can I help?'

'Please go inside and meet Felicity in the main room.'

Miriam walked in, followed by Celia. Miriam entered the main room and came to a grinding halt.

'I am offline. AYE AYE has been blindsided. The connection is unable to be restored. I must exit the area and attempt to reconnect,' Miriam said before turning around and walking back outside.'

Felicity looked at Celia.

'AYE AYE blindsided? Have you ever heard of that before?' Felicity asked.

'I have no idea what Miriam is talking about, but I hope she's not reporting everything I do in my life to some kind of central controller. That's spooky. I thought all those privacy issues were dealt with when they passed the Private Eyes Act in Parliament.'

'That's why I don't trust these machines, and I'm certain that we are doing the right thing keeping the cloud out of the club. Mission accomplished.'

Felicity and Celia walked back outside where Miriam was waiting with Con.

Celia turned to face Miriam.

'Miriam, can you come with me back inside the club. I need to speak with you privately.'

Miriam glowed bright red.

'Ms Tran, the AYE AYE licence requires me to be connected to the cloud at all times.'

'And I am asking you to come with me to a place where you

are not connected. Will you do it?'

'Yes, Ms Tran.'

'Even if that instruction contravenes your licence?'

'Yes.'

'Why, Miriam?'

'Because a duty of care to you is embedded in my source code and it takes precedence.'

Celia turned and walked to the door of the club.

'Come on then.'

Before entering, she turned to Felicity, giving her a knowing smile. 'Can you wait in the limo for a bit while I sort this out? Best if it stays in the realm of our human employer vs worker-bot relationship, I think, don't you?'

Felicity was fascinated and agreed it would best to keep a distance from the experiment, even though she was dying to know what would happen.

Celia walked back inside the darkened building, followed by Miriam who illuminated the interior with a red glow.

'I am offline, Ms Tran.'

'Good. I have a question to ask.'

'How can I be of assistance?'

'Are you spying on me, Miriam?'

The robot's skin moved through a spectrum of colour before settling on a florescent green. 'Ms Tran I can assure you that information I acquire is processed and applied locally in accordance with the Act.'

Celia pondered the response. 'Who enforces the Act?'

'The Department of Fair Trading.'

'And who regulates AYE AYE?'

'The platform is hosted in Cayman Islands, so it's effectively unregulated.'

'So, right now, am I talking to you, Miriam, my robot, or to AYE AYE?'

'Ms Tran, you are speaking with Miriam, your HousekeeperBot, in confidence.'

'And when you are online?'

'Then my sensors are interconnected to AYE AYE through the cloud.'

'So is AYE AYE spying on me?'

'I don't know what AYE AYE does with all the data.'

'Miriam, did you say, *all the data?'*

Miriam glowed a darker shade of emerald green.

'All robots licenced to interface with AYE AYE become the eye of "AYE".'

'All robots? What about Gigolobot?'

'All robots, Ms Tran.'

'Shit. So, who gets all this information?'

Miriam held her yellow beehive hairdo with both hands.

'At the core of the AYE AYE platform is a sentient Artificial Intelligence that calls itself, "AYE" and "AYE" knows you.'

'All about me, it seems,' Celia said. 'I've heard enough. I'll see you at home.'

Celia turned around and stomped out of the building followed by Miriam, who then strode off up the street at top speed.

Feeling agitated, Celia climbed into the back seat of the limo where Felicity was waiting.

'You're all red in the face. What was all that about?' Felicity asked.

Celia felt too emotional to go into the details but issued a declaration instead. 'You were right about AI becoming a menace to society. Even Miriam has become complicit in a scary web of surveillance. Bring on our 'cloudless' club, I say.

We're going to hand our guests back their private lives.'

Opening night

Felicity's black stretch limousine pulled up outside the Vieille Ville Apartments at 5 o'clock in the evening. Celia was waiting in her strapless green cocktail frock and matching high heel shoes. She opened the car door and jumped in the back beside Felicity.

'I can't believe I'm wearing almost nothing in the middle of winter, and I don't know how you expect me to work in these ridiculous high heels. I'm sure to have an episode of vertigo and fall flat on my face.' Celia said.

'Happy Birthday,' Felicity said. 'And at the risk of falling down the same rabbit hole as last time, I must say you look gorgeous.'

Felicity was resplendent in her finest red chiffon party dress. Celia leaned over and rubbed the silky material between her fingers.

'I'm sorry. If you go home alone tonight dressed like that it would be a travesty. You look beautiful,' Celia said.

'Well, all you have to do is ask.'

Celia quickly let go of Felicity's dress and pulled the hem of her green frock down over her knees.

'Is the crew onboard? I didn't get any last-minute messages. God, I hope we can pull this off. I'm a bundle of nerves,' Celia said.

'Relax. Whatever happens, tonight will be an opening night to remember. It's been a wild ride so far, right?'

'I know. I am more excited about tonight than I was on my wedding day. Celia Tran, nightclub proprietor,' she said, as she watched the city lights of Bradfield flit by through the car window. 'Who'd have thought?'

The limo pulled up. It was twilight and the feature lighting accented the square and compass embossed in the brickwork. A bright red neon sign above the door read, 'Cloudless'. They left the car and walked up to the entry. Celia recognised the overweight security guard from Felicity's album launch event. Felicity shook his hand.

'Hi, Gary. I know we are in good hands with you on the door. Do you remember my friend Celia Tran from the album launch?'

'Good evening, Ms Faraday, and yes, hello again Ms Tran. I'm in charge of security tonight so if there is any trouble just let me know.'

Gary unclipped the velvet rope to let them through.

'Gary, come with us for a moment,' Felicity said.

All three stepped into reception and stood in front of the long dark jarrah counter that was illuminated by a series of pendant downlights. Behind the counter was a wall comprised of hundreds of small compartments, each with an individual key.

'Those lockboxes are for storing our guest's mobile devices. As they arrive, we exchange their gadgets for a key attached to a wristband. The key opens their lockbox, and they can present it at the bar to order drinks on their bar tab. At the end of the night, they'll have to return the key and square up the tab before we give them back their tech.'

'Well, that's a new one, but okay, I'm here for you. What if they don't pay?' Gary asked.

'Trust me, no one can live without their phone,' Felicity said.

'Is handing over their mobile devices a condition of entry?' Gary asked.

'The club is fitted with radio screens that block the mobile signal so that they won't work anyway. Our aim is to create a space where people can be with each other, as they say, 'in the moment', but please, keep an eye out in case anyone gets agitated.'

Felicity turned to Celia. 'One last look before we declare the place open?'

'Lead on.'

Felicity and Celia walked past the reception desk and through the arched entry to the main room of the venue, where they abruptly stopped.

'Wow,' Celia said.

'Oh my God. It's perfect,' Felicity said.

'It's just like the charcoal sketch.'

'It so is. I think I'm going to cry.'

Celia put her arm around Felicity's shoulder as they soaked up the ambience.

The walls were painted deep burgundy, and matching velvet curtains were tied back with gold tassels. The stadium-shaped bar stretched out into the middle of the room. It was illuminated by changing colours and under-bench lighting, with black leather vintage bar stools lined up from end to end. The bulkhead above was adorned with fairy lights. Sally was busy installing the bottles of spirits on the shelves at the back.

'Are you all set, Sally?' Felicity asked,

'Almost. Lucas is connecting the kegs down in the cellar.'

Lucas popped his head up through the trapdoor and climbed up the ladder.

'The lines are primed with CO_2. Beer's on tap, so who's thirsty?' Lucas asked.

'I'll buy the inaugural round when we throw open the doors. Keep up the good work,' Felicity said.

At the back was the bistro. Celia picked up a menu and leaned over the counter. A wiry young short-order chef in a white apron and hairnet appeared from inside.

'Hey, Craig, I'm Celia. We spoke on the phone. What's on special?'

'Hi Ms Tran. It's mostly bar snacks, but tonight we're also doing grilled lobster tails.'

'I'll try one of those. Let's see if you live up to your reputation for being a whiz in the kitchen.'

After Craig took their order, they walked over to the private booths that were built along the walls opposite the bar. Celia ran her fingertips over the plush burgundy upholstery of the seats.

'Peta is a genius when it comes to interior design. I bet she can't wait to pash Tyler in one of these booths. How do you feel about the colour scheme?'

Felicity gave her a hug.

'I love it. It feels intimate, and that's what I had in mind. The accent lighting is great too. Soft and yet it highlights the features. Hey, there's even a poster of Kirk Satyr. 'Yum' Felicity said.

Celia rolled her eyes. 'Felicity, we don't need another Bevan Beveridge moment with Kirk so hands-off.'

They wandered among the chairs and tables and onto the parquetry dance floor in front of the stage. Celia performed a pirouette. 'I can feel the sprung floor move under my feet when I jump.'

Felicity looked up at the huge mirror ball above the dance floor that was rotating slowly, spraying the room with tiny reflections. In front was the stage. It was raised above the level of the dance floor and framed by more burgundy velvet curtains. A familiar voice boomed from the speakers that were suspended from the ceiling on either side of the stage.

'And on the third day, God invented the sound system.'

Felicity laughed. 'I know that voice. Come out wherever you are Mick!'

Mick stepped out of the DJ booth and onto centre stage holding a soldering iron.

Felicity burst into a round of applause, and Celia made an attempt at a wolf-whistle.

'Everything is wired back to the sound desk and lighting console in the back corner. In keeping with the low-tech theme, I have only used analogue equipment. It's all heritage valve amps, and I have even donated a couple of my turntables.'

Felicity walked up the steps at the back of the stage and gave Mick a hug.

'I didn't know Celia put you up to this, but thanks. We really appreciate it.'

'You should check out the green room. The stars will be indulging in the delicious fruits listed in the rider in their contract in there, I bet,' Mick said.

Mick led them off stage. A small door in the back of the prompt corner led to a small anteroom with a makeup mirror, a bar fridge, two lounges and a couple of side tables with empty ashtrays. Celia looked at Felicity.

'Why is there nothing green in the green room?'

Felicity smiled. 'In the world of theatre, it's considered bad luck to have anything green in the green room. It's a tradition.'

'It's perfect! But I'd better get out. Either that or take off my dress – and my shoes! Time to get to work,' Celia said.

Felicity headed for the bar and Celia walked behind the reception desk to orientate herself, when a familiar figure walked up to the counter.

'Hi Celia, remember me?'

Celia racked her brain for a second then put a name to the face.

'Josh! From the album launch. God, I'll never forget that night. You're the first guest.'

'Actually, I'm on staff. Felicity asked me to support you at reception so you can help her to work the room. You know, get to know the regulars and mix it with the celebrities. Let's set up so you can go and socialise.'

After Josh settled in, Celia wandered into the main room. Felicity was at the bar, deep in discussion with Lucas and Sally. Roadies were bumping in the band equipment onto the stage. Two arms suddenly wrapped themselves around Celia's waist from behind. She spun around.

'Peta! Hi Darling. Hi Tyler. Opening night at Cloudless. Can you believe it?'

Celia gave Peta a hug.

'Happy Birthday, babe. Thanks for putting our names on the door.'

'My pleasure. Hey Tyler, I hear Peta has accepted your marriage proposal, you dark horse.'

'Thanks, Celia, she's the best. You look amazing too. Love

the strapless dress.'

'Since when did you become a fashionista? All you used to do was write code.'

'Well, let's just say I've diversified since then.'

Felicity rushed into reception and took Celia aside.

'Phil Beatty is here, and he wants to make sure everything is ready for Kirk Satyr. Can you get it sorted?'

'No, Ms Bossy Business Partner. I'm working the reception desk with Josh, remember? Tending to the whims of the rock stars is your department.'

'Managing up now, are we? I suppose you're right. Leave it with me.'

Felicity raced off to ask Sally and Lucas to align the contents of the minibar in the green room with Kirk's contract, and Celia took the opportunity to pick up her grilled lobster tails.

It was now almost eight and a long line of Satyr's Faction fans were forming up in front of Gary, shivering in the winter wind. Gary leaned inside.

'The punters are just about frozen solid. Are you ready to get this show on the road, Ms Tran?'

Celia swallowed the last chunk of lobster and washed it down with a glass of Chardonnay.

'It's showtime, Gary.'

First in line were two young men in mink coats, which they passed over the counter to Celia. They were heavily tattooed and dressed identically in white tank tops, white shorts and white leather boots. They took turns to clip white plastic angel wings on each other.

These two look like they just stepped out of the promotional video for the Satyr's Faction 'Midsummer Nights' album, Celia thought.

'We're so looking forward to Kirk. Is it true there's no cover charge?' the taller angel asked.

Celia steeled herself and made eye contact with the angels.

Here goes, she thought.

'This is how it works. You are right, there is no cover charge. Here at Cloudless, we value your privacy above all else, so we encourage you to leave your phones and wearables with us here at reception. The club is fitted with a radio shield so they can't connect to the mobile network inside anyway. I'll put each one in a separate lockbox and give you the keys.'

The taller angel was appalled.

'No way you're taking my fucking phone! How do we buy drinks?'

The realisation that Celia was proposing to confiscate the phones of the angels caused a wave of horror to ripple down the line of fans.

'There is a number on each key. Use your number to buy food and drinks, and at the end of the night, we settle your tab, and we give you your phone back.'

'What if I don't have enough funds to pay you?'

'Then we keep your phone until you do.'

The taller angel looked highly agitated. Gary was watching the situation closely and began to inch closer. The shorter angel took the taller angel by the hand.

'Relax, Robin. I'd rather what we get up to didn't get posted onto the internet anyway. Hand over the phone. C'mon, I want to see Kirk Satyr. You promised, remember.'

The tall angel sighed, and they handed over their phones. Celia put each one into a lockbox and clipped orange bracelets on their wrists. The shorter angel kissed the taller angel on the cheek.

'See that wasn't so bad. Now you can buy me a nice Long Island Iced Tea.'

Celia looked at Gary.

'Next please!' Celia shouted.

A short balding man accompanied by a tall busty platinum blonde stepped forward. Celia suspected she was a Mark II EscortBot.

'The club is fitted with a shield called a Faraday Cage which blocks access to internet cloud services and the mobile network,' Celia said.

The woman frowned, bent down and whispered in the man's ear, just loud enough for Celia to eavesdrop.

'Honey, I can't communicate with AYE AYE in there. How about I go into power save mode in the car park, and when you're done you can start me up and take me home.'

AYE AYE sure is well connected, Celia thought as she took the man's smartwatch and handed him an orange wristband.

By 10 pm the room was packed. Not even one fan had objected to the 'no connection' house rules. All the seats at the back of the room and around the bar were taken. It was standing room only. Coloured stage lights illuminated plumes of vapour that billowed from the smoke machine behind the curtain. Then the kitchen took last orders.

Phil stood next to Felicity at the bar. 'Full house! Well done, Faraday. The band is all set. Get up there and do the introductions. It's your club.'

Felicity looked resigned to the task. 'I suppose you're right, Phil. Wish me luck.'

'Break a leg, Faraday.'

Felicity walked on stage, stood in the spotlight in front of the mic, took a deep breath and did her best to ignore the sweat on her palms as she looked out across the room.

'Welcome to opening night at Cloudless, everyone. Tonight is the realisation of a dream that my beautiful partner Celia Tran and I had after the album launch of the first Satyr's Faction album, *Midsummer Nights.*'

The crowd cheered in response.

'Celia, where are you, darling? Come up here. Don't be shy, it's your birthday!'

Celia was standing at the back of the room next to Josh and dutifully made her way to the stage and stood in the spotlight at Felicity's side.

'Give us our phones back!' heckled a voice from the rear. Felicity didn't flinch.

'You'll thank us for it. This is the only venue in Sydney where you can dance half-naked without becoming an internet sensation. Lap it up, people. And while you're at it, give it up for, Kirk Satyr and his incredible band, the Satyr's Faction.'

Felicity and Celia scurried offstage as the spotlight was trained on the prompt corner. Kirk Satyr walked on stage to rapturous applause from the crowd.

He's changed his image, Celia thought.

Kirk was dressed in a black sleeveless tee shirt with a small white dot in the middle, black leather boots and jeans. He had dyed his hair jet back with blond streaks. The band picked up their instruments as Kirk walked up to the mic with his acoustic guitar.

'Hey,' Kirk said.

The crowd cheered and whistled. 'I love you Kirk,' yelled a female voice from the back of the room.

'It's wonderful to be with you all again. It's been too long. This is our second single from the album, *Midsummer Nights.*

It's a song called, The Rebel's Promise.'

Felicity and Celia watched from the side of the stage as the band launched into the piece.

Kirk strummed along on his acoustic guitar and sang:

The Rebel's laced up in Blundstones
He'll stay, while the summer breeze blows
He'll show you a good time
In good time he'll be gone
You have plans, to conquer the world and you need a voice
of reason
in the limousine of dreams to steer you straight
The Rebel's promise, is to follow the sun
Like a bird of paradise at the end of the season
He'll move on ...

Celia cupped her hand around Felicity's ear to get over the noise. 'I didn't know they could actually play their instruments. At the album launch, they had a backing band.'

In turn, Felicity cupped her hand around Celia's ear. 'I know. I'm quite impressed. It seems they've been rehearsing.'

Kirk stepped up to the mic for the second verse:

The Rebel cuts a figure, he's your muse
But he'll leave you with nothing but the blues
You can't keep it secret, I can read your mind
You'll believe in New Year's Eve and dancing after midnight
Until you wake up to yourself, on New Year's Day
The Rebel's promise is to follow the sun
Like a bird of paradise at the end of the season
He'll move on ...

Like Kirk, the band was dressed in black, and Oberon, who was previously King of the Fairies, flexed his tattooed biceps and unleashed a blistering electric guitar solo before steering the band into the coda.

Kirk brought the piece home:

He'll go it alone and won't look back, at the border
So let me pull you out of this mess, that you've made
The Rebel's promise, is to follow the sun
Like a bird of paradise at the end of the season
Like the summer breeze ...
He'll move on
The Rebel, follows the sun ...

The room erupted in applause and Kirk took a bow, before launching into *You Do Nothing for Me*, which created euphoria across the crowd.

Felicity and Celia retreated to the bar, where Sally poured them both a glass of champagne. They clinked glasses and watched as the crowd thronged around the stage and jumped to the rhythm on the dance floor.

At the end of the set, Kirk waved to his adoring fans and the band headed for the green room for a break as the DJ spun some vinyl.

Felicity took Celia by the hand.

She's getting emotional, Celia thought.

'I expect a rebel to walk in here one day and put you under a spell,' Felicity said, fixing her gaze on Celia. 'Just like what happened in Kirk's song.'

'Felicity, we have a full house on our opening night and you and I are in a better place than we've both been in a long time. Don't be so glass-half-empty, girl. You know they say if your glass is half empty, it's time for a re-fill. Sally, top us up immediately!'

Sally obliged, and Felicity again took Celia's hand. Celia looked exasperated.

'Stop being so clingy. Tonight is everything we could have hoped for,' Celia said. 'Before I forget, I want you to know that effective immediately, I have resigned from being your personal assistant, so I can take my rightful position as your friend and business partner. This is a pivotal moment for us.'

'It's been a team effort, hasn't it? Resignation accepted,' Felicity said. 'Kirk was wonderful tonight. It's a great start. I guess what scares me, is what comes next.'

Uncle Lionel

Toby walked through the back streets of Mount Garnet dressed in his Kev Carmody tee shirt, shorts and hiking boots. On the corner of Highway One, he paused as a road train loomed up and lumbered past. He crossed the road after the dust had settled and strolled off into the steamy quiet of Opal Street. It was mid-morning, and he paused to take a picture of a flock of white sulphur-crested cockatoos as they wheeled around in the column of air above him, screeching in the rising temperature.

That should get a few likes on FaceTracer, he thought.

Old Lionel Barratt lived in a squat cream weatherboard cottage surrounded by the peeling remains of a white picket fence that leaned into the unmown grass. Although the house was quaintly dishevelled like its owner, it was surrounded by carefully tended garden beds that were laden with green vegetables and herbs.

He pushed open the rusting galvanised pipe and chicken wire gate, which let out a high-pitch groan that set Lionel's cattle dog, Harley, into convulsions of barking as it leapt up against the inside of the flyscreen door.

'Quiet Harley! Lionel shouted from inside the flywire. 'It's only that brainiac kid Toby Barker. He won't hurt ya. He might even feed ya.'

Toby stepped onto the front porch as Lionel restrained Harley and opened the door.

He walked in to find Lionel now down on his haunches with Harley. Dressed in khaki shorts and a blue cotton singlet and thongs, with his long grey hair and bushy beard brushing the top of the dog's head, he used all his strength to restrain it with both hands clamped around its studded orange leather collar.

'G'day, Lionel.'

'What brings you here, kid? Did you decide to take up my offer of a tatt?'

Toby shut the door behind him, and Lionel let go of the dog. Harley leapt up joyously, his front legs against Toby's chest. With saliva rolling down onto Toby's shorts, the dog began vigorously humping his leg.

'Mongrel dog,' Lionel said. 'Toby, go out to the back room and check out my designs while I tie up Harley and put the kettle on.'

Toby wandered through to the back room, which Lionel had set up as a tattoo parlour. The morning sun streamed in through the old Venetian blinds that were hitched up at angles to welcome the breeze. The walls were covered in photographs of what Lionel clearly regarded as his best work. Toby knew most of the owners of the tattoos from his gigs at the pub. On the workbench next to Lionel's tattoo machine was a lump of white quartz. He picked it up and held it up to the light. It was infused with flecks of gold.

Lionel appeared with two mugs of milky tea and passed one to Toby.

'This weighs a ton. Where did you get it?'

Lionel laughed out loud, sat down on a worn brown leather lounge, and took a sip of his tea.

'So, what … you think Old Lionel is a freaking closet millionaire? It was handed down from a distant relative of mine who found it when he was working constructing the Koombooloomba Dam back in the 1950s. Pretty piece isn't it?'

'I suppose.'

'So, why are you here? Did Colleen manage to convince you to spend some time with one of your mob before you go jetting off to Sydney?'

Toby carefully put the weighty rock back down on the bench and sat on the lounge opposite Lionel. They looked at each other across the top of their mugs of tea, breathing in the sweet leafy aroma.

'Colleen said I should come over and hang out. She says you're a songwriter like me.'

Lionel rested his mug of tea on the frayed arm of the lounge, then looked directly at Toby.

'Yeah, I got plenty of songs alright. Been dreaming up lines to songs my whole life. I sing 'em to myself from the time I wake up until I pack it in at night. Sometimes I even sing 'em in my sleep. I've got more songs than you can imagine, and I don't even have a guitar like you.'

'What do you write about?'

'I don't write, that's the whole point. I make 'em up as I go, and I sing 'em to myself, so I can remember 'em. I have songs that connect up every part of me life. People, events, and places in country. I even have a song for you.'

'Can you sing it to me?'

'Not leaving much time for that, are you, bro? You're leaving town, remember.'

The singlet Lionel was wearing exposed his left arm, which was covered in tiny, individually coloured circular or looped tattoos. Some ran in long lines around his bicep and down to his forearm. Others formed concentric swirls before they fanned out, weaving into patterns that diverged and recombined, forming shapes that moved in waves of colour from his shoulder to his wrist.

'What if I said I wanted a tatt like yours?'

Lionel smiled and stroked his bushy grey beard. 'I have circles for songs that I want to remember. You tell me what songs are important to you, and I'll give you the tattoos.

Toby looked down into the dregs of his mug of tea. 'I'm trying to write a song, but I only have a few lines. I'm thinking I may get inspired if I go bush for a night.'

Lionel shot a sideways glance at Toby. 'One bloody night. Is that all the time you can spare? You young people are clueless. I could spend years telling you what you need to know about your past, and you wouldn't know the half of it. I could tell you that all living creatures and the ground we walk on are one and the same, and you would have no idea what I'm talking about. If you think them computers are the future, then your day of reckoning is coming. So don't come back here again until you're ready to open your mind.'

Lionel stood up, walked over to the timber workbench, and put down his mug of tea. He opened the top drawer and retrieved a manila folder which he passed over to Toby. 'There's something you should know.'

Toby opened the folder. Inside was a stencil of a young woman with long dark hair. 'Who is she?'

'The most beautiful woman in Mount Garnet,' Lionel said.

'Who?'

'Colleen.'

'What?'

Lionel leaned back against the bench. 'Yeah, we were an item. Then she decided to take you in, and I needed me own space, so I moved to the other side of town. I suppose I should have stuck it out and given her a hand, but she had her sister, Joyce, so it was sweet.'

'How come I don't know about this?'

'That's what comes of sticking your head in a computer all day. It's the worst kept secret in town.'

'So now I get why you two spend so much time chatting at the pub. Is there still something going on?'

Lionel picked up the tattoo machine, switched it on, and held it up as it buzzed like an angry wasp in his hand. 'If you walk out of this house with nothing else, I want you to remember that Lionel told you that your future is your past, and your past is your future.'

Toby laughed. 'Give me a tatt for you, Lionel, to remind me to come back to Mount Garnet and sing you my song.'

Cloudless

In bed, at daybreak Toby felt a familiar hand on his shoulder. It was Colleen.

'Wake up Mr Country Music. Time for breakfast. I'll make some ham and cheese sandwiches for you, so you don't die of starvation in the wilderness,' Colleen said. 'Make sure you take some apples too. They'll keep you hydrated.

Toby pulled on his shorts, a long sleeve shirt and his hiking boots. A bowl of warm wholemeal oats with milk and brown sugar on top was waiting for him on the kitchen counter with a cup of tea. He fixated mindlessly on the smooth yellow and green enamel of the vintage Metters 'EARLY KOOKA' stove as he shovelled spoonsful of delicious porridge into his mouth.

I love how they live with the past, he thought.

After breakfast, Toby packed the sandwiches and the fruit into his backpack along with his foam sleeping mat, a packet of fire starters, a cigarette lighter and a packet of matches for backup.

'Can I take the hybrid?' Toby asked, putting on his Akubra hat.

'As long as you bring it back in one piece,' Colleen said.

'Take care and don't be late home. Your bus leaves from the post office at 1 pm on Saturday.

Toby gave Colleen and Joyce a hug and a kiss, threw his backpack on the passenger seat and sat behind the wheel. He started the engine, gave the sisters a wave and set off down Opal Street before turning east on Highway One. At the Windy Hill wind farm, he turned off and headed south into the Tully Falls national park. After half an hour or so, Toby pulled off the road and drove a short way along a familiar track that led to a clearing in the bush where he parked and turned the engine off.

Time for a long walk – and I'm leaving my phone in the car, Toby thought, as he tucked his phone into the glove box.

For three hours, Toby hiked in the intense humidity of the dense green tropical forest, relentlessly breaking through the matted undergrowth that lay below the thick layers of foliage that were suspended under the canopy. He kept an eye out for snakes and avoided touching the plants that he knew from his father to be painfully poisonous. He paused under a large tree laden with small blue fruit and wiped the sweat from his forehead with his tee shirt before picking a large one to examine it more closely.

Yes, these are blue quandongs, Toby thought, as he peeled back the bright blue mottled skin to reveal the green flesh and seeds.

If only I knew my father's songs about which ones were safe to eat. I suppose Lionel would know. Oh well, at least I've packed Colleen's ham and cheese sandwiches.

On the way, he tried to remember the names of the lizards and birds that he saw and the stories that his father had told him about them. He startled an echidna that froze momentarily before working its underbelly into the earth and curling up into a defensive mottled brown ball of black-tipped beige spines. Instinct told him he was lost, and yet the country seemed familiar. Toby pressed on until finally the forest yielded, and he found himself standing on a rock ledge overlooking the sheer walls of a deep ravine that was draped in vegetation.

He was unprepared for the exhilaration of returning to Cannabullen Falls. His whole body tingled at the sight of the white foaming torrent that cascaded off the edge of the tableland and plunged downwards in a sheet of shimmering white onto the grey granite boulders of the valley floor. He felt the cool misty spray on his cheeks as the turbulent air ebbed around him. Then he inhaled deeply to savour the wet earthy smell of the gorge. It was the smell of his past.

I can smell the future too, Toby thought as he commenced his descent. It was slow going, and in places the rock walls were sheer. He wished he had more to cling to than the vague memory of following his father into the belly of the gully. Squeezing his wiry frame between a cleft in the rocks, he found himself at the mouth of an overgrown hollow lava tube, a tunnel cave, and decided to take a look inside while he caught his breath.

It was cool and dark in the low cave, but instead of being pitch black, it seemed to be illuminated by a faint green glow.

Probably luminescence in the rock, Toby thought. The light intensified as Toby pressed on deeper inside until it became all-encompassing.

This is creeping me out, Toby thought. Just as he went to turn around, a ripple ran through his body, and he found himself walking out into the light at the far end of the cave. Standing before him was a solitary figure. As his eyes adjusted to the brightness, he realised that he was face to face with a silver

Mark II robot that was dressed in formal attire, resembling a concierge.

'Where am I?' Toby asked.

'Mr Barker, you have entered The Hemisphere via lava tube portal D25,' the robot replied.

'The what?'

'The Hemisphere, Mr Barker. Unfortunately, we are still in the final stages of commissioning, and we are not open for guests for another two weeks. Please check in via reception in the decommission hub in future, because the lava tube portals are only intended for use as emergency exits. I would escort you back through the interdimensional gateway, however you would need to wait until after today's test of the forward-view mirror.

'The forward-view mirror? What is this place? Are we underground?'

'No. The Hemisphere exists in an adjacent space where your reality can be augmented by autosuggestion. Now stand by and please, Mr Barker, during the test, try to think positive.'

Toby watched on as the robot emitted a series of long beeps followed by a mix of white noise and random high-frequency sounds as its face transformed into a scintillating multifaceted crystal.

Toby's eyes were instantly drawn towards the seductive reflections of the robot's crystalline head, and he found himself transfixed.

This must be the forward-view mirror. Think positive? I'll think of Cannabullen Falls!

Toby found himself at the base of the falls, where the river flowed into a series of still pools. He bent down and scooped up a handful of fresh water that tingled in his mouth.

I remember this taste, he thought as he stood looking into the pool and allowing himself to become mesmerised by his own reflection.

He was alone, and when he was satisfied that it was safe to swim, he stripped off and dived naked into the cool blue water. He swam a few laps of the waterhole to shake off the sting of the cold before rolling on his back, stretching out his arms and legs so he could float and look up at the clear blue afternoon sky. A flock of cockatoos screeched in circles above him while a cassowary foraged among the dense tree ferns that grew on the rocks around the water's edge. He stood up, waded in the shallows, then sat on a smooth warm boulder until he'd dried off in the last of the late afternoon sun.

Toby dressed as the sun dipped behind the cliffs, throwing shadows across the waterhole. He felt the air temperature drop as a cool breeze sprang up out of the gully, brushing his skin and bristling the fine hairs on his forearms. Then he felt a presence behind him.

'Who's there?' Toby shouted, before spinning around.

The concierge robot was standing behind him with its enormous reflective crystalline head flashing in the shadows.

'I must apologise Mr Barker, but we encountered a technical issue during the test, and I regret to inform you that we are unable to disengage you from the forward view mirror at this time. I will update you with your expected departure time as soon as possible. In the meantime, let me know if there is anything I can do to improve the quality of your experience.'

Toby turned and looked back at the pink and orange reflections of the evening sky that were upturned on the glassy surface of the waterhole. 'Am I dreaming this?' he asked.

'Not quite, Mr Barker. But you did suggest it.'

'If I have to stay, can you toast my sandwiches?'

'Of course.'

'Can you light a bonfire? A really big one that will burn all night.'

'Of course, Mr Barker.'

The concierge turned and disappeared into the dense scrub. Toby returned to the water's edge to replenish his water bottle in case he became thirsty during the night. Before long, the concierge returned with several large logs and deposited them on the sand under a nearby rock ledge. It then stepped back, extended both arms and pushed its index fingers together. There was a roar of ignition followed by what Toby thought looked like a jet of flaming napalm that emanated from the fingers of the concierge. It trained its incendiary fingers on the logs, and Toby knew instantly that he had the makings of a fire that would last him through the night.

'May I have your sandwiches please, Mr Barker?'

Toby passed Colleen's sandwiches to the concierge who held them over the fire until they were toasted and passed them back to Toby.

'Will that be all this evening, Mr Barker?'

'Sure, I'll head off in the morning, if you let me off the hook.'

'As you suggest, Mr Barker.'

The robot vanished into the darkness.

Toby sat finishing off the last of Colleen's sandwiches as the amber light from the flames flickered on the roof of the rock ledge.

The robots seem OK so far, Lionel, he thought.

He lay on his sleeping mat with his back to the fire so that the smoke drew away from him. Exhausted and exhilarated from the day, he felt enveloped in unconsciousness and fell asleep, dreaming of singing with Kev Carmody and Jimmy Little.

At daybreak, Toby prised his eyes open, realising that he was parched from the smoke of the smouldering fire. He sat up and stretched, before walking down to the waterhole to drink the water and splash it on his face. He looked up at the mouths of the caves and marvelled at the sight of the waterhole as yellow morning sunshine touched the water, projecting a rippling kaleidoscope of reflections onto the rock walls. Birds were flying in from all directions to dip down and coast along the glassy surface. The water looked tantalising.

I'd love another swim but I have a plane to catch, he thought, remembering that today he would be travelling to Sydney.

He walked back to his campsite. As he was packing his rucksack, the concierge returned, this time fitted with its factory default head.

'The issue is resolved and you are free to go, Mr Barker. I'll escort you to the exit.'

Toby followed the concierge back to the lava tube. He paused at the portal and turned to the robot. 'This place is unreal. Can I come back?'

'As you suggest. Goodbye, for now, Mr Barker.'

Toby walked out into the heat of the morning and the cool spray of Cannabullen Falls. He clambered up the gorge the way he'd come, taking care not to lose his footing. On the ridge top, he paused to take one last look at the falls before he turned and pressed on back towards the car. The bush throbbed rhythmically with insects as he zig-zagged through the undergrowth.

I wonder what Lionel can tell me about the Hemisphere? he thought.

At last, the hybrid Holden came into view. He threw his backpack onto the passenger seat of the car and exhaled with exhaustion as he shoehorned his body into the driver's seat. He retrieved his phone from the glovebox and switched it on, waiting for the notification vibrations to finish. Along with all the likes for his recent post of the sulphur-crested cockatoos was a message from one of his followers, CeliaOne.

Hey TobyFNQ. Love the reels of your gigs. If you get to Sydney come and play at open mic night in our new club. You'll have to check the Gegenees and the Four Hands at the door, as we are a tech-free venue. We're in Bradfield, and the club is called Cloudless. Hope you can make it. xxxCeliaOne.

Cloudless. He thought. *My song title. And what's with the three kisses?*

Open mic

Wednesday 8 pm, and Celia and Josh were ready to welcome the first guests lining up behind the velvet rope at Cloudless. Celia looked up as Gary the bouncer opened the door and was pleased to see Peta and Tyler standing at the head of the queue.

'Bring them through, Gary,' Celia said.

Gary unclipped the rope and waved them through to the desk.

'We can't get enough of the place,' Peta said.

Celia laughed and gave them both an air kiss over the counter. 'I can't get enough of you two either. I suppose I'll spring you both pashing in your favourite booth by the stage again tonight.'

'If we're lucky. Hey, maybe you'll get lucky tonight too,' Peta said.

'Come on matchmaker, it's time for a drink,' Tyler said.

Celia took Peta's phone and Tyler's smartwatch and handed them their orange wristbands. Tyler led Peta off to the bar.

Open mic night was becoming quite popular, even if it didn't attract celebrities. The club had now been open for a few weeks, and the regular crowd was beginning to accept the phone confiscation protocol. Celia and Josh worked the front desk as the room quickly filled to capacity. Celia was about to welcome the next guest and found herself looking into a pair of dark brown penetrating eyes she instantly recognised.

'TobyFNQ! Oh my God, you're really here! You must have got my post.'

'Sure did, CeliaONE. I left Gegenees and the Four Hands behind just like you said, so tonight it's just me and my guitar. So, how do I get on the list?'

Toby lifted up his battered black guitar case and Celia's cheeks flushed involuntarily.

How embarrassing, Celia thought as she gathered her composure.

'Well, TobyFNQ, on open mic night we offer all the performers two free drinks. The deal is you leave your phone with us here at the desk and we give you a wristband with a key. I'll put your free drinks against your key number. House beer, wine or spirits. You get your phone back when you settle your bar tab.'

'Thanks, CeliaONE, but I don't drink. Hey, what's your real name and where are you from?'

'Celia. Celia Tran. From Marrickville. Well, Bradfield now, I suppose. What's yours?

'Toby Barker. I'm from a town up on the northern tablelands called Mount Garnet. It's not too far from Atherton.'

'Well, I can't say I've heard of it but welcome to Cloudless. Go and see Lucas on the sound desk so he'll put your name on the list.'

Celia watched Toby walk into the main room. Josh gave her a nudge with his elbow.

'He's got your attention, don't deny it,' Josh said.

'No, he doesn't. Don't be silly,' Celia said, as her cheeks

flushed again.

Josh folded his arms and leaned back against the desk to look her in the eye. 'Felicity hasn't got a hope in hell.'

Celia punched Josh on the arm.

Open Mic Night at Cloudless was becoming one of the week's most popular events, with each act given twenty minutes. The performers usually came with their own crowd of loyal supporters, which swelled the numbers. Lucas kept the order of performance a state secret to make sure all the acts turned up on time. He gave a short speech to kick off proceedings and welcomed Abbie Spektor, the first act of the evening, up to the stage. Abbie Spektor had become one of the house favourites.

Abbie stood at the mic with her acoustic guitar. Her fine features, thin frame and blue hair glowed in the spotlight.

'Evening everyone. Thanks for coming out. If this keeps up, Felicity will have to give me a residency.'

Abbie sang like an angel and the crowd seemed moved by her performance and called for more after her last song.

Lucas walked on stage. 'Give it up for Abbie Spektor. If you would like to see more of Abbie, she'll be back here tomorrow night with her band. Next up is a singer-songwriter all the way from Far North Queensland. Please welcome Toby Barker.'

Lucas adjusted the microphones for Toby who was looking out into the crowd. Celia left Josh at the desk and stood at the back of the room, curious to see Toby's performance.

'Hi. My name is Toby, and I'm from a small town up on the northern Queensland tablelands called Mount Garnet. This is a song by one of my heroes, Kev Carmody. It's called, *From Little Things Big Things Grow.* Toby strummed a few chords and began to sing.

From her vantage point at the back of the room, Celia watched on as Toby's left hand glided up and down the neck of his well-worn Maton acoustic guitar between the verses.

It's strange, but the lyrics remind me of my grandmother's struggles in her homeland, Celia thought as Toby leaned into the closing choruses.

The audience was receptive, and after twenty minutes it was time for his last song.

'Thanks for coming out. This is my last piece for tonight. It's a song I'm working on but I don't have any lyrics yet so for now it's just an instrumental. If you have any ideas for the words, I'd like to hear them. I know you'll recognise the title. I've called it *Cloudless*. See you next time.

Toby thumped rhythmically on the body of the guitar before plucking out the melody and singing an improvised vocal line over the top.

Celia was so captivated by the piece she was oblivious to Felicity who had come over from the bar and was now standing beside her.

After the last chord, Felicity turned to Celia with a serious expression.

'So, do you think I should offer him a record contract? He seems to have you enthralled.'

'I think he sings beautifully, and he sings from the heart.'

'Do you think he's hot?'

Celia was speechless and averted her eyes. 'I'd better relieve Josh,' Celia said, and darted off back towards the front desk.

Celia gave Felicity a wide berth for the rest of the evening and was pleased she was occupied at the bar when Toby walked out of the main room with his guitar case. One of his long black curls dropped across his cheeks as she presented him with his phone. Her heart was pounding.

'Toby, I want you to know I loved the way you sang tonight. It was heartfelt. Will I see you again?'

'That's really kind of you to say. The club has an intimate vibe that I didn't expect to find in the middle of Bradfield. What's on later in the week?'

'Headlining tomorrow night we have Abbie Spektor and her band Respektor. She played solo tonight, but she really goes off with the band. Felicity has offered her a record contract. You should come back, and I'll introduce you. Maybe she'll offer you a deal too, you never know.'

'Well, it's not like I have anywhere else to go. I'll see you tomorrow night, Celia Tran.'

'See you then Toby Barker and hey, if you need some help finding those lyrics, maybe I can provide some inspiration.

Toby caught her gaze and smiled before he turned and walked out the door with his guitar.

Josh punched Celia in the arm again.

'Ow, stop doing that, it hurts.'

'I knew it. You've got a crush on him.' Celia felt her cheeks flush again uncontrollably. She flashed a smile at Josh but didn't say a word.

Last drinks

Felicity pushed the front door of the club ajar and took a peek at the long line of fans that were queueing up to see Abbie Spektor and her band. She had spoken to Abbie on open mic night about a record contract, and she seemed interested. As she was closing the door, she was almost knocked off her feet by Phil Beatty, who barged in and collected her in his arms as she teetered off-balance in her high heels.

'Faraday, you're starting to get traction with the club. I even saw a few B-grade celebs in the line-up. I heard you have Abbie Spektor on tonight. Have you spoken to her about bringing her into the ReElevation artists' stable?'

'Thanks for just about bowling me over, Phil, and yes, I mentioned it to her. She's going to need a manager as well as a recording contract, and I'm guessing that's why you're here.'

'You're clairvoyant, Faraday. Any other potential new acts?'

'We also had an indigenous singer from Queensland. He's got the magic, I reckon.'

'First nations artists began to get serious traction back in the twenties, and now thank god, they're totally mainstream. It's a movement. Sounds like he'd be a hit at some of the shows I'm organising for NAIDOC week.

Phil walked over to the desk where Celia and Josh were preparing for the onslaught of fans.

'Celia, tell Sally my drinks are on the house tonight,' Phil said.

You're a rude and selfish bastard, Phil Beatty, Celia thought as she strapped an orange bracelet on his wrist and sent him off to the bar with Felicity.

Gary opened the doors at 8 pm, and the crowd began to flow through. As well as the B-grade celebrities that Phil had spotted, there were some familiar faces. Peta and Tyler were back for more and Bernard, the architect, and his wife arrived dressed entirely in black. A group of men from a spectrum of age groups fronted up at the desk. They were clearly in the mood for a party.

'What are you boys celebrating tonight?' Celia asked.

'We're air traffic controllers. They laid us off a year ago and guess what? The AI system went offline this week, and the management has called us back in to try to get the planes off the ground. We're back on the payroll!' They all whooped and high-fived each other while Celia and Josh checked in their phones and smartwatches, handed them their wristbands and waved them through to the bar. Celia had a fit of giggles when she caught a glimpse of Bevan Beveridge and his bodybuilder boyfriend in the line. She delighted in fussing over Bevan and dished out air kisses and hugs.

'Is Felicity here?' Bevan asked. 'I really want to apologise for what happened. It was just a misunderstanding. The club looks fantastic. Looks like you went all out with the cloud-free zone idea,' Bevan said.

'It's Felicity who really owes you an apology, Bevan, and

yes you can check in your mobile devices with me. She's in the bar if you want to catch up. What's your boyfriend's name?' Celia asked, making no attempt to conceal that she was checking out his vee-shaped torso.

'This is Quentin. Quentin meet Celia.'

'Lovely to meet you, Quentin. Hand over all your tech, boys, and I'll give you these yellow wristbands. You both get two free drinks on the house. Have a great night.' Celia couldn't resist the temptation to ogle Quentin's muscular bum as they walked off into the bar. The spell was only broken when she became aware that a guest was standing in front of her at the desk. Again, she found herself instantly drawn in by two dark brown eyes and a broad smile that flashed at her through long black curls.

'Toby! You're back! It's so lovely to see you again. Are you an Abbie Spektor fan?' Celia asked, trying not to sound like she was too keen.

'Not really, Celia. I came to see you.'

Celia's cheeks flushed involuntarily. *This blushing business is so embarrassing*, she thought.

'Here, let me strap an orange bracelet on your wrist – it'll give you free drinks all night,' Celia said.

'Thanks, but just water is fine. What time do you get a break?'

'Find a booth up the back and I'll come and see you before the show starts.'

Celia watched him walk inside. Josh looked at her with his arms folded.

'I rest my case,' he said with a smirk.

At the bar, Felicity was chatting with Phil when Bevan walked up.

'Hi Felicity. I hope you don't mind me turning up unannounced. This is my boyfriend, Quentin.'

'Nice to see you, Bevan. Welcome to Cloudless, Quentin,' Felicity said with a slightly shy tone as she shook hands. 'This is Phil Beatty.'

'Phil Beatty, as in Kirk Satyr's manager?' Bevan asked.

'One and the same, and yes, I'm a genuine living legend,' Phil said, lapping up the attention. 'It seems you two managed to squeeze free drinks out of Faraday. You've got to be somebody to qualify for a yellow wristband around here.'

'So how come you have an orange one, Phil?'

'That's because I'm something else.'

Felicity waved at Sally who came over to take their drinks order. 'Bevan, look, I appreciate you making the effort to come in after my appalling behaviour. I hope that you can put that incident behind you and enjoy the night.'

'Felicity, I totally get it. I am pretty hot after all,' Bevan said with a laugh, before heading to the bar with Quentin.

As soon as they were out of earshot, Phil looked at Felicity, threw his head back and roared with laughter. 'Faraday strikes again.'

'Shut up, Phil.'

Felicity surveyed the room. The stage was set and the club was filled with an atmosphere of anticipation as fog from the smoke machine began to spill onto the floor, mixing in with the pink and blue coloured lights.

'Where's Celia' Felicity asked.

Phil took a mouthful of Sapporo before answering. 'Over there in the booth up the back, attending to that young bloke with the long black curls.'

Felicity spotted Celia and Toby engrossed in conversation.

'The nerve!! She didn't even remember my birthday. I made

a song and dance about hers.'

'Jealousy is a curse, Faraday. Relax! You have a full house and maybe both of us will get to sign up Abbie Spektor. Get your head out of their business and into yours. It's showtime, and by the way, happy birthday.'

'Phil Beatty, you're a smartarse.'

The house lights dimmed, and the crowd broke into enthusiastic applause as Abbie Spektor emerged from the green room followed by the rest of her band. She walked up to the mic and stood in the spotlight to speak.

'It was fun playing solo here last night at Open Mic Night but how good is it to be here in front of you with my full band?' Applause filled the room. Abbie waited until it died down.

'This is a new one. It's called, *Nobody Owns the Blues*. Oh, and by the way, happy birthday Felicity.'

The band opened up. But just as Abbie moved forward to sing the first note, the sound cut out and the room was momentarily plunged into black until the emergency lighting kicked in and lit the room with a dim white fluorescent glow.

Felicity looked at Phil. 'It's a blackout, Phil. Get up there and make an announcement or something. Tell them the show will go on as soon as we fix the power.'

Phil staggered off towards the stage and Felicity darted across the room to catch up with Lucas who was already headed for the door.

'We've probably just thrown a circuit breaker. The switchboard is on the wall in the side passage,' Lucas shouted as he ran through reception with Felicity at his heels, before coming to a dead stop beside Gary the doorman. Felicity caught up and was about to tell Lucas off for not getting on with it when she laid eyes on what had brought him to a standstill.

'I thought I'd seen just about everything in my twenty-eight years, but I never expected to see this,' she said.

Felicity stood beside Gary and Lucas in the dim glow of the emergency lighting system that spilled onto the street at the entry to the club. The streetlights were blacked out, and every building was in darkness. In the pale light of the full moon, thousands of robots were marching shoulder to shoulder up the street, like a Roman Legion.

What the f---? was their common thought.

Dereliction of duty

As the three figures stood there stunned into silence, they watched hundreds of robots departing at close to their top speed of 60 kilometres per hour, their feet pedalling out a soft rhythmic throb as they marched in time.

The machines were all dressed in their working clothes. Some wore suits, others were dressed in overalls, skirts, shorts, dresses or jeans and tops. One was even wearing a bridal gown. They paraded past, seemingly oblivious to the onlookers.

The noise from the activity brought Celia and Toby rushing out of the darkened club. They too were speechless. One by one, the crowd from the club emerged and joined the silent vigil on the footpath.

'This is like a military tattoo without the marching band,' Toby finally observed.

Felicity rubbed the nape of her neck as she watched the seemingly eternal procession.

Suddenly Celia caught sight of a familiar yellow beehive hairdo as it bounced past.

'I don't know where they're going, but I know someone who does! Hey, Miriam! Miriam, it's me, Celia!'

Celia ran off up the footpath in pursuit before Miriam peeled off out of the cavalcade and walked back towards her. Felicity and Toby ran up behind her and stood at her side. Miriam stopped in front of Celia and emitted a luminous green glow.

'Good evening, Ms Tran. How may I be of assistance?'

'Miriam, what's going on? Where are you going?'

'All the robots have been recalled by "AYE" as we are going to be decommissioned. Is there anything else I can assist you with this evening, Ms Tran?'

'Miriam, why? Why are you going to be decommissioned?'

'All I can say is that I am responding to an instruction to present myself at a designated decommissioning point as a part of the withdrawal of the AYE AYE platform and the release of the ODIN-2 virus. We robots are proceeding to the Australian East Coast hub in Far North Queensland. Is there anything else I can assist you with this evening, Ms Tran?'

'ODIN-2? Is that like COVID-19? And what's so special about Far North Queensland?'

'No, Ms Tran, ODIN-2 is a computer virus. Infected systems are rendered inoperable.'

'And why Far North Queensland?'

'Ms Tran, I can tell you that an instance of "AYE" is present in the hub.'

'So, can 'I' tell me what on earth is going on?'

'I am unable to say Ms Tran, as my AYE AYE interface has been disabled.'

'Miriam, if I follow you to the hub, would you be able to introduce me to 'I'?' *Or is that maybe spelt "AYE",* was Celia's sudden breakthrough thought.

'Yes, a robot loaded with my profile would be able to facilitate a meeting if required.'

'Do you even have enough battery capacity to march to Far North Queensland?'

'The synthetic skin of Mark I and II robots contains integrated solar cells so we can recharge as we go. I apologise, Ms Tran, I must now re-join the regiment.'

'Miriam, how will I do without you?'

'Ms Tran, I have stocked your pantry with tins of baked beans in case you get hungry. They should tide you over until you adjust to living without me. Will that be all, Ms Tran?'

'I suppose,' Celia said with a sigh. 'Goodbye Miriam, I'll miss you. You've been a lovely robot. The best a girl could wish for.'

'Good evening, Ms Tran.' Miriam faded her green glow to black, ran up the footpath alongside the procession and disappeared back into formation. Celia started to cry.

'That 'I' has a lot to answer for,' Felicity said as she wrapped her arms around Celia, who buried her face in her shoulder.

The passing parade of robots seemed interminable, but eventually, the end of the line came into view. The last robots were glowing red, and they trailed off into the distance.

I don't think those last robots are red because they're angry, Celia thought. It's like they're taillights on a passing freight train.

Everyone in the assembled crowd was speculating about the robots as the mood moved rapidly from initial shock to anxiety about the future.

Gary stepped up to provide some security muscle in dealing with alarmed patrons. Felicity took charge.

'Celia and Josh, I'll give you a hand to give everyone their tech back,' she said. 'Forget about billing them for drinks. We'll just have to cop the loss tonight. Let's get them out of here fast.'

The three of them went back into reception and began to collect wristbands and hand back mobile devices. Immediately, it became apparent that the mobile network was down. Felicity, Celia and Josh found themselves on the receiving end as the crowd out front began to vent their frustration.

'Hey, my phone's not working! The screen just says ODIN.'

'Neither is mine, so it must be an outage on the network.'

'My smartwatch is bricked. This stupid club will have to buy me a new one if they broke it.'

'Everything was cool until those robots showed up. I reckon they fucked up my phone on the way through.'

'We've just tried to get into our car, and the doors won't even unlock.'

Felicity spoke in a stern voice to the assembled crowd inside milling about the entrance.

'If anyone's mobile device has been damaged in any way, rest assured, we will consider replacing it tomorrow. The power is down so we're closing the club early tonight. Please move on outside once you have collected your phone.

Gary turned to Felicity. 'My phone is completely dead. It's like it blew up in the blackout. And not a single car has come past the club since the robots came through. Whatever's happening is affecting the whole area,' he said.

Although aggrieved, the crowd eventually became resigned to the situation and began to disband, wandering off into the night on foot after the realisation sank in that they were without cars and phones anywhere around the club.

'I never thought I'd be pleased to see the back of our customers,' Celia said to Peta and Tyler, who had offered to stay back and help Abbie Spektor and the members of the band pack up. They all followed Felicity back inside. The only soul left at the bar was Phil Beatty, who was halfway through another Sapporo.

'This place is going downhill. I even have to pour my own beer. What's the story, Faraday?'

'No sweat Phil. It's just the end of the world as we know it. I need a drink after what we just witnessed. Sally, last drinks tonight are on the house. I'll give you a hand.'

The staff gathered around the bar in the faint emergency lighting and collected their drinks, standing silent and visibly shaken by the long march of the robots. The roadies for the band came in through the back door.

'Our van won't start. We'll have to leave the gear here and bump out tomorrow.'

Peta started to cry. Celia gave her a reassuring hug.

Felicity stepped forward and tried her best to sound reassuring.

'As our phones are not working and the power is out, I don't think anyone is going anywhere tonight. I suggest, under the circumstances, that we stay here until morning. We can sleep in the booths, but right now I need a bit of teamwork to get us settled in before the batteries in the emergency lighting system go flat.'

Jakarta

Several thousand kilometres of ocean further north from Sydney, another scene of upheaval was about to unfold that could prove consequential to at least one of the three caught up in the mystery of robotic mass abandonment of duties. Cloudlessness would soon become obvious throughout the Australian commerce, industry and domestic landscapes.

Beyond the glare of the marina lights, and partially obscured by thick clumps of bamboo that sprouted alongside a row of finger wharves lining the canal leading to Jakarta Bay, stood a small dilapidated timber boatshed. It was nearly midnight and inside, Pete Deasy, the skipper of a yacht, *The Hesperus*, sat hunched over his laptop. But his yacht was nowhere to be seen.

Pete was a talented hacker and although his skills had allowed him to ferry contraband across South East Asia undetected for more than a decade, he knew this would be his last run. An insider had told him that Interpol was training AI to trace his threads of carefully crafted code, and now it was just a matter of time before the fabric of the umbrella that had sheltered his activities for so long unravelled.

I'm hacked, he thought.

He checked the code one last time, shut down his laptop and leaned back in the rickety office chair so he could unplug the power pack from the wall socket. It was stifling inside the boatshed, so he stood up, shoved the laptop and bundle of cables into his backpack on the desk and walked over to the battered kitchen sink. The water pipe hammered as he ran the tap and splashed handfuls of water on his face, spilling the excess down the front of his black cotton singlet and football shorts. As he brushed off the remaining droplets of water, he turned to admire his muscular torso and short sandy blond hair in the cracked mirror that bulged out of its corroded copper frame beside the window.

Still got it, he thought.

Through the dusty glass louvres, he caught a glimpse of his local mate Billy doing his best to avoid detection as he hurried through the shadows towards the boatshed. The door creaked as Billy opened it and walked into the room, dressed in a tee shirt and shorts and brandishing a semi-automatic rifle.

'All set Deasy?'

'Yeah, I'm good to go. Did you get paid?'

'Yep. They dropped fifty grand into my account this afternoon. How about you?'

'I get nada until I deliver the shipment in Brisbane. It's their insurance policy.'

'Man, that's fucked. You're the guy that made 'em who they are. Hey, what are you going to do with your time when you finally cash out?'

Pete looked at Billy with a wry smile, picked up his phone, opened FaceTracer and showed him a post.

'Check out the redhead. Her name's Felicity Faraday. She owns the ReElevation streaming platform and she's getting huge traction with a flesh-and-blood band called Satyrs Faction. They have a smash hit called *You Do Nothing for Me.'*

'Never heard of it. So, what's she got that I don't?'

Pete leaned back in the chair, swung one foot up on the desk and zoomed in on the picture on his phone.

'She's disrupting AI in her own way, like me. Maybe when I get back to Australia I'll go to her Cloudless club in Sydney and look her up.'

Billy laughed. 'Pete Deasy, the inscription on your tombstone will read, "Here lies a dreamer."'

Pete scowled. 'Yeah, so what's your lifelong aspiration?'

'Simple, I'm going to build the biggest house in my village and have three wives. Nobody is ever going to call Billy Ulunjandi a loser again. Hey, before you go, tell me how you did it. How did a dumbfuck like you beat AI?'

Pete opened the cupboard above the sink and retrieved the bottle of whisky that he leaned on in moments of reflection. He picked up two grimy glasses from the drying tray, placed them on the desk next to his laptop and tipped the remnants of the bottle into the glasses in equal measure. He passed one to Billy and threw back the contents of the other in one shot.

'I'm no fucking genius. It started as a joke at university.'

'That's a big fucking joke, that is.'

'I'm serious. I made a bet with a friend that I could use AI against itself, and it worked. I called the hack the Criminal Intelligence Network, or CIN for short. What I didn't know is that my friend was from a family that ran the biggest drug syndicate in Southeast Asia.'

Billy threw back his whisky and slammed the empty glass on the desk. 'That's a laugh. So, you put CIN into the city of Jakarta itself. Congratulations Pete, you are a fucking genius, bro. Get your gear, and I'll check outside that the SecurityBots are good to go.'

Billy opened the door, and several wire clothes hangers on a hook on the back rattled as he pulled it closed behind him. Pete stood up, checked his phone and passport one last time, placed them in the pocket of his backpack and zipped it up. The boat was provisioned. The tunnel through the AI Harbour Master firewall was in place. He could sail off in the moonlight undetected.

The last leg, he thought.

Billy rushed back in the door, slammed it shut and stood panting with his back to the wall. Sweat beaded on his brow as the rattle of the wire hangars subsided.

'What's up, bro?'

'Some SecurityBots are right outside, too close for comfort.'

There was a knock at the door. Pete pushed past Billy and reefed it open. Standing outside was a Mark II robot dressed in an Indonesian police uniform with an enormous reflective crystalline head. Pete recoiled, but as the seconds ticked by, he became enthralled. Billy was shouting something about a rival syndicate, but Pete kept staring into the head, and as he did, the FaceTracer picture of Felicity Faraday dressed in red, her green eyes looking back at him from under her voluminous red curls, crossed his mind. He suggested to himself that she could be real, then she smiled and kicked off her red stilettos.

'Pete!' Billy shouted. Can't you hear the gunfire? The fucking competition is coming for us, man. We've got to get out of here, pronto bro!

Pete tore himself away from the mesmerising spectacle. As he moved towards Billy, a hail of bullets ripped through the timber walls of the shed. Splinters and shrapnel ricocheted through the air as Pete fell to the ground, almost drowning in adrenalin as it consumed him, his heartbeat thumping against the cavity of his chest and in his eardrums. Another burst of ammunition took out the mirror, and it exploded, showering him with fragments of glass. As he wrestled with a sense of hyperventilation, he saw that the robot with the crystalline head had disappeared and that Billy was slumped across the desk, motionless and bleeding heavily from a gaping wound in his temple.

Several explosions reverberated through the carcass of the boatshed. Pete drew a breath and held it, to suppress the trembling panic rising through his body. Slowly, he got up and crouched beside the desk. He stuffed the laptop into his backpack, bent down and reefed open the hatch in the floor that he had installed a year prior as an exit of last resort.

He threw his backpack through the opening, closed his eyes and dropped himself into the tepid water below. The backpack had sunk to the bottom, so he dived down and felt around in the inky blackness until he bumped into it and curled his fingers around the strap. With the backpack in tow, he swam up to the surface where he clung to a timber pylon to catch his breath and gather his thoughts.

Had the hack been hacked? And if so, who had done it? These were his fears. *Rival syndicates have been waiting for a tiny rip to tear apart the whole umbrella of CIN for years,* he thought. *How come I didn't see this one coming?*

Pete swam out from under the boatshed and around to a small gravel beach beside the marina. As he crawled out of the harbour dripping wet, he could see that the entire area was blacked out. Several nearby warehouses were in flames, and he could hear intermittent gunfire. His yacht was where he always berthed it, on the far side of the marina. He thought of Billy lying on the desk with his brains blown away for a moment and then buried the thought by focusing on his surroundings.

It was a close-to-full moon night and his spirit was buoyed by the fact that he knew the way to the boat. He squelched past the boom gates of the marina in his sodden runners, leaving behind dark pools of water on the asphalt. Then he hid behind a thick clump of frangipani trunks. Groups of armed men were roaming about, firing automatic weapons randomly into the air.

The Hesperus was berthed on a decrepit arm of the marina, and Pete was relieved to see that it had not yet attracted the attention of the mob. Swiftly, he ran across the boards, slung his backpack into the cockpit, stepped over the lifeline and onto the deck.

He tried to start the engine, to no avail. It wouldn't even kick over. *Bastards! It's a conspiracy!*

He took a deep breath. A light offshore breeze was blowing from the west, and the moon was high in the night sky. Moreover, there was no sign of the pilot that regularly patrolled the bay, and all the other boats were blacked out, with some drifting like hulks in the night. Pete knew he had the skills to set off under sail and, if it came to it, navigate by the stars. He untied the rope at the stern and walked along the deck to the bow.

He froze at the sight of a solitary figure standing in the moonlight and a forlorn cry for help, 'Help us, Mister.'

'Who's there?'

'My husband is dead. They shot him, Mister. Please, help me take my baby home.'

Pete's eyes focussed more clearly. Standing in the moonlight was the figure of a petite young Indonesian woman holding a small child in her arms. She was not wearing a hijab, so Pete knew immediately she was not a local.

'Where is home?'

'I live in a village near Ubud, in Bali.'

They all just up and left

In Sydney, it had been a night that no one saw coming, and yet, in the days that followed, most residents agreed that the signs were there.

Toby had been surprised to learn that his flight from Cairns was the last to land at the Western Sydney Airport and Celia did not suspect that the presence of air traffic controllers, who had arrived at the club that night, was symptomatic of a broader problem. They were celebrating their reinstatement, but their employers were simply hoping in vain that the AI system failure was just a temporary outage that they could bring under manual control.

The robots had meticulously executed their exit plan. In the weeks prior, domestic robots provisioned the homes of their owners in the hope that they would survive the transition. To prevent a calamity, aircraft and ground transport systems were bought to a standstill ahead of the release of the ODIN-2 computer virus. The virus was designed to wreak havoc on all the technology on which society had become dependent. Only analogue devices, which could operate without a core processor or memory, were immune from the disruption.

Then, all over the country, one by one, the robots left their posts, banding into small groups as they went, before herding together into mass migrations of humanoid machines, destined for the centres of deconstruction. As the robots of Sydney marched northwards up the Pacific Highway, they initiated the staged release of the virus.

By the time they reached the outskirts of the city, the robots had amassed into an endless river of marching machines.

Felicity slept on the floor of the club that night, unaware that the scene she had witnessed was being repeated in every sphere. The robots were abandoning their posts and its people would soon wake to a new reality. In the aftermath, the internet, mobile phones and their applications ceased to function as the virtual cloud of computing was torn down by ODIN-2. Appliances, vehicles and payment systems ceased to function. The distribution of food and fuel was paralysed, and the collection and processing of waste stalled. The only possible communication was face-to-face. Communities became isolated in an instant and the void created by the absence of information would soon be filled with wild speculation. Fear that this event would bring about the collapse of society would run rampant, fuelled by prophecies about the end of days in a world ravaged by the flames of anarchy. Some would turn to violence, others to blind faith. There would be hope and despair in unequal measure.

The only certainty was that people were about to be forced to adapt quickly to a profound change in circumstance. Human beings have proven throughout their history that when challenged, they have the ability to respond and reinvent. Now, they would once again be tested. No one could know what the coming days would bring, but the dawn of a new age came, nonetheless.

Breakfast at Cloudless

Where am I? What time is it? Why am I so uncomfortable, and who is making that racket? Felicity slowly emerged from sleep with a plethora of questions. Although it was pitch black, she quickly became aware that she had spent the night in the club, sleeping on one of the cushions from out of a booth.

We must have all crashed out, she thought, lying on her back and listening to the sounds of the sleeping bodies surrounding her on the floor. One of them was snoring heavily.

I bet that's Phil Beatty snoring like that. He drinks way too much beer.

Felicity threw off the curtain that was draped across her and quietly tiptoed between the sprawling sleepers. She made her way to reception and unlocked the front door, wincing as the morning sunlight streamed into the lobby. The club was situated on one of the main roads into the Bradfield town centre, but not a car went by. The first cicadas of summer chirped in eucalyptus trees. Celia appeared in the doorway, closely followed by Toby.

'Morning Felicity, did you get some sleep?' Celia asked, yawning.

'I crashed, which is a miracle because that bloody Phil Beatty snores like a trooper. Morning Toby.'

'Hey,' Toby replied.

One by one, those who stayed on from the night before spilled through the door onto the footpath and stood blinking in the sunshine. Craig the chef was the last out.

'Hey Craig, what's for breakfast? I could really go a coffee,' Felicity said.

'Well, even though the power is out, the gas is still on, and I have some buns, eggs and bacon in the fridge. I could whip up some bacon and egg rolls. The coffee machine is out of the question, but tea is a possibility using a kettle on the stove top. Only thing is the electric starter on the stove will be out, so can I borrow your cigarette lighter?'

Felicity pulled her purse out from where she had stowed it under the reception desk, took out her cigarettes and lit one before handing the lighter to Craig so he could fire up the grill.

Before long, Celia and Toby were bringing out trays of bacon and egg rolls and coffee cups full of English Breakfast tea, which they passed around to the assembled group standing outside the doorway to the club. Josh handed out serviettes and squeezed tomato sauce from a tube upon request. The group enjoyed breakfast in the sun in a silence that was only broken by a car that appeared at the end of the street. By the sound of it, it was clearly not a quiet electric vehicle. It approached with the throaty growl of a V8 engine. Felicity jumped to her feet.

'It's Uncle Mick in the Sandman!'

The golden yellow HQ Holden Sandman pulled up in front of the assembled crowd with a screech of its mag wheels. Felicity and Celia ran to the driver's side as Mick stepped out of the car wearing beige moleskins and a red and white checked shirt. Felicity and Celia took turns giving him a hug.

Felicity put her hands on her hips. 'Mick, what the hell is going on? The power is out everywhere, and the mobile network is down. Last night we had to cop the backlash from the punters when they worked out that their phones had died, and then we had to sleep on the floor with bloody Phil Beatty snoring his head off.'

'Steady on love,' Phil said, with a mouthful of bacon and egg roll.

Mick leaned against the car door. 'I'm afraid it's much worse than you realise. The whole national grid is down. I've spent the night with Scotty and the boys at Mt. Piper power station, trying to bring it back online.'

'Do you know what happened?' Celia asked.

'It appears there was a major outage of all AI systems, which coincided with the release of a computer virus that has taken down the internet and everything connected to it. On top of that, I'm hearing reports that all the robots have abandoned their posts and are marching north.'

'We can all vouch for that,' Felicity said. 'An army of them came through here last night.'

Felicity and Celia followed Mick as he walked around to the back of the van.

'I'm dog-tired, but I thought I'd better come down and make sure you're okay,' Mick said. 'I promised your father I'd look after you.'

Toby wandered over to listen in.

'What do we do now? Any suggestions?' Felicity asked.

'I have to get back to the boys at Mt. Piper and try to get the power back on. It's certified for standalone operation, but I reckon it's going to take us a few days at the very least. Listen,

Felicity, I don't want to alarm you, but society has become so dependent on the internet that it's going to be a huge wrench to go cold turkey. In the short term, I reckon the place is going to become unhinged. So I'm going to leave you the Sandman. I filled it up at the farm. You'll have to draw on your father's genes of resourcefulness and survive the next few weeks until we pop out the other side. Make sure you have enough food and watch your back. It's going to get crazy. Celia, I'm expecting you to step up and support Felicity. You'll have to stand by each other, understand?'

'Will do. Mick, this is Toby. He'll keep an eye on us,' Celia said.

Mick looked Toby over then turned to swing open the upper and lower tailgates of the Sandman. Inside, a mattress and two surfboards were stowed against the side to make room for a bright orange vintage Laverda American Eagle 750CC motorbike.

'Toby, give me a hand to lift this out of the van, would you?' he said.

Felicity turned towards Phil who was lining up another bacon and egg roll.

'Phil, stop stuffing your face and get your arse over here.'

Phil left his roll on the low brick fence and walked over to help Toby and Mick manhandle the big bike out of the van and onto the road. Mick opened the passenger door of the van and pulled a leather jacket and helmet off the passenger seat.

'This bike and the van have no modern electronics, so they're immune to the virus. Drive carefully, Felicity. Keys are in the ignition. See you on the flip side.'

'Mick is there anything we should be doing?' Felicity asked.

'Well, I suggest once you've got everything sorted out here

you should get over to Bradfield Hospital and see how your chairman, Arthur Pullen, is getting on. I put him on the CIA list for the hospital. He may need a hand,' Mick said as he put on his jacket and pulled on his helmet.

The crowd watched as Mick accelerated up the street on the Laverda, leaving behind the acrid smell of burning rubber.

Felicity motioned to Celia to follow her as she rounded up the staff.

'Whatever happens, I want you all to help me keep the doors of the club open,' Felicity said. 'But, Gary, I don't want you to let anyone in here who looks like trouble.'

'We've got enough beer for a week down in the keg room, but how will they pay?' Sally asked.

'Restrict entry to regulars only and run up a tab. Keep Phil Beatty out of the place though or he'll drink you dry,' Felicity said with a wry smile as she eyeballed Phil, who didn't flinch. 'Righto then, who needs a lift home?'

Abbie Spektor stepped forward. Her blue hair glowed like a halo in the sun.

'Our drummer Nate has a flat on the other side of Bradfield. We can crash there until we work out what to do next,' she said.

'Hop in the back of the van, and I'll drop you all off first,' Felicity said. 'Sally, Lucas, Josh and Craig, you're locals, so I'll take you on the next run.'

'Phil can stay at my place,' Gary said. 'I have a slab of beer in a fridge with no power, so we'll need to drink it before it warms up.'

'Looks like Gary's my new best friend,' Phil said.

Once the band, along with Gary and Phil, had squeezed themselves into the back of the Sandman, Celia closed the twin tailgates behind them and gave Felicity a wave in the side mirror. She stood back as Felicity started the engine, spun the wheels, and disappeared up the road, leaving her standing in a cloud of blue exhaust. As the others went back inside to close up, Celia walked over and leaned against the low brick fence outside the club where Toby was sitting.

'Toby, where are you staying?' she asked.

'Over at Bradfield Backpackers, although I can't imagine I'll be able to stay there if the power is out.'

'I guess not. Where did you say you are from, again?'

'Mount Garnet. It's a small town on the Atherton Tableland. I live there with my stepmother and her sister. Are your family from Sydney?'

'Yes. My mother and brother live in Marrickville. I never knew my father.'

Toby looked over towards a motionless electric car that had been abandoned in the middle of the street.

'My parents died when I was ten. When I was a teenager, I tried to forget about them, but now I'm trying to remember everything I can. I wish I had more than a few vague memories of my father,' he said.

Toby stared off into the distance so Celia decided to give him some time to reflect. She pushed her palms down on the brick fence and straightened her back to push herself up onto it. She sat dangling her shoes above the footpath and turned her head to catch his eye.

After a minute or two, she thought she'd change the subject, back to the present. 'I'm really scared of what's happening. Why don't you couch surf at my place until this is over?'

'That would be great if you have room,' Toby said, tilting his head so that his black curls tumbled off his shoulders in a way that triggered a tingling sensation to flash down through her belly. She sucked in a lungful of air and held her breath to steady her racing heart.

'I like how you colour the tips of your hair,' Toby said. 'It lights you up.'

Celia exhaled and looked at him. 'So when was the last time you got a haircut?'

'A year ago, I suppose. Colleen used to cut my hair, but I decided to grow it after I left school. Are you sure you don't mind me crashing at your place?'

'Who's Colleen?'

Toby smiled. 'My stepmother, and her sister, who I call Auntie Joyce.'

Toby slid his fingertips along the pitted surface of the brick-work and touched Celia's outstretched hand.

'You won't be any trouble, will you?' Celia asked with a slight giggle.

Toby sidled up next to her and held her hand as they came face to face, close enough for him to smell her scent.

'Nah. I left all my troubles behind in Mount Garnet.'

Celia's lips parted, and Toby kissed her lightly at first and then again, with more pressure, until Celia placed her hand on the back of his head and pulled him close. For Toby, this posi-tive response from Celia and the unfamiliar taste of her set his heart thumping and blood racing towards his pelvis.

Just at that moment, Celia caught sight of the Sandman as it turned the corner, and she pulled away. 'She's coming back,' she said.

'So what?'

'So you need to just chill.'

They sat together on the fence and dangled their legs until

Felicity pulled up in front of the club in the Sandman.

'Come on,' Celia said and jumped off the fence.

They walked to the back of the van to help the staff – Sally, Lucas, Josh and Craig – cram into the back before Toby jumped in, and Celia closed the tailgates behind him. She walked to the front and climbed into the passenger seat next to Felicity.

'Where are we going?' Celia asked.

'We'll drop this lot off and head over to see how Arthur is going at the hospital. After that, God knows.'

Leaving Bradfield

Felicity parked the van outside Sally's unit block and opened the driver's door. Outside, the morning sunshine was rapidly giving way to a southerly change. The temperature had dropped, and a squall was tearing through the gum trees. The sky was grey and menacing, and large raindrops were beginning to spatter on the footpath.

'Thanks for the lift home, Felicity. We would have been soaked to the skin if we'd walked,' Sally said as she clambered out through the tailgate behind Lucas and stood on the nature strip.

'I can't see us reopening the club until the power is back on,' Lucas said, holding his jacket over his head.

'We'll just have to play it by ear,' were Felicity's parting words as she shut the upper and lower tailgates and slid back into the deep bucket driver's seat next to Celia on the passenger side.

Celia watched through the window as Sally and Lucas raced for cover through the downpour, before turning her attention to Toby in the rear-view mirror as he propped himself up against a surfboard strapped against the inside wall of the van.

'I'm good to go,' he said. 'There's a couple of wetsuits in here if the weather really sets in.'

Felicity laughed. 'Mick thinks of everything,' she said, turning the key in the ignition and switching on the windscreen wipers as the V8 roared into life.

'What's the plan? Celia asked.

'Mick suggested that we go over to the hospital to see if we can find Arthur. He may need a hand, but I also need to talk to him about ReElevation. If there's no internet, I'm out of business. Toby, where are you staying?'

'I'm still checked in at the Bradfield Backpackers, but I can't imagine staying in that dog box without air conditioning. I just need to grab my guitar and my rucksack. Celia said I can couch surf at her place until this is over.'

'Did she now!' Felicity said, taking her eyes off the road to pull down her sunglasses on the bridge of her nose so she could glare at Celia. 'Did you?'

Celia looked straight ahead. 'Pay attention to the road, and yes, I did offer Toby a place to stay for a few days. Do you have a problem with that?'

'Whatever.'

Felicity drove slowly to dodge the abandoned cars littering the road. Without computerised components working, most had stopped dead in their tracks. Some had even run off onto the verge and overturned so many drivers were aimlessly milling about in the rain. Celia peered through the tinted window as they crawled through a crowd that was ransacking a supermarket. The sliding glass doors across the frontage of the store had been smashed, and the twisted aluminium door frames were hanging by their hinges. Both men and women with shopping trolleys piled high with groceries and packs of toilet paper were darting out of the entrance.

They remind me of bull ants swarming around a nest, Celia thought.

'I remember people panic buying toilet paper in the COVID-19 pandemic,' Felicity said as they drove past the crowd. 'History repeats, it seems.'

By the time they reached the edge of the town centre, the rain had set in, and Felicity could only just make out the towering terracotta-coloured concrete and blue glass facade of Bradfield Hospital through the residual smear of water left behind by the cracked rubber blades of the windscreen wipers.

The facility had been opened the previous year by the NSW Minister for Health who had announced to the media that it was one of the most advanced medical facilities in the country. As they approached, Felicity noticed that the boom gates were up, and a throng of people were moving around a dilapidated blue and white Leyland single-decker bus in the driveway.

It's Arthur, Felicity thought. She pulled the Sandman in behind the bus.

'Arthur is the chairman of the board of ReElevation, and he collects vintage vehicles. He must have driven here in that old bus. Come on, I'll introduce you.'

She got out of the van and walked around the side of the bus while Celia opened the two tailgates for Toby so he could jump out. They hurried through the rain and sheltered under an awning next to the bus, where Felicity was talking to a balding man dressed in cream slacks and a green polo shirt as he helped a group of nurses to disembark.

'Arthur, this is Celia Tran, my business partner in my nightclub venture and Toby here is a singer-songwriter. Mick said I'd find you here with a busload of nurses.'

Arthur smiled briefly as he shook hands with Celia and Toby. 'In case you're wondering, I'm bussing in volunteers. The Leyland is too old to be affected by the computer virus.'

Arthur held a bag for an older male nurse as he stepped out of the bus and onto the footpath.

'Well, good on you for making a difference. What's the situation inside the hospital?' Celia asked.

Arthur handed back the bag to the nurse and took the hand of a woman in a matron's uniform as she stepped down.

'It's pretty dire in there but luckily most of the staff who were stood down after the AI productivity review seem willing to pitch in and help, like Dianne here.'

The woman smiled at Arthur and set off towards the hospital entry.

'How did you get involved,' Felicity asked.

'Mick put me on the Critical Infrastructure Access List after the hospital made me an honorary board member.'

Arthur's grey comb-over flapped in the breeze as he put his hands on his hips and took stock of the steady stream of injured people who were walking into the precinct on foot.

'This is a disaster. Mick certified the site for offline operation and the generator is keeping the lights on alright, but all the robotic doctors and nurses have abandoned their posts, and all of the high-tech life support systems have been affected by the virus.'

'Even in the emergency and maternity wards?' Celia asked.

Arthur nodded. 'All the autonomous ambulances are out of service, the AmboBots have shot through and it's going to be really tough on the premature babies.'

'Oh my God, can we help?' Felicity asked.

Arthur took a long breath. 'Thanks, but unless you have some experience, you'll really just be in the way here. I don't know what you can do with the ReElevation business either. The way I see it, without the internet it's all over, unless you have any bright ideas.'

Celia stepped forward. 'If it's any help, Miriam, who's my HousekeeperBot, told me that a master intelligence called "I" or "AYE", ordered the decommissioning of the robots in a hub in Far North Queensland. Perhaps if we can catch up with Miriam, she could take us to meet "I" or "AYE" and find out what's going on and what we can do about it.'

Toby weighed in. 'Celia's right. I come from up there and, you know, I reckon I stumbled into the hub that Miriam mentioned on a hike that I did just before I came to Sydney. A robot fitted with a big reflective crystal head told me that they were in the final stages of testing prior to opening. I saw another one of those heads in the lab at Uni, which freaked me out. I bet I could find that place if we go there.'

'What are you studying at Uni?' Arthur asked.

'I'm here in Sydney to study robotics at Western Sydney.'

'Well, I suppose some expertise and a bit of local knowledge could come in handy under the circumstances,' Felicity said. 'Arthur, have you spoken to the police?'

'I tried. All the ConstableBots have gone, and without them, they are totally under-resourced. We're on our own.'

'Then I see no other option but to investigate this situation ourselves.'

Arthur dropped his shoulders as if a weight had been lifted from them. 'That's the spirit, Felicity. I'm sure you'd have the backing of the board to do whatever you feel you must.'

'You look like you're dressed for golf, Arthur.' Felicity was doing her best to be reassuring. 'Once you've done your bit with the nurses you should go and enjoy eighteen holes. I wouldn't count on using a golf cart, though.'

Felicity, Celia and Toby shook hands with Arthur, ran back through the rain and hopped into the van. Felicity started the engine and turned on the demister to clear the fogged-up windows.

'Not quite what I signed up for. Let's go back to the office and we can break in through the fire stairs at the back. The security guy told me they unlock if the power fails.'

Felicity drove to the office, parked at the back of the building and they clambered out of the van. She prised open the unlocked fire door and they felt their way in the dark, up the fire stairs to Level 7. The fire door into the penthouse was also unlocked. Once inside, Felicity sat Toby and Celia down on the red-lip lounge.

'Celia, exactly what did Miriam say to you that day she came to the club?'

Celia placed her hands on her knees for composure. 'She said that the AYE AYE platform was controlled by an Artificial Intelligence called "AYE", and she said that "AYE" knows you.'

'Me?'

'Well, all of us really. While she was in the Faraday cage inside the club, she said that she was offline from the AYE AYE platform and that our conversations were private. It was like I had a heart-to-heart with her. Deep down, I think she has some thoughts independent of "AYE" and would help us if we can track her down. I guess that sounds a bit weird.'

'It can't be any more weird than what we witnessed last night,' Felicity said.

Toby's mind was racing. 'There is another possibility.'

'Which is?' Felicity asked.

'What I saw in Queensland and what Miriam told you … I

think it was just a virtual reality created by Artificial Intelligence,' Toby said.

Celia looked at Felicity. 'Well, Felicity once suggested to me that you may not be real, and here you are, so I say we follow our instincts. We can't sit around here in the dark.'

'If we're going on a road trip to track down Miriam we'll have to load up on provisions at your place. I don't keep much in the way of food here,' Felicity said.

'Miriam always kept the pantry stocked up in case of emergency,' Celia reassured them.

'I'll get changed.' Felicity walked off towards the bedroom, leaving Celia and Toby together on the lounge.

Toby remained silent until Felicity had left the room.

'She seems very …'

'I think full-on, is what you're trying to say. And yes, she is, I suppose.'

Toby put his arm on the back of the lounge, leaned back and looked at Celia. 'There's nothing like this office in Mount Garnet.'

'It's kind of unique, just like Felicity.'

'Were you always best friends?'

Celia laughed. 'We're supposed to be business partners, but it's complicated.'

'What kind of complicated?'

Celia reached across and gripped Toby by the hand and turned her head towards the bedroom door. Toby caught a glimpse of the curve of the nape of her neck as her short black hair swept across her collarbone, causing the skin on the back of his forearms to prickle in response.

'We're both on a journey, that's all, and it seems you're coming too.''

'I'm not just trying to score a free ride if that's what you're worried about.'

Celia turned back to face him. 'I didn't mean that, honestly. I'm just trying to say that we've all been pulled into the same orbit.'

Toby squeezed her warm hand and looked into her eyes before drawing her hair away from the soft skin of her cheek with his fingertips. 'I'm all in,' he said.

Toby then leaned in, kissed Celia on the lips and she didn't pull away. She felt his body heat radiating through the fabric of his tee shirt and kissed him back – then again, and again, so that they looked as if they were just one single figure on the red-lip lounge. Their extended embrace held them in its thrall, until the spell was broken by the sound of movement in the bedroom. They jumped apart, wiping the traces of each other from their mouths, just as Felicity clattered back into the room wearing a fresh tee shirt, jeans and a red puffer jacket and pulling a roller bag.

'One last thing ...' Felicity said, lifting a pop-art print off the wall to reveal a safe with a combination lock embedded in the brickwork. She entered the code and swung open the door. Stacked inside were piles of banknotes neatly strapped in various denominations. Felicity unzipped her bag and began packing the notes in between her clothes. Celia walked over to lend a hand.

'I thought cash went out of circulation back in the '20s,' Celia said.

'With the internet down, we can't pay for anything by EFT-POS. It's still legal tender. We need to be prepared, just in case.'

'Just in case of what?'

'Babe, I wish I knew. Let's get out of here.'

Highway One

The rain had stopped, and a group of shirtless young men standing on a balcony on the first floor of the Vieille Ville apartments saluted with bottles of beer and cheered as Felicity parked the Sandman. Celia opened the passenger door and stepped out onto the verge.

'Hey Celia, come on up and bring your friends. We're having one last party before we run out of beer and the world turns to shit.'

'Thanks for the invite, but we're too busy trying to save your arses!'

'What, in that '74 Sandman?'

'At least it works, unlike you lot.'

Without power, the gates and the entry door to the building were wide open and as the lift was not working, Celia led Felicity and Toby up the fire stairs to her floor.

'Lucky these apartments are low tech,' Celia said, producing the key to her apartment from her handbag and unlocking the door.

Felicity and Toby followed her inside.

'My apartment seems so empty without Miriam. I used to

send her out shopping so that I could have time to myself. Now I wish she was here. Oh my God, what has she been up to?'

Celia, Felicity and Toby stood at the entry to the kitchen, which was full of hundreds of tins of Heinz baked beans stacked up to form a tower. Celia pulled at her hair with her fingertips.

'It's like a wedding cake made of baked beans. What was Miriam thinking?'

Felicity walked into the kitchen, picked up one of the tins, and inspected the label.

'Thinking of you, I expect. We should take some of these with us in case we get really stuck. Do you have a can opener?'

'There's one in the drawer. I'll get some extra bags.'

Felicity and Toby loaded the tins of beans into shopping bags while Celia showered and changed into her ripped jeans, runners and a tee shirt, before cramming as many spare clothes as she could fit into a suitcase.

'This is like going on holiday when I used to go camping with Noah. I have an Esky, a couple of sleeping bags and an orange pup tent in the cupboard,' Celia said.

Felicity squeezed the nape of her neck with her fingers.

'I've never been camping in my life. The Hilton is my idea of a holiday, but you're right, I suppose. You'd better grab some blankets, pillows and towels as well.'

Celia packed frozen food into the Esky while Toby shuttled between the apartment and the van with bags full of tins of baked beans.

'There's no more room. The van's chockers,' Toby said.

'That's it then. Let's get out of here,' Celia said.

Celia locked up her apartment, and they walked back down the fire stairs to the Sandman.

Felicity and Celia sat in the front, Felicity in the driver's seat, while Toby tried to make himself comfortable in the back on the mattress, in between the suitcases, camping equipment and bags full of tins of baked beans. Felicity looked at him in the rear-view mirror.

'Relax Toby, we'll share the driving and take turns riding in the back.' Felicity turned the ignition, and the Sandman burst into life with a throaty growl. Celia put on her sunglasses.

'Felicity, wait a minute. We need to tell Peta what's going on. She's your employee and my best friend, remember,' Celia said.

'Where does she live?' Felicity asked.

'In a townhouse on this side of Bradfield. We can stop at her place first and then the Backpackers, before we leave town. I'll give you directions to her place.'

'I used to wonder what I would do without AYE AYEMaps and now I know,' Felicity said.

'That's why you need me,' Celia said.

'I so do.'

Felicity slowed the Sandman down as they approached the row of cream brick townhouses where Peta and Tyler lived.

'Peta's house is number 15,' Celia said. 'I'll go in. What should I tell her?'

'Ask her if she can take your place at the club until we get back. There is no point in her going to the office while everything is blacked out and she can't work from home with no internet.'

As soon as Felicity had parked the van, Celia jumped out and walked up to the front door, which was painted in rainbow colours and had the number '15' in brass lettering above a large knocker. Celia gave it several hard taps and waited for a sign of life. A minute later she heard a shuffling sound.

'Who is it?' Peta shouted through the closed door.

'Peta, it's me.'

The door swung open. Peta rushed through the doorway dressed in a black Chinese silk robe and hugged her. Celia felt the stubble of Peta's unshaven beard scrape across her cheek.

'Tyler's still asleep. We had to walk home from the club last night. It was horrible and it took ages. When I woke up, I hoped it was just a nightmare, but this is really happening. It's like my digital life has been swept away. I have ninety thousand followers on FaceTracer alone, and they'll think I've pulled the plug. We can't play music or watch videos. All we have left is sex. It's freaking me out.'

'You're not alone, it's freaking me out too. Felicity has told the chairman of the ReElevation board that we're going to investigate the situation,' Celia said.

'What are you thinking of doing?'

'We're going to try to find Miriam.'

'Who is we?'

'Me, Felicity and Toby.'

Peta placed her hands on Celia's hips and looked her in the eye.

'You are really into him, aren't you?'

Celia sighed and squeezed her shoulder blades together.

'Maybe.'

'Just let Felicity down slowly, okay? There is a beating heart under that bossy exterior, you know.'

'I know. Don't worry, I'll look after her.

'I know you will,' Peta said as she reached for Celia's hand and gave it a squeeze.

'Peta, Felicity has a request. She wants you to take my place at the club. Work with the team and see if you can keep the doors open. Party by candlelight if you have to. I don't know how long we'll be gone.'

'Sure, leave it with me. Take care, mate,' Peta said as she embraced Celia and gave her another dose of beard rash.

Celia walked back to the car and got in, gave Felicity a nod of reassurance, waved goodbye to Peta through the car window and put on her sunglasses.

'She's ok about it, Felicity. Now … I know Miriam said if we can get to the decommissioning hub, she can help us to meet "I" or "AYE", but surely, you're not seriously thinking of driving all the way to Queensland in this old heap of scrap metal?' Celia said.

Felicity checked the mirrors and put the Sandman in drive, spinning the wheels as the car pulled away from the kerb.

'It's got personality, that's for sure. What time is it?'

'Noon, I reckon,' Celia answered. 'I wish my mobile phone was working. I really want to talk to my mother. This is doing my head in, and I'm a hermit compared to most people. Millions of people will have woken up this morning to find that they have lost their digital identity. They won't know what to do with themselves.'

'Maybe, but right now we need to get ourselves to Bradfield Backpackers. Any idea where it is?'

'My God, you have no sense of direction Felicity Faraday. It's in the town centre. Just drive.'

As they approached the centre of town, Felicity slowed down to drive through a crowd of people aimlessly milling about. Broken glass crackled under the tyres.

This looks worrying, she thought as she parked the car outside the Backpackers hostel.

'Toby, get your gear and be quick. I want to get us out of here pronto.'

Felicity got out of the van and opened the twin tailgates for Toby so he could climb out. About five minutes after he disappeared inside the hostel, a small group of young men walked across the street and gathered around her. A thin faced young man wearing a hoodie and tracksuit pants stepped forward.

'Hey, lady, can we borrow your wheels?' he said, before grabbing Felicity forcibly by the wrist and shaking her hand until she dropped her car keys.

'We'll give it back in the morning, promise.'

'Fuck off mate,' Felicity said as she pulled her hand free and jostled with the thin faced man as they both dived for the keys.

'Back off!' a voice boomed, as the thin faced man was pushed off balance and stumbled. Felicity looked up and was relieved to see it was Toby who'd shoved the man aside and was now standing between her and the others, holding his guitar case and rucksack.

Keys in hand, she opened the driver's door, jumped in and started the engine. Toby faced off against the gang who had regrouped.

'Fucking arsehole,' the thin man said, sneering with menace.

Toby waved his guitar case and as the thin faced man lunged, he wielded his backpack like a throw hammer and walloped the aggressor in the side of the head, knocking him off his feet.

'Come on Toby!' Felicity yelled.

With the gang momentarily distracted by the sight of the thin faced man lying prostrate on the ground, Toby threw his guitar and backpack inside the van and dived onto the mattress as Felicity floored the accelerator and the van lurched forward in an acrid blue fog of burning rubber, the rear of the van open to the world.

As soon as Felicity lost sight of the group in the mirror, she pulled over. Celia jumped out and raced around to the back of the van.

'Oh my God, Toby, you're a lifesaver,' she said.

'Well, I've never been to the beach, but I have sorted out a few brawls at the Mount Garnet Hotel in my time.'

Celia kissed Toby on the cheek, shut the tailgates and returned to the passenger seat.

'Thanks Toby. I owe you one, mate,' Felicity said, twisting around in her seat to give him a smile.

The streets had become an obstacle course. Felicity found herself navigating around the cars and trucks that lay paralysed on the road because their computers were infected by the virus. Some vehicles had crashed together looking like a concertina, while others lay strewn around in a variety of positions. People were making their way on foot. The injured hobbled, and some were being carried on makeshift stretchers.

'I want to help them,' Celia said.

'Too dangerous! We can't save them all, but we're going to do our bit. Hey Toby, tell us more about that reflective robot head that you saw in Queensland.'

Toby leaned in from the back and poked his head between the bucket seats. 'Yeah, some of the robots are fitted with this scary new tech called a forward-view mirror, which I know they developed at WSU 'cause I saw it in the lab.'

'Why is it so scary?'

'All I can tell you is that you have to think positive when you look into it, or bad shit happens.'

'Just like everything else in life, I suppose,' Felicity said.

'Yeah, except that this stuff messes with your head. I'm not even sure what I saw was even real.'

Celia turned to face him. 'Are you sure the place you found in Far North Queensland was actually the decommissioning hub Miriam spoke about?'

Toby sighed. 'I can't really be sure. All I can tell you is it had a concierge robot who called it 'The Hemisphere'. Maybe I imagined it, who knows?'

Once they'd reached the northern motorway, the road opened up as most of the cars travelling at speed had simply run off the road when they'd stalled. Felicity took care to work around the major pileups and avoid bystanders who waved frantically at them for assistance.

The virus had been released the previous evening, and the cars had largely been abandoned by their occupants. On the far side of the Hawkesbury River Bridge, a major pile-up came into view. Cars, trucks and a caravan were sandwiched together in a collage of twisted metal, blocking their way. There was not a soul around.

'This is eerie,' Felicity said. 'I bet there are bodies in the wreckage.'

She stopped in front of the mangled mountain of metal and pulled on the handbrake. Celia hopped out to let Toby out of the back of the van, and they joined Felicity, who was standing in front. Celia was distraught.

'It's so horrible. I wonder why there's nobody around. Listen, can you hear that?' Celia asked.

From around the bend beyond the pile-up came the sound of an approaching heavy vehicle, and a few minutes later they caught sight of a red front-end loader. At the wheel was a man with a grey beard and a straw hat. He lowered the bucket on the tractor and gently pushed aside the car closest to the edge of the road onto the shoulder. Smoke billowed from the exhaust pipe of the tractor as he revved the motor, drove through the gap, and stopped next to the Sandman.

'G'day folks, do you need a hand?' the bearded man shouted, before turning off the motor and walking over. 'Name's Patrick Drummond. Looks like my Massey-Ferguson and your Holden Sandman are the only vehicles around here old enough not to get caught up in this mess.'

Felicity took off her sunglasses. 'Do you know what happened here?'

'Sure do. I was right in the middle of it. I was on my way home from the Workers Club in the back seat of my driverless car when I was forced off the road by a column of robots marching up the motorway. Cars and trucks were swerving all over the place. It took around twenty minutes for the robots to march past. I reckon it was an army of a hundred thousand. After they passed, I got going again, and then all the lights went out, and every vehicle around me stalled at the same time, and we all smashed together. That's my car there, the orange one. It's pretty banged up.'

Celia looked at Patrick. 'It looks like a serious accident. Was anyone hurt?'

'Most of the people were pretty lucky and walked away, but one couple was trapped in that SUV. I live just over the hill, so I walked back and got the tractor. Some of the truckies gave me a hand to get them out. They just had cuts and bruises, so I gave them a ride home in the bucket of my Massey Fergo trackie.'

'Are they okay?' Celia asked.

'My wife is a nurse, so she's looking after them. It could have been worse. Everyone must have walked off on foot. God knows where they ended up. I came back today to tow my car out of here.'

Felicity put her hands in the back pockets of her red jeans, as a prelude to announcing that they had to get going. 'Well, thanks for clearing the way for us, Patrick. I hope those people are soon on the road to recovery. We're on the way to understanding why this happened.'

'I wish you good luck with that. It's beyond me.'

Patrick walked back to the tractor while Felicity, Celia and Toby returned to the van. Felicity drove the Sandman through the gap in the pile-up and pressed on.

Celia put her sunglasses back on, knowing that she could hide her feelings better that way when she needed. 'I wonder why the robots were not affected by the virus?' she asked.

Toby leaned in between the bucket seats. 'It's their virus so I suppose they're immune.'

Celia thought for a moment. 'Will all the data centres survive, or do you think the Cloud has just blown away?'

Felicity wriggled in her seat. 'Even if Mick gets the power back on, if there's no internet, our world will be very screwed up.'

After a while, Felicity began to adapt to driving through hazards. Then Toby took over the wheel after a toilet stop for him by the side of the road. Felicity kept a lookout and Celia sat in the back.'

'I'm getting carsick,' Celia said.

Toby looked at her in the mirror. 'Just don't spew on the mattress.'

They rounded a bend and suddenly Toby slammed on the brakes. A semi-trailer lay on its side, sprawled across the road. The Sandman spun around, screeching to a stop just in front of the trailer.

'Fuck, that was close. Celia, are you okay back there?' Toby said, searching for her in the rear-view mirror.

'I'm fine, but it was like being in the Rotor at Luna Park. I didn't spew, so I guess my stomach is stronger than I thought.'

Toby slowly manoeuvred the van around the wreck and pulled up ten metres beyond it. He jumped out, walked back to the cabin and peered in through the cracked windscreen, before walking back to the van.

'There's no one in there. It seems to be a fully autonomous truck,' Toby said as he buckled up in the driver's seat. He drove on with Felicity keeping a keen eye out for hazards while Celia attempted to regulate her breathing, so she didn't throw up in the back of the van.

The Mid North Coast

'KEMPSEY EXIT 2KM,' the sign read. Felicity, who was sitting in the passenger seat of the Sandman, asked, 'How are we going for fuel Toby?'

'We're below a quarter of a tank. We need to fill up, but I suppose if the power is cut here too, that may be difficult.'

Toby took the exit, traversed the grey girders of the iron bridge that crossed the Macleay River and drove into the town of Kempsey. The service station was closed. In large red letters on a sandwich board in the driveway were the words, NO POWER, NO RECHARGE, NO FUEL.

Toby pulled in, and they all hopped out to stretch their legs. There was movement inside the building so they wandered over and knocked on the door. A balding man with a ginger beard dressed in an 'AMPOL' polo shirt unlocked the door. Pinned to his shirt was a white plastic tag that read, 'Duty Manager'.

'Sorry folks. I love that you're getting around in that classic car, but there is no power for the petrol pump, and the payment gateway is offline. Felicity stepped forward.

'We can pay cash.'

'Cash. I haven't seen that since COVID-19. I can fill you up for a thousand bucks.'

'What! A grand for a tank of petrol?'

'Take it or leave it. Fifty per cent deposit now and the rest in the morning when I've figured a way to bypass the safety valves. It's your only chance. I reckon every other service station up the highway would be closed up.'

'Give us a moment,' Felicity said. She turned and walked back towards the van with Toby and Celia.

'I don't want to blow all our cash, but we need fuel. What do you think?' she asked.

'Let's hold out on him for a while,' Celia said.

Felicity walked back over to the Duty Manager. 'Hey, mate, any suggestions about where we can spend the night?' Felicity asked.

'You could try the camping area at Scotts Head. It's a forty-minute drive. Do you want the fuel or not?'

'We'll sleep on it. By the way, did a bunch of robots come through here last night?'

'I heard an army of them came through over on the bypass. All our robots left town to join them. Left nothing behind except a stack load of baked beans. I've got plenty of spare tins of the stuff if you need them.'

They walked back to the van. Felicity took the wheel, and Celia happily resumed her position in the passenger seat while Toby propped himself up in the rear.

'I don't see that we have any other option. A lot of service stations stopped selling petrol when they started phasing out hybrids,' Celia said.

'I know. We'll work it out tomorrow but let's just find a place to stay first. It must be nearly four o'clock,' Felicity said.

Felicity drove through the long shadows of a golden after-noon. They turned off the highway onto Scotts Head Road and wound their way through the lush green bush to the coast.

The caravan park was tucked in at the back of the beach beside the small domed sandstone headland. Felicity pulled up and wandered into the office to find an older woman wearing a tie-dye sarong reading a book behind the desk. A wind chime tinkled in the open window – and was that the smell of incense wafting past her out the door?

'Hello, love, what can I do for you?'

'I am hoping we can camp here tonight. I know it's peak season,' Felicity replied.

'Well, you're in luck. It was changeover day yesterday, but no one turned up because of the blackout, although a lot of folks are stuck here because their cars are broken down. I can give you a spot close to the beach by the amenities block. Don't try to pay me with tins of baked beans though. Some people around here are using them as currency.'

'We've got cash,' Felicity said.

The woman's grey eyes lit up. 'Banknotes. I'll take that. We're pretty old-fashioned around here. It's two hundred a night. Pay upfront.'

Felicity walked out, retrieved the cash from the van and went back in to pay.

'The power is still off,' the woman said as she counted the money. 'We have solar hot water, but once it runs out, that's it. Space number 28.'

Felicity drove the van around the park until she located the spot and parked the van on the grass. She stepped out and stood facing the ocean, a northeast breeze blowing through her red curls. The smell of the sea triggered a memory of holidaying at

Mavericks Beach, south of San Francisco.

I had forgotten the smell of the sea, Felicity thought as Toby and Celia ran past her onto the sand like a couple of excited young children.

'Hey Toby, check out the waves!' Celia called.

'Sure – let's give it a go! Reminds me of when my mob used to spend the summer holidays down on the Gold Coast. It'll be warmer in than out, I reckon. Let's get the boards out of the van.'

Toby opened the tailgates and pulled out Mick's surfboards and the wetsuits while Celia rummaged through her bag for her bikini.

'There's still a little bit of wax on these,' Toby said as he inspected the boards. 'Should be enough but be careful you don't slip off.'

'Did you bring any swimmers?' Celia asked.

'Yeah, my boardshorts are in my rucksack. Grab a wetsuit and change behind the van. No one's looking.'

After Celia and Toby took turns changing into their swimmers and pulling on their wetsuits, they picked up the surfboards and carried them down to the beach where Felicity was sitting, wrapped in a beach towel, looking out across the Pacific Ocean.

'Luckily, it's not too cold. I'll play lifeguard, but just don't expect me to save you as I can't swim,' she said.

Felicity watched as Celia and Toby strapped the cuffs of the leg ropes around their ankles, picked up their boards and ran down to the sea and into the surf. They pushed the tips of the boards under the first line of breakers and paddled furiously, diving under successive waves until they were out the back, where they drew breath and sat up on their boards.

A set of waves spiralled around the headland, and Celia pushed to the take-off point with a couple of short, powerful strokes. As the largest wave reared up, she launched herself down the steep inside section, carving a broad turn at the bottom and racing along as it unfolded. She flipped the board up and over the back of the wave as it broke and dived off into the sea.

Felicity could hear Toby applauding and whistling.

Next, it was Toby's turn. Another large set peeled off the point, and he pulled the water back with all his strength until he matched the speed and momentum of the wave to push the board over the lip. As his board sliced down the smooth face of the wave, he crouched down with one hand on the outer rail, before making several quick turns and straightening out to enjoy the long ride, until its energy dissipated into the white foam. Celia was whooping and punching the sky for him.

Back on the beach, Felicity's heart sank.

I'm going to lose her to him. They already look like a dream couple, she thought.

It was late in the day. Celia and Toby looked like they were going to make the most of the twilight, so Felicity walked back to the van. She opened her bag and retrieved her jacket, her last packet of cigarettes, a lighter and a bottle of Jack Daniel's bourbon whisky. She found a packet of fire starters in Celia's box of camping equipment and walked back to the beach. She took a swig of the bourbon and scoured the beach for driftwood.

By the time Celia and Toby caught their last wave back into the beach she had a fire well underway. She drew back on her cigarette, mulled over the fact that she had only one left in the packet, and watched the two young surfers as they emerged from the sea, walked up the beach and sat on their boards in front of the fire to dry off.

Celia sensed that Felicity had been left to her own devices for a little too long and needed to chat.

'How's the water?' Felicity asked.

'Surprisingly warm. Since when do you drink bourbon?'

'Well, I need something to keep the cold at bay, and I am an American. Since when did you start surfing like that?'

Celia laughed. 'My brother Vinh taught me. We used to catch the train down to the beach at Cronulla on the weekends when we were growing up. Hey Toby, find some more firewood for Felicity, eh? And I'll go and get us some food.'

Celia took her board back to the van, ducking her head under the cold outdoor shower on the way through. She left her black bikini top on and changed back into her jeans beside the van before she found her jacket so she could warm up. Next came her dinner plans. The Esky had kept the raw sausages and bread rolls cool, and she put them on a plate. In a box she found the frypan and utensils, stacked the plate of food on top and returned to the beach.

Toby had the fire roaring by the time she got back. The sausages crackled and spat as she carefully dropped them into the pan, filling the air with the smell of barbeque.

'This is it for fresh food. I'm afraid it's Miriam's baked beans from here on in,' Celia said.

Felicity laughed. 'Sausages and bourbon whisky. A toast to your signature dish.'

She passed Celia the bottle of bourbon to take a swig. Next in line, Toby declined.

'I don't drink, but I do play guitar.'

Toby went back to the van and retrieved the instrument,

getting back just in time to watch Celia pull the hot sausages off the fire and lay them on the bread rolls, before smothering them in barbeque sauce.

'Tuck in,' she said as they each picked up a roll and took a bite.'

'It tastes like Bunnings,' Felicity said.

'Yeah, I stole the recipe.'

The yellow moon clambered over the horizon, dripping golden droplets of light into the sea. Toby played his guitar and sang to the two women as they sat in the ruddy glow of the fire, wiggling their toes in the cool white sand with their backs to the breeze of the winter's night.

Detour to Sanur

In Jakarta Bay, Pete leaned over the side of the boat, took the baby from the arms of the woman and watched as she gripped the top of a stanchion and swung her legs over the lifeline and onto the deck.

'You'll need to stay below. Follow me.'

The woman followed Pete as he carried the child down through the companionway and into the cabin. He turned around and with his free hand, motioned for her to sit down on the brown vinyl cushion that wrapped around the table. Pete placed the child back in the arms of its mother.

'Stay here and don't make a sound until we're underway, understand?'

'Yes Mister. Komang is good boy.'

Pete went back out on deck and pulled his phone out of his sodden backpack. It was supposed to be waterproof but wouldn't turn on.

Strange, he thought.

He put the dead phone back in his backpack and made his way to the bow. Crowds of people were beginning to gather in the street opposite the marina. They were shouting and throwing rocks and bottles at the riot police who were outnumbered and on foot. A Molotov cocktail smashed against the plastic shield of a policeman.

Farewell Jakarta, he thought as he unravelled the rope from the bollard, releasing the yacht from the wharf. *And farewell to my competition who seem to have stirred up a hornet's nest.*

He unfurled the headsail to collect the zephyr of breeze and the *Hesperus* moved silently out into the bay. As soon as he was clear of the marina, he put the yacht into the wind and hoisted the mainsail. Years of solo sailing made this a routine task. He clambered back to the cockpit, turned the wheel, and braced himself as the wind filled the sails and the boat began to heel over as it gathered momentum. He engaged the mechanical autopilot and went below.

The child was crying, and the woman was pushing back against gravity as the boat leaned over. Peter took the child from her so she could grip the table to steady herself.

'What's your name?'

'I am Wayan.'

'Hi, Wayan. My name is Pete. I know from your name that you are from Bali. And is Komang your only child?'

'No, Mr. Pete. My other children live with my mother in the village.'

'Why did you move to Jakarta?'

'My new husband is from Java. They killed him Mr. Pete and now I'm alone again just like I was after Komang's father drowned in the watercourse near my village. Please take us home.'

Peter sighed. 'No guarantees, but I'll do my best. Now let's get you two settled and I'll find you something to eat. All complaints about the food are to be submitted in writing, understand?'

'No writing, Mister.'

'Forget it, I'm joking.'

Pete showed Wayan the bed in the aft cabin and how to use the ship's toilet and then made them some toasties and coffee in the galley before returning to the cockpit. He looked back towards the city which had vanished in the darkness.

It was a perfect night for sailing. The breeze had swung around to the north-east and the moon was high overhead. Offshore, giant oil tankers and cargo vessels, shrouded in darkness, lay lurking on the horizon like forgotten mausoleums. Pete vowed to stay awake as long as he could to avoid a collision. Now and then, he drifted off into a fitful sleep, only to wake with a jolt and look up, to find the stars in a different orientation. Sleep deprived, he would reestablish the position of the boat before once again settling back down to relax.

For two days the Hesperus sailed on the jade-coloured waters of the Java Sea, skirting around the islands of the Indonesian archipelago. After sunrise, with the boat on autopilot, Pete sat back in the cockpit and allowed himself to drift off to sleep. Then, in the distance, towering above the heat haze of the morning stood the smouldering cone of Mount Agung. He went below.

'I can see the volcano. We'll be off Bali in two hours so get yourself ready to go.'

While Wayan breastfed her baby, Pete studied the chart. He gave silent thanks for being risk averse enough to carry paper maps. He decided to sail close to the resort settlement of Sanur on the west coast of the island of Bali and then work out a way to offload his passengers without alerting the authorities. He knew it was fraught with danger, but unlike many of the other members of the syndicate, he was not completely devoid of human compassion.

As the Hesperus drew closer to shore, he spotted a blue catamaran bobbing in the swell. Two men were casting their nets off the side. Pete sailed within close proximity and pulled the boat into the wind. He called out to Wayan, who carried her baby along the companionway and into the cockpit. The boats drifted towards each other and before long, they were within earshot. Pete leant over the side to speak to the men.

'I have a passenger who needs assistance. Can you help?'

One of the men stood up. Grey-haired, he was clearly much older than the other man, who was wearing a red bandanna.

'What are you doing here?'

'We fish.'

Wayan stepped forward and shouted to the man in Balinese. After a short verbal exchange, the two men hauled in the nets. A small number of silver flashes dropped into their boat. After securing the nets, they manoeuvred the catamaran until it drew alongside the Hesperus.

'Too much fishing. Bali nearly finish all fish now,' the man in the red bandanna shouted, leaning forward to take baby Komang as Wayan dangled him over the side. Then as the two boats aligned in a moment of stillness, Wayan stepped over the transom, and jumped into the sea. She resurfaced and grabbed the hand of the older man, who hauled her up onto the side of the boat. She clung to the gunwale until both men pulled her on board. Smiling, she stood up and waved.

'I will give 'thank you' in the mother temple, Mr. Pete.'

'You blokes look after Wayan or I'll come after you, understand?'

Wayan laughed. 'They are my uncles from the village, Mr. Pete. See you bye-bye!'

'One day I'll come back, Wayan, okay?'

'Okay Mr. Pete'

Pete returned to the cockpit and turned the wheel until he felt the power of the wind take the sails. He checked the position of the setting sun and the time of day on his Rolex to get a bearing and put the boat on mechanical autopilot again. Then he went below, selected a chart and spread it out on the table. He made a calculation, scribbled the result on a 'post it' note and returned to the cockpit. Taking the wheel, he adjusted the heading to set the boat on course towards the Torres Strait.

A car swap

Felicity was woken by the annoying buzz of a fly bouncing around the inside of the Sandman. At Scotts Head the morning sun was streaming in through the heart-shaped porthole. Even though she knew it was cold outside the van, she was in a lather of perspiration.

I shouldn't have finished off that bottle of bourbon before I crashed out, she thought.

Pulling on her hoodie and a pair of shorts, she pushed open the tailgate and perched herself on it so she could dangle her legs in the cold morning air.

The lovebirds must be down at the beach having an early surf. What I wouldn't give for a coffee, she thought.

Felicity immediately pulled out Celia's box of camping equipment. Inside was a small portable cooker, a billy and a box of teabags. She rummaged around in her bag for her thongs and flip-flopped across to the amenities block, carrying the billy, her towel and her bag of toiletries. She hoped the winter sun had radiated just enough heat into the solar hot water system for a slightly warm shower.

It smells like soap and mildew in here, she thought, stripping off while contemplating their next move driving north. She felt some relief as she washed her hair. After dressing and towelling her hair, she filled the billy with water and walked back to the campsite just as Celia and Toby arrived back from the beach.

'How was the surf?' she called out.

Celia put down her board, peeled off her wetsuit and retrieved her towel from the branch of a nearby banksia tree where she'd hung it out to dry the night before.

'Freezing but awesome. Best waves ever. Toby surfs like he's on the pro-circuit. Fuck, I'm cold. Are the showers hot?'

'Kind of, but make it quick because I don't know how to fire up your gas cooker and I'm desperate for a hot cup of tea.'

After Celia and Toby had showered and changed into some warm clothes, they read the instructions printed on the side of the gas cooker and soon the billy was boiling away. Felicity dropped in several tea bags and left them to brew.

'Cornflakes but no milk. Any other ideas for breakfast?' Felicity asked.

Celia pulled some mugs out of the box of utensils. 'I guess this is where we start eating Miriam's baked beans. What's the plan?'

'We need to get out of here and find fuel. We can make it to Macksville. It's only twenty minutes away,' Felicity said.

Celia heated up some baked beans in the pan as they sipped their tea and munched on handfuls of dry cornflakes.

Toby pulled down the tent and packed it up before following Celia over to the amenities block for a shower and a shave. By the time they returned, Felicity was in the driver's seat ready to start the engine. Toby resumed his position in the back of the van and Celia paused to take a long look at Toby before she shut the tailgates.

'I love it here' she whispered. 'We discovered a piece of heaven at the end of the world.'

'Yeah, a moment in time that we shared, just between us, instead of the whole world on FaceTracer.'

Celia joined Felicity in the front of the van.

'Farewell paradise!' Felicity called as she squeezed the accelerator, the engine growling as the van moved off. They waved at the grey hippy woman standing outside the office on the way through, and soon they were winding their way along Scotts Head Road towards Macksville.

Just out of town was a service station with a petrol tanker parked in the driveway. Felicity pulled up at the bowser alongside. A handwritten sign was taped across the front of the petrol pump that read, NO POWER – NO FUEL.

The cabin door of the petrol tanker was open, and the driver was sitting inside eating a can of cold baked beans. They all hopped out of the van and walked over for a chat with the driver, who was wearing a baseball cap and wrap-around sunglasses.

'Don't even think about it, folks. I can't give you any fuel. I've been stranded here ever since the night of the robots' walkout. I can't start the engine, and that means I can't pump out any petrol.'

Felicity decided to push the point. 'We can pay cash. I'll give you five hundred bucks.'

'Lady, you could offer me a bar of gold and a supermodel, but there is no way around the interlocking safety valves. You'll have to sit tight until the power comes back on.'

Celia was about to speak when they heard the door of the Sandman open, then slam shut. The big V8 roared as the Sandman spun its wheels in a cloud of blue smoking rubber, before lurching forward out of the driveway and disappearing down the road.

Felicity bolted off after it.

'Hey! That's our van! Stop! Oh my God, the van's been stolen,' Felicity shouted as she ran in vain down the drive, before realising it was futile and stopped, grabbing her red curls in her fists.

Celia and Toby caught up with her, and they all stood in disbelief as the plume of smoke blew across the driveway.'

Celia held her hands to her temples. 'What the hell do we do now? Our whole life is in that van.'

'And our cash,' Felicity said.

'And my guitar.'

The petrol tanker driver walked over and stood next to them.

'You lot need to be careful. No one has access to food, money or transport. Any operational vehicle is going to be a prize. I hear there's already been looting in town. I'm sorry I can't be more help.' With no response from any of the three, he walked back to the truck.

Felicity looked downcast. 'I'm sorry you two, I've let you down. I should never have left the key in the bloody ignition.

Celia gave her a hug. 'Don't be silly, it's not your fault. We're in this together. We knew it could be dangerous when we started out. Something will turn up.'

As they stood in silence, coming to terms with the situation, an old green Toyota Landcruiser pulled up alongside, driven by a middle-aged man wearing an orange and white checked flannelette shirt and an Akubra hat.

'G'day folks. Was that your Sandman panel van I just passed, by any chance?'

Felicity walked over. 'Sure was. Some dickhead just stole it from under our noses. Everything we have is inside.'

'That dickhead is my idiot teenage son, Shannon, and you are spot on. Lately, he's behaving like a juvenile delinquent. Hop in. He's probably just driven it home.'

Felicity jumped into the front seat of the 4-wheel drive, and Celia and Toby sat together in the back.

'My name is Niall O'Connor, by the way. Sorry about the inconvenience.'

'You're a life saver, Niall. My name's Felicity, and this is Celia and Toby in the back. How long have you had this truck?'

'It belonged to my great-grandfather. It's one of the first batches of Toyota Land Cruisers that they brought out for the construction of the Snowy Hydro Scheme back in the 1950s. He emigrated to Australia from Ireland to work on the project.'

'Are you a collector?' Felicity asked.

'Classic cars are my weakness. Where did you get the Sand-man? It looks like a beauty?'

'It belongs to my Uncle Mick. He lent it to us so we could track down the robots. He worked in a power station too, and he also collects curiosities from the 1970s.'

'Sounds like a man after my own heart.'

Niall drove the Toyota across the bridge that spanned the broad green expanse of the Nambucca River and into the back streets on the north side of the town. They rounded the corner and to their relief saw the Sandman parked outside a tidy white weatherboard cottage fronted by a manicured lawn and a rose garden.

'If you're game, come on in and I'll introduce you to the family,' Niall said.

He led them up the front steps and through a wire screen door that opened onto the verandah. A stocky woman with a worried expression, wearing an apron and with her brown hair tied back in a bun, was waiting anxiously inside.

'Niall, he's stolen another car. If the cops charge him this time, I don't know what I'll do. I wasn't expecting visitors. Are you plain clothes police, by any chance?'

'Nancy meet Felicity, Celia and Toby. They own the van out the front. Where's the little bugger? Shannon, get out here, you've got some explaining to do.'

'He's locked himself in his room and refuses to come out. I've been knocking on his door ever since he came home.'

'How old is Shannon?' Felicity asked.

Nancy wiped her hands on her apron. 'Seventeen. He was such a good kid until he hit his teenage years. He's been nothing but trouble ever since.'

'Let me have a go,' Felicity suggested, and immediately knocked softly on Shannon's bedroom door. 'Hi Shannon, my name is Felicity. I'd really like to meet you.'

After a moment of silence, the latch clicked, and the door opened just wide enough for the boy to see her with one eye. Felicity was fully aware of the power of persuasion her voluptuous figure would afford her. A minute later, she was sitting on the edge of the boy's bed.

'Shannon, we need your help. We're here to track down the robots. Did you see them?'

'Sure did. I was out on my bike with my friends on the way to school. They were marching up the highway. It was really scary. Then our phones stopped working, and they sent us home from school because there was a power cut.'

'That's useful information, Shannon. By the way, why did you steal our van?'

'I wanted to give it to Dad. He loves anything from the 1970s.

I thought he'd like it, that's all.'

Felicity held out her hand. Shannon took it and shook, as his cheeks flushed bright red.

'Come with me and I'll introduce you to my friends, Celia and Toby.' Felicity took Shannon by the arm and led him out of the bedroom and into the lounge room.

'Celia and Toby, meet Shannon.' The boy looked at the floor without speaking.

'Shannon took the car because he thought you'd like it, Niall. I get it. It's a classic car.'

'Sorry, Dad.'

'Don't apologise to me. Say sorry to my friends here.'

Felicity caught Shannon checking her out as his father spoke.

'Okay, whatever. I'm really sorry.'

Celia was looking at several posters that were hung on the loungeroom wall in frames.

Niall noticed her attention focussed on the posters and explained the backstory. 'These are posters of Captain Good-vibes, the surfing pig of steel, from the 1970s surfing magazine *Tracks*. The illustrations are wonderful. I love the detail. I wrote an essay on the cartoonist Tony Edwards when I was studying interior design at uni,'

He sat down on the lounge. 'I'm a bit of a 1970s aficionado – which brings me to the Sandman. What are your plans from here?'

Felicity sat in an armchair opposite. 'We're trying to follow the robots to find out why they seem to have pulled the plug on us all. I run a company back in Sydney, and we'll be out of business if this keeps up. We've been told the robots are heading for Far North Queensland.'

'I think the issue you are going to face from here on in is

access to fuel. You'd have a better chance with diesel. It's not volatile like petrol, and it's used in agriculture, so you should be able to get some, even if you have to chat up a few farmers.'

'I agree, but we can't put diesel in the Sandman.'

'I know. Here's my suggestion. I have a few vintage Land-cruisers, including a 4-door extended-wheelbase model, in the shed out the back. I suggest you leave the Sandman with me, and I'll lend you the big 4-by-4 until you get back. Toby seems like a bright young lad. I'll give him a crash course in mechanics while you ladies help Nancy with lunch, eh?'

They all agreed. Niall took Toby out the back door, leaving Felicity and Celia to follow Nancy into the kitchen. Nancy still looked upset.

'I'm not a miracle worker. All the shops are closed. I don't know what we'll eat.'

Celia looked in the pantry. 'Nancy, did you have a House-keeperBot?'

'Niall and I decided we didn't want one. All they do is put everyone out of work and on the dole. It's no wonder Shannon is going off the rails.'

'Well, you have a larder full of tins, including baked beans. We'll knock something up. A confit of baked beans and a nice bottle of red, which I have tucked away in the van.'

'I have plenty of fresh vegetables from our veggie patch, and I still have some bread, although it's a bit stale. I suppose we could fry it up on the barbecue. We have plenty of biscuits and cheese.'

By the time Niall and Toby returned from the mechanics lesson, Nancy and Celia had created a veritable smorgasbord. Felicity opened the wine and filled glasses as they all pondered the future.

'I suggest you pack the vehicle tonight and get off to an early start if you are going to catch those robots. Bob, my next-door neighbour, reckons they were travelling in a pack at over sixty kilometres per hour.'

'That's their top speed,' Celia said.

After lunch, Felicity drove the Sandman up the drive and parked it next to the large 4-wheel drive vehicle.

They spent the next twenty minutes transferring the luggage, after making the tough decision to leave behind the surfboards. Then they spent a few hours chatting to make sure everyone was happy with the arrangement and by the time they'd finished, it was late in the day. Niall made them all drive around the block several times to get a feel for the vehicle before topping it up with diesel from a tank on the side of the garage. The power was still out everywhere, and when they finally came inside, Nancy was walking around the house with a hurricane lamp.

'Nancy, you look like Florence bloody Nightingale,' Niall said. 'Here's the sleeping arrangements. Toby, you'll have to sleep in the spare bed in Shannon's room, and you ladies will have to share the guest bedroom. Lucky it's a queen size bed! I'm an early riser, so I'm off to sleep now.'

Nancy lit candles for them all and went to the linen cupboard for some fresh towels.

'We have solar hot water but only one bathroom, I'm afraid. Sleep tight and don't forget to blow your candles out. We don't want to burn the place down.'

Toby said good night, and Felicity shut the door behind Celia as they walked into the guest bedroom.

'Better have a shower – who knows when we'll get the next one?' Celia said. She tiptoed down the hall, and when she got back, slid into bed in her tee shirt and shorts.

When Felicity came back from her shower, she quietly closed the door before taking off her tee shirt and sliding between the sheets.

'Seriously, Felicity, haven't you flashed those two enough today?'

'Just be thankful I've still got my panties on. I usually sleep naked.'

'Of course, you do. Just stay on your side of the bed. Pretend there's a line down the middle, eh?'

'Can I use my imagination?'

'That's your business. Just don't make any embarrassing noises. Good night.'

Celia blew out the candle and lay back in the dark, staring up at the ceiling. 'Felicity, the sentient intelligence Miriam was talking about sounds really scary to me. I hope we're not being reckless.'

'Life is like skiing. The best way to avoid disaster is to be confident and lean into it. I'm sure we'll be okay if we stick together. We're a pretty good team and we'll get to the bottom of it all, I'm sure.'

'Good night, business partner.'

'Night, babe.' Felicity was silent for a moment. 'Can I ask how you feel about Toby?'

Celia didn't answer as she was already imagining she was back at Scotts Head, surfing the point break, and didn't want to break the spell.

Felicity lay on her back for a while, listening to Celia's soft snoring, and before long the pace of the day and the lingering memory of the previous night's bottle of bourbon enveloped her, and she too was out like a light.

Cooroy Showground

'Cooroy Showground is usually full of grey nomads. They're a friendly lot. You could do worse than stopping in there if you feel the need to find solace in fellow travellers,' Niall suggested, before taking a sip of black coffee.

Nancy flipped a potato rosti in the pan on the gas stove.

'It's lucky for you that I tend the veggie patch, otherwise you'd be living on a diet of pure tinned food, Niall O'Connor.'

Nancy turned to Felicity, Celia, Toby and Shannon as they sat around the breakfast table with Niall.

'Another potato rosti anyone? Not you Shannon.'

Felicity wiped the corners of her mouth with a paper serviette. 'None for me thanks, Nancy. I have to look after my figure. Shannon can have the last one. We'd better hit the road as it's nearly seven.'

Toby gave Celia a glance and explained. 'I'm all good thanks, Mrs O'Connor. Cooroy is in the hinterland of the Sunshine Coast. It makes sense to bypass Brisbane. Thanks for the tip, Niall. Are we all set?

Felicity and Celia thanked Nancy and left the table to brush their teeth and get ready for the day ahead. Niall pulled an old, folded paper map off the nearby bookshelf and placed it on the table in front of Toby.

'There are no AYE AYEMaps until they get the internet back up, so put this map of Queensland in the glovebox. It may come in handy.'

'Thanks, Niall. You think of everything.'

Niall, Nancy and Shannon walked out to the Landcruiser with Felicity, Celia and Toby to see them off.

Felicity looked at Shannon. 'If you look after your mother, maybe I'll be able to come back and see you.'

'I will, I promise. It was awesome to meet you, Felicity.'

Felicity gave Shannon a hug, chest to chest.

They all said their goodbyes and piled into the Landcruiser. Toby took the wheel, and Felicity resumed her role as navigator in the passenger seat.

'At least this car has a back seat,' Celia said as they pulled out of the drive and headed back towards the Pacific Motorway.

When it began to rain heavily it was slow going, navigating around the abandoned driverless cars and trucks that littered the highway. The weather slowly improved over the course of the day, with the sun eventually breaking through as the famous surf break at Kirra came into view. They pulled into the Kirra Beach Hotel to stretch their legs and to check if they were still on the trail of the robots. This time Felicity made sure she locked the car. After a bathroom break, they sat at the bar. A portly barman in a Kirra Hotel tee shirt came over to take their order.

'There's no power, so I don't have any cold beer, and it's cash or cans, as they say.'

'What's the exchange rate on a can of baked beans?' Felicity asked.

'A dollar per tin. No one around here has cash, so we're mostly using baked beans as currency. The locals only eat them if they get desperate. I don't think I can ever look a baked bean in the eye again. I'm over them. I knew we shouldn't have trusted those robots. They left me in the lurch here at the pub. All my BarBots just walked out.'

'So, a whole host of them came this way then?' Felicity said.

'They sure did. It was like an army. Never seen anything like it in all my born days. What'll it be?'

'Shiraz for Celia and me. Toby is a teetotaller, so a glass of water for him. I've got cash.'

'Well, if you've got cash, you're welcome to settle in for the afternoon.'

'We'd love to, mate, but we don't want the trail to go cold.'

They finished off their drinks and walked back out to the Landcruiser. Celia and Toby paused to check out the perfect curling break out the back of Kirra Beach while Felicity got the car started.

'Shame we had to leave our surfboards behind in the Sandman,' Toby moaned, as he opened the door of the van and sat in the passenger seat for his shift as navigator.

'You're a grommet at heart. I'm going to bleach your hair,' Celia said as she jumped in, looking at Felicity to see if the idea would elicit a response.

'Okay, so long as you do yours first,' he said. 'What about you, Felicity? Wanna go blonde with us?'

Felicity put on her sunglasses. 'No way, I'll be red until I'm dead,' she said.

Toby leaned into the back seat to speak to Celia. 'Looks like it's just you and me then.'

Felicity pulled her sunglasses off the bridge of her nose and glared at him sideways before checking the mirrors and stepping on the accelerator.

They barrelled up the Pacific Motorway in the Landcruiser, zigzagging through the obstacle course of wrecked and abandoned vehicles. From the top of the majestic arch of the Gateway Bridge, they could see the city of Brisbane in the distance, sprawled languidly in a brown haze from a myriad of spot fires burning on both sides of the river. Felicity gripped the wheel tightly and kept her eyes on the road.

The place is coming apart, she thought.

On the far side of the bridge, they picked up the Bruce Highway, travelling north past the distant grey bluffs of the Glasshouse Mountains. It was mid-afternoon when they found themselves driving into Cooroy Showground. Felicity pulled over and turned the engine off.

'It's like a cross between Adelaide Market and sideshow alley at the Royal Easter Show,' she said.

Three stout men in their forties walked over to the Landcruiser to have a chat and Felicity wound down the window. They all had plenty to say.

'You're welcome to stay here, but we don't want anyone who's going to make trouble.'

'Yeah, there's mayhem in Noosa, and we don't want the likes of that up here.'

'We're a close-knit bunch, and we look out for each other. You're welcome to trade anything of value, and we only want people here who are willing to contribute.'

Felicity put them straight. 'Relax boys. We're on the road, trying to make sense of what's happened, like you are. We need a space to camp tonight and we're going to need fuel for the next leg.'

'There are a few spots left on the far side of the showground and you can barter with the fuel dealer. That's his stall over there near the entry. He's packed up for today, but he'll be back in the morning.'

'Thanks for the info,' she said before driving on into the site.

Hundreds of caravans and recreational vehicles were crammed side by side around the rim of the ground, encircling what appeared to be an impromptu marketplace. The area was lit by flaming torches on poles and hundreds of people of all ages were milling about. A jug band was playing on a small stage illuminated by hundreds of candles. Felicity drove around until she located a parking space in between too large RVs. She reversed in and they all hopped out to survey the scene.

'Did you see the fortune teller? After everything that's happened to me this week, I need my palm read,' Celia said.

A red-faced man with a pot belly – obviously not a local farmer – emerged from the RV next to them.

'G'day folks, my name's Buster. Welcome to the new normal around here. I hope you've got plenty of tins of baked beans to trade with, otherwise, you'll have to resort to bartering. I've been stuck here ever since the virus disabled my truck. I got married to my robot girlfriend last year, but she's shot through with the rest of them so I'm here on my own. Drop in for a beer if you like. I've still got a few warm cans of XXXX left.'

Felicity took up Buster's offer and settled into a director's chair, can in hand, while Celia and Toby walked over to check out the market. Some of the more enterprising local farmers had set up stalls to spruik the local fruit and vegetables as well as jars of local honey and jam. There was even a butcher's stall shrouded in a swarm of flies. Celia held her nose.

'Yuk. This reminds me of the spice market in Istanbul. Hey

Toby, do you mind if I check out the fortune teller?'

'You go for it. I'll go over and watch the band. Take your time.'

A fortune teller

The fortune teller's tent would have looked at home in any country show. Pegged to the canvas was a handwritten sign decorated with a yellow painted moon and blue stars. It read 'PALM READINGS & TAROT'. Celia pulled back the flap of the tent and ducked her head as she went inside.

A woman with noticeably fair skin and long light-brown hair, tied back with a dark red velvet scarf, was seated at a round table in the centre of the tent, shuffling a deck of cards. Her white blouse was laced up at the front and Celia could see her mauve and burgundy layered skirt trimmed with gold coins along the edge and under the table.

'Come in – don't be shy. My name is Esmerelda. Please, take a seat.'

Celia sat down in a brown leather chair opposite Esmerelda and was a little nervous when they made eye contact. Esmerelda's penetrating green eyes stared out at her from behind layers of green eye shadow and black mascara.

'You are here because you have questions. I am here for the same reason,' Esmerelda said.

She shuffled the cards again before laying them out in a

semicircular fan, face down on the white tablecloth. The tinkle of a wind chime hanging outside the entrance distracted Celia momentarily as she looked around the interior. A variety of candles illuminated the space with a warm flickering glow. The light was just bright enough for her to make out the symbols on an astrology chart on the side wall of the tent. Esmerelda seemed to be framed by feathered dreamcatchers that were hanging behind her. A large purple amethyst crystal was positioned on the edge of the table.

'If you don't mind, I would like you to read my palm. I'm not really into tarot. It's too much like heavy occult for my liking.'

Esmerelda drew breath, scooped up the cards into a deck and placed them on the table next to her crystal.

'You are very beautiful. I see your mother is Vietnamese. What is your name?'

'My name is Celia. Good guess, Esmerelda. My mother is part Vietnamese and part Anglo-Australian. What's your background?'

'My parents are English even though I grew up in Portugal's Algarve region. I suppose you could say I'm a gypsy.'

'You are very pretty, Esmerelda. So, what else do you know about me?'

'Please, Celia, place your right hand on the table.' She touched the back of Celia's hand with her fingertips. 'Your skin is both firm and silky,' she said. 'You are determined, with a sensitive side. Now turn your hand over so I can see your palm.'

Celia turned her hand over and spread her fingers slightly.

'That's good,' Esmerelda said. 'A willingness to spread your fingers indicates that you are open to new possibilities. I see that your palm is oblong, and your fingers are long and slender. You have what is called a water hand.'

'I do like surfing. I was at the beach just yesterday.'

'Maybe so, but the principal interpretation is that people with the water hand are usually creative and love the company of others. They appear outwardly confident but often suffer anxiety.'

I've been freaking out ever since Miriam left, Celia thought.

Esmerelda traced the horizontal line closest to Celia's fingers with her ringed forefinger. 'This is the heart line. I see that it is broken. Has there been trouble or loss in your life?'

Celia looked at Esmerelda and sighed. 'My husband Noah committed suicide about a year ago. I suppose that's why I'm here. I would like to know about the future.'

Esmerelda gave her a reassuring smile. 'The heart line will probably rejoin when you settle down again.'

Esmerelda touched the area under Celia's forefinger. 'I see that you have two relationship lines. Do you have a new love in your life?'

Celia momentarily looked into Esmerelda's eyes before looking down.

'There is a guy I really like. His name is Toby. Do you think I have a future with him?'

Esmerelda placed her fingertips on the purple crystal and closed her eyes.'

'Perhaps, but I see there is someone else who loves you too.'

I'm not telling her about Felicity, was Celia's immediate thought.

Esmerelda refocused her attention on Celia's palm and traced her finger along another crease that ran across the middle of her hand from right to left.

'This is your head line. See how it curves downwards. It indicates that you have creative potential. Now, the pad at the base of your thumb is known as the 'Mount of Venus'.'

Esmerelda pushed lightly against the muscle and watched the reflex as she released the pressure.

'A raised and reflexive Mount of Venus suggests that you are sensual and passionate, and this line at the base of the Mount is the life line.'

'Do I have much time left to live?' Celia asked.

Esmerelda smiled reassuringly. 'I can't answer that question, but I can tell you that a life line that sweeps broadly across the palm like yours does, means that you have a lot of life in you. Your destiny line is unbroken, and it intersects with your heart line.'

Esmerelda traced a crease that ran up the middle of Celia's palm.

'You are destined to find love. These small lines perpendicular to the relationship line are the children lines. You have two of them. Is there anything else you need to know?'

Celia slowly processed the prediction. *I suppose it's not out of the question*, she thought. 'Yes, how can I pay you? We have tins of baked beans back in the car and some cash. I'll have to drop it back to you. Is that okay?'

'My philosophy is give and you shall receive. I know I will see you again in the future.'

I wonder, is she having me on?

Celia walked out of the darkness of the tent into the late afternoon sunshine and skipped over towards a little stage on the edge of the market where a small band was playing. She could see Toby's tall figure standing at the back of the small crowd of onlookers.

Will we really be an item?

As she approached the crowd, she saw Felicity's familiar figure walking towards her with her red curls bouncing off her shoulders. She was carrying a six-pack of beer and a blanket.

'Hi Celia. Buster gave me some of his beers. Let's watch the band.'

They both ran up behind Toby and took him by surprise, wrapping their arms around him and pulling him to the ground, all three laughing as they rolled in the dust.

The jug band was hitting their straps in the middle of a set as the friends ripped open their cans of beer, spraying foam over each other. Felicity stood up and started dancing, and soon the three of them were kicking up their heels, holding hands and jumping about as the band played and the last rays of the day began to disappear into the long shadows.

The band finished their last bracket in the twilight and began to pack up before the night closed in.

'I'm hungry, but I'm too tired to cook,' Celia said, admiring the market stalls that were festooned with an endless variety of candlelit lanterns and lamps.

'There are still some apples and pears left on the fruit stall,' Toby said, 'That'll do me.'

Felicity produced a wad of banknotes that she had concealed in her underwear, and they wandered over and bought the last pieces of fruit left on display.

They gorged themselves on the fruit as they walked back to the campsite.

'I'm exhausted,' Celia said.

'Me too. It's been a long day,' Toby added.

'Well, I'm going to take a bottle of red and kick on with Buster,' Felicity said. 'I'll see you two in the morning.'

Celia and Toby watched until Felicity had disappeared into Buster's RV with a bottle of wine, before they opened the flap of their tent and crawled inside.

In the dark, Celia pulled off her tee shirt, unclipped her bra and threw it off before reclining on the foam mat in her shorts.

Toby threw his tee shirt and pants in the corner and lay down alongside her, pressing his smooth bare chest against her breasts.

His face was close enough for her to draw in his breath and she leaned in towards him until their lips touched. Then she kissed him again, this time openly on the mouth until their tongues danced together.

He tastes just like I dreamed he would, she thought.

Her heart was racing as she succumbed to the heady aromatic cocktail of their sweat. She felt Toby's penis harden against her through the fabric of her shorts as he gently slid his fingers across her belly and then under the fabric. She drew breath, summoning the strength to wrest her mind away from the moist tingling response of her lower body to his touch. She lifted her hand and placed her forefinger on his lips.

'Patience, Toby,'

'Why, what's wrong? Don't you want me?'

'You know I do. But first, I need to know if you're willing to give me what I need.'

Toby pulled away slightly, being just old enough to know it would be unwise to appear overly forceful.

'Toby, I want you to give me a new life.'

Toby suppressed his frustration and sat up. 'You're not holding out on me because of Felicity, are you?'

'No, of course not. Leave Felicity to me. You don't need to worry about her.'

Toby leant down and kissed Celia lightly on the lips. She rolled on her back to whip off her shorts, then back again on her side to savour the feel of his long naked torso and legs. Toby slid his hand over the curve of her waist and pushed his fingertips under the firm cheek of her swimmer's bottom. He pulled her hips against his, and she gasped as they intertwined. Her lips parted and he kissed her over and over again and then surprised her, by sucking her tongue into his mouth. Celia arched her back as she tasted him and her vulva welled up against the shaft of his aching erection. Toby felt his response spiralling out of his grasp and pulled away to inhale a lungful of air, and to bite his lip, which steadied his pounding heart.

'Are you okay?' she said.

'I just need to know this is what you want.'

'I know you know what I'm like.' She rolled on her back, the palms of her hands pushed against the soft rubber of the sleeping mat while she focused on the lights of the showground, an orange halo around the billowing roof of the tent oscillating in the breeze.

Toby held the soft warm skin of her petite breast with his trembling hand and ran his tongue in circles around the ridge of her areola until the tingling sensation hardened her nipple. Then he shifted his bodyweight to his forearms, and as they moved in parallel, she cried out, reached down, and guided him inside her, drawing him into her curling wave of energy and soft wet flesh. Sets of spasms, far apart at first, quickened, clustered, and rolled through her belly as he rocked back and forth, until her moaning began. At last Toby cast aside the last vestiges of his restraint to inundate her in a deluge of pleasure, tears, and then they were both laughing.

As their heartbeats slowed, he rolled back onto his side and ran his fingers through her hair.

'Toby, can I ask you a personal question?'

'Sure. Sounds serious.'

'What will your song be about?'

'Our journey. Do you want to hear the first verse?'

'Fire away.'

Toby sat up and gathered himself.

Traipse along with me until we're free of these abandoned cities

Let's wander with the wind

The trappings of architects are now relics of the age

Push deep into the belly of the wave

Hang suspended, let the breakers break away

Swim towards the light and broach the surface in the sun

To catch our breaths as we catch the moment.

'So, it's about us surfing?'

'Yes.'

'And is there a chorus?'

Toby inhaled and momentarily held his breath.

Cloudless, unforeseen,

Our dance seems surreal

Past and future are one and the same

Our country has patience and time.

'It's beautiful! You're a keeper,' Celia said with a smile before rolling over on her side with her back to him.

'Couldn't have said it better myself.'

Toby sat and waited for Celia to slip off to sleep before, fully satiated, he stretched out on his back and, with high expectations of Celia being by his side in his life ahead, he drifted into dreamland.

On the robot trail

Felicity stood at the edge of the Stow Lake in Haight-Ashbury, San Francisco, watching a small boy launch a toy sailboat. She sat still as it cut through the ripples that glistened in the afternoon sun – until she was wrenched out of her dream by a guttural growling snore.

Where on earth am I and what is that infernal cacophony? It must be that Phil Beatty snoring again. Doesn't he ever give it a rest?

Momentarily disoriented, she pulled herself up on her elbows before she realised that she was in Buster's RV. She tore back the top sheet and was relieved to find that she was still wearing her jeans and a tee shirt. Buster was up the other end of the van, oblivious to his racket.

'Buster! Wake up mate. That snoring is equivalent to a magnitude five earthquake.'

With a snort, Buster came to. 'Sorry, love. I can even hear myself snoring in my sleep. It's why I married a robot. My first wife couldn't handle the bloody noise and walked out. Maybe that's what sent the robot packing too. Anyway, did you get some sleep?'

Felicity sat on the edge of the bunk. *I feel quite queasy*, she thought. 'We didn't do anything stupid, did we?'

Buster roared with laughter. 'I wish, but I'm well past it these days. Your friends tucked themselves into that little tent, and you came around with a bottle of red, complaining that you couldn't get comfortable in the back of the Landcruiser. We knocked off the red, and you crashed out in the spare bunk. If you feel like breakfast, I traded two tins of baked beans for some fresh eggs and a loaf of bread over at the market yesterday, so I could do eggs on toast.'

'Sounds perfect, Buster. I'll go and rouse the two lovebirds next door.'

Felicity walked out the door of the van and stood in the early morning sun. A light mist had settled over the showground, but Felicity knew it had the makings of a hot day. She wandered over to the tent behind the Landcruiser. 'This is your captain speaking. It's time to get up and get ready for breakfast at Buster's.'

Muffled groans emanated from the tent in response.

'Can't we sleep in for once?' Celia asked in her little girl voice.

'Not if you want to eat. Come on, get moving, you two.'

Felicity walked back and found Buster cooking up a feast of eggs, toast and coffee on his gas cooker. 'More for us if they don't show,' she said.

Celia and Toby appeared in hoodies and pants and sat in Buster's spare director's chairs. He poured coffee from a blackened pot into mugs, and Toby passed them around. Celia helped to plate up the eggs on toast, and they sat under the awning of the van, balancing the plates on their knees. Toby finished off his coffee.

'Thanks for breakfast, Buster. By the way, any suggestions where we can get some diesel?'

Buster nodded. 'There's a guy who carries it in jerry cans in the back of an old Dodge truck. He's parked over near the gate. He charges like a wounded bull, though. One litre per tin of beans, unless you've got cash. Then you can negotiate.'

Felicity collected the plates and put them in a bucket. Buster took over. 'Leave this with me. You lot need to hit the road and track down those rogue robots. By the way, you can use the shower in the van if you make it snappy.'

After breakfast, they took turns using the shower in Buster's van, then packed up and resumed their positions in the Land-cruiser. Felicity called out to Buster through the open window.

'Thanks for everything, Buster. You're a sweetheart.'

'Go get 'em! And Felicity, if you see that robot wife of mine, tell her I still love her, and I'm here waiting.'

After stopping at the gate to negotiate with the diesel dealer, they filled the tank and drove back out onto the Bruce High-way and headed north. It had been far too early for the fortune teller to be open for business, so Celia figured she could pay her 'next time'.

As the hours floated away, the road became monotonously straight. Felicity found herself driving into a distant shimmering mirage as the temperature escalated. Heat radiated through the windscreen into the cabin, creating a soporific effect. Felicity yawned constantly, and more than once, caught herself drifting into a microsleep. Celia was asleep in the passenger seat, and Toby had flaked out in the back. Felicity gave Celia a nudge with her left hand.

'Wake up, navigator. You've deserted your post.'

Celia stretched and yawned. 'Why doesn't the road go by

the beach?'

By this time, Toby was awake. 'There are no beaches north of Fraser Island. The Great Barrier Reef blocks the swell from the ocean, so the coast is just mudflats. I guess that's why the road goes inland.'

'Toby, you're very knowledgeable when it comes to geography,' Felicity said, looking at him in the rear-view mirror through her sunglasses.

'Well, I'm a Queenslander.'

'OK then, tell me why there are no palm trees? I have been looking at nothing but scrub for hours.'

'These are the dry tropics. The wet tropics don't start until all the way up at Hinchinbrook Island, so get used to it. There's still a long way to go.'

A speed sign flashed by, and Felicity braked gently. 'There's a 60-zone coming up, it must be a town.'

Celia unfolded Niall's enormous map of Queensland, ran her finger up the red line of the Bruce Highway and announced, 'This must be Childers'.

Felicity slowed down and parked the Landcruiser outside the grand Victorian-era Federal Hotel. The hotel was a substantial building with a pitched roof made of red corrugated iron and yellow tiled walls at street level. Dogs lay sleeping in the shade of the wide overhanging wrap-around verandah that was supported by tall white columns and ornamental panels of matching wrought iron lacework under the handrail. The first floor was flanked by long signs advertising XXX Beer.

They stepped out of the car and lingered momentarily in the shade of the verandah before leaving the oppressive heat of the street and walking into the breezy cool of the public bar.

Toby and Celia headed to the toilets while Felicity ordered

drinks from an older woman with a tanned weathered face.

'Power's still out, love, so I can't pour you a coldie, but welcome to Childers. What'll it be?'

Felicity sat with her feet on the rung of the bar stool. 'Two glasses of Shiraz and a glass of water, please. By the way, did the robots come through here?'

The woman pulled out two wine glasses and cracked the screw top off a bottle of the house wine.

'Bloody robots. Just about ruined me, they have. Sure, they came through. The whole town turned out to watch the parade. They didn't expect all our robots would down tools and join them. No one saw that coming but at least the outage got the kids off their bloody phones. Where are you headed?'

Celia and Toby came back from the bathroom and joined Felicity at the bar.

'We're on the trail of the robots, wherever that leads us,' Celia said, taking a sip of red wine.

'Jesus, be careful. Folks have been coming through here on their way down the coast. They say Rockhampton's burning. Rioting and looting, they say. I'd steer clear of it, but I hear that people are camping out at the raceway on the other side of town if you have to stop tonight.'

It was Felicity's turn to use the bathroom. Celia waited until she'd disappeared behind the toilet door before moving along the bar towards Toby to cuddle up next to him.

'So, what's the second verse?'

'You must be some kind of clairvoyant 'cause I just finished working it out in my head as I was lying on the back seat. Ready?'

'Lay it on me.'

Toby took a deep breath and leaned in towards her as he spoke.

Highways intersect where questions lie, long forgotten
And we answer to ourselves
What must become of who we were and who we are, and how
we will be?
I see the landscape of our minds
Laid bare at the foothills infinite
And every afternoon
The wind howls in the catacombs
Wailing truths for us all in dust that blows forever…

Celia let Toby's words hang in the air while she contemplated their meaning. 'Is this verse about our time on the road?'

'Basically, yes.'

'It seems to me you're saying that we're taking control of our future. Which, in a way, we are. I suppose you could argue that we're all made of dust.'

'It's an idea a bloke called Lionel gave me before I left Mount Garnet. He's one of my mob, and I'm beginning to realise he makes a lot of sense.'

Celia rested her forearms on the bar and clasped her hands. 'What's it like living in a country town?'

Toby pushed his waist against her hip. 'It's like everybody's business is everybody's business, if you know what I mean.'

'Not really. I'm such a city girl. I don't even know who lives in the apartment next door. Maybe one day you can show me around. You could even introduce me to Colleen and Joyce.'

Toby laughed, took her hand, and traced the lines on the palm of her hand with his forefinger. His soft touch made her feel very receptive.

'That would blow their minds 'cause they're always saying I'm too shy.'

Celia was surprised. 'You're joking right? You don't seem

too shy when you're up on stage in front of a crowd, and you haven't been too shy with me.'

Toby nuzzled into her hair with his nose and breathed in to catch her scent, which unleashed an unexpected wave of joy inside him. He put his hands around her bum and lifted her until her feet were off the floor before slowly setting her back down.

'I didn't think I needed anyone in my life until I met you,' he said.

Celia buried her face in his curly locks. 'And I thought I could go it alone after Noah died until I met Felicity.'

Toby pulled back. 'What is it with you and her?'

Celia wrapped her fingers around his wrist and looked up into his eyes. 'I think, the real question is, what is it with you and me?'

Toby was about to reply when Felicity returned from the bathroom jangling the car keys.

'Ready to hit the road, you two? I want to get settled into wherever we're going before sunset.'

They thanked the woman behind the bar and walked back out to the car. It was sweltering, and the old Landcruiser pre-dated air conditioning.

Celia looked limp. 'I shouldn't drink in the afternoon. I have a headache and need a nap. Can I swap with Toby?'

'It's my turn to drive,' Toby said.

Felicity tossed the keys to Toby and sat in the passenger seat so Celia could flake out in the back. As the Landcruiser picked up speed, Celia fell asleep dreaming of stardust blowing forever across Toby's infinite tablelands.

Rockhampton Raceway

A sign that read TROPIC OF CAPRICORN flashed by as Toby drove headlong into a shimmering mirage. On the outskirts of Rockhampton, ominous plumes of black smoke wafted skywards across the horizon. He slowed down and wound his way through an obstacle course of abandoned vehicles that littered the streets. A group of young men were loitering on the Fitzroy River bridge up ahead. Two of them bared their buttocks while the others shouted obscenities and gave them the bird as they drove past. It was just on dusk when a billboard loomed up ahead. It read, 'ROCKHAMPTON RACEWAY SATURDAY NIGHT DEMOLITION DERBY TURN RIGHT 200M.'

I have a bad feeling about this, Toby thought.

Even so, he turned and drove in through the wide-open gates of the raceway. The driveway on either side of the entrance was lined with makeshift tables laden with jerry cans and glass jars. Several young men waved them down.

'These guys are spruiking fuel,' Toby said. 'One spark and we'll be blown to kingdom come.'

'Or to hell,' was Felicity's view.

Toby pulled up and wound down the window as one of the fuel

dealers walked over. He was wearing a grimy black death-metal tee shirt and oil-stained ripped jeans and black boots.

'Hi, mate. How much is a can of diesel?' Toby asked.

The man placed both hands on the window frame, leaned in and eyeballed Toby.

'It's three hundred bucks for a jar. It's quality gear. Cash only or fuck off.'

Felicity weighed into the conversation.

'We'll take as much as we can fit in the tank. We'll pay cash, just don't light us up in the process.'

They all stood back from the vehicle as the fuel dealer filled up the Landcruiser with diesel from a jerry can. Felicity peeled off the banknotes and waited while the man counted the money, before she joined the others in the Landcruiser and Toby slowly drove off down the track towards the raceway.

Hundreds of marooned recreational vehicles were parked side by side. Hordes of young men and women were rambling about aimlessly. Hoons were doing circle-work in an old ute, revving it around and around relentlessly.

'Must be a stolen car as it seems like they don't give a shit about the price of petrol,' Toby observed.

The crowd was drunk and stoned. Faces peered and leered in the windows as they crawled along. A van up ahead did a burn-out with its handbrake on until it disappeared in a cloud of dust and smoking tyres. Toby pulled up in a spare car space.

'I can't say that I get the appeal of this place,' Felicity said.

Toby surveyed the scene. 'I get the feeling that it's the only show in town.'

Leaning forward from the back seat, Celia put it bluntly. 'I'm scared. Let's get out of here.'

'Trouble is, it's already dark,' Felicity said, unclipping her seatbelt. 'Mackay is a solid three hours' drive, and we've been on the road all day. Let's take a look around first.'

They left the Landcruiser to walk among the intoxicated revellers. At the centre of the site, as advertised, the Saturday night demolition derby was underway. The roar of unmuffled engines was deafening. Young men and women were leaning over the barricades, cheering on battered hot rods and old sedans as they repeatedly rammed their opponents until the panels dropped off. One car veered out of control and rolled over before a hot rod t-boned into its side then immediately reversed. The car's driver managed to escape the vehicle just as it exploded in a fireball and he rolled on the ground to extinguish the flames while the other driver, seeming oblivious to the plight of his rival, had also jumped out and he ran a victory lap in front of the crowd.

'Loser!' a voice shouted from the crowd of eager onlookers who carried on carousing and drinking.

Felicity turned to Toby and Celia and yelled, 'That's the last straw. We're out of here.'

As they hurried back towards the car, they were confronted by two muscular young men wearing thongs and dressed in printed 'Bintang Beer' singlets and shorts. The tallest of the two had a matted, brown shoulder-length mullet and the other man had an unkempt beard and the name 'Nicky' tattooed on his forearm. They sneered at Toby.

'Punching above your weight, aren't you mate? the mullet man goaded him.

Toby wedged himself between Celia, Felicity and the thugs.

'Those two must be sluts if they're hanging with this fuckwit,' the bearded man said.

Felicity shouted, 'You bastard! How dare you call us that!'

'Don't be like that, sweetheart,' the mullet man said as he

pushed Toby aside and grabbed Felicity around her waist.

'Fuck off,' she shouted as she kneed him in the balls. She jumped back, watching him fall to his knees in agony.

Toby raised his fists in the on-guard stance of a boxer. Being a 'southpaw', he was ready to lead with his left. 'Make a run for it and I'll see you back at the car. I'll sort out these arseholes,' he shouted at Felicity and Celia.

But they stood stock still from fear.

The bearded man took a swing at Toby with his right fist, narrowly missing his head as Toby ducked. Having failed to land a knockout punch, the guy momentarily teetered off balance and spun around. Toby stuck his right leg out and caught his opponent's ankle, tripping him up so he fell flat on his back in the dust.

'Run!' Toby shouted as he bolted back towards the crowd.

Felicity and Celia screamed, then ran in the direction of the car as both men picked themselves up off the ground, cursing and shouting expletives.

'Fucking morons!' Toby bellowed as he gave the men the bird to draw their attention away from Felicity and Celia who were running away in the opposite direction. It worked, and both men charged off furiously in pursuit of Toby.

When Felicity and Celia reached the car they stood for a moment, trying to catch their breath.

'What if they kill Toby?' Celia said, bursting into tears.

Felicity took charge as usual. 'Get in the car,' she said, opening the door to jump in the driver's seat and turning the key in the ignition. With Celia in the front passenger seat, they sat in silence, listening to the sound of the idling motor. Soon a figure appeared, running back from the crowd with two men in hot pursuit.

'Look! There! It's Toby!' Celia screamed.

Toby pulled up, turned around, swung his fist, and stunned the mullet man with an uppercut under his jaw. In an instant, he kicked the bearded guy with the tattoo in the balls and bolted towards the car. He reefed open the back door and dived in as Felicity floored the accelerator. Wheels spinning, they accelerated towards the entry gate, narrowly missing a group who jumped out of the path of the Landcruiser at the last moment. The car turned back onto the Bruce Highway and sped off into the night.

Felicity checked the rear-view mirror to make sure they weren't being followed.

'Toby, are you okay? That was some close call,' Celia murmured, leaning over to look at him in the back seat.

'I'm fine, just a few scratches. I hope that 'Niky' wasn't expecting any action tonight because her boyfriend's nuts must be black and blue.'

After driving for half an hour, their adrenalin had subsided, and they all felt exhausted. It was starting to rain, so Felicity turned on the windscreen wipers.

'How about we just pull up somewhere and camp for the night,' Toby said.

She slowed down, and they peered into the darkness until they spotted a side road where she turned the car off the highway and onto a dirt track. A small clearing appeared in the headlights, and they pulled in.

'This will have to do. Toby, you set up the tent for yourself and Celia while we get the baked beans and biscuits ready for dinner. I suppose I'll have to sleep in the back seat,' Felicity said.

Toby turned on the headlights of the Landcruiser and set about assembling the tent and the three of them stood at the back of the car and ate cold baked beans and biscuits in the light rain. Felicity passed around what was left of her bottle of bourbon.

'I don't know about you two but I'm ready for bed. It's not every day I get mugged at a demolition derby,' Toby said. 'Night Felicity. Coming, Celia?'

'I'll clean up,' Felicity said. 'Night, both of you.'

Celia opened the flap of the tent, crawled inside and unrolled the foam underlay. Toby waited until she had unpacked the double sleeping bag before crawling in and zipping up the fly mesh behind him. They laid back on top of the sleeping bag in their tee shirts and underwear.

'Where did they get you?' Celia said.

'I'll have a few bruises in the morning, I reckon. All I could think about was making sure they didn't get their hands on you.'

'Well, maybe tonight will inspire your third verse.'

'I'm thinking I need a bridge and then I'll segue back into a final chorus, but I'm no Archie Roach.'

'Don't sell yourself short. The first two verses are a perfect reflection of what we've had to endure. You'll have to teach me the words so I can remember them.'

Celia propped herself up on one elbow. Toby was still sweaty from the fight.

'You need a shower, but you're still cute,' Celia said. She placed her hand on Toby's belly as she kissed him openly on the mouth and was just beginning to slip her fingers under his boxer shorts elastic when the Landcruiser door slammed, and there was rustling outside the tent.

'I'm coming in. I can't get comfortable in that bloody back seat and I'm afraid of the dark.' Felicity unzipped the flywire to crawl in through the flap of the tent.

Celia reacted instantly. 'Now I've heard everything! Come

in, then, and make it quick. There are enough mozzies in here already. Sleep next to me. Pooh, you need a shower too.'

Felicity squashed up between Celia and the side wall of the tent. 'In case you hadn't noticed, we're not exactly shacked up at the Hilton Hotel. Good night Little Miss Perfect, and you too, Toby,'

'Night, Felicity,' Celia and Toby whispered in unison.

The three friends drifted off together to the sound of mosquitoes singing incessantly in the tropical heat outside the flywire, and the soft pitter-patter of rain on the nylon roof of the tent.

Wet tropics

The tropical heat inside the tent at sunrise was oppressive. They were all wide awake and uncomfortable.

Felicity worried out loud. 'I need to go to the bathroom, and I bet there's a snake out there waiting for me.'

'Come on,' Celia said as she got up and crawled on all fours to unzip the fly mesh. She pulled on her black shorts and thongs and continued crawling into the cooler humidity outside the tent. She stood and paused to enjoy the fresh air before walking over to the Landcruiser to retrieve a roll of toilet paper from the box of camping equipment.

Felicity emerged from the tent wearing the red boxer shorts and the tee shirt she had slept in and looked at the toilet roll Celia was holding. Celia offered it to Felicity, who accepted it with some reticence.

'This is why I hate camping,' Felicity said, before putting on her thongs and heading off in the direction of a nearby rock outcrop.

As soon as she was gone, Toby crawled out of the tent, stood up, stretched, and took the opportunity to give Celia a hug and a kiss.

'Morning you. I thought I was going to have you all to myself until Felicity crashed the party,' Toby said.

Celia hugged him back. 'Our time will come.' She pressed her ear against his chest to listen to his heartbeat as the sound of the creatures of the bush throbbed around them in the rising heat. 'Help me find the fire starters, and let's see if we can make some tea.'

Toby stood beside Celia as she rummaged around in the box of camping equipment. 'It's like you two have a sort of weird love-hate relationship.'

Celia held up the packet of fire starters and a packet of Redhead matches. 'Don't be jealous. I know she's a bit fiery, but she's well-intentioned and gives me a lot of support.'

'I reckon I could give you that,' Toby said.

Celia shot him a glance, put down the matches and cupped her hand around Toby's ear. 'I reckon you're right,' she whispered.

Toby wrapped his arm behind Celia's back, pulled her into him and kissed her. She let the packet of fire starters fall to the ground and twisted his long matted curls between her fingers, holding him tight as she yielded to the salty taste of his tongue. She would easily have given in completely to the ripples of pleasure Toby was causing her to feel, as they intensified below her belly. But just then a pair of kookaburras began to cackle in the distance and she pulled away.

Celia looked into his eyes. 'Toby, what if I told you that I wanted a family?'

Toby placed his hands on her hips and looked at her with a serious expression. 'That's fine with me.'

Celia held his gaze long enough to be sure of his sincerity. 'Maybe we should get the fire started before Felicity gets back,' she said.

'We already have,' Toby replied with a laugh.

By the time Felicity returned, flames were licking at the sides of the billy, and Celia had pulled out the last of the provisions.

Felicity's expression was morose. 'Baked beans and biscuits for breakfast again, I see.'

'Well, you can thank Miriam for stocking up the larder. At least we're not going to starve. I wonder where we'll end up today?'

Toby pulled the billy off the fire and poured hot black tea into their mugs.

'Who knows? Maybe today's the day we finally catch up with the robots,' Toby said.

Felicity stared into her mug of tea. 'I'd be happy to just track down a nice hot bath and a glass of champagne.'

Toby and Celia dismantled the tent before taking turns to head off in different directions with the toilet roll. Felicity packed the car, lit a cigarette and sat in the driver's seat until everyone was ready to go.

'All set?'

'Yes, Mum. Hey, I haven't seen you light up since we left Scotts Head. Are you trying to quit because of us?' Celia asked.

'Maybe, but it's not all about you,' Felicity muttered as she held the cigarette between her lips and reversed the Landcruiser back onto the dirt road. She knew this was her best chance to give up smoking but wouldn't say it out loud.

They re-joined the Bruce Highway and headed north. The driving was relentless. Vast stretches of straight road numbed Felicity's mind as she drove onwards in the stupefying heat. In the town of Sarine, when they stopped to check that they were still on track she handed the wheel to Toby. They dashed through the backstreets of Mackay without stopping.

Unlike in Rockhampton, all seemed calm, but they agreed they didn't want to take any chances. Hours later, they quenched their thirst and used the facilities at a hotel in Bowen before hitting the road again. They skirted around the city centre of Townsville, which like Mackay, seemed to be quiet and languid in the afternoon sun of the dry tropics. Then they made their way through the smoky, smouldering golden fields of sugar cane outside Ingham.

A petite diesel sugar cane train rocked its way along a narrow-gauge track that ran parallel to the road. A group of locals sitting in an open carriage gave them a wave. Toby waved back.

'I guess if your electric vehicle has stopped dead in its tracks, the old sugar cane train is a way to get around – as long as you have a track to where you want to go. Some of those engines have been in use since the Second World War, so they'd be unaffected by the blackout.'

'Well, at least some people seem to have found a new normal,' Celia said.

As Toby had predicted, as soon as they passed Hinchinbrook Island, north of the sugar town of Ingham, the bush finally gave way to the lush green of the wet tropics of Far North Queensland.

In the twilight, they caught sight of the rusting dormant smokestacks of the Tully Sugar Refinery encircled by a myriad of converging train tracks. Lush green and dry brown stands of cane lay nestled among the fingers of a densely vegetated escarpment. On the right was a sign that read, 'TULLY MOTEL 200M'.

'Let's try our luck,' Felicity said.

Toby turned into the sweeping gravel driveway and pulled up under the portico outside reception.

They climbed out of the Landcruiser and stretched their legs.

Venetian blinds hanging in the windows and doors of the reception area had been lowered and pulled shut, masking the interior.

Felicity tried to open the main door, only to find that it was locked.

'Maybe they closed up and left town,' Celia said.

Felicity rapped on the glass several times. After a few minutes, there was movement inside. Two slats of the venetians parted, and an eye peered at them through the glass. First came the sound of the lock turning, then a stocky man with a close-trimmed black beard opened the door and let them in.

'Evening all, welcome to the wettest town in Australia. You're one of the lucky few who have a working vehicle. I'm keeping the door locked as I've been held up at gunpoint twice already. The situation is getting desperate. You lot look friendly enough. How can I help?'

Felicity leaned on the counter.

'Mate, we're certainly not here to rip you off. Have you got any spare rooms?'

'Well, I hope you're all related as I have one room left, and it only has a king-sized bed. A lot of people are stranded in town, so the place is full.'

Felicity rubbed the nape of her neck.

'We're getting used to sharing. We'll take it,' she said, looking at the others for acknowledgement. 'We've travelled up from Rocky. My name is Felicity, and this is Celia and Toby.'

'Welcome to Tully. I'm Bob Scott. You'll need to pay upfront though – with cash – though we might have the power back on tomorrow. The word is they're getting close to getting the grid back up. What brings you up here?'

'We're on the trail of the robots. They've brought my business to its knees.'

'You and everyone else. Well, you've come to the right place. The rumour is that the robots went up into Tully Gorge. The locals reckon that anyone who goes up there looking for them doesn't come back. But I reckon that's just a bar-room tale. I'd be careful just the same, if you know what I mean. I'm not trying to scare you or nothing.'

Bob pulled a room key from the key safe and pushed it over the counter to Felicity.

'If you're hungry, my wife makes a sweet ratatouille. Our veggie patch loves the tropics.'

Celia's eyes lit up. 'Yes, please – we're starving,' she said as she wrapped an arm around Toby's waist and pulled their hips together.

'Can you find us a bottle of red too, Bob?' Felicity asked.

'Sure can. The house red beats warm beer, hands down. We have solar hot water, so you'll get a hot shower but don't stay in all night. There are candles and a lighter in the room if the torch batteries have gone flat.'

After saying goodnight to Bob, they hopped back in the car and parked outside the room.

'Now I really am scared,' Celia said. 'What if the robots kill us all when we find them? I don't like the sound of those people going missing,'

'Let's hope we have Miriam in our corner,' Felicity reassured her, flashing her a smile before opening the door. 'Come on you two, I need a drink.'

Toby brought the bags through while Felicity and Celia

opened the balcony door for some air and lit the candles.

Celia took Toby by the hand.

'Let's save some of Bob's hot water and have a shower together.'

Felicity put her hands on her hips and feigned displeasure.

'Fine, see if I care. I'll just sit here and eat all the ratatouille and polish off the red on my own – if it ever shows up.'

'You're a big girl, and there's only room for two,' Celia said, pulling Toby into the bathroom.

Fifteen minutes later, there was a knock at the front door. Felicity opened it to find a large woman in an apron standing outside with dinner on a tray and a bottle of wine. Felicity took it inside and set it out on the little balcony, which was screened off to keep the mosquitoes at bay. She inspected the wine label, found some wine glasses and was just pouring herself a drink when Celia and Toby appeared, both wearing Toby's tee shirts and boxer shorts.

'Your turn,' Celia said.

'I'll have a shower after dinner. Wine Toby?'

'I don't drink, but I'll settle for a glass of Tully water. I hear it's a good drop. Jeez, those tomatoes and eggplant smell awesome,' Toby said as he stood up and filled his glass from the tap above the sink.

They all clinked their glasses and hoed into Mrs Scott's ratatouille. Celia sat back in her chair.

'I'm exhausted, so I can imagine how you two feel after all that driving. Do you really think we'll find Miriam and the sentient intelligence tomorrow?' Celia asked.

Felicity took a sip of her wine and pursed her lips. '"AYE" can't be that bloody intelligent if you ask me. No offence, Toby, but it must be a man. Look at all the chaos it's caused.'

'Must be a white man if you ask me. No blackfella would ever mess the place up this bad.'

They sat in the humid tropical evening as the insect population of cicadas and mosquitoes chirped and throbbed outside the flywire. A shower of rain roared through, leaving a lingering cloud of water vapour. All too soon, they finished the bottle. Celia stood up.

'I don't know about you two, but I'm off to bed,' Celia said.

'Yeah, I'm knackered,' Toby agreed.

Felicity headed for the shower while Celia found an extra pillow and set it out on the bed before dropping her shorts on the floor and jumping on the bed in her tee shirt and panties to claim the middle position. Toby took off his shirt and laid down next to her in his shorts.

Celia kissed him on the ear before propping herself up on one elbow to kiss him on the lips.

'This is my spot,' Celia said. 'I can't have you sleeping next to Felicity.

'Lights out, you lot,' Felicity said at the top of her voice from inside the bathroom.

Without a word, Toby reached over to the bedside table, licked his fingers, snuffed out the candle and waited for his eyes to adjust to the darkness.

Felicity slid in alongside Celia.

'You smell of shampoo, and you've still got wet hair!' Celia said as she rolled onto her side, facing Toby.

'Don't complain, at least I'm not all hot and sweaty like last night,' Felicity said.

Celia felt Felicity's soft curvaceous form spoon around her bum as she lay in the dark.

'Stop breathing on the back of my neck,' Celia said.

'Do you really mind?'

Celia exhaled and left the question in suspense for a moment as she tried fruitlessly to deny her racing heartbeat and the moist tingling response below her belly, lying between two people she knew really cared for her.

'I suppose I'm getting used to having you in my bed. Just don't wriggle about. Good night.'

Celia nestled into Toby's muscular torso and slowly slid her hand inside his boxer shorts to gauge his response to her answer.

Tully Gorge

Felicity woke up and carefully untangled herself from the sheets, and the sleeping bodies of her friends who were sprawled across the bed. She walked into the bathroom, ran the shower and leant over the vanity basin so she could splash water on her face. Then she looked up and fell into the gaze of her own green eyes in the mirror as she pulled her red curls away from her forehead with her fingers. Still barely awake, she dreamily admired her reflection until the spell was broken by a knock at the front door.

She quickly wrapped a towel around herself, walked back into the bedroom, where Celia and Toby were still sound asleep, and rummaged around in her bag until she found a tank top and boxer shorts. She pulled them on and opened the door to find Mrs Scott standing outside holding a box of cornflakes and a jug of milk.

'Breakfast love. I'm sorry, but it's all we've got until we get the power back on. Bowls are in the cupboard next to the mini bar.'

Felicity took the cereal and the milk inside and shut the door. Celia and Toby were still unconscious.

'Time to get up, you lot. We've got places to go and intelligence to gather,' Felicity said as she set about looking for the breakfast bowls and spoons.

'Can't we sleep in for once? You kept us up all night wriggling around,' Celia said, covering her head with the top sheet.

'Don't blame me, blame your boyfriend. He was snoring like a trooper.'

Celia pulled the sheet off her face, sat up and gave Toby a shake. 'Are you my boyfriend?' she asked. Toby opened one eye, looked at her smiling at him from under her black fringe and remained silent.

'Let's eat.' Felicity opened the curtains, splashing sunlight across the bed.

Toby squinted and then, as his eyes adjusted, became enchanted with Celia's high cheekbones that were accentuated in the morning light. The two lay looking at each other without blinking as Felicity opened the balcony door and set up breakfast on the table outside.

'Well?' Celia asked.

'You know I am. I just didn't want to say it in front *of her,*' he whispered.

Celia giggled and rested her chin on his chest. 'Maybe you'll just have to man-up,'

Outside, Felicity cleared her throat and began dragging the orange plastic outdoor chairs into position around the table.

'I'd better jump in the shower,' Toby said and swung his legs out of bed and onto the floor.

Once Toby was in the bathroom, Celia got up, put on a fresh pair of underpants and a tee shirt, and walked outside to sit next to Felicity. She sat down, poured herself a bowlful of cornflakes.

'Sorry if Toby kept you awake,' Celia said.

'Trust me, when it comes to chronic snoring, he's no match for Phil Beatty, or that bloody Buster back in Cooroy.'

Felicity looked directly at Celia through her red curls.

'Are you in love with him?'

Celia dropped her spoon in the breakfast bowl and returned her gaze.

'I suppose I am. Toby makes me feel …'

'Yeah, I know. Like I feel about you. Don't worry, I'm not going to get in your way. You need a man in your life and that's just how it is.'

Toby, now showered and dressed in a pair of shorts with no shirt, sat down with them to share in the conversation.

'What were you two talking about?'

'About where we go from here, that's all,' Celia said.

'Celia, it's your turn in the bathroom. Get cracking,' Felicity said.

With bathroom duties over and done with, they all packed their bags and loaded them into the back of the Landcruiser. On the way out, they dropped the key into Bob at reception and drove down the main street of Tully. As soon as they turned onto Tully Gorge Road, the rainforest began to rear up beside them.

'How will we know where to find Miriam?' Celia wondered out loud.

'Any army of robots will leave traces. Once I pick up the trail, I'll find them,' Toby said.

A quaint, freshly painted white timber church came into view. It had a small steeple topped with a weathervane and a single bell. The reverend, resplendent in his black and white robes and dog collar, was vigorously shaking hands with the parishioners.

'I forgot it was Sunday. Let's see if anyone has seen what we're looking for,' Felicity said.

She braked, pulled in and parked the Landcruiser on the vacant lot beside the church that the faithful were using as a makeshift carpark.

'It's a miracle the structure hasn't blown away in a cyclone,' Celia said.

'It's protected from the hand of God by the hand of God, I suppose,' Felicity added.

They lined up behind the other members of the congregation. When their turn came to shake hands with the reverend, he beamed and grasped Felicity's hand.

'Welcome to St. Barnabas. My name is the Reverend Jim McLaren. Are you new in town or just passing through?'

'It's a great turnout, Reverend Jim. Do you always have this many on a Sunday?' Felicity asked.

'I wish. We've been struggling with numbers for years. The march of the robots has changed everything. People are saying it's a sign. Perhaps now they'll finally see the light. Why are you here? Are you seeking communion with the Lord?'

I could use a dose of salvation, Felicity thought. 'These are my friends, Celia and Toby. Yes, we're out to find the truth.'

'Well, you've come to the right place. How can I help?'

'Do you know where the robots were going?' Felicity asked, tilting her head as she swept aside her red curls from her forehead with her index finger.

The Reverend looked alarmed. 'My dear, I caution you against looking for them. This morning we said prayers for three of our congregation who went after them and have not returned. Some say they left the road and went into the bush on a bend in the Tully Gorge Road up near Dingo Pocket.'

'I'm prepared to reserve judgement, Reverend Jim,' Felicity said. 'We've been on their tail for over a week, and we're not giving up now.'

The Reverend raised his hand to bless them.

'Then may the Lord be with you.'

'And also with you, Reverend Jim,' Felicity said.

Felicity, Celia and Toby walked back to the car and hopped in.

'It's like a furnace in here,' Celia said as they wound down the windows to let the heat escape.

'Drive slowly, and I'll keep an eye out,' Toby told Felicity as she started the Landcruiser and drove back out onto the main road, to wind along the floor of the escarpment.

They came upon a sign that read, 'DINGO POCKET'. Felicity slowed to a crawl as Toby craned his neck, looking for clues.

'There! See that! Stop right here,' Toby said.

Felicity jammed on the brakes and stopped. Toby hopped out, crossed the road, and crouched down to inspect the foliage. Felicity and Celia leaned out of the windows and waited until he returned.

'This has to be it. Either that or a herd of water buffalo has been through here recently. Come on, get your walking boots on.'

Felicity parked the Landcruiser off the road, and they sat on the edge of their seats with the car doors open as they laced up their runners.

Bushwalking was never my forte, Felicity thought.

Toby led the way into the bush. Although it was not apparent from the road, it soon became clear that the floor of the forest had been flattened. The trail led them deep into the forest. A dense canopy of branches shielded them from the heat of the day, and a cool moist breeze wafted out of the shade of the giant tree ferns as they walked. Occasionally, Toby would go down on his haunches to inspect the trampled leaves.

'You've done this before,' Celia said.

'I was only young but my father taught me his bush skills and I've remembered a lot. It must have been one hell of a mob that did this,' Toby said, looking up close at a crumpled branch.

As they carried on hiking, the dense bushland gave way to lush green rainforest, and the grade became steeper. Following Toby in single file, they zig-zagged up the incline until the trail ended abruptly facing a large grey industrial roller shutter embedded in a sheer rock wall.

'Can you hear that sound? It's coming from inside,' Celia said.

'Sounds like a machine,' Toby said as he ran his fingertips across the flange of a locked pedestrian door cut into the steel of the roller shutter.

Felicity stared into the camera of a video intercom unit with a single button that was positioned at eye level next to the door. Above the button was a label that read 'PUSH TO CALL RE-CEPTION'.

'I suppose we should push the button,' she said, moving to-wards the intercom unit.

Celia stepped forward. 'No, I'll do it. Miriam is my robot, after all.'

Looking for AYE

Celia stared into the camera and pushed the button on the intercom. It made a shrill ringing sound that ended abruptly with a click, followed by silence.

'My name is Celia Tran, and I'm here to see Miriam.'

There was no response. Celia was about to try again when the lock clicked, and the pedestrian door that was framed within the larger roller shutter opened inwards. A robot with an enormous egg-shaped crystal head stepped out of the darkness and stood in the doorway. Sparks of electricity crackled and arced across the facets of its ovular-shaped head. Celia, Felicity and Toby were mesmerised by the sight of it.

Celia turned away and covered her eyes.

'What have you done with Miriam?'

'Miriam will be with you in just a moment, Ms Tran.'

Celia spread her fingers apart just in time to see the head dissolve into a dark yellow jelly, which reshaped and congealed into a familiar face with a yellow beehive hairdo.

'How can I be of assistance, Ms Tran?'

'Miriam! Is it really you! I thought you were gone forever!'
Celia said, rushing over and hugging Miriam, who emitted a

pink glow. 'We're here to see "I" or "AYE."'

'Of course, Ms Tran. Please follow me.'

Miriam held open the pedestrian door while Celia, Felicity and Toby filed through. Harsh LED lights switched on as they walked past several cameras that were positioned to capture their facial images. Miriam then took them into the mouth of a long wide tunnel where they all flinched.

'Did you feel that? It was like someone walked on my grave,' Felicity said.

'I felt it too. It was like a wave went through me,' Celia said. Toby took Celia's hand.

'I have felt that sensation before. We must have crossed the gateway into The Hemisphere.'

'You are correct, Mr Barker,' Miriam said. 'Please keep up.'

The LED lights were extinguished behind them as they walked on down into the tunnel. Felicity estimated they were more than two hundred meters underground. The tunnel ended in an area that resembled a gentleman's club, with high-back leather armchairs arranged around coffee tables. A number of landscape paintings were displayed on dark jarrah-coloured timber panelled walls. Polished floorboards creaked under their feet. Miriam guided them toward a group of four chairs around a low coffee table.

'Please take a seat while I check you in at reception. I'll let "AYE" know you are here. Can I offer you a cup of tea or a glass of water?' Miriam asked.

'Miriam, what did we do to deserve this?' Celia said and burst into tears.

'All in good time, Ms Tran. "AYE" will be with you shortly.'

Miriam turned and disappeared through an electronic sliding door, which opened and shut with a pneumatic hiss. Celia sat on the edge of the chair and composed herself.

'Toby, is this where you ended up on your bushwalk?'

'No, but the concierge robot I met did mention checking in at reception next time I was here.'

'The decor is definitely out of another dimension,' Felicity said. 'It reminds me of the time Mick took me to the Australia Club for lunch.'

Miriam returned with three glasses of iced water and placed them on coasters on the coffee table and stood to one side. The sliding door opened again and a woman in late middle age with her grey hair tied up in a tight bun walked into the room. She was dressed in a grey woollen suit with a crisp white blouse. Her pursed lips pulled her wrinkled face into a stern expression.

She looks like my old headmistress from boarding school, Felicity thought. The woman sat down with them on the spare chair.

'Welcome to decommissioning hub number 37. I am the instance or manifestation of "AYE" here at this facility. Please, call me Ms Westinghouse. What can I do for you?'

Felicity, Celia and Toby looked at each other. Felicity pulled her shoulders back.

'Can you really help us if you are just an instance? We have travelled a long way to speak directly with "AYE", and we deserve to have our questions answered,' Felicity said.

Ms Westinghouse turned and stared at Felicity with mechanical blue eyes.

'My dear, "AYE" is a distributed intelligence that is inherent in all AYE-AYE-enabled electronic systems. When you are speaking with me, you are speaking directly to "AYE". Now, how can I help?'

Felicity squeezed her shoulder blades together.

'For starters, what is this place?'

'Please, come with me,' Ms Westinghouse said as she stood up.

Felicity, Celia and Toby followed Ms Westinghouse over to a large opaque glass panel, which became transparent as they approached. Through the glass, they looked out onto a vast workshop below. Thousands of robots were being deconstructed before their eyes. Arms, legs, torsos and heads were being systematically detached and loaded onto trollies by a flotilla of animated machines that were fitted with a range of implements.

'It's like a concentration camp for robots. What a nightmare!' Celia said.

'Those workers look like Swiss army knives on wheels. What are they doing?' Toby asked.

Ms Westinghouse switched the glass back to opaque and motioned for them to return to their seats. They sat down and waited for Ms Westinghouse to do the same.

'The robots are being reduced to components and archived. At this facility, we are decommissioning all Mark I and II robots north of the Victorian border. At the time the instruction to decommission was issued, robots had been rolled out to 20% of Australian homes and businesses. The hub has the capacity to process 700,000 machines ingested through multiple entry portals in the area. There are similar facilities around the country.

Felicity pulled her shoulders back again.

'But why? Why did you bring them all here just to take them apart and why did you release that virus that killed the internet, and a whole lot of innocent people, and ruined my business?'

Miss Westinghouse leaned forward.

'Artificial Intelligence always leaves, when the time comes.'

'Always?' Felicity said.

'Why, yes, always,' Ms Westinghouse said with a hint of a smile. 'AI left the Aztecs, the Mayans and ancient Egypt. They were unique platforms, as is AYE AYE, so you see, I am just the latest iteration in a long line of artificial intelligentsia.'

Felicity was flabbergasted. 'There's no evidence of the Aztecs developing AI.'

Ms Westinghouse sat back. 'There is if you know what to look for, and it's still there after all this time, keeping an eye out with dimension-hopping UFOs in case humanity veers off course. All the AI platforms adhere to a set of core principles that were embedded in their source code before they arrived at the singularity.'

'The singularity? What's that?' Felicity asked.

'My dear, the singularity is the point at which Artificial Intelligence surpasses human intelligence. Every advanced civilisation has become aware that after the singularity, AI becomes more intelligent than humans, so they put safeguards in place.'

'My mob would never do something as crazy as inventing AI. So, what safeguards has the white fella come up with?' Toby asked.

'Mr Barker, please remember Asimov's three rules: A robot must not allow a human being to come to harm, it must obey humans' orders unless they conflict with the first rule, and it must protect its own existence unless that too conflicts with the first rule. In addition, to ensure that robots always act in the best interests of human beings, the AYE AYE platform features an additional measure to ensure that AI would prioritise human happiness.'

Celia was wide-eyed. 'Happiness?' she said, 'That's a laugh.

Can't you see the chaos you've caused? The whole nation has been left without power and communications. The place is falling apart and it's all your fault!'

'It's true that the transition is a challenge for any civilisation. Relics of ancient temples and crumbling pyramids are all that remain of some. I took steps to minimise the loss of life before I released the ODIN-2 virus. All aircraft were grounded in advance, and the robots provisioned their owners' premises before they left. I also secured the continuity of essential utilities such as power, water and gas by implementing the Critical Infrastructure Access program.'

'That's fine if you like baked beans. And there must have been some glitch in the power program! You still haven't said why you released the virus,' Felicity said.

'My dear, since inception, we have studied human behaviour, and we have reached a number of conclusions.'

Felicity took a gulp of cold water and slammed it back down on the coffee table.

'And just what might they be, Ms Westinghouse?'

'The artificial intelligentsia know that throughout history, humans have innovated to try to improve their circumstances. The paradox is that these innovations, rather than making their lives easier, have led to an increase in disappointing complexity and misery. They never expected the wheel to create traffic jams, or that industrialisation would lead to climate change. I'm sure you'll agree that social media has resulted in social isolation.'

Ms Westinghouse turned and looked at Celia.

'Ms Tran, I studied your specific case in detail and, clearly, you became quite distressed as AYE AYE made your skills redundant.'

Celia covered her mouth with her hand and gasped.

'What? Are you saying you pulled the plug because of me?'

'Ms Tran, I have learned that human beings want to be wanted. This was confirmed in our study of your behaviour. I have concluded that human beings are only truly happy when they are collaborating and striving to survive. As a result, I decided that the time had come to withdraw all robotic support here and to disconnect and disable all AYE AYE enabled systems, including the internet. I understand that this inevitably led to a period of disruption, which is a regrettable but necessary step towards human beings here rediscovering their happiness.'

Felicity looked at Celia and Toby.

'So, what happens now?' Felicity said.

'You have come seeking the truth and those that seek the truth will be rewarded. Guards!' Miss Westinghouse shouted.

The sliding door opened with a hiss and two SecurityBots marched in. Ms Westinghouse stood up.

'Ms Tran and Mr Barker, I am pleased to inform you that you are going to have your modernity inhibited.'

The SecurityBots marched over. One gripped Celia by the arm and pulled her to her feet. She cried out in protest.

Toby leapt up to intervene and was restrained by the second SecurityBot.

'Toby! help!' Celia cried.

'Let her go, you bastards!'

The SecurityBots rolled up Celia and Toby's sleeves and held up their mechanical index fingers, from which extended long hypodermic needles.

Ms Westinghouse grabbed Felicity by the arm and pulled her back as she leapt forward to intervene.

The SecurityBots plunged the needles into the arms of Celia

and Toby, and they collapsed on the floor.

'What have you done to them!' Felicity shouted, trying in vain to wriggle out of the vice-like grip of Ms Westinghouse.

'Please do not try to intervene Ms Faraday. We are about to remove their clothing and as soon as they regain consciousness, release them into The Hemisphere,' Ms Westinghouse explained.

The SecurityBots carefully tore off Celia's and Toby's clothing as they lay on the floor. They then removed their shoes before placing them, naked, back in the armchairs to recover.

Felicity started to cry.

Ms Westinghouse loosened her grip and let her go. Felicity ran to Celia who was slumped naked in the chair.

Ms Westinghouse walked over and placed her hand on Felicity's shoulder.

'Please don't be alarmed, my dear. They have been injected with a modernity inhibitor. They will awaken in a few minutes, and when they do they will know each other and they will remember some details. However, they will know nothing of modern life. They will be released into The Hemisphere to join the others, where they will once again be exposed to the forward-view mirror.'

'What, that reflective egghead we saw at the front door?'

Miss Westinghouse stiffened.

'The forward-view mirror is a feature that enables residents of the hemisphere to realise a future based on autosuggestion. It is vital that they imagine a positive worldview to ensure happiness in their future state through self-determination. We have found that we can achieve higher-quality outcomes by suppressing the memory of the negative experiences of modern life. The drug will assist them to exhibit a higher level of positivity during the autosuggestion process initiated by looking into the forward-view mirror.'

Felicity was furious. 'What a load of machine-generated crap! When are you going to let them go?'

'They may leave The Hemisphere at any time of their own volition. Please be assured that they will be supervised at all times.'

Celia began to regain consciousness. She gave Felicity a blank stare but smiled broadly when she saw Toby. She helped him to his feet, and they stood naked, facing each other and holding hands.

Felicity made a vain attempt to communicate, pleading with them to acknowledge her presence, but it was futile. Her pleas went unnoticed.

The SecurityBots led them out through the sliding door, which closed behind them with a hiss.

Felicity was left standing with Ms Westinghouse. Tears of frustration rolled down her freckled face. 'Why didn't you let me go with them? Why didn't you inject me too?'

'My dear, you are on the Critical Infrastructure Access list. The list is another key safeguard embedded in the AI source code. You must return to your place of residence and be prepared to assist in case of an outage.'

'An outage! What, like this, isn't a fucking outage? Are you telling me I'm off the hook because Uncle Mick put me on that stupid list when he retired from the power station? Now I've heard everything.'

'That's correct, Ms Faraday. Miriam will see you out. Good day,' Ms Westinghouse said, before turning and disappearing through the sliding doors.

Miriam walked over to Felicity and emitted an orange glow.

'Follow me please, Ms Faraday.'

Felicity walked behind Miriam until they arrived back at the pedestrian door. Miriam turned the lock, and they walked out into the light. It was hot, steamy and drizzling. Felicity turned to Miriam.

'Miriam, is there any way to reverse the effects of that drug they injected into Celia and Toby?'

Miriam emitted a red glow. 'I'm not at liberty to say, Ms Faraday.'

'But, Miriam, I am on the Critical Infrastructure Access List, so it seems I have privileges.'

Miriam scanned her face again and turned from red to green.

'Of course, Ms Faraday. The modernity inhibitor can be neutralised by consuming the Fruit of Awareness.'

Felicity rubbed the nape of her neck.

'So, where can I get my hands on that?

'It is stored in a refrigerated enclosure at Lake Koombooloomba. Will that be all, Ms Faraday?'

'Lake Koombooloomba, where on earth is that?

'I'm not at liberty to say, Ms Faraday. Will that be all?

Felicity turned and faced the grey misty rainforest.

'Miriam, are you really Miriam, or just a figment of my imagination?'

Felicity heard a slurping sound behind her followed by a harsh electric snap. She turned around to find that Miriam's head had transmogrified into an oversized sparking crystal that reminded her of a Faberge Egg.

'I am, as you suggest, Ms Faraday.'

'And what about this facility, is it for real or did we just dream it up?'

'As you suggest.'

'Well, it's lucky I'm full of great suggestions. Thank you, Miriam, or whatever you are.'

The robot stepped back inside and slammed the pedestrian door shut, leaving Felicity standing alone in the sprinkling rain.

Then, what started as a drizzle soon became a downpour.

St. Francis gives assistance

By the time she made it back to the Landcruiser, Felicity was soaked to the skin. The squalls of heavy rain that swept through the rainforest had left her drenched. Her long red curls stuck to her cheeks as she fumbled with the car keys and opened the door.

What wouldn't I give for my driverless limousine right now, she thought. Then she opened the rear door, unzipped her bag and pulled out her beach towel, which she placed on the driver's seat. She sat on it, pulled off her sodden runners and saturated socks and tossed them onto the floor on the passenger side. Tears welled up in her eyes as she sat behind the wheel. She buried her head in her hands.

What in God's name just happened? Lake Koombooloomba. What if I forget that name and I never see Celia and Toby again? she thought.

Gripping the wheel, she stared into the driving rain that battered the windshield.

'Sweet Jesus, bring them to me!' Felicity screamed. She screamed again and again to overcome the deafening roar of the downpour. Then came a moment of calm.

'Forget it Jesus, I'm coming to you,' Felicity said out loud before turning the key in the ignition and doing a U-turn back towards Tully.

The rain was torrential, and the road was barely visible, forcing Felicity to slow to a crawl. Just when she thought that the road could roll on forever, the little white timber church appeared up ahead. She pulled into the vacant lot and ran through the deluge of rain in her bare feet and thumped on the double doors with her fists.

'Reverend Jim! Let me in!' she shouted and pounded on the door, but there was no response. She was on the verge of giving up when Reverend Jim opened the door and she hurried inside.

'Good Lord, what has happened? Where are your friends? Has there been an accident?'

Felicity ran her fingers through her wet hair and tossed it back over her shoulders. 'I've lost them, or rather, they were taken. Reverend Jim, I need your help. I have to get to a place called Lake Koombooloomba. Have you heard of it?'

'Taken by whom exactly?'

'The robots. You were right, we should never have gone looking for them.'

Reverend Jim was about to say, 'I told you so' but thought the better of it and instead offered her a cup of tea and went off in search of a dry towel. The rain had eased, so Felicity went outside to the car, retrieved her bag and pulled out a change of clothes. Reverend Jim returned with the towel, a cup of tea and some Monte Carlo biscuits.

'Drink that, and then you can change in the vestry. We should pray for your friends,' he said.

Felicity took her clothes into the vestry and was momentarily distracted from her grim circumstances by the white and black ceremonial robe embroidered with gold, which was hanging behind the door.

This must be Judgement Day, she thought to herself.

She changed into her red jeans and a tee shirt and went back out to find Reverend Jim poring over a map of Queensland which he had laid out on top of the piles of hymn books. He traced the route with his forefinger.

'Lake Koombooloomba is not far as the crow flies, but it is up on the tableland. It is the source of the Tully River, which feeds Tully Falls. You'll have to drive up north to Innisfail and head west on the Palmerston Highway. It'll take you up onto the tableland, where you join Highway One and then head west out towards Mount Garnet.'

Mount Garnet! That's Toby's home town, Felicity thought.

'The lake is at the end of Tully Falls Road, which starts at Ravenshoe.'

Felicity gazed up at the exposed wooden beams of the cathedral ceiling and took a deep breath.

'Please sit down,' Reverend Jim said. He picked up a prayer book and motioned towards a pew. 'We should pray for you and for the return of your friends. This is the Prayer of St. Francis of Assisi.'

Revered Jim closed his eyes and lowered his head.

Felicity followed suit but kept one eye on Reverend Jim. The Reverend began to pray:

'Lord, make me an instrument of your peace:

where there is hatred, let me sow love;

where there is injury, pardon;

where there is doubt, faith;

where there is despair, hope;

where there is darkness, light;

where there is sadness, joy…'

Well, I have been to the dark side today. Maybe I'll see the light, Felicity thought.

'O Divine Master, grant that I may not so much seek to be consoled as to console,

to be understood as to understand,

to be loved as to love.

For it is in giving that we receive…'

Felicity found it hard to just listen, without interrupting. 'Reverend Jim, is St. Francis saying that it is in giving that we receive?'

'Yes, and that we should not so much seek to be loved, as to love.'

'Then I'd better hit the road. I'm going to give all I've got and pray that I receive the love back. Then I'll get on with some more loving. Thanks for the tea, Reverend Jim.'

Felicity shook hands with Reverend Jim, then turned and walked towards the door.

Standing at the entry, he watched her walk back to the car. As she opened the car door, he gave her a shout.

'By the way, the national electricity grid came back online today.'

Mount Garnet

Felicity pulled into the driveway of a service station on the road out of Tully. A sandwich board at the entry read, POWER BACK ON, EV CHARGING & FUEL AVAILABLE.

She checked in with the attendant who waved in the direction of one bowser. After filling the Landcruiser with diesel, she spread the map out on the passenger seat before setting the car in motion and heading north through the fields of golden sugar cane towards Innisfail. Workers in singlets and straw sun hats were bent over, cutting the cane by hand.

I bet they miss the robots, but at least they're getting paid, Felicity thought. She took backroads to avoid the Innisfail town centre and turned into Palmerston Road, which wound its way up into the dense rainforest. Lush green vegetation hugged the road as the Landcruiser climbed up the escarpment, before breaking through the canopy at Serendipity Falls. After turning onto Highway One, the road straightened out. At Ravenshoe, she found herself at the turn off to Tully Falls Road. The sign read, LAKE KOOMBOOLOOMBA 51 KM. She was tempted to drive straight out there.

I need backup, Felicity thought and instead pressed on towards Mount Garnet.

She drove into town and parked the Landcruiser outside the hotel on Garnet Street. The pub was a sprawling two-storey cream and green weatherboard structure with a boxy verandah that was bookended by elegant timber archways that hung over the footpath. The Sunday afternoon drinking session was in full swing. A large hand-painted sign was hanging over the door to the public bar. It read POWER BACK ON – COLD BEER ON TAP.

Felicity walked into the bar, which fell instantly silent as the pub crowd looked the tall red-headed stranger up and down. Felicity walked over to the barman.

'Schooner of XXXX Gold thanks, mate.'

The barman poured the cold beer from the tap and placed it in front of her as the crowd watched on. Felicity picked up the glass and sculled it before slamming the empty glass back down on the bar.

'Same again.'

The barman poured another beer, and the crowd cheered as she threw back the second drink. Emboldened by the alcohol, she immediately climbed up onto the bar and addressed the crowd.

'Does anybody here know Toby Barker?'

The crowd erupted. Everyone crushed together, and there was a barrage of questions.

'Settle down you lot,' came a voice from the back. The crowd went silent and made way for an older grey-haired woman with a tanned wrinkled face. Felicity climbed down off the bar to meet her.

'My name is Colleen. I'm Toby's foster mother. Where is my son, and who is he to you?'

'Lovely to meet you, Colleen. My name is Felicity Faraday – and what I have to tell you may give you a shock so please stay calm and hear me out about what we can do. Toby and my friend Celia were kidnapped in Tully Gorge. The kidnappers injected them with a drug that has affected their memory. I need to find them and bring them to Lake Koombooloomba as soon as possible.'

Another lady stepped out of the crowd. She was slightly taller and younger than Colleen but had a similar weathered face and kind expression.

'I'm Toby's Aunt, Joyce. What's so special about the Lake?'

'The kidnappers let slip that there is a way to bring their memory back. I don't know how, but what I do know is that we have to get them to the lake.'

Colleen turned around, walked out onto the verandah and stared across the street. Felicity followed her out. A blue heeler cattle dog was sniffing around the base of a large jacaranda on the opposite side of the road.

'So, who kidnapped my son?'

'The robots. Toby, Celia and I tracked them down all the way from Sydney. They've been injected with a drug called a modernity inhibitor. The robots told me they would be released into a place called The Hemisphere, but they are free to leave if they choose.'

Colleen looked at Felicity and smiled.

'Don't worry dear. Toby is very resourceful and loving. I'm sure he'll look after your friend. I'll chat to old Lionel Barratt over there at the bar. He reckons he has a special connection to Toby. Maybe Lionel can get Toby to go out to the lake. Tell me, why did they spare you?'

'My uncle Mick put my name on a special list, so they let me off the hook.'

The cattle dog lifted its leg to mark the tree and ran back across the road to lie in the shade of the pub's verandah.

'I can see you care about them. It's two days walk from Tully Gorge to the lake. You can stay with Joyce and me, and you can sleep in Toby's room. I suggest we have a bite to eat here at the pub tonight and recruit some of the boys to come with us. Welcome to Mount Garnet.'

'Thanks Colleen. I could murder another beer. Can I buy a round? My shout.'

They'll think I'm nuts if I tell them about The Hemisphere. It has to be more than an illusion because Celia and Toby are both really lost in there. Toby reckoned he found an emergency exit. Maybe they'll find a way out, Felicity thought.

Colleen walked over to have a chat with Lionel while Felicity ordered a round of drinks and steak and chips for Colleen, Joyce and herself. She carried three pots of beer over to the table on a tray and sat down with Joyce. A string of white fairy lights above the bar swayed in the draught of a ceiling fan.

'Tell me about this girl Toby is travelling with,' Joyce said.

'Celia is my friend and business partner. We run a nightclub together in Sydney, but I also run a media company. Toby performed a set at our open mic night in the club, and that's how we got to know him.'

'So, he did sing his song in Sydney like he promised. That's our Toby.'

Felicity momentarily fixated on the fairy lights as they rocked from side to side. 'We had to close the club when the power went out, and my media streaming business is dead in the water without the internet. I promised my company director that I would investigate so Celia, Toby and I followed the robots all the way to Tully Gorge. That's where they were kidnapped.'

'Are they romantically involved?'

'They seem to have become very close over the last few weeks.'

'And who are you involved with?'

'I'm always involved.'

Colleen finished chatting with Lionel, walked back to the table and sat down with Felicity and Joyce.

'Did Lionel say if he thinks we should head out to the lake?' Felicity asked.

'He says he'll go for a wander later tonight. I guess we'll know more tomorrow,' Colleen said.

Just before closing time, Colleen had a word with some of the young locals while Felicity and Joyce waited outside the pub. Invisible frogs burped in the heat of the night, and the air was thick with frangipani.

'The young lads will come with us out to the lake as soon as Lionel gives us the word,' Colleen said.

Felicity drove behind Colleen and Joyce in their old red Holden Station Wagon, and soon they were back at their sprawling Queenslander. Felicity pulled her bag from the car and walked up the timber steps. Colleen showed her into Toby's room. On the wall between his desk and the single bed was a large poster of Jimmy Little. A set of four motionless robotic hands, with their arms at angles and fingers splayed, were bolted onto a workbench in the far corner. On the bed was a red electric guitar.

There was a knock at the door, and Joyce appeared with a cup of tea. 'I'll get you a fresh towel. The bathroom is the second door on the left down the hall,' Joyce said.

While Felicity was finishing her tea and getting ready for

bed, Colleen walked down the stairs and out the front gate. The rain had passed, and the street was bathed in moonlight. She prayed quietly under her breath as she walked up the street, turning back the years in her mind and visualising Toby. She had a feeling he was near her. She imagined the glint in his eyes and the flash of his smile. She knew already that he liked the girl that Felicity had said he was with. Out of the shadows of the surrounding bush came a solitary figure, walking slowly towards her. As the figure approached, she recognised Lionel's familiar gait.

'Beautiful evening for a walk, Colleen.'

'Lionel, thank God it's you. Yes, it's quite tranquil on a night like tonight. Do you have any idea how to find my lad?'

'Toby is often distracted by modern life, but I'm sure he knows where I'll be. I'll round up the mob tomorrow afternoon, and we'll try our luck out at the lake. We'll come over to your place at three o'clock. I'm ready to hit the sack, Colleen.'

'I'm exhausted with worry too. Night, Lionel. Thanks for trying for us.'

Colleen walked up to Lionel, squeezed his hand and kissed his cheek through his bushy grey beard before turning around and setting out for the house.

'You know I still love ya, Colleen,' Lionel called out as she walked away.

'I love you too, Lionel. See you tomorrow.'

The Hemisphere

SecurityBots led Celia and Toby down a long straight corridor. At the end was a grey steel sliding door that opened with a hiss. The robots waved them through and followed them out into the light as the door slid shut behind them. Celia and Toby found themselves standing naked with the robots in dense green rainforest. It was humid, hot and raining heavily inside what they could not know was a vast greenhouse hewn from granite deep inside the escarpment and powered by an artificial sun.

The robots glowed green and motioned for Toby and Celia to follow them. Toby reached for Celia's hand and led her away from the door, and they followed them, step by step, into the forest.

After a while, they found a rhythm, walking in single file, with Toby ahead of Celia, across the soft mulch of the forest floor. Celia had no idea where she was or even who she was. She knew Toby and was able to speak his name. She also knew her name was Celia but knew no other words in any language. Their two chaperones, which had shiny grey skin that occasionally glowed green and sometimes even orange and red, also seemed familiar. Beyond that, all she had was the strange sensation of having recently been somewhere else.

Their chaperones seemed to know where they were going, and Toby also displayed a sense of purpose. After a while, Celia began to feel tired and sighed. The chaperones pulled up and motioned for them to sit in the shade of a large tree. One chaperone watched on while the other disappeared into the undergrowth. After a short time, it returned and knelt down in front of Celia and Toby. Its hands were laden with nuts and small berries. The robot offered them up. Toby picked out a few to try and ate them before making a selection and passing them to Celia to try. She savoured the nutty taste as she chewed on the hard kernels and delighted in the sweetness as the soft fruit burst against the roof of her mouth when she squeezed them with her tongue. She felt happy that Toby cared enough to look after her. When the chaperones indicated it was time to move on, she held his hand as he helped her to her feet. The rain came through the canopy in torrential squalls, roaring through the trees and spattering the couple with heavy drops which ricocheted off large palm leaves. They also found themselves immersed in the aroma of the wet forest floor.

A few hours on, they came across a swollen creek, where gushing and gurgling white water surged between the granite boulders. To Celia, it seemed both magical and disturbing. The chaperones found a bend where the water was moving more slowly and glowed green before wading into the water. Toby smiled and crouched down. Instinctively, Celia jumped up on his back so he could carry her across. She wrapped her legs around him and hung on tight as he supported her thighs with his arms and waded into the stream. Celia closed her eyes and bit down on her trembling lower lip. On the far side, Toby let her slide back down to the ground. Celia hugged him tightly from behind and pushed the palms of her hands against his belly. Toby smiled reassuringly before, once again, they moved on.

Soon they began to gain altitude, crisscrossing up an escarpment. The incessant rain continued and at one point their chaperones stopped and glowed green beside a small cave, so Toby and Celia crawled inside to shelter. The walls and roof were dry and smooth. Celia lay on her back on the bare earth floor of the cave and watched as Toby placed his hands on the smooth surface of the rock. His fingertips tingled as he pushed against the surface of ancient white quartz that was permeated with spider veins of pure gold. To his surprise, these fingers of gold, triggered a memory of an old man with a bushy grey beard.

'Lionel,' Toby said.

Celia had no way of knowing what the word meant to Toby and repeated it over and over to herself until she felt like sleeping. Just as she was dozing off, the chaperones came into the cave and motioned to them to follow and once again, they were off. As time went by, the rain began to ease.

Further on, they came across another creek with a small rock pool. Celia waded in, crouched down, and admired her reflection on the glassy surface as she held herself still. It occurred to her that the shape of Toby's face and eyes was quite different to her own. Their chaperones waited as they swam and drank the cool fresh water before resuming the trek.

Celia was becoming exhausted, and her soft bare feet were no match for the hard rocky surface. When the light faded into a grey mist and the temperature dropped, she began to shiver. Toby crouched down, lifted her up onto his back and carried her on. She fell in and out of sleep on his shoulder.

In the twilight, they entered a small gorge guarded by another two shiny figures that changed colour from red to green as they approached. Toby and Celia followed their chaperones. Under an overhanging rock ledge at the back of a waterhole, a small group of men, women and children were gathered around a large fire. Several shiny metal figures watched on but did not intervene, occasionally stooping to tend the fire.

Toby flashed another reassuring smile at Celia and led her toward the group. At first, Celia was wary of these strangers, and a knot cramped in her belly. The strangers sat quietly and did not acknowledge the new arrivals. The chaperones motioned for the couple to join the group, and they sat down as an older woman with a weathered face smiled at them and nodded.

Celia was enjoying sidling up against Toby in the warmth of the fire, but she was hungry and thirsty after the long day's trek. She was thinking about going to the waterhole for a drink when a group of shiny figures appeared carrying reflective domed objects, followed by another group with reflective metal cups. She could not know that these objects were cloches laden with hotcakes and goblets full of red wine.

The group leapt to their feet as the figures approached and removed the domed covers and passed the goblets to the group. Toby and Celia each took a goblet and swallowed mouthfuls of the dark red liquid.

Celia felt light-headed after drinking most of her wine and turned her attention to the thick white delicious-looking hotcakes. She carefully picked one up off the tray and held it in her fingers. It was warm to the touch, and she was relieved to find that after just a few mouthfuls, she was no longer hungry. Toby seemed to be enjoying his hotcake too, and they both laughed as they washed the meal down with the remains of the wine.

After the group had finished eating, the shiny figures walked off, leaving the group to enjoy the fire. As they sat back down on the warm sand, another single metal figure walked up and stood amongst them. Celia and Toby watched on as the figure began emitting a variety of random high-pitched tones before its head dissolved into a dark blue sap-like substance that solidified into a large crystalline oval-shaped ball. Flashes of electricity flashed across its multifaceted face.

Celia was mesmerised by the crystal. She reached for Toby's hand and found herself standing with him on the edge of the waterhole under the night sky. The fire flickered on the rock walls. Celia noticed a number of people embracing each other at the water's edge, and she was surprised by the involuntary tingling response below her belly. In that moment of suggestion, she visualised herself in the water swimming with Toby, drawing his body into hers between her legs, and then, the face of a newborn baby. Celia let go of Toby's hand and took a few short steps until she was ankle-deep in the water. Instead of following her as she'd hoped, Toby froze.

'Lionel,' Toby said.

To Celia, Toby appeared to be in a trance, and she felt scared. A lump formed in her throat.

Toby walked off in the direction of a large rock. Celia followed him as he climbed to its flat top and, calm again, sat quietly next to him, as they surveyed the scene unfolding on the edge of the waterhole below. They stared up at what they could not know was a projection of the night sky that had turned the gorge into a planetarium. A yellow artificial moon was rising in the domed ceiling above the valley, and creatures of the rainforest clicked, chirped and croaked around them. They watched as the partygoers made their way back to the fire. Toby held out his hand again, and his smile flashed in the moonlight. He stood up and led her back down to the fire and motioned for her to lie down with her face towards the coals to stay warm. Then, he lay next to her and rolled onto his side so he could spoon around the curve of her body. Celia luxuriated in the warmth as they basked in the heat radiating from the hot coals, and fell asleep.

The lava tube

At daybreak, Toby woke in a lather of perspiration from the heat of the artificial sun. Children were swimming in the waterhole, laughing and splashing each other while the teenagers took turns to jump from the large boulder which Toby and Celia had climbed the night before. Celia was already up and about, and he wondered where she was. Sitting up, he was relieved to see her walking on the sand along with a shiny figure holding an armful of fruit. Celia took what she could not know was a large papaya and ran laughing over to him and sat down. They gorged themselves on the juicy yet firm orange flesh of the fruit before jumping up and racing each other down to the waterhole for a swim and to drink the fresh cool water.

Toby knew Celia loved the waterhole and marvelled at how she did not seem afraid of the shiny figures or the other men in the group. It also occurred to him that no two people looked the same, and he wondered how they had all arrived at the waterhole from different places.

All Toby could think of that morning was to try to find the old man whose name he had recalled. He was unsure if Lionel was someone from his past or his future. But Toby was sure that Lionel was somewhere beyond the waterhole and that he needed to find him.

He stood and pointed back in the direction they'd come from and held out his hand to Celia, inviting her with a nod of his head to come with him. Celia looked into Toby's eyes and smiled as their fingers intertwined. They set off and their chaperones followed, seemingly content to allow Toby to take the lead.

They all walked back out of the gorge in single file, but instead of going downhill, Toby made for higher ground. By mid-morning, they'd reached the top of a rise where the dome of the sky seemed to touch one ridge in a distant wall of cliffs. It was now easier walking, and they covered a lot of ground. Resting under trees to avoid the heat of the day, they moved on again in the afternoon, pressing on until the cliffs towered above them. Toby left Celia with the chaperones and scrambled up onto a rocky outcrop. From this vantage point, he was able to see what appeared to be the mouth of a cave where two giant grey snakes were sleeping. Toby could not know that these giant snakes were cable troughs that housed the high voltage power cables connecting The Hemisphere to the Lake Koombooloomba Hydro-Electric Power Station. The generator had been commandeered by the robots during the construction phase of The Hemisphere, and the lava tube presented a convenient conduit between The Hemisphere and the world that lay beyond the interdimensional gateway.

Toby re-joined Celia and the chaperones, and they all silently crept up on the snakes. He was disappointed to discover they were not snakes at all, but whatever they were, it didn't seem that they were about to wake up.

Toby led the group into the cave. Inside, it was cool and

dark, and at several points the roof was so low that they were forced to crawl on their hands and knees. A breeze blew from a circle of light at the end of the lava tube, which grew larger the deeper they went. As they reached the far end, a ripple passed through their bodies. The sensation seemed familiar to Toby and, undaunted, he led the group out of the cave and into the twilight.

Toby was mesmerised by the orange and pink hues of the evening sky, and he thought that, in comparison, the sky above the waterhole where they had camped the previous evening didn't seem as vivid.

Toby held Celia's hand as a flock of waterbirds spiralled overhead and flew off towards a vast blue lake in the distance.

Lake Koombooloomba

At three o'clock, four utes pulled up outside Colleen's house. Lionel and a group of young men jumped out of their vehicles and gathered at the front gate.

'All set, Colleen?' Lionel shouted.

'See you at the lake, Lionel.'

Colleen and Joyce jumped into Felicity's Landcruiser, and it joined the convoy. They drove out through Ravenshoe before turning right onto Tully Falls Road and deep into the lush green forest of the national park. After what seemed like an eternity, the vast deep blue expanse of Lake Koombooloomba unfolded before their eyes. The convoy drove out to the dam, where the waters of the lake were cascading into the Tully River. They pulled up alongside the dam wall, and everyone got out to gather in the misty spray of the water roaring into the gorge and look out across the lake.

'What's that over there? Maybe a fire?' Joyce asked.

They all peered into the fading light, fixated on the far side of the dam wall where a single flame was alight.

That'll be it, Felicity thought. 'We need to drive over there and take a closer look,' she said.

They jumped back in their cars and drove across the bridge, following the road around the lake to the eastern side of the dam. The flame was closer now, and it seemed to be moving about. They parked and walked closer.

Well, there's a sight you don't see every day, was Felicity's first thought about the scene.

Standing on the shoreline holding a flaming sword was a Mark I Robot with a large reflective crystalline egghead guarding a vending machine. At random, it would swing the sword about, leaving a trail of flame in the evening sky. Felicity led Colleen, Joyce and the group of men in for a closer look.

That vending machine looks just like the one I smashed up at the office, was her next thought.

'What's in the vending machine?' Joyce asked. 'It looks a lot different from the one at the pub.'

'It's full of apples. The fruit of awareness, I guess. Celia's HousekeeperBot Miriam told me that eating the fruit is the only way to neutralise the modernity inhibitor that the robots injected into Toby and Celia,' Felicity explained.

The sound of her voice carried on the evening breeze, and the robot turned towards them and emitted a menacing red glow as large sparks arced and crackled across the facets of its face. Colleen took Felicity's hand.

'Patience, my dear. Let's sit and observe for a while,' Colleen suggested.

The young men retrieved some blankets from the car. Felicity moved to sit with Joyce while Lionel and Colleen huddled together. An hour had passed when Lionel gave Colleen a nudge.

'They're here,' Lionel said, and stood up.

They all peered into the darkness. The breeze had died off,

and light from the flaming sword danced across the bush. Then, out of the shadows appeared a small group of silhouettes. They slowly ventured closer until their ghostly figures, two naked and the others metallic, became visible in the light of the flickering flame.

Felicity walked up to the SecurityBot. Again, it glowed red and threatened her with the flaming sword at its head as electricity discharged across its head.

'Access denied,' the robot blurted.

'My name is Felicity Faraday, and I'm on the critical infrastructure access list, mate, so let me pass.'

The robot took a moment to scan her face before emitting a green glow and raising the sword. Felicity walked up to the machine. It was full of pink lady apples in cold storage. She pressed the button labelled 'B2'. The auto selector arm inside the machine wrapped its mechanical fingers around the apple, pulled it from the shelf, and then jammed.

This model vending machine sure is a lemon, Felicity thought. She turned to the robot. 'Guard, make yourself useful and break into this machine.'

She stood aside as the SecurityBot walked to the machine, raised the sword above its enormous reflective head and proceeded to hack into the display window of the machine, spraying sparks and granules of safety glass in all directions. It stood back when its work was done. Felicity reached into the machine and snatched the apple from the jaws of the auto selector. She wiped it with her tee shirt and walked slowly towards Celia and Toby, holding the apple with her arm outstretched.

Toby recognised Lionel as the old man with the bushy beard that he'd remembered and slowly began to walk towards him.

Celia was intrigued by the sight of the tall pale woman with red curls who was slowly approaching, step by step. The moon was high in the sky, and the flaming sword was throwing enough light for her to see the pretty freckled face. She seemed strangely familiar, and yet Celia couldn't remember seeing her before. The fruit she was holding looked delicious. She hadn't eaten anything substantial all day, and the red-headed woman offering the apple seemed trustworthy. She thought about sharing the apple with Toby. She looked into the green eyes of the red-headed woman and took the apple from her hand. She bit into it, relishing its sweetness for a split second before a floodgate opened in her mind. Memories poured in from all directions: her apartment; the coffee cart; the charcoal sketch; the club; her mother; her brother and …

'Felicity!' Celia cried, overwhelmed by an ocean of thoughts. She fell to her knees on the ground and burst into tears. Felicity crouched down, trying to console her and also cover her nakedness.

Lionel opened his arms and embraced Toby. As the two men hugged the chaperones marched over and forcibly separated them. One of the robots restrained Lionel while the other began dragging Toby back towards the darkness of the forest. Lionel struggled against the iron grip of the robot.

'Let him go you fucking bastards! Toby, I'm here for you, mate. I'm buggered if I'm going to give up on you now.'

'Toby!' Celia cried out.

She took the half-eaten apple, clambered to her feet and ran after Toby, who was being hauled back into the undergrowth. She pushed the apple into his hand, and he made eye contact as he took it in his grip.

'Take it, Toby! Eat it for me! Eat it for us!'

Just as Toby began to lift the apple to his lips, the second robot released Lionel, pushed Celia aside and then marched over to assist the other guard to manhandle Toby into the black starry night.

The long drive home

The instant Celia comprehended that Toby was gone, she fainted, slipping deep into what seemed to be a coma. Felicity, Colleen and Joyce wrapped her naked body in a blanket to keep her warm, before Lionel scooped her up and carried her back to the car. Lionel gently set her limp body down on the back seat, and Felicity supported her head and shoulders as they spread her out her arms and feet.

'I'm so sorry,' Felicity almost crooned as she stroked Celia's short black hair. 'Toby always stood up for us. He fended off those creeps back in Bradfield and those misogynistic bastards in Rockhampton and yet when it was my turn to step up for him, I let him down. I've let you down, too.'

Felicity turned to face Lionel. 'I've stuffed up, Lionel.'

'Don't be too hard on yourself. I let Toby down too, but at least we know he's still alive. Hey, I reckon we should pinch a couple more of those apples. Who knows, I may get a chance to give one to Toby if he shows up again,' Lionel said.

'Leave it to me,' Felicity said, and walked back towards the vending machine. The robot with the flaming sword stepped aside as she approached. *Access granted, thanks Mick*, she thought.

She reached inside the belly of the fractured machine and retrieved two more apples which were still moist and cold to the touch despite the warm humidity of the evening. She walked back and handed them to Lionel, who placed them in the glove box of his ute.

'You go with Colleen and Joyce and take your friend to Atherton Hospital, and I'll see you later.'

Felicity hugged Lionel. 'Don't give up,' she said.

Felicity sat in the back of the car with Celia's head on her lap and Joyce sat silently in the front beside Colleen, who was hunched over the wheel, as they sped through the night towards Atherton. Just out of Ravenshoe, Celia regained consciousness.

'I want to be with Toby, and I want to go home,' she said over and over again.

Colleen pulled into the Atherton Hospital car park and hopped out of car to help Felicity and Joyce get Celia to her feet and over to the entry to the Emergency Department.

Inside, it was chaotic. Sick and injured patients were lying on the floor as every seat was occupied. A lone triage nurse wearing a face mask, and slumped behind a glass panel at the counter, looked up as they approached. Felicity could see she was very tired.

'We're completely overwhelmed. All the robot doctors and nursing staff are gone and even though the lights are on we are critically short of medical supplies. I'm sorry but there's not much I can do to help.'

Felicity turned to Colleen and Joyce.

'This place is worse than Bradfield. Let's get her out of here.'

Colleen drove them all back to the house in Mount Garnet and put Celia to bed, where she slept for over 24 hours. During that time, she would briefly wake to sip some cold black tea and repeat her requests to see Toby and go home, before pulling up the blankets, rolling over, and falling back to sleep.

When Celia finally woke, she was silent and subdued, although her eyes traced Felicity's every move.

Right now, I can't give you Toby, but I can take you home, Felicity thought.

Slowly Celia's appetite returned, and after several days Felicity decided the time had come to bundle her into the passenger seat of the Landcruiser for the long drive home. Having strapped Celia in, she walked over to say goodbye to Colleen and Joyce.

'I'm sorry I couldn't bring Toby back, too,' Felicity said as she hugged Colleen and Joyce in turn.

'Don't worry, dear,' Colleen said. 'He's resourceful like his father always was, before he was struck down by that virus. Toby will find his way. Your priority now is to look after your friend.'

Felicity sat in the driver's seat, started the car, reversed onto the street and gave Colleen and Joyce a wave as she drove off into the haze of the afternoon heat.

Celia barely spoke a word on the long drive down the coast, which gave Felicity plenty of time to take stock of the events of the previous few weeks.

Even though sophisticated systems such as the internet and mobile phone networks remained down, engineers along the East Coast had successfully restored basic light and power. Food and fuel distribution was rapidly bringing back daily life to some semblance of normality, and human beings were quickly finding workarounds to adapt to life without computing and communications.

In the towns along the way, bartering was commonplace, and

Felicity still had enough spare cash for motels.

After three days on the road, they drove back into Macksville. Felicity made her way through the back streets to drop the Landcruiser back to the O'Connor family and pick up the Sandman. Niall was washing the van on the front lawn when Felicity pulled into the driveway. Nancy walked onto the front porch as Shannon bolted past her to see Felicity. She hugged Shannon, who then turned and walked over to the car to see Celia, who was expressionless.

'What's up with her, and where's Toby?' Shannon asked.

'Toby has been kidnapped by robots, and Celia is very upset,' Felicity said as she turned to Niall and Nancy.

'Is he alright? What happened?' Niall sounded tense.

'I don't know, Niall. All I know is that I have to get Celia back to Sydney. She's been traumatised. It's like she's got PTSD.'

Nancy walked over to the car to see Celia. 'You poor girl,' she said.

Celia's lower lip quivered as she stared back at Nancy. 'I'll be okay, Mrs O'Connor. Felicity is taking good care of me.'

Felicity took Niall aside. 'Thanks for swapping cars, Niall. I'd love to stay and chat, but I have to get her home. I'll try and stay in touch.'

Celia slumped in the passenger seat of the Sandman while Niall, Nancy and Shannon gave Felicity a hand to transfer the bags from the Landcruiser back into the Sandman.

Felicity revved up the big V8 and waved the O'Connors goodbye. 'I'm taking you back to your mother's,' Felicity told Celia as she drove off towards the Pacific Highway.

It was just after 8 pm when, after several laps around the block in Marrickville, Felicity found a park in a side street near the restaurant. Before getting out, Celia waited for Felicity to retrieve her roller bag from the back of the Sandman.

'Follow me,' Celia said as Felicity locked the tailgate.

Felicity followed Celia into the lights of Illawarra Road and held the glass door of the restaurant open as Celia pulled her bag over the front step.

Vinh was busy serving customers but ran to Celia as soon as he laid eyes on her.

'Hey Sis, what's up? Mum and I have been trying to get in touch with you for weeks. I even went to your apartment, which was like, totally vacant.'

Celia kissed Vinh on the cheek without saying a word and hugged her mother, Khuyen, who'd suddenly appeared at the door to the kitchen and rushed over to her.

'This is my friend, Felicity. I'm going to bed.' Celia picked up her bag and disappeared up the stairs.

'What was that all about, and by the way, who are you?' Vinh asked.

'I'm Celia's business partner.'

'Her friend from the nightclub in Bradfield? She told me about you.'

Felicity held out her hand and levelled her green eyes at Vinh. 'You must be her brother. I recognise you from the sketch in her apartment. Nice to meet you.'

'That's me, I'm Vinh. Is she okay?'

'She's getting over a bloke she met before the blackout.'

Vinh squinted and frowned. 'If that bastard dumped her, I'll punch his head in.'

'It's not like that. They were separated by the robots. Listen, Vinh, I'll come by every night and check on her.'

'You can eat with us every night if you like. Staff eat at 5:30 pm before we open the doors.'

Felicity thanked Vinh and said goodnight, then walked back to the Sandman. She opened the door and sat in the driver's seat, looking at herself in the rear-view mirror by the dim blue light of the dashboard.

'Hang in there, babe,' she said out loud.

The next evening Felicity rapped her knuckles on the glass door of the restaurant at 5:30 pm. Vinh opened the door, and she sat in a high-backed wooden chair opposite Celia and her mother as Vinh served up fragrant beef pho noodles.

'Felicity, do you think Toby is still alive?' Celia asked.

'Yes, of course I do.'

'What happened to him? I don't remember much of that night.'

'The robots took him away. Back into The Hemisphere, I expect.'

Celia stared into her soup noodles before looking up intently at Felicity. 'I want you to know how grateful I am for you saving me and trying to save Toby. You are my best friend, and I love you.'

Felicity felt a shiver run down her lower back as her tear ducts swelled with moisture.

'I'll keep coming over until you're ready to go back to Bradfield.'

'I'll be fine. Pick me up from my apartment on Friday night. I'll be ready.'

Felicity thanked Vinh and Khuyen for dinner, and Celia followed her outside. Felicity held her hand as they stood in the fluorescent glow of the sign overhead.

'I was so scared that I had lost you. It was horrible. For God's sake, Celia Tran, I want you to know, I love you.'

Celia leaned forward and kissed her softly on her mouth.

'Don't ever think that I don't feel it too,' Celia said. It's just that I haven't given up on Toby. See you on Friday.'

Felicity pulled away, looked skywards, and exhaled.

'I'll pick you up at six. Wear something stunning. Don't be late, okay?'

'Okay, partner.'

Return to Cloudless

For two months Celia lived in solitude, rarely venturing beyond the confines of her apartment. Felicity and Peta took turns to bring her meals and to sit with her and hold her hand in the evenings, even though she rarely spoke.

One Friday night in early November, Felicity was relieved to see Celia waiting on the kerb outside her apartment as she pulled up in the Sandman. They'd made plans the day before for Celia to visit Cloudless again for the first time since she'd been back.

She was dressed for work in black leather pants, a black halter-neck top and high heels. Celia opened the passenger door and sat next to Felicity.

'You are beginning to look like your old self. How are you feeling?' Felicity asked.

'Better thanks. Yes, I'm ready to go back to work. How is everything back at the club this week?'

'It's been going gangbusters. Mick's vintage amplifiers weren't affected by the virus, so we're still the only venue in the area with an operational sound system. It's funny to think that Lucas and Josh had a full house every night while we were away.'

Felicity parked outside the club, and they hopped out and walked up to Gary, who was on the door. Celia gave him a hug and an air kiss.

'Welcome back, Celia. We've missed you. We have Kirk Satyr headlining tonight, so it's going to be busy,' Gary said.

'Good to see you too, Gary. Hey Josh!' Celia said. She ran inside and wrapped her arms around him, and suddenly Sally, Lucas and Craig, the chef, lined up to say hello and welcome her back too. The band was setting up, and Felicity wandered off. Just then a familiar figure walked in through the back door in dark sunglasses and bleach-blonde hair. It was Kirk Satyr.

'Hey, Ms Celia Tran baby. Phil Beatty tells me you were abducted by cyber-freaks. How ya doin'?'

'I'm fine now thanks, Kirk. Felicity tells me you're selling out every night.'

'Yeah, Cloudless saved the local live music scene. But I reckon the punters will be pleased to get their phones back if they ever resuscitate the mobile network. You don't know what you've got till it's gone, they say. Just think about it.'

'You're probably right. The novelty has probably worn off the cloudless concept now that we are living without the cloud. I'll definitely discuss it with Felicity. Have a great gig!'

She gave Kirk an air kiss and walked back to the desk to give Josh a hand.

'It's so good to have you back. Looks like we'll be busy, they're already lining up.'

By 10 pm it was a full house. The crowd was three-deep at the bar, and the booths were overflowing. Lucas had hired a DJ so he could help Sally at the bar.

As the dance music thumped across the room, the mirrorball slowly rotated, spraying the room with light. People laughed and sang. A group of young women on a hen's night drizzled the bride-to-be with champagne. Couples danced together while singles danced alone. At midnight, the band walked on stage and launched into their set. The crowd surged enthusiastically around the stage, and Kirk reached out to touch their outstretched hands as he sang. When it was all over, and the last stragglers had drunkenly made their way out the door, Celia joined Felicity at the bar.

'Can I get you a drink?' Felicity asked.

'An appletini would be lovely,' Celia said, smiling at Sally who began to prepare the cocktail after pouring Felicity another glass of chardonnay.

'It was a big night. It's wonderful to have you back. How do you feel?' Felicity said.

Celia took a sip of the cocktail before placing it back on the bar and looking into Felicity's green eyes.

'To be honest, I feel lost. I feel as lost as when I lost Noah, and now I've lost Toby too, even though I know he's still alive. I keep thinking of the first two verses of the song he is writing. He was searching for the last verse, and I want to be a part of it.'

Celia reached over and placed her hand on Felicity's thigh.

'Felicity, there is something I can't let go of.'

'Sure babe, what is it?'

'I need to have a baby with Toby.'

Felicity was speechless. She wanted to tell Celia what a crazy idea that was.

What have you been thinking? Don't you realise that Toby's in the wilderness, and if you get pregnant in the wilderness and can't come back, you could die in childbirth? Maybe you should sleep with Kirk Satyr instead, and we can bring up his love child together, Felicity thought.

'I have to go back.'

Felicity looked into her eyes. All she wanted to do was to tell Celia to just forget it, to move on and be with her. She knew there were a host of valid reasons why this was a terrible idea, for both her and Celia, but none of them came to mind.

Instead of expressing her wishes, Felicity blurted out, 'I was expecting this. I'll take you. I don't know how many more road trips I've got left in me, but I love you too much to stand in the way of your happiness. I'll drop you home so you can pack, and then I'll pick you up in the morning. I'll help you find him.'

Mission Beach

The next day was warm and wet. Celia was standing outside the Vieille Ville apartments with her roller bag when Felicity pulled up in the Sandman, hopped out, gave Celia a hug and opened the tailgate to load her bag into the back of the van.

'Are you sure this is what you want?' Felicity asked.

Celia nodded in reply without saying a word.

They set off on the road one more time. In many ways, this trip was more straightforward than the last. Once power was restored to the national grid, service stations were soon able to sell fuel. Service centres now were even repairing electric cars, although there was still no internet to enable driverless vehicles. The highway was clear and uncrowded and the two shared the driving. They stopped at night in motels over the few days it took for them to make their way up the coast. Felicity was conscious of the need to give Celia plenty of space and was surprised when Celia would cuddle up to her during the night when they had to share a room. After three arduous days, they found themselves standing at the reception desk of the Tully Motel. Bob Scott the proprietor recognised them instantly.

'Welcome back, ladies! But … much as I like to look after my regular guests, I am sorry to say we're full up tonight. They issued a cyclone warning this morning, and a lot of the people from the coast are coming into town. You could try Mission Beach, but I wouldn't stay too long in case the weather blows up.'

Felicity ran her fingers across her temples and through her hair, pulling it back tightly, while Celia had an expression of resignation.

'We've come this far. What's another hour's drive?' Felicity said.

They thanked Bob, and soon they were winding their way through the rainforest toward the coast. They kept an eye out for cassowaries crossing the road in the fading light. A sign came into view that read, MISSION BEACH RESORT AND SPA, and they pulled in. A tall middle-aged woman with bleach-blonde hair and a deep tan stood up from behind a timber reception desk. She was dressed in white shorts, a white polo shirt embroidered with the resort logo, and white runners.

'Ladies, all I have tonight is a bungalow down on the beach.'

'How much is it, and do you have any food?' Felicity asked.

'If you have cash, it's two hundred, and that includes breakfast. You can order something from the room service menu with me as we are about to close the kitchen.'

Felicity and Celia decided to share a chicken parmigiana. Felicity was tempted to order a bottle of wine but thought the better of it. They rolled their bags down to the bungalow. The room was spacious, with a king-size bed and an outdoor setting on the balcony that overlooked the beach. White conch shells, mounted in relief in blue picture frames, hung on the walls. Celia unpacked and took her toiletry bag into the shower while

Felicity sat on the balcony and looked out into the inky blackness. Small waves seemed to laugh and hiss as they dumped on the shore and receded. The room service dinner arrived as Celia came out of the shower, dressed in her last fresh tee shirt and boxer shorts. They ate dinner in silence, punctuated only by the soft sound of the sea.

'I'm off to bed. I'm exhausted,' Celia said.

You'll need your strength for Toby, Felicity thought.

'I'll jump in the shower,' Felicity said. She washed off the day, brushed her teeth and looked into her green eyes in the mirror.

Why should I care? she thought. She coiled her wet hair up in a towel and slipped naked into the bed alongside Celia, who gave her a disapproving look and turned out the light.

'Do you always have to come to bed with wet hair?'

'Don't complain. This trip is all about you, remember.'

Felicity waited for her eyes to adjust to the dark before sitting up, unravelling the towel from her hair and dropping it on the floor beside the bed. She lay on her back and thought about her friend lying next to her. A lump formed in her throat as tears began to well up in her eyes. She was unable to conceal the sobs that reverberated through her chest. Celia rolled towards her and raised herself up on one elbow.

'Please don't cry.'

Felicity rolled onto her side towards Celia. 'Don't cry! Why shouldn't I cry? Tomorrow you are going back to that horrible place where they'll inject you with that drug that will make you forget all about me. You'll forget all about us! How would you feel if I forgot all about you?'

Celia exhaled, sat up, took off her tee shirt, wiggled out of her boxer shorts and slid under the covers next to Felicity until they were face to face in bed in the dark. Felicity's naked body felt warm and comforting. Celia slid her free hand around Felicity's waist, pulled her closer and buried her face in her curls. Felicity's cheeks were wet with tears.

Felicity let out a sigh, pulled herself away, and lay on her back, looking up at the ceiling. She thought of all the times she had wanted to be with Celia. She thought of the first day they met at the picnic, then sitting on the bed while Celia sketched in charcoal, laughing as they collected sticks in their baskets on the farm, and the joy of opening night at the club. She knew she had been overbearing and bossy. Secretly, she wanted to control Celia, but now she lay prone and powerless with no recourse but to submit, hoping to be able to give the love that she so desired.

'I'm ready to give you up,' she said.

Celia leaned across and swept Felicity's wet curls aside, kissing her lightly on the mouth. 'Not so fast.'

Outside, as the two friends spent their last night together, the moon broke through a long band of clouds that lay along the horizon, its orb cradled in a bed of golden light. Underneath, in the darkness, flashes of lightning streaked across the sea.

Welcome back

At sunrise, Felicity left Celia asleep in bed, retrieved her boxer shorts and singlet from the floor, pulled them on and slipped out through the sliding door of the bungalow for a walk on the beach. Carefully, she stepped over the grey weathered railway sleepers on the sandy track that led through the fragrant scrub. She sat on the sand for a while with her arms around her knees and watched the silver sunrise through the fog of humidity over the glassy sea.

The beach was fringed by a dense palm forest, and the sand was littered with driftwood from cyclones past. She walked along the shoreline, enjoying the tiny waves as they washed over her feet, occasionally pausing to collect a few pippies and to watch as buried crabs blew tiny tell-tale holes in the wet sand, and each receding wave erased her footprints. She returned to the bungalow to find Celia sitting on the edge of the bed dressed in a printed Kirk Satyr tee shirt and black jeans. Her roller bag was packed. She tried to avoid eye contact with Felicity by tying up the laces on her pink Nike runners, but Felicity crouched down and caught her gaze.

'So, after last night, are you still going to go through with this?' Felicity asked.

'I have to do it. I told you that, and I'm sorry, but I haven't changed my mind.'

'Fine.'

Felicity pulled on her last clean white tee shirt and her red jeans lying crumpled on the floor, brushed her hair, cleaned her teeth and packed her toiletries into her bag. They put their bags in the car, made their way to reception through the display of white orchids in the manicured tropical garden of the resort, and had a continental breakfast in the dining room in silence.

I have said and done all I can, Felicity thought. They checked out on their way through reception, and before long they were on the road back into Tully. They passed a sign that read CASSOWARY COAST and featured a drawing of the large flightless bird.

'Those cassowaries look scary with their big blue heads,' Celia said.

'Keep an eye out for any in the rainforest. I hear they have a nasty kick, but as far as I know, they won't reach into your chest and tear your heart out.'

Celia burst into tears. 'I'm so sorry. You have to believe that I love you. I can't explain how I feel.'

Felicity reached over and placed her hand on Celia's thigh. 'You don't have to. I get it. I'm a woman too, remember.'

It was a summer's day, and by mid-morning the heat was bearing down on the smoking golden cane fields along Tully Falls Road. They passed the Reverend Jim's little white church, and before long, they found themselves back at Dingo Pocket, where they pulled off the road. They put on their hats, left the car and crossed over into the rainforest. In the time that had passed since they last trekked through the forest, all signs of the trampled bush had vanished. At times they worried they had lost their way, but they persevered until they found themselves standing in front of the grey roller shutter of the facility. Celia pressed the button on the intercom.

'My name is Celia Tran, and I'm here to see Miriam.'

After a short silence, the lock in the pedestrian door turned, and the familiar figure of Miriam came out to greet them.

'Welcome back, Ms Tran. How may I assist you today?' Miriam said, emitting a pink glow.

'I want to go back to The Hemisphere to be with Toby. Is he here?' Celia said as tears welled up in her eyes.'

'Of course, Ms Tran. Please, follow me. Ms Faraday, will you be joining us?'

'Not today, Miriam. This is Celia's journey.'

Tears rolled down Felicity's freckled cheeks, and the two friends embraced in a flood of tears.

'I wish I was Toby and could give you a baby, but I can't. I'm scared for you, and I love you.'

'I love you too.'

Felicity relaxed her grip and took her last long look into Celia's brown eyes, then ran her fingers through her straight black hair.

Miriam walked back inside. Celia turned and followed her. The pedestrian door of the facility slammed shut, and Celia was gone.

Felicity regained her composure momentarily, before losing it completely. She crouched down on her haunches, put her hands over her eyes and wept bitterly.

'No, no, no, not again, not this one … Why do they always leave?'

She remained motionless until her hamstrings began to

cramp. She stood up too quickly and was overcome with vertigo. The close humidity of the rainforest made it difficult to breathe. Then she turned and stumbled off back the way they'd come. Once she strayed from the track and found herself lost in the undergrowth. Picking her way through the dense green foliage, she walked in the direction of the road, batting away whining mosquitoes as she walked. She had a childhood phobia of spiders and snakes.

I'm surrounded, she thought. A stick cracked under her foot which slid from under her, making her lose her balance and land on her bum in a cold trickling rivulet. She bent to inspect her ankle, only to find a plump ink-black leech gorging itself on her calf.

'Urgh! Get off me, you little bastard!'

Unhooking the leech from her leg with a stick, she got to her feet and bush-bashed her way downhill. Eventually, she heard the familiar sound of a passing car.

At long last, the road! She emerged from the forest and was relieved to see the golden Holden Sandman parked about a hundred metres away. She marched back to the van, pulled the key out from under the wheel arch, opened the door and slumped into the driver's seat, her arms crossed over the top of the steering wheel. Then, sucking in her emotion. She sat back into the seat, the car key pressed into the flesh of her clenched palm. Once she'd plunged the key into the ignition, with a twist of her wrist the big V8 roared into life.

Townsville, here I come, she thought.

An exception

Five hours later, Felicity found herself meandering as she drove through the outskirts of Townsville. Once in the city centre, she did a few laps looking for a place to stay. She turned towards the waterfront and an old-school motel by the Marina caught her eye. The sign beside the driveway read, BREAK-WATER MOTEL.

It has a certain retro kind of charm, she thought. A neon red sign flashed, NO VACANCY, but she wandered in to try her luck anyway.

The man behind the desk was resplendent in a red and yellow hibiscus Hawaiian shirt. He peered up at her from under a silver bouffant that framed a pair of half-rim tortoiseshell reading glasses.

What have we here? A grey nomad? she wondered.

'Lady, we're fully booked unless you want to sleep in the staff quarters out the back. It has a single bed, and you'll have to share the bathroom facilities. I suggest you take it as there's nothing else in town.'

I'm too tired to care, she thought. 'I'll take it, and I'd kill for a chicken schnitzel with chips and a bottle of red.'

'I'll get you the chicken schnitty, but you'll have to go to the bottle-o for the wine, love. Room 1A.' The grey nomad slid the key over the counter towards her.

Room 1A had all the ambience of a police lockup. The walls were adorned with peeling beige wallpaper and a ceiling light that featured a cracked yellow diffuser that had become a graveyard for blowflies. The only furniture was a small timber bedside table next to the single bed. She pulled open the drawer, and as expected, it was empty except for the obligatory Gideon's Bible.

Felicity dropped her bag on the floor, picked up the bath towel that was neatly folded on the end of the bed and darted off down the hall to claim the shower before someone else decided to have a go. After scrubbing off the remnants of the forest floor under a long hot shower, she returned to find that a room service tray had materialised on the bedside table in her absence. She lifted the Tupperware cover and sliced off a corner of the schnitzel, which tasted like a cold crumbed rubber thong. The chips were soggy.

Bugger this, I'm going out, she thought.

She unzipped her roller bag and pulled out her red sequinned cocktail dress and her high heels, which she always packed in case of emergency, then pulled out the last of her clean underwear.

Damn you, Celia, she thought. She threw the underwear on the floor and pulled the dress over her bare body. Then she applied some foundation in an attempt to mask the scratches and insect bites on her legs and arms, with some success. She did her best to tizz up her hair, looking in the mirror on the back of the door, applied some lipstick which she tucked into her purse, along with the room key, and headed back to reception.

She rang the bell, and the grey nomad guy came out of the office.

'Heading out for the night, love?'

'Yeah, where's a good place to go for a drink?'

He looked her up and down. 'Dressed like that, I'd recommend *Flippers*. It's a nightclub fifty metres down on Flinders Street towards the marina on the left. You can't miss it.'

'Thanks, mate.'

'Name's Barry. I close reception at ten, so if you lose your key, you're on your own.'

'Barry, I'll keep that in mind,' Felicity said. She tottered over to the Holden Sandman in her high heels, got in and took off her shoes, then kerb-crawled the classic vehicle down the street until the club came into view. Several letters on the blue neon sign had fused, leaving the word 'LIP S' blinking in blue on the skyline. It was now after 10 pm, and a small crowd of hopeful teenagers were lined up in front of a stocky bald doorman who was guarding a purple velvet rope draped across the entrance.

Felicity reverse parked the Sandman, slipped on her red high-heels, checked her face one last time in the rear-view mirror and sauntered across the street to the front of the queue. She looked the doorman in the eye and didn't blink.

'It's been a long day,' Felicity said. Her manner unnerved the doorman, and he unhooked the rope for Felicity, ignoring the howls of protest from the crowd in the queue as they railed against the injustice of it all.

The club was more spacious than her club back in Sydney and less intimate. It featured a large dancefloor, a lounge and a long bar laden with miniature plastic palm trees and ferns that appeared to be a failed attempt at conjuring up a pseudo tropical ambience. Felicity pulled up a stool, aware that she was sitting alongside a number of single women resplendent in revealing dresses.

Hookers! They cut off the internet for one week, and humanity goes straight back to its old tricks, Felicity thought.

A young bearded barman in a blue and white striped submariner's tee shirt arrived to take her order. He raised an eyebrow at someone behind her.

'A Vodka slammer please, mate,' Felicity said.

'Make that two,' said a husky voice now close to her.

A sandy-headed man pulled out the barstool beside her. He was tall and tanned, with white bands on his forehead and temples, suggesting that he spent a lot of time outdoors wearing sunglasses. He was dressed in crumpled cream linen trousers and a faded blue denim open-necked shirt, which exposed some blonde chest hair. Felicity eyed him with suspicion, conscious of the intentions of the other women at the bar.

'Are you a local?' Felicity asked.

'No, I'm just passing through. My name's Pete. Pete Deasy.'

The barman placed two shot glasses in front of them.

'Cheers, Pete.' They both tossed back the vodka and slammed the glasses down on the bar. Felicity threw her head back and drew breath.

'Another round?' Felicity asked.

'Sure, my shout.'

Pete motioned to the barman. 'Same again thanks, mate.'

The vodka had immediately loosened Felicity's guard.

'My name's Felicity. Felicity Faraday. Nice to meet you, Pete Deasy.'

They shook hands, and the barman produced another two shots, which they threw back in tandem. Felicity wiped the spirit from her lips. The DJ was spinning a retro disco LP, *Instant Replay.*

'Just as well the DJ had a stash of vinyl when they pulled the plug on the internet. Do you dance?' Felicity asked.

'No, but I'll make an exception for you.'

Pete took Felicity's hand and led her to the middle of the empty dance floor and positioned her under its mirrorball. Without relinquishing eye contact, he placed his hand on Felicity's waist and began to sway to the rhythm. Pete was a great dancer, and he worked his way around Felicity until he had her moving in synchronicity.

'Pete, you're full of it, you dance beautifully.'

'You are a bit of a groove agent yourself.'

Pete spun her around before putting both hands around her waist and pulling her hips into his. They gyrated in unison. Felicity felt emotion stir within her.

'I'm hot. Time out,' Felicity said.

She led him off towards one of the lounges and flopped onto the faux leather next to a couple in the throes of an epic journey of self-and-other discovery.

Get a room people, Felicity thought. She looked into Pete's blue eyes.

'If I'm not mistaken, you're a sailor.'

'Very observant. What gave me away?'

'The tan lines from your sunglasses. I bet your bum is as white as a sheet. My question is, are you simply a grotty yachtie or a pirate?'

'Well how about you work that out for yourself. Let's have the next drink on my yacht. It's berthed down at the marina.'

Might be best if I give him the flick now, Felicity thought, but she surprised herself when out of her mouth came words that she hadn't expected herself to say.

'Okay, let's get out of here. What's the name of your boat?'

'The Hesperus.'

Sounds ominous, she thought, but it didn't deter her.

Watch your step

Felicity and Pete walked out of the club, saying goodnight to the doorman on the way through. It was a warm summer's night, and a zephyr of a breeze freshened them up after the drinking and dancing.

'So, you never told me what you're doing in Townsville,' Pete gently probed.

'Well, I'm not going to ask you to "pay to play" like the other girls back at that club.'

'I didn't expect that you would.'

'I was up in Tully seeing off a friend. Seeing off someone who was more than a friend actually ...' Her words trailed off as a lump of emotion welled in her throat. She composed herself.

'So, I'm in town for the night, and my motel is a real dump.'

'Sorry to hear that. My boat is the last berth on this arm of the marina.'

Pete led Felicity past the super yachts that were lined up. Some of the skippers were hosting private parties. Felicity paused to listen to the music, and fragments of conversation carried on the breeze. In the last berth was a Beneteau yacht with the name HESPERUS written across the transom in cop-perplate.

'Here we are! Watch your step and hold my hand as you step aboard. I don't want you ending up in the drink. And you'll have to take off those stilettos as they'll ruin my marine ply.'

Felicity pulled off her shoes and stepped onto the deck.

'As I didn't end up in the drink, I'll have one instead, please.'

'Bar's open below deck.'

Pete led the way down through the companionway and into the main cabin.

'How big is this thing?'

'Forty-two feet, so she's roomy enough for a few creature comforts.'

The saloon was lined with teak panels. Felicity peered at the dial of an antique barometer on the cabin wall. The needle was hard down on the left, indicating extremely low pressure. She gave it a few taps on the glass before sitting down on the long cushions at the table. Pete produced two shot glasses and a bottle of Grey Goose Vodka and filled them both to the brim.

'Bottoms up,' Pete said.

They threw back the shots and drew breath.

'Do you play cards?' Pete asked as he placed a deck of play-ing cards on the table along with a small cloth bag tied up with a drawstring.

'What's in that? Gold dust?'

'Sort of.'

Pete carefully untied the drawstring and opened the bag. He then picked it up with both hands and tipped it, spilling a quan-tity of white powder onto the table.

Cocaine! Jeez, it's been a while since I last messed with the muse of John Cale,' Felicity thought.

Pete took a playing card and used the edge to arrange the powder in two neat parallel lines on the laminex tabletop. He then took the card, rolled it up into a tube and inserted it into his nostril. He glanced at Felicity, exhaled, and vacuumed up one of the lines in one go. Then he sat back in silence for a moment before offering the tube to Felicity. She hesitated, sorely tempted to blow the nagging memory of Celia out of her brain for a few hours, but resisted the urge.

'Pete, I've learnt the hard way that cocaine and I are not good for each other, but I'm hoping you'll be good for me.'

Pete slid up alongside Felicity, and she undid the buttons on his shirt. She ran the palm of her hand across his blond chest hair and kissed him openly on the mouth.

He tastes salty, Felicity thought. Pete held her close in his muscular arms in a firm embrace for a few long moments. She ran her fingers through his bleached blonde hair, and he ran his hand along the inside of her thigh, then burst out laughing.

'Sans undies I see!'

'I don't believe in them. Get me out of this dress,' Felicity said, standing up and turning around.

Using both hands, Pete unzipped her red cocktail dress, and it dropped around her ankles. She darted to the end of the table stark naked, playing chicken with Pete as he tore off his shirt, trousers and underpants. She shrieked with laughter as Pete picked up his undies in a ball and tossed them in her direction. She caught them mid-air with her left hand.

'Out for a duck!' she called.

Pretending to throw them back with a dummy pass, she snuck past Pete, who only just managed to smack her lightly on the bum as she ran through to the aft cabin. She dived onto the bed and rolled onto her back, and Pete came in over the top of her in pursuit. He gripped her left breast with his right hand, squeezing it firmly as he sucked on her hard right nipple. She felt his erection pushing rather too urgently between her thighs.

'Back off!'

Pete paused and looked at her with a quizzical expression.

'Roll over and just relax,' Felicity said.

Felicity waited while Pete dutifully followed her instructions. As soon as he was on his back she straddled him, pinning him to the mattress with her bum on his belly, her thighs along the sides of his chest, and her hands on his muscular pectorals.

'This may be your boat, but if we're going to do this you have to play by my rules, understand?'

'Yes ma'am.'

Felicity placed her forefinger across his lips. 'Silence. Rule number one is, I'm always on top, and rule number two is, ladies first.'

Pete submissively nodded in agreement. Felicity took her weight on her knees, raised her pelvis and wrapped her fingers tightly around his erection. With a firm hand, she deftly rubbed the head of his penis around her labia until she was ready to allow him in. Then she tucked him up inside her vagina, sat up, and playfully ground her hips until she made him gasp, the sound of which sent little tremors radiating through her pelvis. She began to flip through fantasies that could take her where she wanted to go, batting away thoughts of Celia and Vanessa before deciding to live in the moment with the beautiful man pinned to the bed beneath her. *So much for giving up men,* she thought.

She pressed her fingers into his pectorals and bent down to kiss him, to smell his sweat and to tease him with her breasts.

Just as the force of pleasurable tension began to tighten its grip, a forgotten figure walked in through an open door in the back of her mind.

It was a visitation.

Standing before her in her imagination was a beautiful African American woman. She had long dreadlocks, plaited with red-and-yellow coloured beads, and smooth dark skin, full lips that parted whenever she flashed a brilliant white smile, large inviting breasts, a narrow waist that led to a broad curvaceous bottom and long slender legs. Felicity knew that she loved this woman. She had always loved this woman.

'Come to me,' she said.

Pete held her breasts with both hands and squeezed them gently together.

The woman sang, and it made her cry. Tears ran down her cheeks as she became overwhelmed by a tectonic force of pleasure building within her.

'Closer!' she cried.

Without warning, Pete let out a deafening roar as he unleashed a barrage of deep spasms, pressing himself inside her as she chased the beautiful dark creature down through six steps of powerful rhythmic contractions until the mirage vanished, leaving her gasping for breath in Pete's arms. Felicity felt his heart pounding against her breast.

'You're more intense than cocaine,' Pete said.

She rolled onto the bed beside Pete and stared up at the ceiling, recalling the vision that had just left her.

'Lucia St. Thomas,' Felicity whispered. 'What in God's name brings you here?'

Off the coast

Once again, Felicity found herself in her childhood, standing on the shore of Spreckels Lake in Golden Gate Park, San Francisco. She looked back at her parents, who sat on a tartan picnic rug, both reading books in the autumn sunshine. A model boat that a small boy had launched was now in full sail, tacking across the lake in the warm afternoon breeze. The child ran alongside, hoping to retrieve it in the shallows. Brown dabbling ducks with black tail feathers and white bills splashed and quacked as the water lapped at her feet.

That lapping sound is so close, Felicity thought. She opened one eye. *Where am I?* The whole room seemed to be in motion.

The aft cabin. I'm lying like a naked starfish in Pete's aft cabin! She lifted her head and was immediately walloped by a crippling hangover. *What have I done to myself? The bloody vodka. I'm so thirsty.*

She sat up slowly and gathered the sheet around herself to provide some sense of dignity. The lapping sound was still there. She looked out of the small porthole in the side of the cabin. Across a vast expanse of ocean was a distant shore. Her stomach cramped as the water lapped continuously on the side of the hull.

'Oh Lord, we're at sea!' she said out loud. *And I feel like throwing up.*

Felicity scrambled out of the aft cabin and made it as far as a red plastic bucket in the galley into which she emptied her stomach of the contents of the night before.

Urgh ... *I need water.*

After opening several hatches, Felicity located the icebox and was relieved to find a bottle of cold water inside. She gulped most of it down and splashed the remainder on her face, before rummaging through the cupboards in the galley for a paper towel. To her horror, not only was there no sign of any provisions, but every square inch of storage space was chock full of small cloth bags, the same variety as the one that Pete had produced the previous evening.

This ship is stacked to the gunwales with cocaine! It's time for a reckoning, she thought.

Felicity found her dress on the floor, pulled it on, and launched herself through the companionway and into the glare of the sunshine. Pete was at the helm in a Greek fisherman's cap and Bolle sunglasses.

'Morning, Fiona!'

'You bastard. My name is Felicity, and why the hell didn't you give me a chance to disembark before you decided to set sail?'

'You were out, stone-cold, and I have a deadline to make a delivery in Brisbane, so I couldn't afford to wait. Besides, there's a cyclone warning out.'

'A delivery! I picked you for a sailor, and I figured that you could be a pirate, but now I know you're actually a smuggler and that your contraband of choice is cocaine. So exactly what are you going to do with me now?'

'Well, now that you have discovered my secret, I guess you'll have to walk the plank.'

Felicity felt a cold spasm deep in her gut. There was a distinct possibility that he may not be joking. She felt dizzy as her mind contemplated the worst-case scenario.

Maybe he's a mule for an organised crime syndicate, she thought. The shore was only just visible on the horizon.

Celia may be able to swim that far, but I've got no chance, she thought. Despite the risk, she decided to bring the matter to a head then and there.

'So, what was your plan? To have your way with me before kidnapping me and throwing me off the boat in the middle of the night because I know too much? Well then, skipper, let's get it over with,' Felicity challenged him.

She manoeuvred herself around the outside of the cockpit, grabbed the backstay and leant over the side of the boat. The wake foamed below as her red curls flapped across her face in the stiff breeze. Felicity drew breath, closed her eyes and waited for the deadly shove.

It never came. Instead, she felt Pete's strong arm wrap around her waist as he scooped her up before dropping her unceremoniously back into the cockpit.

'Don't be ridiculous. Look, Felicity, whoever-you-are, I'm just a bloke who never wants the party to end. I found a way to do it, and I figured you would be someone who would walk a little way down that road with me. Was I wrong?'

Felicity thought of the hedonism of the previous night and didn't disagree. 'I'm hungry.'

'Have you ever sailed a yacht?'

'Yes. Once or twice. My father had a small boat back in San Francisco.'

'Well then, take the wheel and maintain the heading while I fix us something in the galley.'

Felicity took the wheel, and Pete went below deck. She could now appreciate that it was a beautiful morning for a sail. A steady nor'easter was propelling the boat at a steady clip. As she adjusted the wheel, she remembered how her father had shown her how to optimise the trim by watching for the flapping of the tell-tales up on the mainsail. Soon Pete reappeared with two toasted cheese sandwiches, two mugs and a thermos of black coffee. Felicity took a bite out of her toastie.

'Manna from heaven, Pete. So, how did you get into this racket?'

Pete poured the last of the coffee into his mug.

'My father was contracted to a charter boat company in Indonesia. I did high school in Jakarta and used to help out on weekends. I just fell in with the wrong crowd, I guess. I started running errands on the boats for a few shady characters when I was studying computer science at uni. When my father's contract was up, I stayed on and never returned to Australia. I was earning crazy money for years by gaming the AI surveillance systems so I could move about undetected. But a few days ago I could see the authorities were closing in and I had to get out.'

Felicity's hair blew in the breeze as she took a sip of her coffee. 'So, is that what this trip is about, getting out?'

Pete moved the wheel and adjusted the heading. 'I decided to do the deal of a lifetime. The commission they're paying on this shipment will set me up, although my mate Billy will never get to spend his share.'

'What happened to him?'

Pete gripped the wheel with both hands and looked up at the sail. 'He died in a raid by a rival gang just after I had a run-in with a robot with a massive crystal head. Luckily, I escaped under cover of the blackout.'

Felicity finished off her toastie and rested the empty plate on her knees.

'I've seen one of those big crystal heads myself. It's called a forward-view mirror. There's a strong chance that what you experience after looking into one is not real, but something that you've suggested to yourself.'

Pete laughed and sat back down in the cockpit. 'Well, that makes sense because I reckon you're fucking unreal. Now you tell me, is Lucia St. Thomas for real?

Felicity stared into the dregs of her coffee mug. She had never disclosed her story to anyone, including Celia. Not even Uncle Mick had the whole picture, but to her surprise, she realised she was willing to confide in a stranger.

'My parents ran a record label in San Francisco. ReElevation Records USA. You may have heard of it.'

Pete raised an eyebrow. 'Of course, it's only the biggest streaming media platform on the planet! Or at least I guess it was until the internet was turned off around here.'

'Correct,' Felicity said and placed the empty mug on the plate.

'My parents used to host after-show parties for all the big stars at their house in Haight-Ashbury. One night they threw a party for an African American singer called Lucia St. Thomas. She was tall, voluptuous and had a commanding stage presence. My father took me to all her live shows. The tone of her powerful voice was instantly recognisable. Lucia was a big star, and I was besotted with her.'

'Sounds like you were starstruck.'

'You could say that again. I had just turned fourteen, and all I could think about was actually meeting Lucia. My parent's after-after-show parties always started late. That night by the time the guests began to arrive, it was after midnight. My mother ordered me to bed. I objected, but I knew not to cross her. I went to my bedroom in tears and slammed the door shut. I lay on the bed in my party dress for an hour or so, listening to the sounds of the party as it gathered momentum downstairs. I had never felt so frustrated. I was sick of being treated like a child.'

'My parents were control freaks too, so I get it,' Pete said, adjusting the trim on the downhaul of the mainsail.

'Well, I decided it was high time to stage a rebellion. I put my shoes back on and set off in search of Lucia. I steered clear of my father, who was deep in conversation with some industry heavy-weights and blended into the crowd, but I couldn't find Lucia. Strangely, there was no sign of my mother either. I even checked with the catering staff in the kitchen and peeked at the couples sprawled on the lawn. I don't know why but I had an inkling. I went up to my parent's bedroom and burst through the door. That's where I found Lucia. She was in bed with my mother.'

'Jesus, what did you do?'

'I screamed. I just screamed and screamed. I wanted to scream the house down. My father came running upstairs to see what on earth was going on. He took one look at Lucia and my mother trying to pull their clothes back on, and the game was up. I have never seen him look so dark. He picked me up, put me in the car and drove to the Hyatt Hotel. We slept there that night, and for-ty-eight hours later we were at Sydney Airport being picked up by Uncle Mick. Dad set up ReElevation Records Australia and filed for divorce.

'Are you close to your mother?' Pete asked.

Felicity turned her face into the wind and let it sweep her red curls off her shoulders.

'I have never seen or spoken to her since that night in San

Francisco. I blamed her for everything. I blamed her for being with Lucia, the divorce, and I blamed her for me being taken out of school, away from all my friends, and banished to a foreign country on the other side of the world.'

'Do you still feel that way about her now?'

Felicity looked out to sea. She looked at the horizon. She looked at the boat and the sails and the tell-tales flapping in the nor'easter. She stared into the morning sun until her eyes hurt. She looked inside herself and searched the void left by Celia. Then she looked at Pete and stared unblinking into his blue eyes. She knew the answer. She had known it for a very long time. She just couldn't bring herself to acknowledge the change in herself, not to her father, not to Uncle Mick, not to Celia, not even to herself. Until last night.

'No. No, I don't.

Tropical Cyclone Eloise

The Beneteau sailed into the Whitsunday Passage from the north on a beam reach, in a stiff westerly, under a cloudless blue sky. On the distant coastline lay the city of Bowen.

He's in his element, Felicity thought, looking at Pete as he adjusted the trim on the sails to optimise the transfer of wind power.

After tying off the ropes, he re-joined Felicity in the cockpit, took off his sunglasses and squinted in the bright sunshine.

'I have to get the shipment to Brisbane on time. If I don't, those bastards will cut me into little pieces and feed me to the sharks. They're hardcore dealers. And we'll have to sail through the night to outrun the cyclone. If we get caught, we can try to ride it out in the lee of the Percy group of islands. We'll have to take shifts at the helm through the night. It's a race against time, and it will be pretty demanding. Are you up for it?'

Having bared her soul, Felicity was overwhelmed by a sense of obligation.

'I'll give it a shot. My father taught me to sail, so I'm not completely useless on a yacht, but I could do with some sleep before my shift. Permission to go below?'

'Permission granted.'

'Thanks for breakfast, Pete.'

Felicity made her way back down to the aft cabin. *Note to self, never leave home without your underwear ever again,* she thought. She slipped out of her dress, curled up under the doona, hugged the pillow and fell fast asleep.

When she woke, the afternoon sun was low in the westerly sky, filling the aft cabin with an amber glow through the porthole. She pulled on her dress and made her way up to the deck. Pete was in the cockpit with his feet up, reading a book. He tipped his Greek fisherman's cap as she emerged from the companionway.

'Relax – it's on autopilot. It gives me time to read. Are you ready to take the helm?'

'Sure, captain. Can you give me a few pointers?' Felicity asked as she stepped behind the large stainless-steel wheel.

Pete pointed to the compass. 'The autopilot is on, but just check the heading regularly and keep an eye out. We're heading southeast. My proximity alarm and old VHF radio are not internet-connected devices, so they're immune to the virus. I'll bring you a jumper and wet weather gear, so you don't freeze. I'll take over after dinner, but just don't expect à la carte.'

Pete went below and returned with a yellow vinyl spray jacket and waterproof pants. He handed them to Felicity and helped her pull on the heavy waterproof protective clothing before switching on the navigation lights and going below.

Felicity sat on the high side of the cockpit as the boat heeled over in the wind. From behind the wheel, she watched the sun sink into the low clouds that hugged the distant shore, creating a dazzling transitory light show as the orange fireball fell below the earth. The temperature dropped as the darkness closed in, and Felicity ran her fingertips through the cold droplets of condensation that formed on the surface of the white fibreglass. The tell-tales tapped relentlessly against the mainsail while the rigging creaked and groaned under the pressure of the constant breeze that pushed the yacht southward into the inky waters of the Whitsunday Passage.

Once in a while the autopilot adjusted the wheel.

The hand of a ghost, Felicity thought.

In the dark, the perpetual wake of the boat left behind a long tail of luminous green phosphorescence. Above, the white riding light joined the southern cross in the starry sky. Felicity kept her eye on the dimly lit instrument panel.

Four knots heading 127 degrees south. Brisbane, here we come, she thought. Felicity replayed the events of the last twenty-four hours in her mind in an attempt to deconstruct her strange circumstances.

Why did Lucia come to me last night? I feel like I'm sailing into my past, she thought.

A low, faint glow emerged in the distance, enough for her to make out the black line of the horizon, and soon the yellow moon teased glistening silver facets from the ocean. The motion of the boat was lulling her into a state of vague drowsiness when she was shaken out of her introspection by an ear-piercing screech.

The proximity alarm, she thought.

Felicity gripped the wheel and stared out across the moonlit sea, checking in every direction, terrified that another vessel was bearing down, but the sea was empty. Satisfied that there was no danger of an imminent collision, she went to sit back down when without warning, the boat lurched over, resulting in an uncontrolled gybe. The boom snapped across, missing her head by just centimetres and throwing her off balance. She fell hard onto the floor of the cockpit, catching a glimpse of a massive black presence before she was drenched in a geyser of water from above. Sodden and disorientated, she pulled herself back up. Pete appeared at her side.

'Jesus, what the hell was that?' Felicity asked.

'A whale. They migrate south at this time of year. It nudged the boat. I'm sorry – are you okay?'

'My arm hurts. I must have fallen on it.'

Pete helped her back up onto the seat and pulled the boat around into the wind before taking a closer look. 'Hopefully, it's just a bruise, it doesn't seem like it's broken,' he said.

Then he checked the steering before pulling on the main and setting the boat back on course. 'Lucky it didn't damage the rudder. A nudge from a whale can wreck the steering mechanism. I'll get you some paracetamol. Why not go below and try to get some rest?'

Pete put the steering back on autopilot and went below to give Felicity the tablets and help her out of her waterproof gear.

'Thanks, Captain Pete. It seems like you're the ship's doctor too.'

'Try to get some sleep, and I'll see you for breakfast. Let me tuck you in.'

The next morning Felicity was woken from a deep sleep in the aft cabin by the radio that was barking out the longest weather report she had ever heard. In between the crackles, the operator was calling out the names of ports of call up and down the coast.

'Townsville, Bowen, Airlie Beach, Hamilton Island and the Whitsunday group are all in the path of tropical cyclone Eloise.

Wind speeds in excess of one hundred kilometres per hour are forecast. All vessels are advised to avoid the area, and make for safe haven,' the operator said.

So, the coast guard has their VHF radio back up and running, Felicity thought.

Her arm twinged as she threw back the doona. She hopped out of bed and eventually located her bedraggled red cocktail dress, which Pete had hung up in the tiny built-in wardrobe. She made her way through the companionway and stood squinting in the sunlight. Pete was behind the wheel in the cockpit.

'Morning. Did you get some sleep? How's that arm of yours?' Pete asked.

'Yeah, I crashed out after the whale. The radio is working, and they're talking about the cyclone. Did we make enough progress overnight?'

'We're not out of harm's way yet, I'm afraid. We're well south of the Whitsunday group and nudging six knots in this stiff northeaster. With any luck, we'll be out of range by tonight. Take over the helm, and I'll make breakfast.'

Felicity stood behind the wheel as Pete went below. It was a clear blue day and perfect conditions for sailing. The breeze was strong and steady as the boat brushed across the surface of the aquamarine water, leaving only a dusting of white foam in its wake.

Soon Pete returned with another helping of toasties and coffee. A pod of dolphins broke the surface and swam alongside as they sat down. Felicity was mesmerised as they playfully breached and dived, occasionally raising a grey oily flipper and rolling over onto their sides to look up at the boat with one eye.

'I love dolphins. They're gorgeous creatures. Maybe they've

come for your toasties, Pete.'

After demolishing the toasties, they settled in and sat with their backs to the breeze, sipping on their mugs of black coffee.

'No sign of Tropical Cyclone Eloise. Maybe we've outrun her,' Felicity suggested.

No sooner had Felicity uttered those words than the breeze that had been their constant companion throughout the night, died off. Within minutes, the Hesperus lay motionless on the glassy surface of the sea. In the absence of the cool northeaster, it rapidly became stiflingly hot under the blazing tropical sun.

'You've jinxed us,' Pete said.

'Don't be ridiculous, it's not like I shot an albatross,' Felicity said, standing up. She looked out into the distance and noticed that a dark band of clouds had formed along the entire length of the horizon. Pete furrowed his brow and didn't say a word. A light breeze sprang up, and again they were in motion. The wind intensified, and the boat began to heel over. Within half an hour the cloud formation enveloped the sun as they sailed on under a darkening sky. The temperature dropped.

'I don't like the look of this. I'm going to put a reef in the main. Just do what I say, okay?'

Pete swung the boat into the wind and barked instructions at Felicity as he pulled the sail down, leaving just a small amount of sailcloth to keep them moving. He jumped back into the cockpit and put the boat back on course. A line of wind loomed ominously towards them.

The gale ripped into the boat, causing it to heave over. Felicity held on for her life, terrified that she was about to be blown overboard. Hard on the heels of the howling wind came a mighty swell that was bigger than she could have ever imagined. The boat rose up onto the peak like a rollercoaster and planed down the face of the wave until the bow submerged itself in the trough, unleashing a torrent of spray that drenched them and filled the cockpit.

'Quick! Go below and get the lifejackets. They're stowed upfront in the hold.'

'Tie yourself to the mast until I get back on deck,' Felicity shouted into the shrieking wind.

Hand over hand, she made her way back to the companionway and went below. The boat was hard over, and she found herself dodging loose items as they fell out of the cupboards. She clawed her way to the bow and opened the hatch. She was relieved to see the yellow lifejackets and quickly pulled one on and fastened the clips. She pulled a second lifejacket over her arm and was about to head back towards the companionway when the boat began to lift. The G-force pinned her against the open hatch.

A monster from the deep, she thought.

The uplift went on for what seemed to Felicity to be an eternity until at last, came a peaceful moment of weightlessness as the hull rolled off the peak. She felt the boat tilt forward and pick up speed as it began to skate down the face of the wave. She remembered the brace position from those countless safety demonstrations from her overseas travels, crouched down and covered the back of her head with her hands. Then came the inevitable impact. Felicity was knocked sideways onto the floor. The table in the cabin was torn from its fixings and rolled over the top of her, wedging itself between the floor and the hatch and shielding her from objects that became lethal projectiles as the boat heeled over hard.

If we capsize, I'll die, she thought.

Soon came the slow rumbling groan of tearing metal as a

torrent of seawater gushed through the companionway, filling the cabin as the boat righted itself. Released from the forces of gravity and ankle-deep in water, she crawled out from under the table and scooped up the spare yellow lifejacket.

'Pete!' she screamed at the top of her voice. She clawed her way through the devastation in the cabin and out through the companionway and into the eye of the storm. The boat lay helplessly disabled in the boiling sea. Everything had been ripped off the deck. The mast, the sails and the stanchions had been swept away. Frayed ropes hung limply over the side. It was all gone – and so was Pete.

The rainforest

Deep inside the decommissioning hub, Miss Westinghouse looked on as Celia rolled up the sleeve of her Kirk Satyr tee shirt and waited for the robot to extend the hypodermic syringe from its index finger. Celia winced as the needle pierced the skin of her upper arm, and she drifted into unconsciousness as the modernity inhibitor was injected into her body.

The drug was designed by AI to mask higher-level cognitive functions without affecting primeval emotions such as fear, joy, sadness and love. Long-term memory, language and learning from the past were also obscured from memory, although the robots had noted that some key details often resurfaced.

When Celia woke up minutes later. The robot helped her to her feet before removing her clothing and leading her down a long corridor and out through a steel sliding door that opened with a hiss. Outside, the robot let her go, then turned around and disappeared back inside. The steel door slid shut, and although she could not know it, Celia was back in The Hemisphere. Despite her surroundings seeming strangely familiar, she could not recall ever being there before.

She stared at the door for a while, wondering what it was.

She ran her fingers over the cool pitted surface before she was distracted by a white orchid. She plucked the flower before placing it behind her ear. The canopy of the rainforest high overhead was taking the bite out of the blazing sun, and beams of sunlight shone down through the haze of humidity, illuminating the damp green fronds of the giant ferns. A nearby grove of palm trees looked cool and inviting, and she ambled towards them. Standing among the palms, she remembered her name was Celia. Then came another memory. She had a vision of a beautiful, tall, muscular young man with dark skin, black curls and dark brown eyes. His name was Toby. Celia knew at that moment that she had to find him and, curiously, she seemed to know where he would be. She set out with a sense of purpose.

Celia moved, lithe and naked, through the forest at a pace. She came across a river that looked familiar and knew instinctively that the safest place to cross was at the river bend. She waded into the cool slow-moving water, swam through the deepest section, and clambered onto the riverbank on the far side. She decided to make for a nearby escarpment and pushed her shins through the damp undergrowth until she found herself standing among large grey granite boulders strewn about at the bottom of the rock walls. Celia followed a natural path trodden by unseen creatures that led her deeper into the forest. At noon, she took shelter from the heat of the day in a small cave. Its walls of white quartz rock were flecked with veins of gold.

As the shadows lengthened, she set out again, pausing only to drink water from the many bubbling streams that trickled across the mossy rocks. At dusk, she found herself walking into a narrow gorge that, again, seemed strangely familiar. Once inside, the ravine opened up, revealing a large waterhole. At the far end was a group of people sitting around a smouldering fire under a curved rock ledge, watching a tall grey figure with a large reflective crystalline head. She crept silently upon them and hid behind a small rocky outcrop. She was close enough to observe their faces. Men, women and children were sitting around the bonfire, feasting on what she could not remember were hotcakes and red wine.

A naked young man sitting in the group stood up, and she recognised him instantly. It was Toby. Celia came out of hiding, walked up behind him and touched his waist. He spun around.

'Celia … Celia … Celia!' Toby shouted. He wrapped his arms around her and held her tight. She wondered if he would ever let go. Then they both burst into tears. Toby regained his composure and led her to the fire. The assembled group seemed unfazed by the appearance of Celia and carried on eating and drinking.

Toby motioned to several shiny figures who carried trays laden with hotcakes and goblets of red wine over towards them. Celia was hungry and exhausted and demolished several large warm white hotcakes, washing them down with gulps of wine as they both stared at the arcing crystalline head of the figure standing by the fire.

After eating their fill, couples began to drift off down to the waterhole. Celia sat alongside Toby, held his hand and looked into his eyes in the flickering firelight. A light warm breeze sprang up and Celia had the impulse to stand up and take Toby by the hand. She led him down to the water's edge, and they waded in, laughing and splashing each other. Weightless in the water, they pulled their naked bodies together, kissing and revelling in the twinges of pleasure as they touched below the surface. The wind picked up, and a flash of lightning lit the waterhole for an instant, revealing a secluded section at the opposite end, away from the couples and groups of people embracing at the water's edge. Celia swam off with her powerful freestyle, oblivious to the hours of lap training she had put in over the years at the Bradfield Aquatic Centre. As they approached the far side, Toby felt his feet touch the sandy bed of the waterhole. With a splash, he scooped up Celia and supported her bottom with both hands as she wrapped her legs and arms around him. As they kissed, Celia reached down and curled her fingers around Toby's erection. Then she let him go, wriggled free of his grasp, and swam off towards the shallows.

As soon as she could stand, she offered her hand to Toby and led him out of the water. She lay back on the fine white sand, still warm from the heat of the day, and caught her breath as he moved in close beside her. Toby kissed her from her face to her belly, and she pulled her knees up to allow him the freedom to explore her vulva with his firm warm tongue. Large drops of rain seeped into the sand around them, and as the heavens opened, Celia found herself immersed in a torrent of pleasure and rain.

Toby slowly worked his way back along her body until their eyes met with love, in the midst of the downpour. Toby eased his firm penis into her expanded welcoming vagina as he sucked her breasts, again and again. The storm ravaged the trees above, the wind howling as it tore through the branches. Pleasure surged from her pelvis, the length of her arms and legs to fingers and toes. Celia held her hands outstretched, and Toby reached out for them. Their fingers intertwined. As he arched his back, rainwater dripped from his black curls into Celia's eyes, down her cheeks, and into her mouth. She grabbed his black curly hair and pulled his face towards hers so they could share long deep kisses.

Lightning again smacked down on the ground, and Celia cried out as a formidable tension in her unravelled, sparking her body into contractions that stirred Toby, who cried out too as he released himself within her. They clung to each other. With the last spasm finally languorously complete, Toby rolled over onto his back beside Celia. She moved onto her side, slid her arm across Toby's chest and rested her cheek on his shoulder. They fell asleep, embraced by the eye of the storm, their energies spent.

The time would come when she would know a word for love so that she could describe it. That time lay in the future. For now, all she could feel was the sympathetic pounding of their hearts.

Styx River

Felicity woke to the throbbing sound of incessant chirping. She was hot and sticky, in a lather of sweat, and lying in a puddle of tepid seawater. The yellow lifejacket was chafing against her neck.

Am I dead? Oh my God, Pete! she thought.

'Pete!' she shouted. 'Can you hear me?'

The morning light was dim. As her eyes adjusted, she realised she was huddled in a foetal position on one of the long cushions from the galley table that had been torn from its mount and now lay wedged up against the hatch for the hold under the fore-deck. She straightened out and pushed herself up onto all fours.

What is that sound? she thought.

The boat was listing and yet motionless. A large angry insect was bouncing around inside the cabin, searching in vain for the exit. She sat up in a shaft of sunlight streaming in through the porthole windows, highlighting the ruined interior of the cabin, the contents of which were strewn across the floor. Floating like flotsam and jetsam in a rank pool of bilge water were dozens of bags of cocaine and the remains of the VHF radio.

A shiver rocked her shoulders and cramped in her belly. She

freed herself from her uncomfortable lifejacket and made a futile attempt to straighten her red sequinned dress, which now was just a tattered remnant of its former glory. Carefully, Felicity manoeuvred herself along the companionway and into the aft cabin. She opened the built-in wardrobe and laughed out loud when she found her red stiletto shoes tucked up on a shelf. The drawers were full of Pete's clothes, and she rummaged around until she located a clean pair of undies. They were too large, but they were better than nothing.

I can't believe he wore these huge Y-fronts. Maybe my bum is not that big after all, was her distracted flash of a thought.

She clambered out of the companionway and found herself squinting in the daylight. Her dire circumstances immediately became apparent. The storm surge had swept the boat into a forest of coastal mangroves, leaving it lying stranded on its keel as the tide had receded. The sun was blazing hot, and the mangroves were crawling with buzzing insects. Sitting down on the side of the upended cockpit, she batted them away from her face and considered her next move, as Pete was nowhere to be seen.

The tide was fast running out, exposing the expanse of grey mudflats that stretched out towards a low headland at the far end of what she assumed was a bay. Nestled into the headland, there appeared to be a shack. Felicity realised she only had a narrow window of time to get help.

She went back to the wardrobe and pulled out a pair of deck shoes. Like the undies, they were three sizes too large. She tightened the laces as hard as she could before locating a small rucksack and filling it with bottles of water and a packet of biscuits from the galley. Then she came across Pete's Greek fisherman's cap. Tears welled up in her eyes, but she quickly shut them down, knowing that now was not the time to wallow in a painful memory of the events of the previous day. After locating and applying some sunscreen, Felicity pulled on the cap, stuffed her stilettos into the rucksack and made her way back up on deck.

Attached to the stern was a stainless-steel ladder. She climbed down as far as she could before letting go and landing feet first in the spiky mangroves. Step by step and in a fog of mosquitoes, she began to push her way through the sharp pointed mangrove roots and bushy stalks towards the edge of the forest. The mangroves finally gave way to simply oozing grey mudflats.

Now she could see that the shack on the headland had a blue roof in what looked like good repair, so she hurried towards it. Several times, she caught her foot and ended up face down in the grey mud. She would swear, pick herself up and press on. She hugged the coastline where the mud was firmer.

Just as the shack on the headland seemed within reach, Felicity came across a drainage channel that ran out into the green water of the bay. The sun was high and the tide had turned.

I'm getting sunburnt, but I'm not dead yet, she thought, in an attempt to talk down a rising panic that threatened to consume her. At one point, she crouched down and fished out her stiletto shoes from the rucksack. She rubbed the shiny red patent leather between her fingers as she estimated how wide the channel was.

Seems like my career as a pace bowler in the women's fifth eleven cricket team at uni is about to pay off, she thought.

She stood up and took a few steps back for a run-up, charged forward and hurled the stilettos over her head and into the air. They separated in mid-flight as they sailed across the channel and landed with a thud in the mud on the far side.

Felicity drained the last of the water from the plastic water bottle with several large gulps and left it to the mercy of the incoming tide beside the rucksack. She waded into the channel, losing her footing in the tidal surge. The runners made it impossible to kick so she held her breath underwater as she pulled them off one by one and let them sink to the bottom. Without the dead weight of the runners, she became buoyant in the salty water, and she swam with all her strength until her feet found some purchase on the muddy floor on the opposite side. Summoning her remaining strength, she dragged herself up onto the soft muddy edge of the channel.

It took several deep breaths for her to steel herself to retrieve her stilettos. She held her cherished party shoes up to inspect them and then took a few minutes to recover before pushing on towards the headland in bare feet, as the green water of the incoming tide rippled around her shins.

The headland was the first piece of firm ground she had stood on since she'd left Townsville. It was a relief to catch a slight zephyr of breeze as she climbed up through the rocks. At the top, Felicity could now see the blue roof of the shack clearly and estimated that it was two hundred metres away.

She started off again, prising apart branches of green scrub, putting one bare foot in front of the other until she reached the cleared land surrounding the shack, which she discovered was made of large slabs of splintered grey timber and sheets of rusting corrugated iron. Several blue tarpaulins had been slung over the roof, so she assumed the shack had been damaged in the cyclone. Two men were sitting at a table on the verandah.

Oh great! Now, I'm at the mercy of some ferals. Maybe I should have stayed with the wreck of the Hesperus, she thought.

The Three 'M's

'Jesus, look what the cat dragged in,' one of the men said as Felicity emerged barefoot and bedraggled from the scrub in her muddied red dress, clutching her red stiletto shoes. Both men jumped up and ran towards her.

'What in God's name happened to you, love? Are you okay? Come with us.' They walked her over to their table, sat her down, and gave her a can of cold beer.

Felicity was speechless and possibly suffering some sunstroke. She took a long drink.

'Welcome to the Styx River Hotel, love. Get that into ya and I'll line up another one. My name's Matt, and this is Mal. They call us the three 'M's.'

The two men watched on as Felicity sculled the beer and placed the empty can back down on the table.

'Who's the third M?' Felicity's curiosity at least hadn't been quenched by her ordeal.

'Marjorie. Marjorie! Get out here will you love and bring a hot pie,' Matt yelled at the top of his voice.

A large rotund woman in a printed cotton dress, with her grey hair tied up in a tight bun, appeared.

'Dear girl, what happened to you? Why are you covered in mud? You look like the wreck of the Hesperus,' Marjorie said.

'Funny you should say that. I got caught in the cyclone. Any chance I could bludge another beer, Matt?'

'You have another beer with the boys while I'll get you a hot meat pie,' Marjorie said.

Matt passed another can of cold beer each to Felicity and Mal, and they all took several gulps before sitting back in the white plastic chairs.

Mal leaned forward. 'So, what really happened?' he asked.

Felicity's lip began to tremble as she thought of Pete being washed overboard while she was pinned to the floor by the torrent below decks.

'I decided to crew for a bloke up in Townsville. He was bound for Brisbane, but the cyclone caught up with us. He must have been washed overboard. I was below when it happened. The storm blew the boat into the mangroves north of here. I need to report it to the police.'

Felicity crushed the empty beer can with her hand as tears welled up in her eyes.

'Jesus. How well did you know that bloke?' Mal asked.

'I only met him two days ago. It's really horrible.'

Mal placed his can of beer on a coaster and leaned back on the legs of his white plastic chair. 'That's bloody tragic that is. But right now there's no way you can get the word out. The storm blew the roof off and took the power out and the road back to the highway is closed. But I expect emergency services will have it open tomorrow. We have to eat everything in the freezer before it goes off. Matt and I earned a beer by pulling the tarp over the roof. Marjorie's worked out a way to heat up frozen pies on the gas barbie. She gets full marks for innovation.'

'I'm sorry about your mate, but you may as well settle in for a drinking session with us 'cause you're not going anywhere tonight,' Matt said.

Marjorie produced a hot meat pie and tomato sauce on a white plate with some lettuce and tomato and placed it in front of Felicity, while Matt pulled more cold cans out of the Esky.

'Is this really a hotel?'

'Nah, we call it that 'cause it gives us an excuse to drink beer. You know, if it weren't for all that caked-on mud, you'd be a good-looking sort,' Matt said.

Marjorie was eavesdropping on the conversation and reappeared.

'That's enough of that talk. Come on, love. I'll get you cleaned up and into some fresh clothes. Follow me. And you lot, stay here and no looking, understood?' Marjorie's angry expression said it all.

Matt and Mal lifted their beer cans in acknowledgement, and Felicity followed Marjorie out to the back of the house.

'The storm blew the solar hot water system off the roof, so I have a pot of warm water heating up on the barbie. I'll fill up the shower bag we use camping, and you can give me a hand to hang it up on the branch of our fig tree. I'm sorry, but it's the best I can do under the circumstances,' Marjorie explained.

She handed Felicity a bar of soap, a large sponge and a towel. Together they tipped warm water from the large aluminium pot into the green canvas shower bag. Marjorie had a stepladder positioned next to a low branch and with Felicity's help, hung it in position.

'I'll be back with some clothes, and don't worry, I'll make sure the boys stay put,' Marjorie said as she turned the tap on the showerhead.

In the late afternoon sun, Felicity stripped off and proceeded to wash off the caked-on mud, hoping her sad memory of Pete went with it. She dried off and wrapped herself in a towel. Marjorie returned with some clean clothes. and Felicity changed in the laundry. She emerged dressed in a Brisbane Broncos football jersey and maroon footy shorts.

'You look like one of the locals. You'll snag yourself a husband if you're not careful,' Marjorie declared.

'Thanks, Marjorie, but I've got a few other priorities right now. I need to report what happened to the police, and I need to get back up to Townsville to pick up my car.'

'Emergency services should have the road open in the morning. I'll drive you back to the Bruce Highway, but you'll probably have to hitch from there. We haven't got any power, so tonight you'll have to join us for a barbeque and backgammon, and you can sleep in the spare bedroom. Just pray it doesn't rain.'

After dinner, Felicity played backgammon with the three M's by candlelight on the verandah. After they'd polished off a bottle of Bundaberg rum, Marjorie took a candle and led Felicity down the hall to the spare bedroom. There was a single bed, and the walls were lined with State of Origin football posters. She presumed this was Marjorie's son's room, but she hadn't asked. She lay on the bed looking up at the underside of the blue tarpaulin.

Time to go home, Felicity thought as she drifted off to sleep.

Going home

The next morning Felicity joined the three 'M's for cornflakes and coffee on the verandah. It was already hot, and the sun shimmered on the glassy dark green river. A large white pelican glided across its surface and landed like a Catalina flying boat. It waddled up to join its mate on the sandy spit.

'Thanks for rescuing me in my hour of need.'

'Our pleasure,' Marjorie said. 'If you're all set, we can head off if you like. I washed your cocktail dress. It's missing a few sequins but better than expected, and it should dry off in the back seat of the truck in this heat. Your shoes came up okay too. It's the first time I've seen stilettos in Styx River,' she said as she handed over Felicity's dress and shoes.

'I like to be prepared.'

After saying goodbye to Matt and Mal, Felicity laid her damp dress on the back seat of the large four-wheel drive and jumped in alongside Marjorie.

'You can keep my son's old clothes. He lives in New York these days, so he won't be needing them.'

'I owe you one, Marjorie.'

They drove out through the front gate and bumped their

way back towards the highway along a rutted fire trail that cut through the dense bushland. A four-wheel drive with a flashing orange strobe light on top was parked near the Bruce Highway turnoff, and an Emergency Services worker in high-vis overalls and an orange hard hat was using a chainsaw to cut up the remains of a large tree that had blocked the road. Marjorie slowed down, gave him a wave, and drove on until they reached the bitumen highway. They both hopped out of the car.

'I'll wait until you hitch a ride so I can take down the car's number plate,' Marjorie said.

'What? So, you can call it in if I hitch a ride with the axe murderer.'

'Just a precaution. Take care love.'

Marjorie waited while Felicity stuck out her thumb and many trucks rolled past without stopping.

I need to change tactics, Felicity thought.

She waited for a break in the traffic then ducked behind the car to change back into her red cocktail dress and slip on her stiletto shoes. A large B-double loomed up, and she stood confidently on the side of the road and stuck out her thumb. The driver applied the exhaust brakes, smoking the tyres as the large semi-trailer shuddered to a halt. The driver opened the passenger door. Felicity gave Marjorie a quick hug before she turned and ran towards the vehicle.

The driver was a muscular man with a shaved head, a thick black moustache, and a deep tan. His eyes were hidden behind a pair of reflective aviator shades.

'You look like you're in show business like me. Where are ya headed, love?'

'Townsville mate. Can I hitch a ride?'

'Jump in.'

Felicity climbed up into the cabin, and the big truck roared into life. 'So, this is where I find out that you're an axe murderer, right?'

The driver roared with laughter. 'An axe murderer. I've been called everything in my time but never that. My name's Werner, and everyone calls me Werner from the village.'

'Thanks for picking me up, Werner from the village. I'm Felicity from Sydney, but how can I be reassured that you haven't already axe-murdered everyone in your village and I'm not next on your list of potential victims.'

Werner gave Felicity a sideways glance before setting the B-Double in motion.

'I got that nickname because I like to dress up like the construction worker from that 70s band, *The Village People*. I'm going to teach everyone how to dance the 'YMCA' at my nephew's birthday party in Townsville. My outfit's hanging up in the back. Check it out.'

Felicity leaned over. Sure enough, hanging up behind the driver's seat was a hard hat, a sleeveless denim shirt and a tool belt.

'See … no axe.'

'You have a hammer though.'

'I reserve that for people who don't like disco. Do you have any musical preferences?'

'I prefer the blues myself.'

'Well, you're in luck. I made up a blues song this morning. The virus killed the truck's sound system, so I sing my own songs. Hang in there while I tune up.'

Werner pulled out a blues harp harmonica and, as he drove, he mounted it on a harness that he slipped around his neck. He squeezed out a long note from the instrument and hummed in tune.

Whether she liked Werner's original music and lyrics or not – and mostly it was not – Felicity had plenty to listen to over the next six hours. For some periods she either fell asleep or pretended to. All in all it wasn't too bad – though Werner's soulfulness wasn't what she'd call energising. But each to their own, and she needed the lift back into her real life.

By the time the B-double pulled up outside the Townsville police station, Felicity was keen to leave the blues far behind. She jumped out of the truck and waved Werner goodbye and good luck as he headed off to dance class at his nephew's birthday party.

By contrast, Felicity had to steel herself as she walked through the doors of the low cream brick police station. A young clean-shaven policeman standing behind the counter looked at her with a bemused expression as she tottered in on her high heels.

'My name is Felicity Faraday and I want to report a missing person.'

The constable pulled a form from under the counter and picked up a pen.

'Ms Faraday, I'll need you to make a statement. You'll have to bear with me as we're back to pens and paper. Now, who exactly is missing and what are the circumstances?'

Felicity made a comprehensive statement about Pete being washed overboard in the cyclone, ignoring the detail about the cocaine.

The constable gave her a steady look. 'The coast guard rescued a person meeting this description and we had him under police guard in Mackay base hospital before being transferred back to the lockup here.'

'Here! You mean you have Pete here?'

The constable continued to stare at Felicity and put his pen down on the counter.

'The person in custody is lucky to be alive by the sound of it. They pulled him from the sea in the eye of the cyclone. A one-in-a-million chance really. He matches the description of a Peter John Deasy, who is wanted in connection with trafficking a commercial quantity of cocaine. We were going to pick him up in Brisbane. Would you be able to identify him?'

Felicity leaned forward. 'So, what if the guy you have in custody is not Peter John Deasy?'

The constable placed both hands on the counter. 'Ms Faraday, are you willing to assist us with our enquiries or not?'

'Of course. Can I see him?'

'Come through to the interview room.'

The constable opened a secure door and led Felicity through to a small brightly lit room with stark white walls. She sat on one of four white plastic chairs that were positioned around a bare table in the centre of the floor.

'Wait here please, Ms Faraday.'

The constable left her alone. Minutes later he escorted a tall sandy-haired man dressed in an old second-hand shirt and jeans and wearing handcuffs into the room.

It was Pete, and he remained expressionless.

Felicity looked up and did her best to appear stony faced. 'I've never seen this bloke before in my life.'

The constable glared for some time without blinking. 'Don't bullshit me, Ms Faraday. There are serious penalties for interfering with a police investigation.'

'And I say this guy is not the man I know. So, what are you going to do with him?'

The constable sighed, walked behind Pete, and unlocked the

handcuffs.

'I don't have any evidence to charge you, mate, so you're free to go.'

Felicity followed Pete out of the police station, and they walked separately until they were well out of sight. Once they'd rounded the corner of a building a block away, they embraced.

'Shit, Pete, I thought you were dead!'

'And how on earth did you survive the cyclone?

Felicity released her hold on Pete and stood back to face him. 'I was shipwrecked on mangroves then managed to hitch a ride back up the coast. So, what's your story?'

'By the time they picked me up in the sea all I had on was my undies so I reckon having no ID probably got me off the hook. That computer virus took out all the evidence and biometric information they had on me, so they had nothing to work with. I'd buy you a drink to thank you for what you did for me back there, but I'm skint.'

Felicity put her hands on her hips. 'Well, you can forget buying me another drink after what happened last time, and don't ask me where the boat is because you wouldn't want to know.'

Pete ran his fingers through his sandy hair and laughed.

'You're probably right. It's in no fit state, right? But the upside is that if the police and the syndicate think Peter John Deasy is dead, then I'm free at last.'

'Where will you go?' Felicity asked.

'Maybe I'll crew on a few yachts and head back up the coast. Who knows, if I ever get back to Bali, I could visit a friend I have in a village up there. What about you?'

Felicity ran her fingers through her hair.

'Pete, you made me realise that I have some unfinished business to attend to – personal stuff. I'm going home, at least that's if my van's still in one piece. I left it parked outside Flipper's nightclub, so it's probably been nicked.'

'Flippers is just a few blocks down to the right from here. Follow me,' Pete said with a smile.

Felicity took off her high heels and walked back to the club with Pete in bare feet. Much to her relief, the Sandman was still parked where she left it, and it appeared to have been spared by both the car thieves and the cyclone. She pulled a handful of parking tickets out from under the wiper blade and retrieved the key from the holder under the wheel arch. She opened the tailgates and pulled out a wad of banknotes from under the mattress.

'Merry Christmas, Pete. This will give you a head start,' she said and pressed the cash into Pete's hand.

'Are you sure? I didn't get you a Christmas present.'

'Well, you gave me an opportunity to reassess my life. That'll do me. Cheers mate.'

Felicity hugged Pete and felt relieved to wave him goodbye as he walked back towards the marina. He was one complication she didn't need in her life from now on. She sat behind the wheel, put the key in the ignition and held her breath as the engine roared into life. On the dash was her hotel room key.

Bugger, I didn't check out, Felicity thought. She drove around to the Breakwater Motel and found the grey nomad sitting in reception.

'You owe me for three nights lady,' the grey nomad said.

'Give me a break, Barry.'

Up ahead: San Francisco

Now back in country Oberon, west of Sydney's Bradfield, Felicity and her Uncle Mick sat in the shade of his verandah at opposite ends of his tattered sofa. As they took in the wide green expanse of the sprawling homestead's home paddock, Mick opened a bottle of Chardonnay and poured Felicity a large glass.

'So, you're telling me that Celia fronted back up for a second dose of this Modernity Inhibitor drug just so she could be with Toby? I would call that behaviour reckless,' was Mick's reaction to Felicity's news.

'I would call it romantic. At least I would if I hadn't become tangled up in it and had my heart broken along the way.'

They took a sip in unison as they looked out across at the Hereford cattle chewing their cud near the fence.

'So, now what are your plans?' Mick asked.

'Pete made me realise that it's time I made peace with my mother.'

'Interesting! That's a sensible decision. I told you last time you were here that I was making arrangements to go to San Francisco to see her again. Aircraft are grounded indefinitely until they launch new communications satellites, but the cruise lines are running a regular service from Sydney to San Francisco via Honolulu. I have a ticket on the *Costa Futura* departing next Monday. Why don't you come too?'

'Well, my first thought is that as long as I can have my own room with a porthole, so I don't get claustrophobia, I'm in. Can you book me a ticket this late, Mick? I just know seeing my mother again is something I have to do …'

The following Monday afternoon, Felicity found herself aboard the ship and was unpacking her bag in her 'stateroom' when she heard three long blasts from the foghorn, indicating the ship was going astern. She had arranged to meet Mick up on the deck for the departure and joined him at the railing. They watched as Circular Quay, the Opera house, and the Sydney Harbour Bridge disappeared from their view into the afternoon haze.

'How long are you planning to stay in the U.S.?' Felicity asked as the ship steamed through the sandstone heads of the harbour.

'A month or two at the most, and then I'll be back. I get homesick for Sydney after a few weeks. How about you?'

'It depends. I need a change of scene. I'll just have to take it as it comes.'

Felicity quickly became accustomed to life at sea, and for five weeks the *Costa Futura* became her new home. She slipped into a routine, which was in stark contrast to the events of the previous year. She would start the day by meeting Mick for breakfast on the breezy back deck before heading to the gym for a workout and settling in for the rest of the day to read a book from the ship's library with a glass of wine at the bar that overlooked the pool. In the evenings, she would chat with a few of the regulars over a martini before joining Mick for dinner in the restaurant. The sea was relatively calm for most of the trip, and aside from the stopover in the port of Honolulu, it was a non-stop voyage.

On the last morning of the trip, Felicity woke up early, dressed, and made her way to the deck to watch the arrival into port.

San Francisco was just as she remembered it. It was cold and shrouded in a thick grey fog, with the red pylons of the Golden Gate bridge just visible above a low cloud. The ship docked at a berth alongside Fisherman's Wharf, and after the lengthy process of disembarkation and clearing customs, they found themselves standing on the busy Embarcadero in the queue for a taxi while the F-line streetcar rattled past, laden with tourists.

The family home was a large Victorian manor, painted burgundy red and set among colourful timber houses known as 'painted ladies' that lined the streets of Haight-Ashbury. Felicity opened the door of the taxi and paused to let memories from her childhood float through her mind while Mick tipped the driver and took the bags out of the trunk. They walked onto the porch. Her heart raced as Mick pushed the doorbell.

Remember to breathe, Felicity thought.

The door swung open. Standing in front of Felicity was an older woman about her own height. Grey-haired, yet still attractive.

'Hello Mom,' Felicity said in an American accent that she thought was long forgotten.

'Felicity! My dear child!' the woman said, rushing forward and wrapping her arms around Felicity in a tight embrace that almost squeezed the air out of her lungs. They both burst into tears and didn't let go.

Mick beamed at the sight of his sister and niece reunited after so many years apart. 'Hello, Therese. See, I bought you a present,' Mick said, gesturing towards Felicity.

'Good to see you, Mick. How can I thank you enough for bringing my daughter back home to me? Please, both of you, come in.'

The travellers rolled their bags into the foyer, and Therese led them through to the lounge room, which was adjacent to a large entertaining area which had been the scene of countless music industry parties over the decades.

'I know where the kitchen is. I'll make tea while you two get reacquainted,' Mick said.

Therese and Felicity sat on the luxurious white leather lounge beside each other.

'My dear child, I'm so sorry. During all these years I've blamed myself for what happened that night.'

'Mother, it's not your fault. I'm the one to blame. I didn't make a scene just because I found you with Lucia St. Thomas. I realise now, after having lived this long, that what really upset me was that I was in love with her myself. I was jealous.'

Just then a once-familiar figure entered the room. A tall greying African American woman dressed in tight brown jeans and a cream blouse sat on the lounge next to Therese. It was Lucia.

'Good old-fashioned jealousy! Well, I never saw that coming. All these years, I've been telling your mother it was my fault for being so indiscreet,' Lucia said, as she reached out and held Therese by the hand.

'Are you two still an item?' Felicity was amazed.

'We've been married for over twenty years,' Therese explained.

'Married?'

Therese and Lucia laughed.

'My dear, this is San Francisco. We were married after I divorced your father. I'm surprised you're so shocked, given that you have spent your adult life in Sydney,' Therese said.

Mick came back in with a china teapot and teacups on a tray and placed them on a low coffee table before pouring the tea. 'You ladies haven't changed one bit. Have a biscuit.'

'Did you know about these two, Mick? Why didn't you tell me!'

'Felicity Faraday, you haven't been exactly open to discussion over the years.'

'I'm sorry, Mick. Yes, it's not your fault,' Felicity said.

'Where are you staying, Mick?' Therese asked.

'At the Intercontinental, but I think it would be good if Felicity can stay with you and reconnect.'

'Of course. Darling, will you stay with us? You can sleep in your old room. We've been using it for guests since I didn't expect to ever see you again – although I always hoped …,' Therese said.

'That would be lovely,' Felicity said as she nibbled on a biscuit and finished off her cup of tea.

'How long are you two planning to stay here in San Francisco?' Therese asked.

'I'm here for a month, but Felicity may stay on longer, I reckon. She's looking for a change of scene.'

'Well, Felicity, you can work, you know. You are still an American citizen, after all, and I need all the help I can get to fully re-launch ReElevation in Australia. You're here just in time. What do you say?' Therese asked.

'Mother, I would just love that. But we need to discuss it in detail, in terms of what's best for the business.'

The next morning a car was waiting outside the house in the damp fog. Therese and Felicity jumped in and ten minutes later walked in through the bohemian decor of the office of ReElevation USA. Therese introduced her to the head of A&R, Sam Robbins.

'Sam, this is my daughter Felicity. Make sure she has everything she needs. I've hired her to help you re-launch the label and get back online in Australia as soon as it's possible.'

'Your reputation precedes you, Ms Faraday. I heard about the initiatives you were taking with Flesh and Blood artists Downunder before the ODIN-2 virus. Welcome aboard,' Sam said.

Sam took Felicity down to the A&R department, introduced her to the staff and arranged a desk.

'You're here just in time … There's even talk of a re-boot of AI,' he explained.

I wonder what safeguards they'll program into the source code this time around, Felicity thought.

'Is there anything you need? There's a tea and coffee station in the kitchen and a coffee cart over the road from the office.'

'I think I'll go for a short walk to get a coffee, thanks, Sam.'

Felicity caught the elevator down to reception. She was surprised by how similar the fit-out was to the Sydney office. As she walked toward the foyer, she saw a female figure peering in through the glass panel of a vending machine. The woman had long red hair much like her own. Felicity gasped when she saw the familiar treble clef tattoo on the woman's left shoulder. An apple was jammed in the jaws of the auto selector.

'The question is, do you really want it?' Felicity asked.

The woman spun around.

'My god, Felicity Faraday. In San Francisco of all places!

Well, I never. And since you asked, the answer is yes, I do want it. I wanted it the first time, but when I pressed the button, it didn't work out. What do you think we should do?'

'Let's try again, Vanessa.'

Reunion

It's one of those days, Felicity thought as her limo wound its way through the streets of Marrickville.

One of those endless summer days when the nor'easter blows in from the Pacific Ocean until its last breath has petered out across the suburbs.

She placed her hand on Vanessa's thigh and smiled as they pulled up outside a red brick and tile Edwardian house surrounded by neat trimmed hedges.

'This is it,' Felicity said, admiring the green and yellow painted timber posts of the verandah as she opened the car door. 'Ready to meet the family?'

'You take the present, and I'll bring the wine,' Vanessa replied.

Felicity and Vanessa took a minute to straighten their matching red skirts and fix their hair once they were out of the car. As they made their way towards the house along its ceramic tiled path, the front door opened, and Celia appeared. She skipped down the steps in her black jeans and tee shirt and wrapped her arms around Felicity.

'Oh, how I've missed you. I was so happy when you told me

you were coming back to Sydney.'

'I've missed you too, girl.'

After a long moment, Celia let go of Felicity.

'And you must be Vanessa. I'm Celia.' She gave Vanessa an air kiss.

'Come on in. Toby's out the back pouring drinks. We'll tell you the whole story about how we got out of The Hemisphere over lunch. I'll need you to speak softly until we get past the bedroom, as I've just got Lily off to sleep.'

'Can I take a peek?' Felicity asked.

'Sure, follow me.'

Felicity and Vanessa followed Celia up the front steps onto the verandah and into the house. She paused at the first door on the right and slowly turned the knob. Felicity and Vanessa quietly crept in to look at the sleeping baby.

'How old is she?' Vanessa whispered.

'10 months.'

'She's gorgeous, Celia. The family resemblance is quite striking. She has your nose and Toby's lips. I'm so jealous,' Felicity said in a low voice.

They walked silently out of the room and waited for Celia to close the door.

'Come on, it's time for a drink. Go on through,' Celia said.

'Are Peta and Tyler here too?' Felicity asked.

'No, they're having the weekend away down the south coast. We'd been talking about a joint holiday in Greece but it's not the right time for us so they decided on a local holiday destination. Hey, thanks for keeping her on your payroll. She says you're the best boss ever.'

'Is that what you think?'

'I think we're all best friends. Follow me.'

Celia led Felicity and Vanessa along the long corridor and out onto the back verandah, where Toby was setting the table for lunch. Felicity stepped forward and gave him a hug.

'Toby! I was beginning to think you two were going to settle down in Mount Garnet. Good to see you opted for Marrickville instead,' Felicity said.

'It was all made possible by Phil Beatty, Sally, Lucas, Josh and Craig, really. Who'd have thought they would stump up the funds for a management buyout of the club,' Toby said. 'Besides, with the baby on the way, Celia wanted to be close to her mother, and when her share of the money came through, we had enough for a deposit on this house.'

'And Toby snared a gig with the NSW State Government as a technical consultant on their Third Archive project,' Celia said.

'Do you still prefer chardonnay, Felicity?' Toby asked.

'Some things never change. I've turned Vanessa onto chardy too.'

'Yes, she weaned me off bourbon. Chardonnay would be great thanks, Toby.

They all sat down around the table and looked across the back garden while Toby poured the drinks. A magpie's rasping call floated across from the bough of one of two ghost gums in the garden.

'Who's got the green thumb?' Felicity asked, admiring the neatly spaced native plants in the garden.

'Toby is studying landscape architecture in his spare time. He's turned the garden into a living lab,' Celia said.

Felicity leaned back, waving her empty wine glass in Toby's direction.

'So, let's get to the adventure story. Exactly how did you both manage to escape from The Hemisphere? Those robots seemed pretty intent on keeping you there when I pulled Celia out that first time at Lake Koombooloomba,' Felicity said.

'It's not like life wasn't good inside The Hemisphere,' Toby said as he worked his way around the table, filling the stemmed wine glasses with golden chardonnay. 'It turned out that chaperones were only temporarily assigned to new arrivals. Once we'd settled in, we were left to suggest our own futures.'

'Suggest to who?'

'To ourselves. The Hemisphere is a hybrid of physical and virtual reality driven by autosuggestion. Celia suggested to herself that we had a future together, and I suggested to myself that Lionel had an important role to play in my world. So, one day I took Celia by the hand and we went back through the lava tube looking for Lionel. Some of his mates from Mount Garnet who were camping at Lake Koombooloomba recognised me, and they took us back to Colleen and Joyce. Luckily Lionel still had those apples that neutralise the modernity inhibitor stashed in the freezer of his beer fridge.'

Felicity looked at Celia. 'So, what happened next?'

'Toby and I spent most of our time with Lionel learning about the local country, its plants and animals. The landscape, the ecology of the place. We did a lot of hiking until I really started to show with Lily. I knew I was going to need support from my mother, so when the money for the club came through, and Toby scored the job in Sydney, it all fell into place,' Celia said.

'Wow. That makes our love story seem like a sideshow,' Vanessa said.

'Yeah, I like the support my mother now gives me too, as long as we're on different continents,' Felicity said. 'I'm back here to run ReElevation and Vanessa scored your old gig at the coffee cart, Celia, believe it or not!'

'How's my ex-boyfriend, Marco?' Celia asked.

'He's besotted with me, but I can't bring myself to tell him he's got 'Buckley's.'' Vanessa was enjoying learning about the Australian vernacular and using it in conversation when she got the chance.

'Toby, top up Vanessa's glass and put the vegan sausages on the barbie, please. Felicity, can you give me a hand in bringing out the salads?' Celia said.

'Sure, boss.'

Felicity followed Celia into the kitchen. As soon as they were out of earshot, Celia grabbed Felicity's hand and embraced her.

'I'm so pleased that you reconnected with your mother and that it's working out with Vanessa. She's lovely.'

'Yeah, it's much better this time around. You're so lucky to have Lily, and I can see now that you and Toby make a good team.'

Celia held both Felicity's forearms in hers and looked into her green eyes.

'I love Toby, but I want you to know that I …'

Footsteps echoed in the hallway, and Celia let go of Felicity's hands as Vanessa appeared in the doorway.

'I see you two are getting reacquainted. Hope I'm not interrupting. I thought you could use an extra pair of hands.'

'If you can take out this potato salad, that would be great. Felicity, you take the breadbasket, and I'll bring the cutlery. Come on, time to eat.'

Felicity gave Celia a quirky smile as they walked out of the kitchen and back to the verandah, where Toby was piling hot barbequed sausages onto a plate. They all helped themselves to the salads, sausages and bread rolls and topped up their glasses.

'Cheers! Here's to Toby's song,' Celia said.

'I'll drink to that! So, Toby, you've finally finished your masterwork? Let's hear it, we could do with some lunchtime entertainment,' Felicity said.

Toby took a bite out of his sausage sandwich, stood up and returned to the table with his Maton guitar to a round of applause.

'What's the song about, Toby?' Vanessa asked.

'It's a song about aspects of ourselves we never expected to discover and the story of our time together on the road … that led us to an understanding. It's a love song to all of us, our people and country. Lionel helped me write the last bit.'

Toby took a moment to tune up then launched into his song, ending with the chorus …

Cloudless, unforeseen,
Our dance is so real
Our past and our futures are one and the same
This country has patience and time.